Heaven to Betsy
and
Betsy in Spite of Herself

The Betsy-Tacy Books

Book 1: *Betsy-Tacy*

Book 2: *Betsy-Tacy and Tib*

Book 3: *Betsy and Tacy Go Over the Big Hill*

Book 4: *Betsy and Tacy Go Downtown*

Book 5: *Heaven to Betsy*

Book 6: *Betsy in Spite of Herself*

Book 7: *Betsy Was a Junior*

Book 8: *Betsy and Joe*

Book 9: *Betsy and the Great World*

Book 10: *Betsy's Wedding*

The Deep Valley Books

Winona's Pony Cart

Carney's House Party

Emily of Deep Valley

Heaven to Betsy
and
Betsy in Spite of Herself

Maud Hart Lovelace

Illustrated by Vera Neville

HARPER**PERENNIAL** ● MODERN**CLASSICS**

NEW YORK ● LONDON ● TORONTO ● SYDNEY ● NEW DELHI ● AUCKLAND

HARPERPERENNIAL ● MODERNCLASSICS

HarperCollins books may be purchased for educational, business, or sales
promotional use. For information, please e-mail the Special Markets Department at SPsales@harpercollins.com.

Heaven to Betsy was first published in 1945 by Thomas Y. Crowell Company.
First Harper Trophy edition published 1980.

Betsy in Spite of Herself was first published in 1946 by Thomas Y. Crowell
Company. First Harper Trophy edition published 1979.

FIRST HARPER PERENNIAL MODERN CLASSICS EDITION PUBLISHED 2009.

Library of Congress Cataloging-in-Publication Data is available upon request.

ISBN 978-0-06-179469-8

22 LSC 20 19 18 17 16 15 14 13 12

Foreword

It's a rite of girlhood that almost everyone knows. A beloved friend disappears for a year or two, during that crucial middle school period. Perhaps she lives in another school district or her family relocates temporarily for a parent's job. Reunited with your old classmate in high school, you are shocked at how she has changed physically. Where she was once short and stocky with pigtails, she is now tall and slender, willowy even, with a cloud of dark hair. Her clothes are much more grown-up, fashion-forward. You approach this newly glamorous creature with caution, wondering if she will have any use for you. Then she throws back her head and laughs her familiar laugh, showing teeth that are still parted in the middle, and you realize she hasn't changed in the ways that matter.

Betsy Ray, the heroine of Maud Hart Lovelace's beloved series, underwent such a transformation between the ages of twelve and fourteen. After four books in which she was depicted by the delightful line drawings of Lois Lenski, she graduated to high school and the dreamily flattering pen of Vera Neville. But she was still Betsy—warm, stubborn, imaginative.

Now I read pretty widely as a kid—I am the daughter of a children's librarian, after all—and discovered many kindred spirits in literature. But no character meant as much to me as Betsy Ray in her high school years. At a time when library shelves groaned with books about modern teenagers facing all sorts of modern dilemmas, Betsy was the most relatable character I could find. True, she was a small-town Minnesota girl at the turn of the century, and I was living in a relatively big city in the 1970s. But she seemed more real to me than my contemporaneous counterparts, the girls who watched television and cruised McDonald's, worrying about how to fill their training bras. Sure, I did those things, too, but they didn't *define* me.

So much about Betsy elicited an inner cry of "Me, too!" She liked boys. She didn't have a clue what to do about them. Outgoing and friendly, she also was intensely private, even within the safe confines of a loving family. She was endlessly self-critical, bemoaning her straight hair, the part in her teeth, and her freckles. Actually, I was okay with my teeth and had no freckles, but oh, how I hated my hair.

The primary reason I identified with Betsy, however, is that she wanted to be a writer, not a wife and mother. Oh, she planned to have a family one day. But first, she had other things to do. In *Heaven to Betsy*, the story of her freshman year at Deep Valley High School, "she had been almost appalled, when she started going around with Carney and Bonnie, to discover how fixed their ideas of marriage were. . . . When Betsy and Tacy and Tib talked about their future, they planned to be writers, dancers, circus acrobats."

More amazingly—it is the early twentieth century, after all, before women have won the right to vote—no one close to Betsy ever tries to disabuse her of this ambition. Her family, in fact, could not be more supportive. Loyal Tacy adores everything she writes. And while her other friends tease her—the boys call her "The Little Poetess" because she once published some verse in the local paper—it's done with admiration and affection.

No, the person who comes between Betsy and her writing in her first two years of high school is . . . Betsy. As a freshman, trying to find her place with a new crowd, she makes the mistake of thinking she shouldn't write because the other girls don't. She learns the hard way that her writing is a gift that she must never neglect, and that one should never follow the crowd if it means sacrificing one's true identity.

Then, as a sophomore in *Betsy in Spite of Herself*, Betsy has an essentially existential crisis that once again challenges writing's place in her life. Methodically, she reinvents herself as a reserved, poised siren, a persona that helps her win the attention of a desirable boy. She gets the boy, but at what cost to her writing?

Her new beau isn't the only person who gets between Betsy and writing. A pedantic English teacher seems to find a strange pleasure in challenging Betsy, mocking her light verse, and downgrading her short stories for perceived factual errors. But even Betsy's supportive father advises her that such criticism is a constant in a writer's life.

Consider this exchange at the Ray dinner table:

"It wouldn't do Betsy any harm to learn about commas," Mr. Ray said. "I've noticed myself that she scatters them like grass seed."

"Who reads Shakespeare for the commas?" [Betsy's mother retorted.]

"Maybe . . ." Mr. Ray's eyes twinkled. "I duck when I say it . . . Maybe Betsy isn't in Shakespeare's class?"

That drew [older sister] Julia into the fray.

"How do you know she isn't? Maybe this generation is going to produce another Shakespeare and maybe it's Betsy."

"It wouldn't surprise me a bit," interjected Mrs. Ray.

Talk about Minnesota nice! I've met archetypal Jewish mothers who don't have this much pride in their offspring.

     ❧ x ❧

Okay, Betsy wasn't Shakespeare, but she went on to enjoy a career not unlike Maud Hart Lovelace's, publishing her first short stories while still quite young. The last time we see her, in *Betsy's Wedding*, her husband is encouraging her to write a novel, and I firmly believe she took his advice.

"Role model" has become a cliché, a banality, but Betsy Ray was that for me, and more, a BFF before there were BFFs. I reread these books every year, marveling at how a world so quaint—shirtwaists! pompadours! Merry Widow hats!—can feature a heroine who is undeniably modern. Today, sixty-plus years after these two books first appeared, Betsy remains a vibrant, inspiring presence, with a heart large enough to embrace many new friends. Although, just so you know: Tacy will always have first position.

—LAURA LIPPMAN
Baltimore, Maryland
2009

Heaven to Betsy

For
TOM *and* STELLA

Contents

All things must change
To something new, to something strange . . .

—HENRY W. LONGFELLOW

1

The Farm

BETSY WAS VISITING at the Taggarts' farm. It was Wednesday, and soon the kitchen would swim with warm delicious odors. It was ninety-six in the shade outside, and the wood-burning range gave off a fiery heat, but Mrs. Taggart baked on Wednesday just as inflexibly as she washed on Monday and ironed on Tuesday. Heat or no heat, she would bake today . . . cake, cookies, pie, bread, biscuits. It was sad that Betsy who usually liked such mouth-watering items felt she would choke on every morsel.

Betsy smiled brightly.

"I'll walk on down for the mail," she said, "if there's nothing more I can do."

"Not a thing," answered Mrs. Taggart cheerfully, setting out bowls, an egg beater, a flour sifter, pans. She was a short, bright-eyed pouter pigeon of a woman in an apron that crackled with starch. "It isn't time for Mr. Simmons yet, though."

"That's all right. I like sitting down by the road."

"You're sure you're not homesick, Betsy?"

"Oh, no, Mrs. Taggart!"

"Take Shep along for company," Mrs. Taggart said.

Shep plainly expected to go. In the eight days of Betsy's visit, the old collie who had been a pet of the Taggarts' Mattie, now married and gone, had come to look forward to this morning walk. He rose now, brushed against her ankle-length skirts, and barked.

Betsy took a sunbonnet from a row of hooks on the kitchen wall and climbed to the prim, low-ceiled room which had once been Mattie's. She crossed to the bureau and tied on her sunbonnet, looking anxiously into the mirror.

Every time she looked into a mirror Betsy hoped to

find that her looks had changed. They had certainly changed enough in the last two years. At twelve she had been short, straight and chunky with perky braids and a freckled smiling face. At fourteen she was tall, very slender, with a tendency to stoop. Her brown hair waved softly by reason of eight kid rollers, four on either side, in which she slept at night. Her one braid was turned up with a large hair ribbon, red today, matching the tie of her dark blue sailor suit. Freckles were fading out of a pink and white skin, the delicacy of which she guarded carefully.

"It's the only pretty thing about me," she often muttered savagely while rubbing in creams at night. "Straight hair! Teeth parted in the middle! Mighty good thing I have a decent complexion!"

As a matter of fact what one noticed first and liked best in Betsy were her eyes, clear hazel, under dark brows and lashes. But her frown, as she tied on the sunbonnet, expressed disapproval of her entire physiognomy. She picked up a pad of paper and a pencil, ran down the stairs and out the kitchen door, saying good-by to Mrs. Taggart gaily, and calling out to Shep an invitation to race. This, in view of the heat and his age, he sensibly ignored.

Shep was not fooled by Betsy's vivacity. And in spite of laughing denials, Betsy was homesick. She was . . . to put it mildly . . . wretchedly, desperately, nightmarishly homesick, and had been ever since she came to visit the Taggarts.

Mr. Taggart, a friend of her father's, had come into the store to buy shoes. Seeing Betsy and noticing her droopy thinness, he had told her father that the young lady needed some country milk and eggs. How about letting her come out to visit Mrs. Taggart who felt lost since Mattie had married? Betsy had felt important and flattered. She had been delighted to go.

Tacy Kelly, her best friend, who lived across the street, had been thrilled too. When Betsy drove away on the high seat of the farm wagon beside bearded, mild Mr. Taggart, Tacy waved enthusiastically along with Betsy's sisters, Julia and Margaret. Betsy waved back with a shining face but she had not left Deep Valley behind before this sickish misery invaded her being.

It seemed to her that she had to burst out crying and ask Mr. Taggart to turn around and go back. She couldn't do that, of course, and they drove farther and farther away . . . out Front Street and through the wooded river valley, scene of so many family picnics. They climbed Pigeon Hill, and it was worse after that for the country was not even familiar.

The town of Deep Valley was set amidst hills, and Hill Street where Betsy had lived all her life was barricaded by tree-covered slopes. Beyond Pigeon Hill lay prairie, treeless except for planted groves around the widely separated houses. There were only telephone wires for the birds to perch on. Prairie, poles and wires! Prairie, poles and wires! On the seat beside Mr. Taggart Betsy grew quieter and quieter.

"See what I've brought home, Mamma." Mr. Taggart had presented her proudly in the dooryard of a small grey house dwarfed by a windmill and a big red barn and the planted windbreak of trees.

In response to Mrs. Taggart's welcoming kindness, Betsy had ground her teeth and smiled.

It was Julia, and not Betsy, who had a talent for the stage, but Betsy had done a wonderful job of acting through eight endless days. She had swallowed food over a lump in her throat and exclaimed over its goodness. She had chatted in a grown-up way borrowed from Julia, listened radiantly to Mrs. Taggart's brisk domestic conversation when she could hardly keep the tears back. Sometimes she knew she could not keep them back and fled to the barn pretending sudden interest in the calf or baby pigs. There in dark solitude she buried her head in her arms while waves of desolation broke against her.

The hardest time of each day came at the end. Every evening her family called her on the telephone.

It was one thing to fool Mr. and Mrs. Taggart. They were strangers, and easily taken in. Fooling her loving, keen-witted mother was quite another matter. But Betsy felt she would rather die than let her family know that she was homesick. Julia went visiting alone, and she was only two years older.

It wasn't necessary for her to stay. The merest hint over the 'phone, and her mother would find a reason for summoning her home. But Betsy wouldn't give it. She had been invited for two weeks, and she would not by her own act cut those two weeks short. Betsy looked these days like a somewhat wilted lily, but going into her teens hadn't changed *one* thing about her. She was still as stubborn as a mule.

A hundred times a day she checked off on her fingers the days that must elapse before she went home. She checked them off now . . . one, two, three, four, five, six . . . as she walked down the long narrow road to the mailbox. This was the happiest hour of her day; not because of the walk . . . that was hot and dusty . . . but because of the blessed anticipation of mail. Tacy wrote faithfully, and sometimes there were letters from Tib, who used to live in Deep Valley but had moved back to her native city of Milwaukee.

Betsy and Tacy had mourned at first when Tib moved away. They had not known then the fun and fascination to be found in correspondence. Now letters flew from Deep Valley to Milwaukee and back like fat, gossipy birds.

"Maybe there'll be a letter from Tib today," thought Betsy as she and Shep plodded along in the burning heat.

The roadsides offered no shade, only thickets of purple spiked leadplant and gaudy butterfly weed. To the right and the left stretched golden fields where rye was in shock. But down at the main road where the Taggart R.F.D. box waited hungrily on a fence post, stood an elderberry bush. Betsy sat down in its patch of shade and Shep gratefully eased himself to the ground. She took off her sunbonnet. Her curls had quite flattened out in the heat, but fortunately she did not know it. She fanned herself and Shep with the generous bonnet.

A short yard away a picket pin gopher appeared, erect on his haunches. From the telephone wire a meadow lark soared into the air, broke the hot stillness with a cool cascade of notes, dropped into the meadow. Betsy groped in her pocket for the pencil and the pad of paper. She scribbled dreamily:

"*I sit by the side of the road,*
Thinking of times gone by,
Thinking of home far away,
'til a tear springs into my eye.
Then a gopher springs up to amuse me,
And a meadow lark sings me a song,

When the world is so full of God's creatures,
To be homesick is certainly wrong."

She read this over and changed the first "springs" to "wells." She read it over again, and frowned. The word "certainly" didn't seem very poetic. But before she had found an adverb she liked better, she heard a clop clop of hoofs and saw the mail wagon's halo of dust. She jumped to her feet. Mr. Simmons, red faced and genial, handed her a card from Sears Roebuck for Mrs. Taggart, and a letter bearing Tacy's dear angular script.

"But it's thin," Betsy thought as she told Mr. Simmons that Mr. Taggart was haying today, that it *was* hot enough for her, and that she would see him tomorrow.

When he was gone she sat down again. She did not hurry about opening her letter. The moment was too precious to be hurried. She examined the postmark: Deep Valley, Minn. July 25, 1906. Sometimes Tacy enlivened the envelope by putting the stamp on upside down to signify love, or by addressing her with some grandiloquent string of names such as Miss Elizabetha Gwendolyn Madeline Angeline Rosemond Ray, or by adding BC for Best Chum or HHAS for Herbert Humphreys Admiration Society. Herbert Humphreys, large and bright-blond, had been the beau ideal of the girls through grade school.

Today, however, Tacy's envelope was lacking in lively decorations, and when Betsy opened it, there was, as she had feared, only a single page inside. But its message was potent to hold homesickness at bay.

"*Dear Betsy. I don't dare to write much for fear I'll give something away. Your mother said I could tell you that they have a surprise for you, but of course I can't tell you what it is. It's nice for you, but not so nice for me, but that's all right. In a way it's nice for me, too. I'd better stop. You see how it is. If I write I'm sure to give it away. Love. Your sincere friend. Tacy.*"

Betsy jumped up, her eyes sparkling. Shep sprang up, too, and barked, sending echoes over the fields.

"Shep! What is it? What *can* it be?"

Shep barked as though guessing a bone.

A Peter Thompson suit? thought Betsy, striding up the road. But that would not be not nice for Tacy. A bike? Her father had suggested buying her a bike, for it was a long walk from Hill Street to the High School which Betsy and Tacy would enter this fall. But Tacy didn't have a bike, and the town, he had said, would fall down with surprise if Betsy and Tacy stopped going to school together. What could it be?

17

Betsy hurried into the house to get Mrs. Taggart's guess.

Mrs. Taggart promptly guessed a baby, and Betsy laughingly told her that once she had gone to visit on a farm and had come home to find a baby sister. But that wouldn't happen now. She was, she explained complacently, old enough to be told. Besides, Tacy liked babies. What could possibly be nice for Betsy that Tacy would not like?

She puzzled while she shelled peas and at dinner Mr. Taggart joined affably in the guessing. But when Betsy started to eat, the misery came back. The surprise seemed suddenly unimportant and it was nightmarish again that she, Betsy, was out here alone among strangers. She started the now familiar business of pushing food around her plate.

"I never knew a growing girl to take so little interest in her victuals," Mrs. Taggart said when Betsy declared that she really didn't have room for fresh peach pie.

Misery kept her company through the dragging afternoon. Then there was supper to be eaten, harder even than dinner. When the dishes were washed Betsy went out to sit on the back fence and watch the sunset. She had always liked sunsets, and tonight the west was turquoise blue, with banked clouds turning from peach color to pink. But shortly the clouds became grey, the sky dark. The orchard trees moved slowly in an imperceptible breeze, and the crickets began.

The worst thing about farm evenings was the crickets. The cows were bad enough with their dreary lowing, and the birds flying urgently homeward at nightfall when Betsy could not fly home to Hill Street. But those crickets!

"I must, I must get to feeling better before Mamma 'phones," Betsy thought, jumping off the fence.

Winking rapidly, she walked toward the house. The lamps were not yet lighted; Mrs. Taggart was sitting in the dooryard for coolness while Mr. Taggart finished his chores. And just as Betsy came up the telephone bell inside the kitchen rang. Two long and three short rings, the Taggarts' call.

"It's sure to be for you, Betsy," Mrs. Taggart said. "Make your mamma tell you what that secret is."

"I'll certainly try," Betsy answered merrily. She put the receiver to her ear.

"Hello. Bettina?" Julia always called her Bettina. "How're you?"

"Dandy," said Betsy. "I'm having a dandy time."

"Not too dandy, I hope," Julia answered, and laughed excitedly. "I mean . . . there's a wonderful surprise here. Papa and Mamma want to know if you'd just as soon hurry up your visit."

"Hurry up . . . my visit?"

"And come home ahead of time . . . tomorrow."

Betsy clung to the receiver as though holding fast to Julia's words.

"Why, all right," she said slowly, after a pause. "Of course, I hate like the dickens to leave."

"But this surprise won't keep," said Julia. "That is, you might hear about it. You might read it in the paper."

"In the *paper?*"

Julia laughed out loud.

"I'd better ring off, or I'll give it away. Mamma's too busy to talk, if you're coming home tomorrow."

"I'll come," Betsy said. "Wait. I'll find out what time." Holding the receiver, she spoke to Mrs. Taggart.

"Why, Mr. Simmons can take you along to Butternut Center tomorrow," she said. "There's a train at two-three. Tell your mamma we hope you'll come again."

"I'd love to come again," Betsy cried.

When she rang off the kitchen seemed transformed. Mrs. Taggart had lighted the lamps, and the glow was as cozy as home lamplight. Betsy played with Shep, and ate the piece of pie she had spurned at dinner, said goodnight gaily and ran gaily upstairs to the prim little room that had once been Mattie's.

Whistling to herself she undressed and put on her

long-sleeved cambric night gown. Smilingly, she washed in the flowered bowl, and brushed her teeth, and rubbed cream into her face, and wound her hair on eight kid rollers. Briskly, she lifted off the pillow shams . . . one said Good Night, and one said Good Morning . . . and folded back the patchwork quilt and blew out the lamp. After she had raced through her prayers, she climbed into bed and lay there peacefully.

The room still held the heat of the day, but the air coming through the screened windows was cool. Outside the crickets were singing.

"Yes, I must come here again sometime," thought Betsy happily, listening to their tune.

2

Butternut Center

BETSY'S FIRST THOUGHT on awakening was that she
was going home. She lay in bed and thought about
Hill Street with adoration.

It took its name from the fact that it ended in a hill.
Her house and Tacy's, across the street, were the last
two houses in the town. The rolling, tree-covered slopes
seemed but an extension of the lawns surrounding

the white rambling Kelly house and the yellow Ray cottage.

This was growing altogether too small. When they kept a hired girl, Julia, Betsy and Margaret had to share one bedroom. The house had almost none of the modern improvements, Betsy had heard her mother remark disparagingly. Never mind, Betsy loved it, from the butternut tree standing like a sentinel in front, to Old Mag's barn behind the garden, not forgetting the lilac bush by the side kitchen door and the backyard maple.

She thought about Hill Street through breakfast and farewells. But homeward bound beside Mr. Simmons, she began to give a little attention to the surprise. She told him about it, they discussed it pro and con while the wagon rolled from mailbox to mailbox, between swaying cornfields where red-winged blackbirds foraged. By the time they reached Butternut Center Mr. Simmons was quite worked up about the surprise.

"I'll drop you a card to tell you what it is," Betsy promised at the depot.

Tall and slim in her blue sailor suit, with her flat hat and spreading hairbow, she felt very much the young lady. Butternut Center wasn't exactly Paris, but it was adventurous to be there alone. She went into the small red depot and asked the agent whether she might leave her valise; he said, "Sure." She walked along the platform, past wagons full of milk cans, found a shady spot and ate the lunch Mrs. Taggart had put up. It was magnificent; ham sandwiches, dill pickles, hard-boiled eggs, a chunk of layer cake and cookies. She ate looking off at the fields, her back to Butternut Center, feeling that lunch out of doors, out of a box, was slightly undignified. Her lunch eaten, however, and the box disposed of, she set out to see the town.

There wasn't much of it. Except for a white church and burying ground out on the prairie, it lay along a single road. This was dusty now, but its ruts and gulches showed how rich its mud would be at other seasons. It led in one direction to the grain elevator, in the other past a handful of houses to the general store. The store reminded her that in the excitement of her unexpected return, she had forgotten to buy presents. No Ray ever came home from a trip without bringing presents for the rest.

"I'd like to get something for Tacy, too," Betsy thought, hurrying toward the store.

Willard's Emporium, said the sign above the door. It was one of those stores, perfect for her purpose, where everything under the sun was for sale. A single glance revealed kitchen stoves, buggy whips, corset covers and crackers. Betsy browsed happily along the overflowing counters until a boy sitting in a corner, eating an apple and reading a book, threw away the apple and came forward.

She was struck by the way he walked, with a slight challenging swing. He had very light hair brushed back in a pompadour, blue eyes under thick light brows and healthy red lips with the lower one pushed out as though seeming to dare the world to knock the chip off his shoulder. It was a sturdy well-built shoulder, in a faded blue cotton shirt. He hardly looked at her, but keeping his finger in the partly closed book . . . it was, she noticed, *The Three Musketeers* . . . asked what he could do for her in a tone that implied he hoped she would answer, "Nothing. I'm just looking."

"Nothing, thanks. I'm just looking," said Betsy obligingly. Then, realizing that she really had to buy five presents even though it meant delaying D'Artagnan's greatest feat she added, "That is, I can look around a few minutes if you're in an exciting place."

The boy grinned. "Oh, I've read it six times. Swell book! What are you looking for?"

"Presents. Five of them." She explained, talking very fast, that no Ray ever came home from a visit without bringing presents. "It's an old family custom," she said.

25

"Hallelujah!" he exclaimed, shutting the book. "That'll be fun, picking out five presents. I hope you have a brother. There's a corking jack-knife here."

"Not a sign of a brother," Betsy answered. "Just two sisters. And Margaret's so young she'd cut herself on a jack-knife, and Julia wouldn't care for one. She's sixteen."

"What's Julia interested in?" he asked.

"Oh, music and boys."

Betsy hadn't intended to be funny, and when the boy laughed, she blushed.

"Well," he said. "We've got a mouth organ."

"But she likes classical music. A mouth organ might do for Tacy, though."

"Who's Tacy?"

"My best friend. I want to take her something, too, if I've got money enough."

"How much do you have?" he asked. He put *The Three Musketeers* aside completely and hoisted himself to a counter, smiling. Betsy sat down on a barrel and opened her pocketbook.

"Three dollars."

"A ticket to Deep Valley is only forty cents."

"But I have to take the hack home. That costs a quarter."

"Can't you walk?"

"In our family," said Betsy, "when we come home on the train, we take the hack."

Again he burst into laughter.

"You have a lot of customs in your family. Haven't you?" he asked.

Pleased and pink, she tried to make it clear. "The hack is part of the fun of the trip."

"All right. Forty plus twenty-five, that's sixty-five. So you have two dollars and thirty-five cents to spend for presents."

"But I want to buy some things on the train. Caramels, maybe, and a magazine. It's . . ."

"I know, I know," he interrupted. "It's one of those old family customs. You never travel without caramels."

Betsy's blushes sank to the V of her sailor suit.

"We'll give you a quarter for caramels, then, and get on with the presents. Would your father like a moustache cup?"

"My father," said Betsy, "hasn't a moustache any more, and moustache cups are out of style." She looked around the store. "He likes cheese," she said, nodding toward a row of giant cheeses.

"Fine. Cheese for your father. Sharp or mild?"

"Sharp."

"If you brought home mild cheese, he wouldn't let you in, I'll bet."

"He'd use it for the mousetrap."

They joked like old friends, choosing the presents. For her father he cut a wedge of cheese so sharp that

Betsy could smell it even after it was wrapped. For her mother, they found a glass butter dish. Tacy got the mouth organ; Julia, side combs decorated with rhinestones. They hadn't found a present for Margaret when they heard the hooting whistle of the train.

"You don't need to rush," he said. "They take on all the milk cans."

But in spite of this reassurance, Betsy felt hurried. She had to pick up her valise. She decided quickly on doll dishes for Margaret. Her purchases came to a dollar and sixty cents.

"Fifty cents for the pig bank," said the boy. "Well, back to *The Three Musketeers*."

Betsy hesitated, trying to think what to say. She had no brothers, and she hadn't started going around with boys. Julia would have known how to convey to this one that she liked him and appreciated his help. In fact, thought Betsy enviously, Julia would have him taking the next train to Deep Valley to call. But Betsy didn't know how to do it.

Should she tell him that her name was Betsy? He knew it was Ray. Should she ask him to come up to Hill Street when he came to Deep Valley? Perhaps she ought to mention that she was starting high school this fall? That would make him understand that she was old enough to have callers. Before she could decide anything, the train whistled again.

The boy had picked up *The Three Musketeers*. He was acting almost as though he regretted having been so friendly. Betsy blurted out:

"What's your name?"

"Joe Willard."

"Willard's Emporium?"

"I'm just a poor relation."

"Well, thank you," Betsy said. "Thank you a lot."

It wasn't satisfactory, but it was the best she could manage. At least he smiled again.

"Don't eat the cheese before you get home," he said.

The brakeman ushered her into the day coach, and she sat down in a red plush seat. All the passengers seemed to be eating, bananas chiefly, and an endless line of hot, restless children trotted to and from the water fountain.

Betsy bought a box of Cracker Jack. She bought a box of caramels and a copy of *The Ladies' Home Journal*.

"Like traveling?" asked the train boy.

"Love it," she answered.

"I'd like to travel all over the world," she thought, munching Cracker Jack. "I think I'd like Paris especially. I think I just belong in Paris."

Paris reminded her of *The Three Musketeers*, and

that brought Joe Willard back into her thoughts.

"He's handsomer than Herbert Humphreys," she decided. "Tacy'll never believe it though."

The speed of the train swallowed up the prairie. In no time at all the river came into sight. They passed a waterfall she recognized; then the train descended along the side of a bluff.

The brakeman called, "Deep Valley!" and at once the car was in confusion. Hats were pinned on; small bonnets tied; all traces of banana wiped away. Valises and suit cases were dragged down from the rack. The train slowed to a stop.

Holding her valise in one hand and the package from Willard's Emporium in the other, Betsy found Mr. Thumbler's hack.

"Good afternoon, Mr. Thumbler," she said. "333 Hill Street, please." As though he didn't know where the Ray family lived! The hack rolled up Front Street, past her father's shoe store. It crossed to Broad Street and rolled past Lincoln Park, and began to climb.

Betsy tried to sit back in careless calm, but a smile as bright as her hair ribbon spread across her face. Neighbors darted out to see who was coming in the hack. Children waved, and dogs barked. It was a triumphal return. And not only was she back on her beloved Hill Street . . . the surprise was still ahead.

"Now for the surprise!" thought Betsy, trying not to bounce.

3
The Surprise

BETSY DIDN'T KNOW exactly what she had expected,
but certainly not to find everything at home going
forward just as usual on a summer afternoon. Margaret was playing with her dolls on the front porch.
Julia was at the piano, vocalizing.

"Ni-po-tu-la-he-" Her voice floated out the window
as the hack stopped in front of the yellow cottage.

Betsy dug twenty-five cents from her pocket book.

"Thank you, Mr. Thumbler," she said politely, and thanked him again with downright gratitude when he carried her valise up the steps, just as though she were grown up.

Margaret gave a welcoming cry, and Julia rushed out, closely followed by Mrs. Ray in a dressing sacque with her curly red hair falling on her shoulders. She had just been changing into an afternoon dress.

Mrs. Ray was tall and slim; younger and gayer, Betsy was pleasantly aware, than most mothers. She did not seem much older than Julia who was old for sixteen.

None of the Ray girls looked like their mother. They all had their father's dark hair. But Julia's hair was wavy, not straight like Betsy's. It waved in a high pompadour above a truly beautiful face . . . arched brows, violet eyes, classic nose, even teeth and a delicate pink and white skin like the one Betsy cherished.

Much to her chagrin . . . for she planned to be an opera singer, and longed to be tall and queenly . . . Julia was small. She had a tiny waist, dainty hands and feet, and an air of complete poise. Julia, Betsy often heard, had never had an awkward age. Betsy never heard this said about herself and suspected strongly that she was in the midst of one, but she admired Julia without resentment. During the last year all big-sister, little-sister friction had miraculously melted away.

Margaret was eight years old, and not at all the sort of little girl that either of her sisters had been. She did not have Julia's diamond-bright precocity nor Betsy's gregariousness. Betsy at eight had been habitually surrounded by children, cheerfully smudged and disheveled if five minutes away from the wash bowl. Margaret played sedately alone or with one child at a time, and her brown English bob was always glossy, her starched dresses immaculate. She had large black-lashed blue eyes, and a grave expression. She held herself erect just as Mr. Ray did. It was amusing to see the pair, one so big and one so little, but both with squared shoulders, walking hand in hand. And Hill Street saw this often.

"She's my boy," Mr. Ray used to joke. "All the boy I've got."

She came down the steps now with her usual flawless dignity but her small face was covered with smiles. She hugged and kissed Betsy, and so did Julia, and so did Mrs. Ray.

When these greetings were over Betsy waited to hear some word of the surprise, but none was spoken. They all trooped into Mrs. Ray's room so that she could finish dressing while Betsy told the story of her visit.

"I had the dandiest time," she kept repeating.

"And you weren't homesick?" asked Julia. "Bettina, you're wonderful! I die with homesickness when I go away."

"You're temperamental," said Betsy. "You're a temperamental prima donna." To Tacy, and to Tacy alone would she confess how homesick she had been.

Shortly Tacy came running across the street. Politeness had kept her away until she was sure the family reunion was over. Tacy too had grown tall, taller even than Betsy, and she too wore skirts down to her ankles. Her ringlets were gone, and thick auburn braids were bound about her head. She and Betsy hugged tempestuously, rocking back and forth.

They all sat on the porch then, and Julia made lemonade. At intervals Betsy saw her mother and Julia, or Julia and Tacy, or Margaret and her mother, exchange mysterious glances. She wished she had asked about the surprise the minute she stepped out of the hack. Now she didn't know how.

"I must go and unpack," she said. "I brought some presents. Shall I give Tacy hers and put the others on the supper table? We don't want to open them, of course, until Papa comes home."

Margaret looked at her mother and then spoke, beaming.

"We aren't eating supper here."

"Not . . . why not?"

"Papa's taking us to a restaurant."

"But why? It isn't Sunday, or a holiday, or anything."

"Oh, he likes to give me a rest once in a while," Mrs. Ray put in breezily, "when we're not keeping a hired girl."

"And there really isn't room for a hired girl in this house," added Julia with an exaggerated sigh.

"What the dickens!" thought Betsy. But she was too stubborn to ask about the surprise since she hadn't done it in the first place.

"I'll give Tacy hers anyway," she said.

Tacy proved to have a talent for the mouth organ. After experimenting only a short time, she said, "This is in Betsy's honor," and began a recognizable, "Home, sweet home."

"Be it ever so humble,
There's no place like home . . ."

Betsy and Julia and Mrs. Ray intoned in close harmony. They all fell to laughing, but Betsy thought secretly how suitable the sentiment was.

"Come on, Tacy," she said. "Let's look around."

They inspected the front lawn and the back lawn, backyard maple, garden, empty buggy shed and barn.

They ran across the street and Betsy said "hello" to Mrs. Kelly, and to Katie, Tacy's sister, Julia's age, and to Paul, their youngest brother.

"Let's go up on the hill," said Betsy, still holding Tacy's hand. She wouldn't really feel she was at home until she and Tacy had been up on the hill. "Let's go up to our bench and talk."

But to her surprise Tacy refused.

"I don't dare," she replied. "I'm afraid . . ." She broke off, but Betsy knew what she meant. She was afraid that alone on the hill she would give away the secret. "You see," said Tacy hesitantly. "I'm going downtown with you."

"You're what?"

"Going down to the restaurant . . . for supper. Your father invited me. There comes your father now," she cried, sounding relieved.

Sure enough Old Mag was climbing up Hill Street, drawing the surrey.

"But it isn't five o'clock yet!" exclaimed Betsy. "What's Papa coming home for?"

"You'll know! You'll see!" Tacy cried.

All the Kellys began to laugh, and when Betsy and Tacy raced across the street, Mr. Ray was smiling, Mrs. Ray and Julia were hugging one another, and Margaret for all her dignity was jumping up and down.

She whispered to her mother; then, ran into the house.

"And a safety pin, Margaret," Mrs. Ray called.

Margaret returned with a table napkin and a safety pin.

"Sit down, Bettina," Julia commanded.

"But why? What for?"

"We're going to blindfold you. No questions, please."

Betsy sat down on the porch steps. She looked around at the laughing faces. She looked up at the loved green hill which seemed to be smiling, too, and down Hill Street. Obediently she closed her eyes and Julia with deft fingers adjusted the blindfold.

"I'll help her."

"No, let me!"

Betsy was surrounded with clamoring voices. She was interested to discover how helpless she felt with her eyes bandaged.

"It's like this to be blind," she thought.

A soft hand took one of hers. That was Julia. Slender, rougher fingers took her other hand. That was Tacy. A whiff of violet perfume rushed by. That was her mother. There were light feet, Margaret's, and her father's firm tread.

"Bring her along. This way. Careful of the stairs."

"Step up, now!" That was the hitching block.

"Again. That's right. Sit down."

She was in the back seat of the surrey. Julia and Tacy squeezed in on either side. Margaret, no doubt, was sitting with Papa and Mamma up in front.

"Good-by! Surprise on Betsy!" Katie and Paul were calling from the Kellys' hitching block. The surrey began to move.

"We're on Hill Street, going down," thought Betsy. She resolved to keep track of where they were going. But she couldn't. Right turn, left turn, down hill, up hill. She soon lost her way.

"I give up. Where *are* we? And what's it all about?"

Tacy giggled and squeezed her hand.

"We're on our way to California to see Grandma," said her mother.

"We're on our way to Washington to call on the Teddy Roosevelts," said her father.

"We're almost there," said Margaret. "Oh, Betsy! You're going to be so surprised!"

The clop clop of Old Mag's hoofs stopped at last, and the surrey, too, halted. Betsy was helped out by agitated hands. She was led up a flight of stairs and across a level space and up another flight of stairs.

"You're fooling me!" she cried. "We're back home again."

Everyone laughed uproariously.

"You're not far wrong, at that," Mr. Ray remarked.

A door opened. There was a smell of fresh paint, of new wood, of the paste they stick wall paper on with. Betsy was pushed forward, turned around three times, and her blindfold taken off.

She stood blinking in a small square room, empty of all but sunshine. A golden oak staircase went up at the right. The wall paper, a design of dark green leaves, was set in gold panels. The floor was oiled and shone with newness.

"It's the music room," Julia cried. "The piano will stand right here, under the stairs."

Turning Betsy to the left they led her through an archway into another, larger room with a big window pushing out at the front. This was papered in lighter green with loops of roses for a border.

"It's the parlor," everyone cried.

Behind that, through another archway, was a room with a plate rail, papered above with pears and grapes. There was a fireplace in one corner, and a glittering gold-fringed lamp was suspended by a gold chain from the ceiling.

"It's the dining room," came the shout.

They pushed through a swinging door into a pantry, into a kitchen, empty and smelling of newness.

Returning by a small door to the music room they

climbed the golden oak stairs. There were two bed-rooms at the front. Margaret rushed into the right-hand room.

"Papa's and Mamma's room!" she cried.

She rushed into the left-hand room which had a window seat.

"Julia's room!" she chanted.

Back in the hall three doors remained unopened. Mrs. Ray opened the one at the head of the stairs.

"This room is yours, Betsy," she said.

"And down the hall is a bathroom," cried Julia. "A bathroom, Bettina! No more baths in a tub in the kitchen."

"And down at the end of the hall is *my* room," said Margaret, standing very straight. "I can arrange the bureau to suit myself."

"There's a room on the third floor for the hired girl when we get one," Mrs. Ray explained. "But now come in and see your room. It's your very own."

"You don't need to put up with me and my untidiness any more," said Julia, putting her arm around Betsy.

Everyone was talking very fast, perhaps because Betsy was saying so little. She had made a few excla-mations of surprise, but for Betsy, who was usually such a talker, she was very quiet indeed.

She looked around the generous room which was

to be hers alone, with a great pang of loneliness for Julia who had always slept in the same room, in the very same bed, and for Margaret who when they had a hired girl slept in a small bed in the corner. She forced her lips into a smile and walked to one of the windows.

She saw somebody's house, some stranger's dull ordinary house. Across from her window at home was Tacy's house with tall trees behind it and the sunset behind that. She thought of the hill, the dear green hill where she and Tacy had picnicked ever since they were old enough to take their supper plates up to the bench.

"I won't cry! I won't!" she thought, staring out the window. She forced the smile to her face again. It felt as though her lips were stretched tight against her teeth. But she must have managed a pretty fair imitation of a smile for her father who had been looking anxious smiled in return.

"It's ours, Betsy!" he said. "I've bought it. Mamma has her modern improvements at last."

Mrs. Ray danced across the empty room to hug him.

"I'm going to take one bath after another all day long."

"But what about the new gas stove, Mrs. Ray?" asked Tacy. "You have to stop between baths long enough to cook on that."

"Oh, yes! My darling gas stove! No more horrid wood fires to build."

"And no more lamps to clean," said Julia. "This house is lighted all over by gas. See the fixtures, Betsy?"

"And it's heated by a furnace," Mr. Ray said. "No coal stove in the parlor."

Betsy thought her heart would break. Didn't they know how much she loved that coal stove beside which she had read so many books while the tea kettle sang and the little flames leaped behind the isinglass window? Didn't they know how she loved the yellow lamplight over the small cottage rooms? And she thought it was cozy to take baths in the kitchen beside the old wood-burning range! But her father's face was so proud, and her mother's so radiant . . . Julia and Margaret looked so happy . . . she couldn't say a word. She glanced at Tacy. Tacy, she saw, understood. Tacy smiled now and said, "It's just two blocks from the high school, Betsy. I'm going to stop in here before school and after school, every single day."

"Tacy is going to practically live here," said Mrs. Ray. "Oh, my beautiful house! My beautiful new house!" And she hugged Mr. Ray again, and picked up her long skirts and waltzed around the empty room. Julia began to waltz with her, and Mr. Ray began to waltz in his stately way with Margaret, and

Tacy caught Betsy. Everybody waltzed singing, "In the Good Old Summertime," until they were laughing too hard either to waltz or to sing.

Betsy laughed harder than anyone, and she and Tacy, hand in hand, raced all over the house. They looked into every nook and corner, and into the closets, and out the windows. And when they had finished they all went down to the restaurant for supper. There everyone talked at once about the new house, and about how the furniture would be arranged, and what new things would have to be bought.

Betsy talked harder and faster than anyone, but inside she felt terrible. She felt as though she had fallen downstairs and had all her breath knocked out. She felt even worse than when she was visiting the Taggarts.

4
High Street

IN A BREATHLESSLY SHORT space of time the Rays had moved from Hill Street where Betsy had lived all her life, to the new house at the windy junction of High Street and Plum.

High Street, like Hill Street, was on a hill for Deep Valley was built upon the river bluffs. But where Hill Street ran up a hill like a finger pointing to the top,

High Street ran lengthwise, one of a layer of streets of which the lowest was Front Street, parallel to the river.

Two blocks from the Ray house, on the same side of the street, stood the red brick, turreted high school. Opposite were other houses with trees and shady lawns. Above them rows of rooftops indicated layers of streets, all the way to the top of High Street's hill, where the sun came up behind a German Catholic College. It was different from the Hill Street hill, with its gifts of flowers and snow.

Betsy's room looked south to Plum Street. Behind Plum Street's houses the road dipped into a ravine. There was a store where Margaret bought candy as Betsy and Tacy had once bought it at Mrs. Chubbock's store. The road forked, at a watering trough, and one branch led off to Cemetery Hill; the other, with several jogs invisible from Betsy's window, found its way to Hill Street.

"At least," Betsy thought with moody satisfaction, "I'm looking in the right direction."

The house sat proudly on a terrace. It was freshly painted, green. It looked at the moment a little bare but that wouldn't last long. Mr. Ray was transplanting vines from the Hill Street house. The new home would be covered with the old familiar pattern by next summer. Mrs. Ray planned to hang baskets filled with daisies, geraniums and long trailing vines around the porch. Bridal wreath and hydrangeas would be set out on the lawn. This house had no garden, no orchard, no grape arbor; not even a buggy shed and barn. Old Mag lived in a barn Mr. Ray had rented down the street. Betsy missed the comfortable litter, the familiar smell of the barnyard. She wondered whether Old Mag wasn't homesick, and she and Margaret secretly made frequent trips to see her, taking sugar.

On moving day Betsy had been caught up into the excitement of the occasion. While men carried the furniture out of the yellow cottage, all the children and dogs of the neighborhood had looked on and rushed about. With scarcely a glance into the startled empty rooms, the family had hurried off in the surrey to reach High Street ahead of the dray.

Tacy had gone along, bearing a cake from her mother, a bowl of potato salad from Mrs. Rivers, and various contributions from the other neighbors. Mr. Ray tucked a coffee pot under the surrey seat. They had picnicked gaily in the midst of the confusion, and the moment the piano was set down in the music room . . . some people would have called this room a hall, but Julia insisted upon music room . . . Julia sat down and began to trill "ni-po-tu-la-he. . . ." There hadn't been time or opportunity to feel lonely for Hill Street.

But when the new house was comparatively settled and serene, the impact of the move struck Betsy with delayed force. Her mother was still blissfully busy with curtains and new purchases. Julia had joined the Girls' Choir of St. John's Episcopal Church which was directed by her singing teacher, Mrs. Poppy. She was busy with choir rehearsals, talking a language of vestments and te deums that Betsy did not even understand. She had also a new boy on the string, a solid, sober, well-dressed boy named Fred.

Betsy turned to Margaret, but Margaret was six years her junior; Betsy with ankle-length skirts and turned-up braid felt foolish playing childish games. She went up to see Tacy often, but the windows of the empty yellow cottage stared like reproachful eyes. She took to writing long letters to Tib, and when she could find solitude adequate enough, she wrote poems, about childhood and Hill Street and Tacy. But there didn't seem to be a place to write poems in the new house. Her Uncle Keith's trunk was not in the spacious new room.

Keith Warrington, her mother's brother, was an actor. And his trunk, a real trouper's trunk, flat-topped, four-square, had long served Betsy as a desk. It did not seem to belong in the new room, somehow. At Betsy's own suggestion, on moving day, it had been put in the attic.

"Papa and I will buy you a new desk," her mother said absently. Betsy disliked the new desk in advance. Sometimes she climbed to the attic and stuffed smudged, scribbled papers furtively into the trunk, standing forlorn in a dark corner. On such occasions she often cried a little; never much, for it always occurred to her how romantic it was to be crying about her trunk, and then she stopped, and couldn't start again.

"I'll be glad when school begins," she thought one day, sitting on the porch steps, looking across the street at older lawns and gardens where late summer flowers gave the look of fall.

Her mother came out of the house just then, wearing the abstracted beatific look she had worn since moving day. Her red hair was tied up in a towel and she carried a hammer.

She tip-toed out to the muddy lawn and squinted at the big front window.

"I'm putting the new curtains up," she explained. "Just wanted to get the effect. I'm fixing them in a stunning new way, crossed over, sort of. What I need for that window is a big brass bowl, with a palm in it, you know . . ." She stopped, sensing Betsy's disinterest.

Betsy spoke crossly. "I'll be glad when school begins."

Mrs. Ray came out of her trance. She sat down

on the steps, looking troubled.

"I'm sure you will. You'll be happier, too, when you get acquainted with some boys and girls. I don't know why you haven't already. You were always such a one for other children."

"There aren't any around here," said Betsy gloomily.

"Why, there's the Edwards boy."

Betsy could not deny it. The Rays' back lawn ended in an alley, and across the alley was the Edwards' barn. Their house looked the other way, fronting on the street below High Street, but it was as close as Tacy's house had been. And there was an Edwards boy just about her age named Caleb. People called him Cab.

"I don't know him; he went to the other school. And he's always busy with boys, playing ball," Betsy said.

"Go out and play with them."

"Mamma! You seem to think I'm no older than Margaret."

Mrs. Ray sighed. She looked at the stooped slender Betsy.

"Sit up straight, Betsy," she said in an irritated tone, but Betsy only stooped the more. Secretly she thought the stoop attractive. She did not consider it a stoop, but a droop, such as Miss Ethel Barrymore had. She had read in the newspapers about the Ethel Barrymore droop, and she hoped that the Betsy Ray droop was equally fascinating.

Mrs. Ray was yearning to get at her windows but she made another attempt.

"Why don't you go down to the Sibleys?" she asked. "They live so near, and Caroline is such a lovely girl."

Mrs. Ray never mentioned Caroline Sibley without adding that she was a lovely girl which always annoyed Betsy.

"Caroline Sibley is a stick," she said.

"Why, Betsy, you hardly know her. I'm sure she isn't a stick. And they have such a big beautiful lawn, and there's always a crowd of young people there. . . ."

"And her father's a banker," Betsy put in rudely.

Mrs. Ray rose.

"Betsy, I really can't let you talk to me like that. You know perfectly well it makes no difference to me that Caroline Sibley's father is a banker. What interests me is that she is a very nice girl with a circle of friends who ought to be your friends, now that you live near. But there's no use in my talking. I see that I can't help you, at least in your present mood. And I'm busy. I wish to goodness I could get some help."

"Hasn't anyone answered your advertisement, Mamma?" asked Betsy, trying to sound pleasant because she felt ashamed.

"Not a soul. And I'm willing to pay top wages, two dollars a week."

"Can I help you?"

"Not with the curtains, thanks. I just have to fuss until I get them right." Thoughts of the new lace curtains, and the big shiny front window, brought the gleam back to Mrs. Ray's eyes. "Why don't you go to the Majestic?" she asked.

"Oh, Mamma! May I?" Betsy jumped up, smiling. "I haven't a cent," she added.

"Take a nickel out of my brown purse, and another nickel for ice cream," Mrs. Ray answered, and went back to her curtains, swinging the hammer and humming.

Betsy rushed upstairs to wash. The new bathroom *was* nice, she admitted, running hot water into the bowl. She combed her hair freshly, taking care not to comb out the curls, and tied the big taffeta hair ribbon which matched her pink lawn jumper. She scowled at a shiny nose.

"I think I'll run Mamma's chamois skin over my face," she said to herself. "Julia does it sometimes. It isn't really powdering."

Having beautified herself, she took ten cents from the brown pocket book, caught up a pink ruffled parasol and ran downstairs to kiss her mother penitently.

Starting down Plum Street she saw the Edwards

boy sawing wood in his back yard. She had seen him first over the back fence the day they moved in, and several times since. He was about her own height, which was tall for a girl but not for a boy. He was thin and wiry with black hair, snapping green eyes and a dark monkeyish face which was not handsome but undeniably attractive, especially when, as now, he grinned.

A year or two before Betsy would have given him a cheerful hello. Today, although she returned his smile, she did not speak or pause. She knew that her pink lawn jumper was becoming, and hoped that her Ethel Barrymore droop was fascinating, as she sauntered past his back yard and his front yard and on down the hill.

Crossing Broad Street she saw the Sibleys' house, and in spite of the indifference she had shown in talking to her mother, she glanced toward it wistfully. It was a large blue-grey frame house with a generous porch. At the side was a large lawn with a trampled comfortable look. Caroline had several brothers, and there was usually a game of some sort going on.

Betsy acknowledged now that she was prejudiced against Caroline Sibley; perhaps because her mother always praised her so highly.

"Probably I'd like her if I knew her better," Betsy conceded, and at that moment caught sight of her, walking arm in arm with a girl whom Betsy did not know at all. She was short, with smooth yellow hair, a round figure, and skirts a shade longer than the other girls wore. Betsy wondered who she was, but although Caroline Sibley called, "Hello!" and Betsy answered, she did not pause to be introduced. As soon as she had left them behind, she was sorry.

"I don't know what ails me," she thought dejectedly, and hurried on, glad to be going to the Majestic.

The Majestic Theatre, now . . . according to the sign . . . a High Class Place of Amusement, with Up-to-date Moving Picture Entertainment, Especially for Ladies and Children . . . had been just a short time before an ordinary Front Street store. Moving Picture Entertainment had been only a rumor emanating from nearby St. Paul and Minneapolis. There, travelers said, pictures moved on a screen. Deep Valley had seen them move only in nickelodeons, small boxes into which one dropped a nickel and peeped at jerky horse races, prize fights or dancing girls. Then talk of a moving picture called "The Great Train Robbery" rolled over the country like a tidal wave. In Deep Valley as in thousands of other towns a store front was painted red and yellow; a screen was put up inside; a projection machine, a piano and rows of chairs were moved in. The first program was "The Great Train Robbery," and Mr. Ray took the family to see it.

Today the picture was a fantasy called "The Astronomer's Dream." That was the kind Betsy liked best. She sat on the hard chair in the dim stuffy show house and watched the flickering scenes in an enchanted silence. After the main picture there was an illustrated song. The girl who played the piano sang, as colored slides were flashed on the screen.

"Keep a little cozy corner,
In your heart for me,
Just for me. . . ."

Betsy knew it well, for Julia played it.

She had an ice cream soda at Heinz's afterwards, but walking home under her pink ruffled parasol, she felt blue again. A game of prisoners' base was in progress now on the Sibleys' lawn. Cab Edwards had disappeared.

"Down at the Sibleys, probably," Betsy thought.

She was returning more despondent than she had been when she left. And that wasn't fair after her mother had spent ten cents to cheer her up. She didn't know what she could do about it, though. Then in a twinkling she didn't feel blue any more. Her spirits perked up like a terrier's ears. For Mr. Thumbler's hack was driving away from her house, and on the steps stood a stout woman wearing an elegant purple silk dress, a large hat trimmed with feathers, and a feather boa which, flung over one shoulder, shimmered down her ample body. She wasn't just a caller, for she carried a valise. A visitor! How thrilling!

Betsy collapsed her parasol, patted her curls. After the visitor had rung the bell and had been admitted and a suitable short interval had elapsed, Betsy put on her Ethel Barrymore droop and sauntered into the house.

5

Anna

HER MOTHER AND THE visitor were seated in the parlor. The curtains had been hung. Mrs. Ray's hair was no longer concealed by a towel but rose in its usual high red pompadour, and she was wearing a becoming waist and skirt.

She called, "Come in, dear!" and said to the visitor . . . in a somewhat choked voice, Betsy thought . . .

"This is my middle daughter, Betsy. Betsy, this is Anna Swenson who has come to work for us."

"I'm pleased to meet you," Betsy murmured.

Under the feathered hat she saw a wide good-natured face.

"Why, lovey!" said Anna Swenson. "How puny you look! Almost as puny as you are, lovey," she added, to Mrs. Ray.

"We're a very puny family," Mrs. Ray answered in the same choked voice.

Anna nodded.

"So were the McCloskeys. They're the folks I used to work for, lovey. My, how they liked my raised biscuits and my meat balls and my chocolate layer cake! And every last one of them was puny. Charley used to say to me, 'Anna, aren't those McCloskeys the puniest folks?' and I'd say, 'Ja, Charley! They're certainly puny.' They were tony, too."

"And who is Charley?" asked Mrs. Ray while Betsy slipped into a chair and stared with fascinated eyes.

"My beau," Anna answered, smiling broadly. "A bartender down at the Corner Café."

"Is he puny, too?"

"Na," answered Anna regretfully, shaking her head. "He's not puny. He's a nice fellow, Charley is, and a good spender. But I'd never call him puny."

"Are you engaged to him?" asked Betsy, hoping that if she was they would not be married soon.

"I'm not much on the marrying," Anna reassured her. "What I like to do is cook. You may think you know how to cook," she said to Mrs. Ray, who certainly *did* think she knew how to cook and started to say so, but Anna waved her down. "You may think you know how to cook, but wait 'til you taste my cinnamon buns. They melt in your mouth. 'Anna,' Mrs. McCloskey used to say to me, 'your cinnamon buns just melt in my mouth.'" She turned to Betsy. "The McCloskey girl," she added, "always said the same."

"Are you really coming to work for us?" cried Betsy.

"Certainly I am," Anna replied, beaming. "I said so to Charley last night. We were out buggy riding. A hired rig, but very tony. He's a good spender, Charley is. I showed him your ad in the paper. Mrs. Robert Ray of High Street wants a hired girl, five in the family, two dollars a week. I said to Charley, 'That's my place, Charley.' 'Well,' he said, 'I hope you'll like them as well as you liked the McCloskeys.'"

"Do you think you will?" Betsy asked eagerly.

Anna looked around the parlor, and Mrs. Ray flashed Betsy a proud confident glance. The new lace curtains were draped with a dazzling effect. Embroidered pillows made a tidy nest at the head of the leather sofa. A gas lamp with a green shade stood on the mission oak table and photographs marched along a mission oak bookcase. Framed pictures dotted the walls.

Anna spoke reflectively.

"The McCloskeys' house was tonier," she said.

For a moment Betsy wasn't sure whether her mother would let Anna work for them or not. She wanted to hiss "cinnamon buns" warningly across the room. But to her relief her mother's blue eyes began to dance. She jumped up and took Anna's hands.

"Anna," she said. "It's going to be our ambition in life to make you like us as well as you did the McCloskeys."

Julia came in then, swinging her music roll and looking very pretty. Margaret, too, appeared. She had been visiting a neighbor, Mrs. Wheat, on whom she called almost every afternoon. Anna was introduced, and pronounced them both puny. It was dawning upon Betsy that Anna did not give "puny" its usual insignificant meaning, that it was, on the contrary, the most complimentary word in her vocabulary.

Followed by her daughters Mrs. Ray showed Anna the dining room, the pantry, the shining kitchen. Anna surveyed them with pursed thoughtful lips. She did not say how they compared with the McCloskeys', but it was clear they did not quite measure up.

"I'll show her to her room, Mamma," Betsy offered, picking up the valise. It was very heavy.

"Thank you, lovey," Anna said, and Betsy led the way to the second floor and the third, across the open attic where Uncle Keith's trunk stood.

Up to this moment she had thought the hired girl's room very nice. It reminded her of her own room on Hill Street, being slant-roofed and small. There were an iron bed, a bureau, a wash stand with bowl and pitcher, a rocking chair beside the single window, a rag rug on the clean pine floor. It was neat as a pin and looked very inviting, but thinking about the Mc-Closkeys Betsy waited anxiously.

Anna looked around and smiled.

"I'll get along fine up here," she said.

"I like it, too," said Betsy, much relieved. "I'll come up and see you sometimes if you want me to."

"I'd like to have you, lovey. You can stay now and watch me unpack."

Betsy sat down in the rocking chair.

Anna took off her feather boa, smoothed it lovingly and hung it in the closet. She removed her big feathered hat and placed it on the closet shelf. Her hair was wound in a big tight knob that made her broad face look even broader than it was. Her forehead was seamed.

She opened her valise and unrolled a flannel night

gown in which an alarm clock had been wrapped. She put that on the bureau. She unrolled another night gown and took out a tall, gilt-topped bottle.

"Perfume," she said. "Jasmine. Do you want some, lovey?"

"Why, thank you," Betsy answered. "I love perfume."

Anna sprinkled her liberally and put the bottle on the bureau. She returned to the valise and lifted out a black silk dress.

"This is my best dress," she remarked. "I wear it to weddings and funerals. I'll wear it to your wedding, lovey, but I hope I won't wear it to your funeral."

"I hope so, too," said Betsy, but the idea was not entirely unpleasant. It was quite romantic.

"The dress I have on is second best," Anna continued.

"It's very stylish," Betsy said.

Anna took out a blue cotton dress, a red cotton dress, and a green cotton dress.

"House dresses," she commented. She hung them all on hangers in the closet and added a well worn wrapper. She took out a pile of aprons, and folded suits of underwear and disposed of them neatly in the bureau drawers. She ranged a pair of worn shoes and a pair of slippers in the closet.

Last of all she lifted out a large square box covered

with purple plush. She carried this to the bureau and proudly threw back the lid. Gleaming on white satin were a hand mirror, a comb and brush, a button hook, a shoe horn, a finger nail cleaner and a buffer.

"My dresser set. Charley gave it to me for Christmas."

"It's beautiful!"

"It's mother-of-pearl."

"I'd like to brush my hair with such a beautiful brush," Betsy cried.

"Come up and use it any time," said Anna generously.

She closed the valise, put it in the closet and sat down on the bed. The clothing, the alarm clock, the bottle of perfume and the plush-encased dresser set seemed to complete the list of her possessions. Bureaus in the Ray bedrooms bore cherished photographs. There wasn't a single picture on Anna's bureau. Not of Charley, not of the McCloskeys, not of her mother or father or sisters or brothers or home.

"Anna," said Betsy suddenly. "Where is your home?"

Anna's broad seamed face broke into a smile of unexpected gentleness.

"Why, lovey!" she answered. "This is my home."

Anna had found a home . . . or had borrowed one as hired girls do . . . and Betsy had found a friend, her first friend on High Street. She walked to the lofty window and looked out, and for the first time saw beauty in the German Catholic College, grey and dour, on the heights.

"The sun comes up behind that college," she remarked.

She sat down again to tell Anna about Hill Street, and Tacy.

"Is she puny?" Anna asked.

"The puniest girl I know," Betsy answered, and praised Tacy's curly auburn hair. "I wish I were punier," she confided abruptly.

"You're plenty puny, lovey," Anna answered. "You're almost as puny as the McCloskey girl."

This Betsy knew now, was real praise. And Anna had more than compliments to give. She knew about a cream that took off freckles in a week.

"I'll buy you some on Thursday."

She knew about metal curlers . . . Magic Wavers, they were called . . . that produced a curl so tight and lasting it put kid rollers to shame.

"I'll find you some on Thursday, too," she promised.

They had a beautiful time until Anna looked at her clock and said it was time to change her dress and go down to start supper.

"What would you like me to make, lovey? It's too late for chocolate cake, and cinnamon buns have to raise, but I could stir up a floating island."

"I love floating island!" cried Betsy.

She bounded down the stairs, spreading waves of jasmine perfume.

Betsy liked High Street better after Anna came, and the rest of August slipped by swiftly. Margaret was still busy with her friend, Mrs. Wheat.

"She's a perfect little lady," Mrs. Wheat said.

Julia was busy with the Episcopal Choir, and "nipo-tu-la-he," and the new beau named Fred. He had a fine voice and liked to sing and Julia played his accompaniments.

"Love me . . . and the world is mine," he bellowed with such feeling that his face grew red.

He brought Margaret a grey and white kitten which she named Washington. He joked with Betsy about how green she would be on her first day at high school. He enlivened life considerably and so, in a different way, did Miss Mix, the dressmaker who . . . toward the last of the month . . . came to the Rays every day for a week.

"I'm certainly lucky to have her . . . best dressmaker in town . . . three girls and myself to get ready for fall . . ."

Mrs. Ray kept repeating this with variations for Miss Mix's semi-annual visits always upset the house. She sewed only in Mrs. Ray's bedroom, but bright scraps of cloth and snarls of thread, like the hum of her machine, permeated everywhere.

Mr. Ray could find no peaceful spot in which to read his paper. He was irritable. Mrs. Ray was nervous and abstracted, and even Anna was jumpy. Every meal was a challenge; company food, and the best silver and dishes. Miss Mix, wherever she went, expected and received the best.

Miss Mix was a favored character. She went to the twin cities often, bringing back the latest styles, the newest coiffures, not only in fashion books but on her person. Moreover she wore rouge. Women in Deep Valley did not use rouge; not even Julia's singing teacher, Mrs. Poppy, whose husband owned the opera house and the hotel and who used to be an actress. Mrs. Ray sometimes surreptitiously darkened her eyebrows with a burned match, but she never even considered using rouge. Miss Mix used it unreproved . . . on her grave lips, her unsmiling middle-aged cheeks. Unlike most dressmakers she was not talkative. She worked silently, swiftly, intent upon materials, trimmings, patterns, seeming to take little interest in the wearers of the beautiful clothes she produced.

So the sewing machine hummed in a littered bedroom, and Anna baked, and the ends of the maples in lawns along High Street turned yellow.

6
The First Day of High School

SCHOOL OPENED ON THE DAY after Labor Day. Betsy was awake at six o'clock. She hadn't slept well, for the Magic Wavers weren't as comfortable as the familiar kid rollers. They made a firm curl, though, and a dazzling entrance into high school was worth any discomfort.

She was glad to be up early in order to have plenty of time in the bathroom. She could get in before her father started shaving and ahead of Julia, Margaret and her mother. She had taken a warm bath the night before but this morning she took the quick cold one which . . . she understood from novels, chiefly English . . . brought a glow to the cheek and a shine to the eye. Looking into the mirror afterwards she was not at all sure it had had this effect; she looked a trifle blue and chilly. But it gave her a good feeling, and she didn't worry about her color knowing that her cheeks always flushed obligingly on exciting occasions.

They were gratifyingly pink when, giddy with curls, wearing a large and jaunty pale blue hair ribbon and a pale blue and white sailor suit, closely belted to make her waist look even smaller than it was, Betsy descended the stairs. The family wasn't down yet so she went out to the kitchen.

"Do I look puny, Anna?"

"Lovey, you do!" cried Anna admiringly. "I was saying to Charley last night that you get punier all the time."

"What smells so good?"

"Muffins. They're on account of it's the first day of school. At the McCloskeys I always made muffins for the first day of school."

"The McCloskeys had the nicest customs," said Betsy with a sigh. "Where did they live, Anna? What's become of them?"

She had asked these questions before, but Anna was always evasive.

"They've moved away," she answered vaguely. "They lived in a big tony house. Take the coffee in for me, will you, lovey? And strike the gong? I hear your father coming down."

Betsy took in the coffee and beat a tattoo on the gong. She also ran upstairs to prod Julia. It was Julia's practise to tumble out of bed, not when she was called but after the breakfast gong sounded. Betsy hurried her along now with a tantalizing reference to muffins and rushed back to the dining room where her father, mother and Margaret were assembled. The checked taffeta hair ribbon atop Margaret's English bob was as stiff with newness as her checked gingham dress. Her small face was sober for she, too, was starting at a new school and unlike Betsy was not sure that she was going to like it.

"Where is Julia?" asked Mr. Ray as usual.

"We won't wait for her," said Mrs. Ray quickly, and they sat down at the table. Mr. Ray asked the blessing while Betsy peeked into the sideboard mirror pleased to note the pinkness of her cheeks and the pronounced curl of her hair.

"When I was a boy," said Mr. Ray as soon as the blessing was over, "every child in the family was on time for every meal. There were ten of us, too."

Mr. Ray was a great one to joke, but he wasn't joking now. He had been raised on a farm and believed in early rising, that habit so repugnant to Julia.

Mrs. Ray hurried his coffee across the table and Betsy, as usual, tried to create a diversion.

"I'm starting high school today, Papa. How do you like the new sailor suit Miss Mix made for me?"

"Margaret has a new dress, too," said Mrs. Ray.

"I'm glad you have something to show for all that fuss," said Mr. Ray, serving the bacon and eggs. He forgot Julia for a moment, but when Anna brought in the muffins he looked around.

"My dear," he said to Mrs. Ray. "It's too bad for Julia not to get down while these muffins are hot."

"I told her about the muffins, Papa. She's hurrying," Betsy said and tried to think of another diversion. A sharp ring at the doorbell provided one. Betsy ran to the door and came back with Tacy whose arrival put Mr. Ray into such good humor that Julia slipped into her chair without a reprimand.

"Well, well!" said Mr. Ray. "Betsy and Tacy starting high school together! How many years have you gone off together on the first day of school?"

"This is the tenth," Tacy said. "It's too bad Tib isn't here to go along."

"Sit down and have a muffin and a cup of cocoa with Betsy," Mrs. Ray urged and Tacy slipped into a chair. Betsy's pink cheeks looked pale beside Tacy's which were sheets of scarlet. Under a round hat even her ears were red; and her eyes were shining.

"I'm almost too scared to eat," she said. "Not quite, though. These muffins look so good."

"Well, don't cry and try to go home like you did in kindergarten," Betsy responded.

"And remember, both of you, all Katie and I have told you," Julia said mischievously. "Don't put Mr. or Miss in front of a teacher's name. Except when you're speaking to one, of course. You always say Bangeter, Clarke, O'Rourke, and so on. Not *Miss* Bangeter, *Miss* Clarke, *Miss* O'Rourke."

"Yes, ma'am," replied Tacy meekly. "What else, ma'am?"

"Did you ever hear of a Social Room?" asked Julia. "Do you know what a vacant period is?"

"Certainly," said Tacy. "I know what it means to flunk, too, and I only hope I won't do it."

"Well, don't act like freshies. Be a credit to Katie and me."

"Don't worry," said Betsy. "We'll act as though we owned the school. We'll saunter in with bored expressions. Won't we, Tacy?"

"Absolutely," said Tacy. "And we'd better stop eating muffins if we're going to saunter in early enough to get those seats."

"What seats?" asked Mr. Ray.

"The back corner seats in the freshman row. They're the seats everyone tries to get."

"I forbid you to choose those seats," Mr. Ray said. "Front seats for both of you. You need to be where Miss Bangeter can keep her eyes on you."

But his hazel eyes were twinkling now.

"It isn't eight o'clock yet," said Mrs. Ray. "School doesn't begin until nine."

"We want to be there when the doors open. All the kids are after those back corner seats."

"Winona Root is after one. And you know we have to hump to get ahead of Winona."

"Good-by, Mamma. Good-by, Papa." Betsy kissed them hurriedly.

"The muffins were grand, Anna. Hope you get a nice teacher, Margaret."

"I'll see you in school," Julia cried.

Betsy put on her hat before the music room mirror, picked up a new tablet and a freshly sharpened pencil. Tacy carried a spanking new tablet and pencil, too. Joining hands, they ran.

Outside there was sunshine. The air smelled and tasted like September, like the first day of school. The flood of schoolbound children was not yet loosed. Betsy and Tacy had High Street to themselves.

At the high school, the grizzled janitor was opening

the big front doors. Betsy and Tacy rushed in. They rushed up the broad stairs which turned at a landing where a statue of Mercury was placed, through the spacious upper hall and the girls' cloakroom into the big assembly room, empty and silent.

Freshmen, they knew, were always assigned to the last half dozen rows on the far side of the room. They ran at once to these, and followed the last two rows back to the end. The back seats in these rows had advantages other than the obvious one of being so far from the presiding teacher's desk. They were next to a bulging many-windowed alcove which served as the school library and could also . . . so they had heard from Julia and Katie . . . provide a sociable retreat. The alcove held not only a dictionary on an easel, an encyclopedia and other reference books, but offered a view over descending rooftops all the way to Front Street and the river. Betsy and Tacy paused to look at their own Deep Valley spread out before them on this momentous day.

They sat down breathless, smiling at each other. They examined the inkwells, the grooves for pens and pencils where each one placed her pencil now, the empty interiors of the desks.

"Let's leave our tablets out on top," said Betsy. "They'll stake our claim to the seats while we look around."

So leaving the tablets as evidence of ownership, they drifted down the aisle. They investigated the assembly room. Betsy even went up on the platform where stood a piano, two armchairs and a high reading desk.

"Betsy! Come down! You shouldn't!" hissed Tacy as Betsy sat down in one of the armchairs and tried to imitate tall, erect, queenly Miss Bangeter.

Betsy ran down the steps at the other side of the platform and into the girls' cloakroom again.

Here they were delighted to find Winona Root hanging up a red hat. Winona was tall, thin, angular, yet jauntily graceful. She had heavy black hair worn in Grecian braids like Tacy's but given a different effect by a red hair ribbon at the back. She had gleaming black eyes, gleaming white teeth and an habitual teasing smile. It vanished now when she saw Betsy and Tacy. For Winona too was carrying a tablet and pencil, and she too was breathless, obviously headed for one of the prized back seats.

"Don't bother to go in," Betsy sang out. "We've got them."

"Got what?"

"Got you know what."

"Got what you're after yourself."

"Phooey!" cried Winona, and made a dash for the assembly room, Betsy and Tacy following.

At the back of the room a scuffle ensued, but accepting defeat Winona placed her tablet and pencil on the back seat next to Tacy's and they all raced to the front again. Winona ran up on the platform as Betsy had done, but her imitation of Miss Bangeter was much more daring. She stood up at the reading desk, threw out her chest and said, "Students of the Deep Valley High School . . ." with the strong Boston accent which characterized Miss Bangeter's speech. Boys and girls were flooding in from the cloakrooms now.

"Winona!" Betsy and Tacy pleaded. "Come down!"

And Winona, flashing her white teeth, jumped down from the platform, ignoring the steps. She and Betsy and Tacy ran through the girls' cloakroom, out into the hall, inspected, one after another, the empty classrooms that made a half circle around it, peeped into the Social Room where upper classmen were gathered, and looked at the trophy cups displayed behind glass in a case in the big hall.

"Know which society you're going to join?" Betsy asked Winona. The students were divided between Philomathians and Zetamathians, societies which competed in athletics, in debate and in essay writing as the three cups testified. "Tacy and I are going to be Zets," she added.

"Then I'll be a Philomathian," said Winona sticking out her tongue.

"Just because we got the best seats!" jibed Tacy.

"No. To make things interesting. Besides, the cutest boys are Philos." Winona tossed her head and smiled. She looked around abruptly. "Who's *that* cute boy?" she asked.

Betsy and Tacy followed her penetrating gaze, and Betsy saw a yellow pompadour, an out-thrust lower lip. She looked almost directly into blue eyes which were puzzlingly familiar. While she hesitated the boy passed on. Then she remembered.

"That's Joe Willard . . . Tacy, you know . . . the boy from Butternut Center." She started to run after him, but at that moment a gong clanged. There was a rush for the assembly room, and Joe Willard disappeared.

"Do you know him?" Winona asked eagerly. "Gosh, introduce me! Have you heard that Tom Slade's gone to Cox Military? Weep, weep! Herbert Humphreys is back, though. Don't run like freshies. That's only the first gong." And Winona led the way nonchalantly to the girls' cloakroom. They took turns at the mirror, Betsy and Tacy striving to act as nonchalant as Winona. They delayed so successfully that when Betsy and Tacy were halfway up the aisle the second gong sounded and quiet descended upon the big assembly room.

"A good thing we've got our seats," Betsy thought, trying not to hurry. Tacy was frankly hurrying and her ears, Betsy saw, were as red as fire. Betsy felt all eyes upon them and remembered to assume her Ethel Barrymore droop. Three-quarters of the way up the aisle, however, she stood upright. For lounging comfortably in the choice back corner seats were two boys. Herbert Humphreys and Cab Edwards!

Tacy stopped stock still. If anything was going to be done, Betsy realized, she would have to do it. Forcing a smile she approached them.

"Pardon me," she said politely, in an undertone, "but these are our seats."

"They're ours now," said Herbert Humphreys, grinning.

"We put our tablets on to hold them," Betsy said.

"Looking for these?" asked Cab, pulling two tablets and two pencils out of his desk. He too grinned at them impudently.

Everyone else in the room was seated now. Miss Bangeter was rapping for order. There were several vacant seats in the freshman rows . . . far front, not together, most undesirable. Tacy nudged Betsy and pointed to them. She was agonized with embarrassment.

But Betsy was stubborn.

"We came early to get those seats," she said in a loud whisper. The boys looked at each other and grinned. Betsy forgot herself. She blushed furiously, but not from shyness. "They belong to us. You get out!" she said.

To her amazement the boys, with one accord, slipped out of the seats.

"Take it easy! Take it easy!" Herbert Humphreys said.

"And she looks so sweet and gentle, walking past my house," Cab whispered.

Covering their retreat with muttered witticisms, they hurried down the aisle.

Betsy and Tacy sat down, breathing hard. All about them necks were craned. A wave of giggling swept through the room. Miss Bangeter rapped for order again.

Then to Betsy's horror, Miss Bangeter turned and descended the platform. She walked rapidly up the last aisle. Heads were turned to follow her progress. Betsy saw Julia's anxious face, Katie's.

Miss Bangeter drew nearer. No feeble imitation of Betsy's or Winona's had conveyed her height, her sternness, her black-haired majesty. Betsy stole a glance at Tacy who had turned pale, and seemed frozen to her seat.

Miss Bangeter drew nearer the two culprits, nearer, nearer . . .

She passed them by, and going into the alcove, efficiently opened a window.

7
Cab

EXCEPT FOR THE ADVENTURE of the Two Back Seats, the first day at high school did not amount to much. There were the usual opening exercises. The school joined lustily in singing a hymn, and for the first time Betsy and Tacy heard Miss Bangeter, with stern sincerity and an impressive Boston accent, read a psalm and lead in the Lord's Prayer. Long before noon school was dismissed for the day.

In the afternoon Betsy, Tacy and Winona went down to Cook's Book Store to buy school supplies. They went to Heinz's Restaurant for banana splits and back to the Ray house where . . . joined by Julia, Katie and Mrs. Ray . . . they discussed the morning. The banana splits proving insufficient, they made fudge. And Julia played, and all of them sang.

Julia preferred operatic music. Some time before she had written to a music store in Minneapolis, grandly opened an account, asked for a list of their opera scores and ordered . . . because it was cheapest . . . the opera of Pagliacci. When alone, she played and sang Pagliacci by the hour. Not just the soprano part of Nedda, but all the parts . . . tenors, baritones, even the villagers. She told Betsy the story of the clown's betrayal and Betsy almost wept at first when Julia sang, "Laugh, Pagliaccio," with a sob in her voice. But the Rays had grown callous to the sorrows of the strolling players.

When contemporaries were around, as now, Julia played popular songs and with such contagious zest that everyone gathered arm in arm around the piano and sang.

After supper, Betsy telephoned Tacy and Winona for prolonged conversations, then went upstairs to wind her hair on Magic Wavers, take a warm bath with some of Julia's bath salts in it, and rub the new freckle cream into her face. Wrapped in a kimono she sat down to manicure her nails.

She still felt a little strange in the new bedroom. It was always so neat. . . . Julia had kept the old room cozily untidy. And she missed Uncle Keith's trunk, gathering dust in the attic. She had to admit that the room was pretty, though; Mrs. Ray joyfully called it a typical girl's room.

It was papered in a pattern of large blue and white flowers clambering up vines. There were blue ruffled curtains at the windows, blue matting on the floor, a blue, white-tufted bedspread on the white iron bed. The furniture was Mrs. Ray's old Hill Street bedroom set, freshly painted white.

"You'll have a set of bird's eye maple some day," her mother promised. But Betsy rather liked the low old-fashioned bureau with a tier of shelves at the side, and the chest and rocking chair in their shining new white coats. The walls were liberally sprinkled with photographs and Gibson Girls.

"I'm going to get me a Deep Valley High School pennant," Betsy planned, buffing luxuriously.

Julia and Fred were downstairs. Betsy could hear their voices in the parlor, and that brought to her mind a question dormant since morning. Winona had created it with her talk about boys. Tacy didn't care about boys, and with Tacy Betsy almost forgot how important they were.

But she was in high school now. Would boys start coming to see her, as they came to see Julia?

Tom Slade had come of course, since he was a little boy, but that was because his mother and Mrs. Ray were friends. And Tom had gone away to the military school that Julia's friend Jerry had once attended. She knew Herbert Humphreys pretty well; his parents too were friends of her parents, and at intervals he and his older brother joined the Rays at a family party. But she couldn't imagine Herbert coming to the house independent of his parents.

She giggled to herself remembering the morning's encounter with him and Cab.

"No more H.H.A.S.," Tacy had leaned out to whisper after Miss Bangeter returned to the platform. And Betsy agreed although admitting to herself that Herbert, in vacation tan, blonder, bigger and brawnier than ever, was outstandingly good looking. Cab Edwards was cute, too.

"I wish I were prettier," she thought, depression, like a sudden fog, invading the room. She put away her manicure set, took off her kimono, turned out the gas, said her prayers and slipped into bed.

"I wish I had golden hair," she continued in the darkness. "Wavy golden hair, a yard long. And big blue eyes, and pink cheeks, and teeth close together like Julia's. Or maybe it would be nicer to have heavy black ringlets, and big black eyes with curly lashes, and a white satiny skin."

Before she could decide which she preferred, she fell asleep.

The next day was the first day of real school, and the prospect was almost as exciting as it had been the day before. There weren't muffins for breakfast, but there were pancakes with sausage and maple syrup. While the Rays were at the table, the doorbell rang.

"Tacy, probably," Betsy said, as Margaret went to answer it, and Julia slipped into her chair, late, as usual.

Margaret came back, looking surprised.

"It's a boy," she said. "He asked for Betsy."

"For *me*?" Betsy was sure Margaret had misunderstood.

"Ask him to come in," said Mrs. Ray, and Margaret went back. She returned with the dark monkeyish face of Cab Edwards grinning behind her.

"Good morning, Cab," said Mr. Ray who had sold him his shoes for many years.

"Good morning," said Mrs. Ray.

"Hello," said Julia.

"Hello," said Betsy blushing. Anna who had come to the doorway rolled her eyes at Betsy.

"Won't you sit down?" asked Mrs. Ray. "Maybe you'd like a pancake?"

"Gosh, I should say I would!" said Cab. He drew up a chair beside Betsy's, and Betsy jumping up to get him a plate and knife and fork and spoon managed a hasty glance at her curls in the sideboard mirror. They were still Magically Waved, thank goodness!

"Have you heard how your daughter treated me yesterday, Mr. Ray?" asked Cab.

"Isn't she behaving?"

"Well, did you bring her up to steal? Cold blood-edly steal?"

"She's stolen my pencils for years," said Mr. Ray.

"And my perfume," said Julia.

"And my handkerchiefs," said Mrs. Ray.

"We did not steal those seats. You go jump in the lake," said Betsy. She was enormously pleased. Cab had dropped in to walk to school with her. There was no doubt of it.

To be sure, he wasn't gazing at her soulfully as Julia's beaux gazed. He was devouring pancakes and syrup, and Anna was plying him with more. But he must like her, or he wouldn't have come.

The doorbell rang again, and this time it was Tacy. She looked surprised and confused when she saw Cab. Then the significance of his presence dawned and she flashed Betsy a congratulatory glance. On invitation, she too sat down for a pancake.

"Tacy," said Cab, "was as bad as Betsy."

"Worse, probably," Mr. Ray returned. "These redheads! I know all about them. I've been married to one for twenty years. She's terrific to live with; isn't she, Anna?"

Anna was not yet accustomed to Mr. Ray's teasing. Moreover she thought that Mrs. Ray's beautiful red hair was a curse which it was indelicate to mention.

"Lovey," she said to Mrs. Ray, "I don't think your hair is really red. Just last night, Charley said to me, 'I think Mrs. Ray's hair is more brown than red.'"

"No, Anna," said Mr. Ray. "You can't get around it. She's a carrot top. But I've stood it for twenty years, and I can stand it for twenty more if you'll only bring me another plate of pancakes."

"Betsy, can I walk to school with you every day forever? I like your groceries," said Cab.

"Don't they feed you at home?" asked Betsy. "If you're coming with Tacy and me, you'll have to hurry."

She tried to conceal her gratification at having a masculine escort as she and Tacy joined the river of schoolbound boys and girls.

"Who is that girl with Caroline Sibley?" she asked as Caroline passed, arm in arm with the yellow-haired girl she had noticed before.

"Don't you know?" Cab replied. "Bonnie Andrews. Her father's the new minister at the Presbyterian Church. She's the reason all the boys have started going to Christian Endeavor."

"Where did she come from?"

"Gosh, don't you know anything? From Paris."

"Paris! Not Paris, France?"

"What other Paris is there? There isn't any Paris, Minnesota, that I've ever heard of."

Betsy was thrilled.

"But what's the connection between being a Presbyterian minister and living in Paris?"

"Let's go down to the Sibleys' some day and ask," Cab replied. "We'd find her there," he added. "Everyone gangs up on the Sibleys' lawn."

It was just what her mother had said. Betsy felt ashamed of the remote bad-tempered Betsy of the days before high school began. "Let's," she replied.

There were real lessons today. Betsy and Tacy had enrolled for Latin, algebra, ancient history and composition. In most classes they sat together, and they needed companionship for high school subjects seemed very strange.

Latin! A language, so Mr. Morse said, that nobody living spoke familiarly now. It was mystifying that one should have to study it. And algebra baffled Betsy from the first, but she liked the algebra teacher. Miss

O'Rourke had curly hair and smiling eyes and looked trimly lovely in a white shirt waist and collar.

Miss Clarke, the ancient-history teacher, was nice, too. She wore glasses, but she was pretty, with dark wings of hair and soft white skin. She was gentle; she trusted everyone. Ancient history, therefore, was supposed to be a snap. Mr. Gaston who taught composition had a reputation for stiffness, but that didn't worry Betsy.

"You're sure to be the best in the class," Tacy remarked, voicing Betsy's own thought.

Joe Willard was in the composition class. Remembering *The Three Musketeers*, Betsy had an idea that he too might be good; and she soon found out that he was. Several times during the first week she tried to catch his eye, but she never succeeded. He must, she thought regretfully, have thought she was snubbing him on the first day of school. He sat in the back row and always slipped out promptly, so she never found a chance to make things right.

Returning to school after dinner one day, Betsy and Tacy went into the Social Room. Freshmen were unwelcome there usually, but not today; today they were fawned on by seniors, juniors and sophomores; for this afternoon they would choose their societies, and rivalry between Philomathians and Zetamathians was keen. Betsy and Tacy were sure to be Zetamathians, because Julia and Katie were, so no upperclassmen wasted time on them. But they basked in the short-lived popularity of freshmen and inspected the Social Room.

It was only a classroom, furnished with desks and black boards, but it was particularly pleasant, located in one of the turrets as the library alcove was; and it was given over to social intercourse during all school intermissions.

Julia and Katie, busily wooing Cab, waved at them. Fred hailed them, and so did Leo who went with Katie, and another friend of their sisters', dark-eyed Dorothy Drew. Caroline Sibley was there with Bonnie Andrews and the Humphreys boys.

"This Social Room makes school as good as a party," Tacy observed. "Only no refreshments."

After the afternoon classes there was a big assembly. Miss Bangeter explained about the two societies, about the cups . . . for athletics, debating and essay writing . . . for which they annually competed. The presidents of the societies spoke, and there was rooting:

"Zet! Zet! Zetamathian!"

"Philo! Philo! Philomathian!"

Then lists were passed and Betsy and Tacy became Zetamathians. They were given turquoise blue bows.

"Zet! Zet! Zetamathian!" they chanted in the cloakroom.

"Philo! Philo! Philomathian!" Winona, wearing an orange bow, threw her red hat in the air. "The cute new boy's a Philo. Did you know?"

She meant Joe Willard. Betsy saw him on the steps and he was wearing an orange bow.

Cab, wearing a turquoise blue bow, joined Betsy and Tacy on High Street. They all dropped into the Ray house for cookies and some singing. Then Cab proposed, "How about going down to the Sibleys'? Find out who went what?"

"I can't," said Tacy. "I have to go home."

"I'll go. Love to," said Betsy. She avoided her mother's eyes as she fluffed up her curls in the mirror.

Tacy walked with Cab and Betsy down the Plum Street hill to Broad Street, and left them at the Sibleys' lawn.

"You'll like Carney; she's lots of fun," said Cab as he and Betsy strolled toward a group of boys and girls.

"Is Carney, Caroline?"

"Sure."

"I hope Bonnie Andrews is here," Betsy remarked.

It was exciting to be going to the Sibleys; and gratifying to have a boy by her side. But most thrilling of all was the thought of meeting someone who came from Paris, France.

8

The Sibleys' Side Lawn

IT WAS TO DEVELOP LATER that the younger high
school crowd had the most indoor fun at the Ray
house and the most outdoor fun at the Sibleys . . . on
the wide, trampled side lawn, and the porch running
across the front and around the side of the house. The
porch was unscreened and shaded by vines, now
turning red. It was broad enough to hold a hammock

and some chairs and a table, but nothing too good, nothing rain would hurt.

The porch was deserted today. A bonfire smouldered in the driveway; rakes lay beside it, and a crowd composed of Caroline Sibley's brothers, Herbert Humphreys and his older brother Lawrence, Caroline and Bonnie, were seated on the leaf-strewn lawn. Cab and Betsy dropped down beside them and no one seemed to think it strange that Betsy had come. Caroline said, "Hello," showing a surprising solitary dimple, and introduced Bonnie.

Caroline Sibley was the only girl Betsy had ever seen who had only one dimple. She was also the only girl Betsy had ever seen who looked prettier in glasses than she could possibly have looked without them. They were eye glasses and suited her demure, piquant face. She had slightly irregular teeth which folded over in front, twinkling eyes, and a skin like apple blossoms. Her straight brown hair was parted and combed smoothly back to an always crisp hair ribbon. Her shirt waist was unbelievably white, the slender waist-band neat. Caroline's people came from New England, and she had a prim New Englandish air that contrasted with the dimple in a fascinating way.

Bonnie's blonde hair was as smooth as Caroline's and her shirt waist as snowy and fresh. Betsy's hair was forever coming loose, and her waists had a way of pulling out from her skirts just as soon as she forgot them and began to have a good time. She immediately admired Caroline's and Bonnie's trimness.

"Of course they're sophomores," she told herself consolingly. "Probably by the time I'm a sophomore I can keep my waist tucked in, too."

Bonnie had calm blue eyes. She was short, but her figure was more mature than Caroline's and her skirts were sedately long. She had small, plump, very soft hands, and a soft, chuckling laugh that flowed continuously through the conversation. In spite of the laugh, however, she seemed womanly and serious, as befitted a minister's daughter.

Lawrence Humphreys was as dark as Herbert was light, as big or bigger, and equally handsome. But he was quiet. He lacked Herbert's wild high spirits. Not that these were apparent, today. Herbert seemed glum, subdued, and most of the time gazed moodily at Bonnie.

"He has a crush on Bonnie," Betsy thought, proud of her acumen.

Lawrence, whom they all called Larry, played football on the first team. After Saturday, he said, he'd be in training and he had told the girls to spoil him while they could.

Caroline was making a wreath of red ivy leaves

from the porch. She was going to crown him, she explained, as the Romans crowned guests at their banquets. She and Bonnie and Larry were all studying Caesar or Cicero and were full of Latin quotations.

"*O di immortales!*" was Caroline's favorite exclamation. It made Betsy's Latin come considerably alive.

While waiting for his crown, Lawrence was being fed peanuts by Bonnie to the accompaniment of her soft giggle.

"Heck! I'm going out for football, too. What about me?" Herbert protested.

"And what about me?" asked Cab, flexing his muscles. "Boy, what football material!"

Caroline's brothers, all still in grade school, laughed appreciatively.

The Humphreys were Philos, Betsy discovered, and Caroline and Bonnie were Zets.

"What do Philomathian and Zetamathian mean, I wonder?" asked Betsy.

Bonnie knew. Philomathian meant Lover of Learning and Zetamathian, Investigator.

"My father told me," she explained, tossing off her knowledge.

Betsy liked her. She liked Carney, too. Already she was calling Caroline Carney, Lawrence Larry, and exclaiming *O di immortales!* with the rest of the crowd. At last Carney's brothers went back to their raking which reminded Larry and Herbert that they too had a lawn.

"And, gosh, I've got a paper route!" Cab said. "But if you'll go home now, Betsy, I'll escort you. Always the perfect gentleman, by gum!"

"I can find my way," said Betsy. "Me and my trained bloodhound!"

"Betsy isn't going to hurry," said Carney. She smiled up at Larry. "I think you're mean to go. You haven't worn your wreath."

"You wear it. You'll look nice in it."

"All right. And I'll make one for Bonnie and one for Betsy!"

"Hey! You'll be a Triumvirate!" What, Betsy wondered, was a Triumvirate?

"Girls! We're a Triumvirate!" cried Carney, flashing her dimple. "I want to be Caesar. He's so cute in the pictures. You can be Crassus, Bonnie, and Betsy, you can be Pompey."

"A Triumvirate of Lady Bugs!" jeered Larry.

"There are three of you boys, too," cried Bonnie, soft giggles bubbling. "You're a Triumvirate your own selves. What's the name of yours? Make one up, somebody."

"They're a Triumvirate of Potato Bugs," said Betsy.

This was a triumph. The boys, departing, yelped, and Carney and Bonnie doubled up with appreciative mirth. Their laughter continued while they robbed the porch of ivy leaves and Carney made wreaths. Carney and Bonnie laughed at everything Betsy said.

"Betsy, you're so *funny!*" Bonnie kept gasping. And Betsy, delighted, laughed so hard at her own wit that she could hardly keep on being witty.

When the wreaths were finished she put hers on askew, over the left eye. Carney put hers on over the right eye. Bonnie hung hers on one ear. They leered drunkenly, imitating Romans. Exhausted, at last, they rolled in the grass.

Carney sat up suddenly and said, "I hereby invite the Triumvirate to go riding tomorrow after school."

"Will we wear crowns?" asked Betsy.

"We ought to wrap up in bedsheets like those old Romans."

"*O di immortales!*" cried Carney, rocking back and forth. "We'd scare Dandy."

"Who's Dandy?"

"He's our horse. All our horses are named Dandy."

"All our horses are named Old Mag," said Betsy "whether they're girls or boys."

This struck Carney and Bonnie as so supremely comical that they were obliged to fall shrieking into the grass again. But the Big Mill whistle, blowing for six o'clock, brought them all to their feet.

"Gee, I didn't know it was that late," Betsy said.

"I ought to be in helping my mother," cried Carney.

"Walk home with me, Bonnie," Betsy urged. "I hate to think of that long walk all alone."

"But I'd have to walk back all alone."

"No you wouldn't. I'd walk halfway back with you. That would make everything fair."

So Bonnie walked home with Betsy, and having gained the new green house on High Street, they turned around and Betsy walked halfway back with Bonnie. From the time they said good-by to Carney until they said good-by to each other, they didn't laugh at all. In a sudden shift of mood, Betsy asked Bonnie about Paris, and Bonnie told her a little about it, but she failed to create any picture of Paris in Betsy's mind.

"There are lots of hacks," she said. "They drive like mad. And there was a merry-go-round—carousels, they call them—in the park where I played after school."

"Do you speak French?"

"Of course. Father was in the pastorate there for four years."

"Say some for me," said Betsy.

Bonnie looked embarrassed but obediently murmured something.

"What does that mean?"

"It means I like Deep Valley better than Paris."

Betsy remembered that many years ago Tib had said she liked Deep Valley better than Milwaukee.

Deep Valley, Betsy thought, looking up at the hills and down at the town, must be a pretty nice place.

She told Bonnie about Tib . . . how pretty she was, small and dainty with yellow curls. She told her that Tib was going to be a dancer.

"She and Tacy are my two best friends," Betsy explained.

"Carney's my best friend," said Bonnie. "It's wonderful having a chum. We're having our Sunday dresses made just alike."

"Exactly alike?"

"Exactly. Miss Mix is making them."

"How marvelous!" cried Betsy. She wished that she and Tacy had thought of doing that.

"Carney's going with Lawrence. Did you know it?"

"I guessed it," said Betsy.

"Do you go with anyone?" asked Bonnie.

With a feeling of unutterable thankfulness Betsy answered carelessly, "Only Cab. He's just a neighbor, of course."

"I'll tell you something, Betsy," said Bonnie. "Promise not to tell a soul. Herbert has a crush on me."

"I noticed it," said Betsy. "I think it's thrilling. Herbert was just the idol of all the girls in grade school. We trembled when we saw him, practically."

"But he's such a *child*," cried Bonnie. "He's such

an *infant*. Why, he's only a freshman, and I'm a sophomore. I wish I could hand him over to you."

"And I wish I could find a nice sophomore boy for you," said Betsy. "Not that you need anybody found for you," she added, and repeated what Cab had said about Bonnie having greatly increased attendance at Christian Endeavor.

"How silly!" said Bonnie. "I try not to think about boys at Christian Endeavor." She looked so sincerely devout that Betsy was impressed.

They parted at a point on Plum Street which was exactly halfway between High Street and Broad.

Betsy instead of Julia was late for supper that night. Her father gave her a reproving glance when she entered the dining room, but he relented quickly; she looked so radiantly happy. She was full of talk all through supper. Anna, clearing the plates, paused to listen.

"But who *is* this Bonnie?" Mr. Ray asked.

"Bonnie Andrews. Her father is the new Presbyterian minister."

"And Carney?"

"Caroline Sibley. Don't be surprised, though, if I call her Julius Caesar. We've formed a Triumvirate."

"What is a Triumvirate?" asked Margaret, looking up from her plate.

"She doesn't even know what a Triumvirate is! O *di immortales!*" Betsy cried.

9
The Triumvirate of Lady Bugs

CAB APPEARED AS USUAL the next day to walk to
school with them, and Betsy and Tacy had small
chance for private conversation. During the morning,
however, Betsy was able to give some idea of the fun
she had had at the Sibleys. And at noon they walked
around and around the school block for a really confidential talk.

Betsy told her about Carney and Bonnie.

"They're oceans of fun. You'll be crazy about them."

She told her about the two Triumvirates.

Tacy was not the kind of best friend who felt jealous of a Triumvirate of Lady Bugs which left her out. Of course she and Betsy both knew that any group which included Betsy would shortly expand to take in Tacy too. Betsy said as much and Tacy agreed, but with a reservation.

"You know, Betsy, I'm not interested in boys. When those Triumvirates do things together, I'd just as soon not be there."

"But what do you have against boys?" asked Betsy. "You like Cab, don't you?"

"Yes. Cab's nice."

"You always liked Tom Slade."

"Yes, but he's gone away. And anyway, Betsy, it's not that I don't like boys all right. I don't know how to act when they're around like you and Julia do."

Betsy was flattered to be classed with Julia.

"You're just bashful, Tacy. But, listen! I've got a plan. Herbert Humphreys has a crush on Bonnie, and Bonnie doesn't want him because he's a freshman. So she said she'd hand him over to me, but I don't really need him because I've got Cab, sort of. So I could hand Herbert over to you."

Tacy burst out laughing.

"You can't hand boys around as though they were pieces of cake," she said. "Don't worry about getting a boy for me, Betsy. Boys just don't seem important to me. They don't seem any more important to me than they ever did."

"Tacy!" said Betsy. "You're beyond me!"

"Well!" said Tacy. "That's the way I am."

So after school she went off contentedly with Alice, who was a friend from the Hill Street neighborhood, a tall blonde girl with glasses, and Betsy dropped her books at home, preparatory to going down to the Sibleys'. She took Carney and Bonnie in to meet her mother. They liked her, as all the girls did, and chattered easily while Betsy foraged. She came back from the kitchen flourishing a box of crackers.

"Nourishment for the ride!"

"I'll get some olives at home," Carney said.

"Those old Romans didn't eat crackers and olives," objected Bonnie with her bubbling laugh.

"They drank wine," said Carney. "But don't forget you're a minister's daughter, miss."

At the Sibleys', they went in to speak to Mrs. Sibley, a slender dark-haired woman with twinkling eyes who looked much as Carney would look at her age. Carney got the olives, and the three girls hitched the bay horse to the surrey.

"I like horses better than automobiles. Don't you?" asked Betsy.

"Yes. Papa's threatening to get an automobile, though."

"Are you allowed to take Dandy out often?"

"Quite often. Papa walks to the bank."

"Papa lets Julia and me drive Old Mag too. I love to go riding," Betsy said.

It was a perfect day for a ride. The sky was greenish blue and misty over Deep Valley's hills. The air was warm, and smelled of bonfires.

They left Broad Street at the Episcopal Church and took the road leading to Cemetery Hill. They passed the watering trough and the little store where Margaret had bought candy, and the road began to climb.

Carney knew this hill as Betsy and Tacy knew the Hill Street Hill. She coasted down it every winter.

"Larry steers. He's wonderful," she said. "How he misses the watering trough is just beyond me!"

The dry gulch beside the road became a brook in the spring, she said. She and her brothers used to float boats there.

Today it was full of yellow leaves and bordered by flaming sumac. On the right, at the crest of the hill, rose the solemn white arch of the cemetery gate.

"Shall we go in?" asked Betsy. "I love to look at gravestones."

"Not today," said Carney. "I'm not in the mood for it."

"Neither am I," said Bonnie. "I feel perfectly wild."

"Let's scream then," said Betsy, and she screamed, and they all screamed. Dandy didn't turn his head, but a flock of blackbirds rose in alarm.

"I think I'll ride Dandy. Would he mind?" Betsy asked.

"Not a bit. He's used to it."

"I could climb on from that fencepost. Pompey always rode horseback." Betsy scrambled down.

"He didn't either," shouted Bonnie. "He rode in a chariot!"

"They raced," yelled Carney. "Whoopee! Remember Ben Hur?"

But Betsy thought Dandy's back was better than any chariot. She sat astride, pretending to be a cowboy, while Carney and Bonnie rolled in the seat with laughter. Her hair came down, and lost its curl in the breeze. Her waist pulled out of her skirt. She didn't mind.

"Look what I see!" she cried suddenly.

"What?"

"Grapes!" She pointed to an old elm, laden with clustering vines.

"Pompey has discovered wine!" shrieked Bonnie.

"He's the noblest Roman of them all," cried Carney.

She and Bonnie tumbled out of the surrey while Betsy, with some difficulty, got down from Dandy's back. The grapes were ripe and they picked handfuls.

"There's a good place to eat," said Carney pointing to a field that was empty except for golden-rod, asters and thistles and a jeweled apple tree.

"Swell! We can steal apples."

"Listen to the minister's daughter!"

"I'll get some. My father is only an elder." Carney ran to the tree, returned with six apples and tossed two to each of the girls.

"*Gallia est omnis divisa in partes tres.*"

"*Amo, amas, amat,*" shouted Betsy, not to be outdone.

"Freshie!" the others yelled.

Carney loosened Dandy's checkrein, and he stood without hitching during the Roman feast.

While they ate they talked about boys. Betsy repeated Tacy's remark about passing boys around like pieces of cake. Carney and Bonnie thought it was killing. Bonnie said she was going to entertain the two Triumvirates Friday night. She bewailed Herbert's youth, and Betsy said she was going to ask Julia to look out for a junior boy for Bonnie.

"A junior! Betsy, you angel!"

"Do you like them?"

"I adore them!"

"Larry is nicer than any old junior," said Carney, munching her stolen fruit.

"He is not."

"He is so."

"Herbie's nice too."

"That baby!"

They had a wonderful time, and after eating they made themselves as tidy as they could. Bonnie and Carney weren't very mussed, but they tucked in Betsy's waist and tied her hair up with a ribbon.

"Heavens, I hope we won't meet any boys going home!" Betsy said. "If we do, make Dandy gallop; will you, Carney?"

"He forgot how years ago."

"Besides, if we galloped the boys would think they had to rescue us," said Bonnie.

"Let 'em try," said Betsy. "They couldn't catch up. And we'd yell, 'Help! Help! Help!' like this. 'Help! Help! Help!'"

They raced across the field crying, "Help! Help! Help!" Fortunately nobody heard them but Dandy who ignored them. Laughter drifted behind them like smoke all the way down Cemetery Hill.

Betsy parted from Carney and Bonnie at the watering trough. She raced home through the early twilight and had just time to wash before supper. She could use, she found, a good bit of washing.

After supper she was supposed to do homework but first she telephoned Tacy to tell her about the ride. And Bonnie telephoned to giggle over how funny Betsy had looked on Dandy. And Betsy telephoned Carney to bring her up to date on the other two conversations.

Julia was out at choir practice, and when she returned Betsy went into her room to drum up a junior boy for Bonnie.

Betsy always liked to go into Julia's room. It smelled like her, of a sweet cologne she used. It was often in disorder for Julia was untidy, but she was untidy in a dainty way. The pile of clothes that Betsy now moved from the window seat, in order to sit down, was fresh, lacy and sweet-smelling.

Betsy loved this window seat, which looked up at the Catholic College. She settled into it cozily now while Julia in a white night gown sat down at the dressing table to take pins out of her hair. Julia didn't wear a hair ribbon any more. She wore her hair in a pompadour all around her head with a knot on top.

Julia was not one of a crowd of girls as Betsy was. She never had been. Katie and Dorothy were her friends, but she didn't feel that she must telephone them every night, nor see them every day. She wasn't inclined either toward a crowd of boys. She preferred one completely devoted swain, but she always tired of him and went on to another, indifferent to the sufferings of the discarded one.

"He'll get over it," was her callous answer to tender Betsy's protests.

She had liked Jerry best, but he had gone away to West Point, and none of them could compete in her interest with music. Her mind was upon music now, while Betsy talked.

"Of course I'll introduce Bonnie to some junior boys," she said. "But Bettina, listen! The choir needs altos badly and Mrs. Poppy wants you to come and try out."

"I'd love to!" cried Betsy. She thought rapturously of wearing vestments and of marching through candlelight. "But, Julia, I'm sure I can't sing well enough. Mrs. Poppy just thinks I can because I'm your sister."

"No, Bettina, you could do it. I wouldn't say so if I didn't believe it. You're really musical. Perhaps because we've always had so much music at home." She laughed as she shook out her hair. "You know, Mamma raised us on the Gilbert and Sullivan operas. She sang them to us while we were nursing. And I've been banging a piano in your ears for centuries now. You could carry the alto part without coming up to the soprano all the time the way so many girls do."

"The way I used to do when Tacy and I sang the Cat Duet," said Betsy.

"You've learned since then," said Julia, "shouting around the piano."

"Do you suppose Papa and Mamma would mind?" asked Betsy after a thoughtful moment. "They don't mind *your* doing it because you have such a talent for music, and they know it's good training. But they might not like to have me going all the time to the Episcopal Church."

"They'd still have Margaret to go to the Baptist Church with them," said Julia. She turned from the mirror to look solemnly into Betsy's face.

"Bettina," she said. "I love the Episcopal Church. I want to be an Episcopalian."

"Julia!" cried Betsy, hardly believing her ears.

"I don't think I was ever cut out to be a Baptist," Julia said.

Betsy was genuinely shocked. It had not occurred to her that one could change one's church any more than one could change one's skin. She was silent, and Julia went on:

"Just because Papa and Mamma are Baptists is no reason I should be a Baptist. People are different. I'm myself."

"But Julia!" Betsy protested. "You've been baptized."

She well remembered Julia's baptism several years before. At the front of the Baptist Church, behind the pulpit, hung a painted landscape of the River Jordan. Where the canvas river ended there was a deep recess which could be made into an actual pool. On the days when people were baptized, the minister stood there in a rubber coat; each devotee in turn walked down the steps and was dipped beneath the water.

Julia had seemed like an angel coming down. The other girls had looked self-conscious or frightened, but Julia had looked rapt and grave. The people were singing, "Shall we gather at the river?" and Julia had looked as though she were listening to heavenly choirs. The other girls had come up from their immersion sputtering and gasping, but Julia, although her long hair hung like sea weed, had kept a grave, rapt profile.

Betsy had not yet been baptized. And she knew that she could not hope to emulate Julia. She was religious. But she was religious only when she prayed, and when she wrote poetry, and when she talked with Tacy about God and Heaven. Her religion had nothing whatever to do with the Baptist Church. It came to her now that perhaps she, like Julia, was not cut out to be a Baptist.

"But you can't hurt Papa's and Mamma's feelings," she said, coming back to Julia's problem which was suddenly unmistakably her own.

"I'd die first," said Julia.

"What are you going to do about it?"

"I don't know. You'll have to help me, Bettina."

Julia had a way of leaning on Betsy, of coming to her for advice, which was wine to Betsy's soul. Julia was looking at her now out of tragic, dark-blue eyes, her classic face strained.

"Betsy, I *have* to be an Episcopalian!"

"Girls!" came Mrs. Ray's voice. "It's ten o'clock."

"I'm going to bed, Mamma," Betsy called. She whispered to Julia, "I'll think up something."

"Thank you, darling. Turn out the light, will you?" Julia asked, jumping into bed.

Before she turned out the gas Betsy looked at the vivid face framed in a cloud of dark hair on the pillow. Julia had no need to put her hair up on curlers. She hadn't put cream on her face or rubbed her hands with lemon or done a single thing to make herself look pretty on the morrow. But Betsy knew how pretty she would look.

Betsy turned out the gas and went to the bathroom to begin her nightly ritual. She loved Julia dearly, and could not be jealous of her. Yet as her thoughts returned to the two Triumvirates, to Bonnie's party, boys, she felt a little bitter. She wound her hair on Magic Wavers, and scrubbed her face and rubbed in the freckle cream; it was supposed to remove freckles practically overnight, but Betsy had been using it for two weeks now, and the soft brown sprinkle on her nose was as plain as ever.

10

And the Triumvirate
of Potato Bugs

As Bonnie's evening party for the two Triumvirates
drew near, Betsy began to worry. It was not the first
time she had gone to a party boys attended, but it was
the first time since boys had emerged from the pest
and nuisance class. She wished ardently that one of
them would ask to be her escort.

Thursday night, after winding her hair on the Wavers

with special care, she even included in her prayers a request that a boy invite her to the party. It seemed a little frivolous, but she felt sure God wouldn't mind.

Cab walked to school with her Friday morning, and she thought he would surely mention Bonnie's party, but he didn't; he talked about the scrub football team. Betsy listened with what she hoped seemed radiant attention.

"Did I act interested in that football business?" she asked Tacy in the cloakroom.

"You certainly did," Tacy replied. "You acted as though your life depended on whether he made the team or not."

"That's the way you have to be with boys," said Betsy. "Beam about their old football when you're dying to know whether they're going to take you to a party."

Tacy knew all about Betsy's worry.

"Of course, he'll ask you," she said. "Hasn't he called for you almost every morning since school began? I think you're foolish to want to go with boys, but I must say you're not having any trouble doing it."

Betsy glowed at this. She had a secret suspicion that the easy hospitality of her home attracted Cab at least as much as she did, but it was gratifying to hear Tacy's opinion.

"Well, if he's going to call for me, why doesn't he ask me?" she groaned.

"Oh, boys just like to be annoying."

Betsy waited hopefully for Cab to drop in that afternoon. He didn't. But of course, she consoled herself, the scrubs might be practising late. As supper time approached she waited for the telephone to ring. It didn't.

During supper, her mother said casually, "Betsy's going out tonight, a party at Bonnie Andrews'."

"What time shall I call for you?" her father asked.

Betsy was grateful to them for assuming that she would be called for as usual when she went out in the evening.

"I'll telephone you," she said.

"Not to come," added Julia in a whisper. This was cheering, for it meant that though Julia had noticed no boy was taking her, she felt sure one would ask to walk home with her. Betsy's spirits began to rise. She excused herself while the rest were still eating dessert and went upstairs to dress.

She wished she could take a bath in the tub but she didn't dare; the steam would uncurl her hair. She sponged carefully, however, put on her prettiest underwear, and pinned starched ruffles across her chest to give her figure an Anna Held curve.

This wasn't a real dress-up party to which she could wear the blue silk mull trimmed with insertion medallions which Miss Mix had made. She felt sure that Bonnie and Carney would wear waists and skirts. So she wore a white openwork waist over a pale blue cambric underwaist, a white duck skirt which Anna had carefully pressed, and a large pale blue hair ribbon.

Julia did her hair . . . she had a gift with Betsy's hair . . . and tied the hair ribbon. Mrs. Ray came in with her best perfume which she sprayed over Betsy's waist. Margaret sat with Washington on her lap and watched with awed eyes. Only Mr. Ray remained in the parlor reading his newspaper.

Betsy's cheeks had flushed a vivid pink. The reflection she saw in the mirror was pleasant. She was excited and happy, but not so happy as she would have been if a boy were calling for her.

Her mother and Julia kept tactfully away from the subject of boys calling for girls.

"Just telephone Papa when . . ." Mrs. Ray was saying when a bell rang sharply below.

"Oh, let it be the telephone!" Betsy prayed. But it wasn't. It was the doorbell.

Anna answered it. She always hurried to answer the doorbell in the evening even though she was washing dishes. She took a great interest in Julia's beaux.

"Tell him I'll be down in a minute," Julia called without even waiting for Anna to tell her who was there. She was intent on Betsy's ribbon.

Anna did not reply, but her feet mounted the stairs. She came into Betsy's room, still wiping her hands on her apron.

"Stars in the sky!" she said. "It's for Betsy."

"I had an idea Cab might drop in to walk down with you," Mrs. Ray said carelessly.

"It ain't Cab," said Anna. "It's the puniest young fellow I ever laid eyes on."

Everyone turned toward her.

"What's his name?"

"He didn't say. He just said he'd come to call for Betsy, and he went into the parlor and shook hands with your pa."

Betsy felt a surge of joy.

"It must be Herbert," she said. "He's extremely puny."

"There's a piece of pie left from dinner," Anna said. "Do you suppose he'd like a piece of pie?"

"Anna," said Mrs. Ray, "did you ever know a boy who didn't like a piece of pie?"

Everybody laughed, and Betsy was very glad to laugh for she felt shaky with joy. An evening party, and a boy had called for her, and Herbert Humphreys at that!

Anna hurried down, and Betsy twirled before the mirror, to make sure that her waist was tucked in neatly, and that no petticoats showed. She was glad she had a slender waist, and pretty ankles when the petticoats whirled; the starched ruffles gave her bust the proper curve.

"Keep him waiting. It's always a good plan," said Julia.

"Especially when he's eating a piece of Anna's pie," said Mrs. Ray, and they all laughed again.

While they were still laughing the bell rang again. Again Anna raced to the door.

"Right down, Anna," Julia called, fastening her best new bracelet on Betsy's wrist.

Again Anna's heavy steps were heard on the stairs, and she burst into the room, her eyes gleaming.

"But 't' ain't for you, Julia. It's Cab, and he said he came to call for Betsy, and then he saw that Herbert sitting in the parlor, looking so puny, and eating the pie. And he said, 'Anna, what's he doing with my pie? There'd better be a piece of pie for me too,' he said. (But there ain't.) He said to Herbert, 'Why don't you get yourself a girl of your own?'"

"Aren't they silly?" asked Betsy blissfully, going to the closet for her jacket.

"I hope you can find Cab at least a cookie," said Mrs. Ray, laughing.

"Bettina," said Julia. "I'm going to keep my beaux away from you. Sisters' beaux are sacred. Do you hear?"

It was glorious. Drooping in her most Barrymorish manner, she floated down the stairs. Margaret and Washington, Mrs. Ray and Anna came behind. Julia stayed upstairs to primp for Fred, but she peeked down to watch Betsy's departure.

Curled and flushed, treading on air, a boy on either side, Betsy went out into the crisp September night.

On the way down to Bonnie's house, the boys continued to wrangle. Bonnie not being present, Herbert was his usual hilarious self, and he and Cab joked and tussled, with Betsy an appreciative audience.

"Ever been to the Andrews' before?" Herbert asked Betsy as they approached the parsonage. It was opposite the Sibleys', a sprawling old house, set back from the road.

"No, it looks romantic."

"It's something, all right."

And Betsy knew what he meant as soon as she entered the hall. The house had a foreign flavor. Bonnie now seemed almost like other Deep Valley girls but her home spoke of far away places.

At the end of the hall a door stood open. Betsy saw books in rich abundance, not in cases behind glass, but on open shelves, up to the ceiling.

"That's Dr. Andrews' library," said Carney, who was taking Betsy's jacket.

"Think of having that many books right at home!" Betsy exclaimed.

"It's a fascinating room. It's full of things the Andrewses have brought from Europe and the Holy Land. The pictures are prints of paintings from European galleries. Bonnie has seen the originals. Just think!" Betsy was enthralled.

They did not go into the library, although Betsy longed to, but turned into the parlor. This too was remarkable, but in a different way. It was richly carpeted, with curtains of cream-colored lace, paintings in gold frames, damask-covered sofas, small polished tables with statuettes and little boxes on them. A huge, light tan grand piano filled one wall.

"This isn't a parlor, it's a drawing room," thought Betsy. "I'm in a drawing room for the first time in my life."

She stayed there only a moment, for the elegance of the room was unsuited to the occasion, and the two Triumvirates instinctively moved on to the cozy crowded back parlor.

Dr. Andrews, impressive in a beard, came in to welcome them. He left, but Mrs. Andrews stayed on for a time and seemed, indeed, to hate to go. She obviously liked young people and greeted their sallies with a duplicate of Bonnie's flowing laugh.

Her hair was dark and crisply curly. She wore garnet ear rings, and beautiful rings, and a watch pinned to her shirt waist. Her speech had a slight odd twist which charmed Betsy.

"Is she French?" Betsy whispered to Carney who shook her head.

"English. But he met her in Paris."

How romantic! Betsy thought.

After Mrs. Andrews left, the two Triumvirates played Consequences and Fortunes. Later they trooped to the kitchen and made cocoa and drank it with cookies and cake.

For a while Betsy remembered her Ethel Barrymore droop; and she tried to imitate Julia's manner with boys. But before the end of the evening she had forgotten the droop, and Julia's manner just didn't work. Boys worshiped Julia, but they teased Betsy. They teased her about her blushing; they teased her about her curls which they had discovered were manufactured; they teased her about using perfume and about her writing. She had had a poem published long ago in the *Deep Valley Sun*, and Herbert remembered it. He and Larry started calling her The Little Poetess, and Cab took it up.

"Betsy, The Little Poetess!" they mocked, and Betsy pretended to be angry.

Cab and Herbert both walked home with her. Before they reached High Street they were joined by Larry; Carney's mother did not permit a lingering goodnight. Betsy's mother did not permit it either, as Betsy well knew from injunctions she had heard given to Julia. But she paused a moment on the porch steps enjoying the tangy autumn chill, the brilliance of the stars, and the satisfying presence of three boys pushing one another about and making jokes for her amusement.

"Why don't you come to Christian Endeavor Sunday night?" Herbert asked.

"I'm a Baptist."

"Well, Larry and I are Episcopalians but we turn Presbyterian on Sunday night."

"I'm Welsh Calvinistic Methodist," said Cab, "but I turn Presbyterian for Christian Endeavor. I'll call for you if you'll go."

"Not this Sunday night," Betsy said. Tacy was coming for Sunday night lunch. "Some time I'll go."

She ran into the house and up to Julia's room where a light was burning. She had barely bounced to the foot of her sister's bed when her mother came in, in a bathrobe. She too curled up on the bed and Betsy told them all about the evening . . . about the grandeur of the Andrews' house, how nice Mrs. Andrews was, how Carney was undoubtedly going with Larry, and more about Herbert's crush on Bonnie.

The next day she told the whole story to Tacy on the telephone, and she told it again in even more detail on Sunday night when Tacy came to lunch.

11

Sunday Night Lunch

SUNDAY NIGHT LUNCH was an institution at the Ray
house. They never called it supper; and they scorned
folks who called it tea. The drink of the evening was
coffee, which Mrs. Ray loved, and although Betsy
and Margaret still took cocoa, their loyalty was to
coffee for her sake.

The meal was prepared by Mr. Ray. This was a

custom of many years' standing. No one else was allowed in the kitchen except in the role of admiring audience. He didn't object when Anna or Mrs. Ray made a cake earlier in the day; he didn't mind the girls putting a cloth on the dining room table. But in the kitchen on Sunday evenings he was supreme.

First he put the coffee on. He made it with egg, crushing shell and all into the pot, mixing it with plenty of coffee and filling the pot with cold water. He put this to simmer and while it came to a boil, slowly filling the kitchen with delicious coffee fragrance, he made the sandwiches.

He got out a wooden breadboard, and a sharp knife which he always proceeded to sharpen further. He sliced the bread in sensibly thick slices and he never cut off the crusts. Mr. Ray's opinion of sandwiches without crusts matched Mrs. Ray's opinion of tea on Sunday nights. The butter had been put to soften, and now around the breadboard he ranged everything he could find in the ice box. Sometimes there was cold roast beef, sometimes chicken, sometimes cheese. If nothing else was available he made his sandwiches of onions. He used slices of mild Bermuda onions, sprinkled with vinegar and dusted with pepper and salt. About the use of pepper and salt Mr. Ray had very positive ideas. He used his condiments with the care and precision of a gourmet.

Not too much! Not too little! And spread so evenly that each bite had the heavenly seasoning of the one before.

"I'm not," he used to say with sedate pride, "the sort of sandwich maker who puts salt and pepper all in one place with a shovel. No, siree!" And then he would add, for emphasis, "No siree, BOB!"

The onion sandwiches were most popular of all with the boys who flocked to the Ray house.

Mr. Ray didn't mind company for Sunday night lunch; in fact, he liked it. The larger his audience, the more skill and ingenuity he displayed in his sandwich combinations. Tall, black haired, big-nosed, benevolent, an apron tied around his widening middle, he perched on a stool in the pantry with assorted guests all around.

The guests were of all ages. Friends of Mrs. Ray and himself . . . the High Fly Whist Club crowd . . . friends of Julia, Betsy and Margaret were equally welcome. Old and young gathered in the dining room around the table beneath the hanging lamp. The big platter of sandwiches was placed in the center. A cake sat on one side, a dish of pickles on the other. There was the pot of steaming coffee, of course; but the sandwiches were king of the meal.

After the Rays moved to High Street, there was always a fire in the dining room grate for Sunday night lunch. Often the crowd spilled over to pillows ranged around the fire. Almost everyone ended there, with a second cup of coffee and his cake. Talk flourished, until Julia went to the piano. Mr. Ray always made her play, "Everybody Works but Father."

Tacy came often for Sunday night lunch. And often she stayed all night. She stayed all night on the Sunday after Bonnie's party. Betsy had 'phoned her, of course, to report that not one boy but two had taken her to the party. And in the course of the sandwich making, the sandwich eating, the general talk and singing, she gave her a few more high points. But not until she and Tacy went up to her room did Betsy do the party justice.

Betsy talked on and on, and Tacy listened eagerly, undressing beneath a ballooning night gown, after the modest custom of Deep Valley girls.

"It's like a novel," said Tacy at last, "by Robert W. Chambers. Imagine a house with a library, and a drawing room!"

"You'll be going there soon, Tacy. Carney and Bonnie both are anxious to get better acquainted."

"I'd love to go. It sounds marvelous. And Betsy you're marvelous, too. Other girls think they're doing well to get one boy for a party, and you had three."

"Not really," Betsy objected, although pleased by the remark. "Larry only wanted to walk home with

Herbert, and Herbert, of course, has a case on Bonnie." Honesty compelled a further admission. "Cab likes me, but just as a friend. Mostly he likes coming to our house."

"Who doesn't?" Tacy asked.

"But I mean . . . it isn't very romantic. Cab doesn't feel the least bit romantic about me."

She had finished undressing and now she sat down in the middle of the bed, drawing her knees into her arms.

"To tell the truth, Tacy," she said, "I don't feel romantic about any of these boys. I've known Herbert all my life, almost, and Cab's a neighbor. When I feel romantic about a boy," she added, "he'll be somebody dark and mysterious, a stranger."

Tacy began to laugh.

"A Tall, Dark Stranger."

"That's right. Like in Rena's novels." Rena had been the Rays' hired girl on Hill Street and Betsy and Tacy had read her paper-backed novels. Betsy joined in Tacy's laughter, but after a moment she grew serious again. "I'm just practising on these boys," she said, "so I'll know how to act when my Tall Dark Stranger comes along."

"How *does* a girl act with boys, exactly?" Tacy asked.

"Oh," said Betsy airily, "you just curl your hair

and use a lot of perfume and act plagued when they tease you."

September rolled on its slowly goldening way. The stairs and halls, the cloakrooms and classrooms of the high school became familiar ground. Betsy started singing in the Episcopalian choir. Her father and mother didn't object at all. Julia had a birthday, her seventeenth, and Anna made a birthday cake and Fred was invited to supper.

Chauncey Olcott came to Deep Valley in his play, *Aileen Asthore*. Mr. Ray took the family to hear him. Usually Betsy saw her rare plays at matinees with Winona who had passes because her father was editor of the *Deep Valley Sun*. But once a year when Chauncey Olcott came, she went to the Opera House in the evening with her parents.

The Irish tenor was growing old and stout, but his swagger was as gallant as ever, his voice as honey sweet. Always in the course of the evening the audience made him sing a hit song of earlier years called, "My Wild Irish Rose." At the end of the second act when he came out to take his curtain calls, someone in the audience would shout, "My Wild Irish Rose," and others would take up the cry. Chauncey Olcott would laugh, shake his head, make gestures of protest, but the cries would continue, and at last the curtain would go up again, he would hoist himself a trifle heavily to a table or bench, and the orchestra would begin the much-loved song.

Mr. Ray would take Mrs. Ray's hand then. Julia, Betsy and Margaret . . . whose eyes were blazing like stars in the excitement of going to the Opera House . . . would settle back to enjoy each honied note.

"Of course," Julia said to Betsy afterwards, "that isn't great music."

"Why, the idea!" cried Betsy. "If that isn't great music, I'd like to know what is."

"Grand Opera," answered Julia.

"Like that Pagliacci you sing?"

"Of course. But Chauncey Olcott is a sweet old thing."

A sweet old thing! Betsy was indignant. She and Tacy agreed that Chauncey Olcott was the finest singer in the world.

September brought the first football game . . . the game with Red Feather. Carney, Bonnie, Betsy, Tacy, Winona and Alice drove in Sibleys' surrey to the football field at the far end of town. The school colors were pinned to their coats, bows of maroon and gold, with yard-long streamers.

Larry was halfback on the team which made Carney very important. Once Larry was knocked out for a few seconds and Carney turned white, and Bonnie held her hand. Cab and Herbert sat with the scrub team praying for an accident which would give them a chance to play.

Betsy didn't understand the game very well but she tried to shout and groan at the proper places. Bonnie didn't understand it either, and she was earnest about trying to learn. Carney and Tacy and Alice, having brothers, knew all the fine points and watched the game with interest. Winona excelled at cheering. They all chanted together:

> *"One, two, three, four, five, six, seven,*
> *All good children, go to heaven,*
> *When we get there, we will shout,*
> *'Red Feather High School, you get out!'"*

But Red Feather High School didn't get out. It played to a triumphant score of forty to nothing.

"Larry will feel bad," Carney said soberly as they crowded back into the surrey. They returned to the Sibleys' for cocoa, and Cab and Herbert came shortly, but not Larry.

"He's got the blues," Herbert explained.

"He shouldn't have. He played well," said Carney. "I'd send him some cakes except that he's in training."

"Those Red Feather players weigh two hundred pounds apiece," said Cab.

"Everybody knows," said Herbert scornfully, "that

they're practically grown men. They only stay in school for the football season."

Everyone was indignant, and the cocoa tasted very good.

In September also, Betsy entertained the two Triumvirates. It was the last time the Triumvirates were to meet. The group was bursting out in all directions, outgrowing its fixed mould of three boys and three girls. For one thing Betsy did not like leaving Tacy out, and Carney and Bonnie had grown fond of her too; and Tacy wasn't bashful with Cab or Herbert or Larry although she still refused to consider them important. Then, Bonnie had a new junior boy to whom Julia had introduced her, a tall, thin, freckled boy nicknamed Pin, who had gone around with Katie but didn't any more because Katie was busy with Leo.

The two Triumvirates merged into what was called simply, The Crowd.

"When are you going with The Crowd to Christian Endeavor?" Cab asked Betsy.

"I'll go next Sunday night," Betsy replied.

"Good!" put in Herbert. "I'll call for you at a quarter to seven."

"*You'll* call for her, you big stiff!" said Cab.

"And both of you come back here for Sunday night lunch afterwards," said Betsy.

No boy ever objected to that.

12

The Tall Dark Stranger

THE PRESBYTERIAN CHURCH stood on a corner of Broad Street. It was built of white stone with a pointed steeple and a round stained glass window on one side. But no colored light flowed from this window in the early Sunday evening when Cab, Herbert and Betsy approached to attend Christian Endeavor.

"Christian Endeavor's held in the Sunday School

room," Cab explained, heading for the side door.

"What's it like, anyway?" Betsy asked. She paused in the doorway to settle her hat.

"Religious exercises first," said Cab. "But a social hour afterwards."

"Refreshments?"

"Only cocoa on Sunday nights. Once a month they have a Friday meeting with games and real grub. The Presbyterians give you a good time; and then of course there's Bonnie."

"Bonnie's president," said Herbert. His tone was gloomy. Bonnie now walked to Christian Endeavor with Pin.

In the spacious Sunday School room, rows of folding chairs were ranged in one corner, and Carney and Larry were sitting there in devout silence with Pin. Cab, Herbert and Betsy tiptoed to seats beside them. They too sat in devout silence while at a table in front Bonnie conferred with another girl in whispers. She did not even glance their way.

The chairs were filling up, and Betsy saw that the boys had been telling the truth when they said that almost all denominations came to Christian Endeavor. She saw fellow Baptists, and boys and girls she knew were Methodists, Congregationalists, Camelites, Lutherans. The Humphreys represented the Episcopal Church, and Cab, of course, was a Welsh Calvinistic Methodist.

Bonnie looked sweet enough to have drawn them all. She gazed over the group with calm blue eyes. Then, grave and efficient, she called the meeting to order. She announced a hymn and they all stood up and sang: "Let a Little Sunshine In."

Cab, Herbert and Betsy looked on one book. Betsy took the alto part, and they sang loudly and with spirit.

Bonnie prayed. It was amazing to Betsy that a 'teen-age girl could pray just like a minister. She didn't use a prayer book, either, as they did in the Episcopal Church. She made it all up out of her head. At the end she led the others in saying the Lord's Prayer. Then she turned the meeting over to her companion. It was the practise, she explained, for a different member to take charge each week.

The new presiding officer read haltingly from the Scriptures. Bonnie paid conscientious attention but the boys began to grow restive. Cab found a pencil and scribbled:

"Gosh, I feel religious. How about you?"

"Me, too," scribbled Betsy, and passed the note to Carney who wrote, "Me, too," and passed it on to Larry who wrote, "Maybe our Little Poetess will write an appropriate poem," and passed it to Betsy who wrote "Brute!" and passed it back.

Herbert, the usually irrepressible, would take no part in these doings. He could not remove his adoring eyes from Bonnie. Herbert would stop being crazy about Bonnie, and then he would see her presiding at Christian Endeavor and it would all come back on him. So he had told Betsy one day in a confidential moment.

The meeting ended and the social hour began. It wasn't a full hour; it merely spanned the interval between Christian Endeavor and the Sunday evening service. Members of the hospitality committee had slipped out to the kitchen during the final hymn and now came in with trays full of steaming cups. Bonnie in her friendly way was calling everybody to come and get cocoa when the door opened and two boys entered.

One of them was familiar to Betsy; he was a sophomore boy named Pete. The other she had never seen before.

"They've got their nerve," muttered Cab. "If you drink the Presbyterians' cocoa, you ought to come for their prayers. Don't you think so, Betsy?"

But Betsy only nodded absently. The second boy was Tall, Dark, and a Stranger. He might almost have walked out of her conversation with Tacy. She stared with fascinated eyes.

He walked with a slouch that was inexplicably attractive. His hair, parted at the left side, stood up on the right side in a black curly bush. He had heavy eyebrows and large sleepy dark eyes and full lips. He looked about with an almost scornful expression which melted as Bonnie, mindful of her duties as president, crossed the room and held out her hand.

"I am Bonnie Andrews," she said.

"My name's Tony Markham," Betsy heard him reply in a voice deeper than the voices of most of the other boys.

Bonnie shook hands with Pete, too.

"We're having some cocoa," she said. "Won't you join us? Just introduce yourself," she added to Tony. "We're very informal around here."

Tony smiled out of his sleepy eyes, and sauntered toward the table.

Tony Markham! Tony Markham! Betsy said his name over and over to herself. Cab brought her some cocoa, and she drank it, thankful for the banter between Herbert and Cab which made it unnecessary for her to talk very much. She looked between people's heads and over their shoulders at Tony.

"You're certainly taking a look at Christian Endeavor," Cab remarked.

"Well," she answered, "that's what I'm here for."

"Do you feel yourself turning just slightly Presbyterian?"

"Um . . . what did you say?"

When the meeting broke up Bonnie sought out

Tony again. Betsy, Carney, Larry, Cab and Herbert were all within earshot.

"Christian Endeavor begins at seven," she said. "I hope you will come next week for the first part of the meeting." She smiled but the rebuke was apparent.

"Maybe I will," Tony replied. His joking tone robbed the answer of rudeness. But Bonnie would not flirt at Christian Endeavor.

"I'm sure you'll remember," she said with a cool smile.

"Oh, you are, are you?" asked Tony. But he could not get a response in kind. Bonnie smiled again, reprovingly, and hurried away.

"What kind of a girl is that anyway?" asked Tony, turning to The Crowd.

"She's president of Christian Endeavor," said Carney. "She's a wonderful girl."

"She'd make a good school teacher," said Tony.

Herbert stiffened.

"Nobody's asking you to come here," he said. "Why don't you try staying away?"

"Aw, come off!" said Tony with his lazy smile. "I was only fooling. Some school teachers are fine and dandy."

Carney remembered her duties as a bona fide Presbyterian.

"Don't mind Herbert," she said. "We all hope you'll come regularly to Christian Endeavor. And *on time.*" She stressed the last two words but she showed her mischievous solitary dimple.

Tony turned to Pete.

"I didn't think," he said, "that Christian Endeavor was much in my line, but I'm getting to like it better all the time."

Everyone laughed. They moved out into the darkness, and Tony and Pete walked away.

Betsy's heart was pounding. The Tall Dark Stranger, the Tall Dark Stranger, she said under her breath.

Climbing the Plum Street hill Herbert and Cab wrangled and brawled as usual, but Betsy was very quiet. In her mind she was reconstructing Tony's image, recalling his curly bush of hair and the laughter in his eyes. She was startled out of her reverie by hearing Herbert say to Cab, "Who is this Markham guy, anyway?"

"He must be new in town," answered Cab. "I never saw him before. Fresh, isn't he?"

"So fresh he'll get his nose punched if he doesn't look out," Herbert replied.

Betsy shuddered; Herbert was extremely brawny.

"Aw, he didn't mean any harm," Cab said soothingly. "Bonnie isn't sacred, you know. She isn't a plaster saint, with a ring around her head."

Herbert kicked sulkily at the curb. But he cheered as they opened the door of the Ray house with its firelight, and piano music, and the festive smell of coffee. Herbert and Cab ignored the piano and the clamor of Julia's crowd, to charge into the dining room where they pounced upon Mr. Ray's sandwiches and Anna's chocolate cake. Betsy put off her coat and hat and pushed into the kitchen to the niche beside the cellar door where the telephone was placed. She gave the Kellys' number and when Mr. Kelly answered, she called breathlessly for Tacy.

"Tacy, this is Betsy."

"Hello. You sound excited."

"I am. Can you hear me? The piano is making such a racket."

"I can hear you. Heavens, what is it?"

"I have to be careful for the boys might come in. Herbert and Cab are here. Tacy, I've seen the T.D.S."

"The what?"

"The T.D.S. You remember our conversation . . ."

There was a bewildered silence.

"Think hard," said Betsy. "The T.D.S. What I could be romantic about."

"Oh-h-h-h-h-h-h!" Tacy's voice swelled with illumination. "Where?"

"At Christian Endeavor. I'll tell you all about it in the morning."

"I'll call for you early."

"Oh, do! I don't expect to sleep a wink tonight. . . ." The swinging door from the dining room opened, and her father came in followed by Herbert and Cab. He was going to make more sandwiches, and they wanted to watch him, of course.

"Yes, the algebra lesson is on page ninety-six," said Betsy changing her tone. "Ten problems. They're hard as the dickens, too."

"I hope you've done them," said her father sharpening the knife as Betsy hung up the receiver.

"Julia helped me."

"Mr. Ray," said Cab. "In algebra, your daughter is not quite bright."

"Just leave off the 'in algebra,'" Herbert put in, and Betsy made a face, and thought for the first time to go to the mirror to see whether her hair was still in curl.

Beside the fire she munched an onion sandwich dreamily. And after the boys had gone, clearing the dining room table with her mother and Julia she was still silent and dreamy.

Julia came into her room to undress. She was full of talk to which Betsy gave but abstracted attention.

"Bettina," said Julia. "Do you have something on your mind?"

"Not a thing," said Betsy.

"You didn't meet anybody new at Christian Endeavor, did you?"

"Not a soul."

"I didn't meet him; I only saw him," she whispered after Julia was gone.

She turned out the gas and went to the window and looked out into the night.

"The Tall Dark Stranger, The Tall Dark Stranger," she murmured dreamily, liking the sound of the words.

Bonnie
Carney
Mrs. Ray
Julia — Betsy Tacy

13
The Freshman Party

TACY CAME SO EARLY the next morning that Betsy was not yet downstairs. Red-cheeked from her long walk, bright-eyed with curiosity, Tacy burst into the bedroom and found Betsy, fully dressed, standing before the mirror staring into her own hazel eyes.

"Oh, Tacy!" she said in a lowered voice. "I wish I was prettier."

"Why, Betsy, you're plenty pretty enough. You're better than pretty."

"I don't want to be better than pretty. I'm tired of being better than pretty. Sweet looking! Interesting looking! Pooh for that! I want to be plain pretty like you are."

"Look at my freckles," said Tacy.

"But look at your beautiful auburn curly hair and big blue eyes. And you have the reddest lips, and not a quarter as many freckles as you used to have."

"Neither have you," said Tacy. "Your skin is peaches and cream."

"It's the only decent thing about me."

"It isn't either. You have the smallest waist of any girl in The Crowd and the prettiest hands and ankles."

"My ankles aren't half as pretty as Carney's, and she has a dimple besides."

"Betsy, don't wish to change the way you look," said Tacy indignantly. And putting down her school books, she gave Betsy a hug to which Betsy responded by snuggling her head for a long comforting moment on Tacy's shoulder.

"But he's so unutterably marvelous, Tacy."

"So are you."

"Betsy!" came Mr. Ray's stern voice from below. "Your breakfast is getting cold. And will you see whether your sister Julia is ready to come down?"

When Mr. Ray said, "your sister Julia," he was really annoyed. Straightening up, Betsy called, "Coming, Papa!" She ran into Julia's room, pulled the covers off the bed and threw them on the floor.

"Papa's mad," she hissed. Then she rushed downstairs, followed by Tacy.

She ate hurriedly so that they could get away before Cab arrived. For once they did not want a boy's company. They went to the high school and sat down on the lawn, littered with colored leaves. The maples were all yellow now, or coral pink, or crimson. It was a beautiful place to sit and talk about a Tall Dark Stranger.

"But who is he?" asked Tacy after Betsy had finished her description of the upstanding curly black hair, the black eyes, the lazy saunter.

"His name's Tony Markham. That's all I know."

"His family must have just moved here. But why hasn't he come to school?"

"He will. Oh, Tacy, I hope he doesn't show up in any of my classes! I couldn't recite! I'd drop through the floor!"

"You'd do no such thing," replied Tacy. "You'd put on your Ethel Barrymore droop and fascinate him like you do Cab and Herbert."

Betsy knew that she didn't really fascinate Cab and Herbert, but it was good of Tacy to say so.

"Look at you!" Tacy continued. "Only in high school a month, and two boys on the string. You'll have this Tony too. See if you don't!"

Silently Betsy squeezed Tacy's hand.

"I hear the first gong," she said after a moment.

Tony did not appear at school that day, or the next, or the next. There wasn't a sign of him anywhere, although Betsy and Tacy looked both in school and out of it. They had agreed that if she saw him Betsy was to say, "T.D.S." But the week passed without a sign of the Tall Dark Stranger.

By the end of the week they were almost talked out on the subject. Betsy could not even remember just exactly how he looked, nor just why she had been so crazy about him. She began to take some interest in the Freshman Party, scheduled for Friday night.

A get-together, it was called. Ten cents admission. Cab had not invited Betsy to go, and she suspected that the ten cents was standing in the way. Cab earned his pocket money by delivering papers; his family thought this was good for him; and it undoubtedly was, for when he had money he spent it lavishly. There weren't many spare dimes clinking in his pocket.

"If no boy asks you, come with Alice and me," said Tacy. "But I'm sure some boy will, worse luck!"

Betsy didn't particularly care whether one did or

not, unless it were the Tall Dark Stranger, but on Friday morning she received a note from Herbert.

"Dear, dear Betsy,
    It makes no difference to me which way you take the following. Will you accompany me to the High School this evening? My mother is going to serve punch, and I'm glad because then you can't flirt with me. Of course, you'll have to pay your own way. If you answer this, and if affirmative, tell me when to call. I remain
                        Yours very truly
                        Herbert W. Humphreys."

Betsy passed the note to Tacy and both of them rocked with mirth, to the great satisfaction of Herbert, who had turned around in his seat to watch the reception of this masterpiece of wit.

After much pencil-chewing Betsy produced an answer Tacy approved, and they passed it furtively down the aisle.

"Dear Herbert,
    I'm surprised that you don't want me to pay your way too. Are you sure you wouldn't like me to rob a bank for you? I am glad your mother is going to be there for she won't let you

monopolize the punch bowl. I saw you in action
at Christian Endeavor, remember. I'll be ready at
half past seven with a rose in my hair.
                    Your obedient servant,
                    Betsy Warrington Ray."

Betsy almost forgot about the Tall Dark Stranger in the fun of getting ready for the party. Here was an occasion suitable for her pale blue silk mull. Worn with a large hair ribbon and with stockings of the same soft blue, it was very becoming, and as usual on important occasions Julia dressed her hair.

Herbert called for her early, thinking perhaps that there might be an extra piece of pie, and when Betsy appeared he was eating it. He looked very big and handsome in his best blue serge suit. Anna was stealing admiring glances around the swinging door. Among all the boys who came to the Ray house, Herbert was Anna's favorite.

When he saw Betsy he actually was startled into a compliment.

"Golly, you look nice!"

"For a change," said Betsy pertly.

"I'm going to pay for you. Darned if I'm not!"

"Triumph of triumphs!" said Betsy.

She kissed her father and mother, Julia and Margaret . . . the Rays were great ones for kissing one another . . . and started off in a glow. She did look pretty, and she knew it.

At the corner they found Cab waiting.

"Well of all the bums!" said Herbert. "Can't raise a dime to take a girl himself, so he horns in on me and my girl."

"I thought you needed a chaperone," Cab grinned. "Betsy's getting to be a terrible flirt."

"These poetesses!" said Herbert. "When they get started they're worse than any girls."

"You two behave yourselves!" said Betsy blissfully. She floated into the high school between them. And in the cloakroom she encountered Tacy who remarked at once upon how pretty she looked.

"If only I could wear blue silk mull all the time!" Betsy sighed, fluffing out her curls.

Everyone looked festive, the girls in their prettiest dresses, the boys in their Sunday suits. The women teachers looked curiously unnatural wearing trailing silk dresses instead of shirtwaist suits. And the upper hall looked unnatural, decorated with potted palms, and with rugs and cushions brought from people's houses by the decorating committee. An unnatural air of propriety hung over it.

But presently a program of games was begun. Ruth and Jacob, Going to Jerusalem, Bird, Beast or Fish, Jenkins Says Thumbs Up. The air of propriety gave way to increasing noise and confusion. Betsy, having a very good time, forgot about her curls and the becomingness of blue silk mull.

In the game of Pass the Ring she found herself next to Joe Willard. This surprised her for he was not much in evidence outside of classes. He worked after school, Cab had told her. He worked at the creamery; couldn't even go out for football. He didn't have much to do with girls. Winona had tried in vain to fascinate him.

Knowing that she looked pretty now, feeling successful and gay, Betsy smiled.

"How do you like high school?" she asked.

"I like it. Do you?"

"I think it's just Heaven."

"Heaven to Betsy!" he said.

She paid this sally the tribute of a laugh so hearty that he laughed himself. The hunter found the ring just then, and there was a scramble while a new hunter took his place in the center, then Joe Willard asked: "How did your family like the presents?"

"Crazy about them. My mother adored the butter dish." She had a daring impulse. "Wouldn't you like to come to see how it looks on our dining room table?"

"Maybe I could walk home with you tonight and find out where you live?" he answered. He said it stiffly as though it were an effort for him to make the request.

"Oh, I'm sorry!" said Betsy. "But I came with a boy . . . two boys, that is." She didn't mean to sound braggy, but she realized at once that he might think she had. She felt confused, and all the more so when he said, "Request withdrawn," not as though he had thought she was bragging but as though he thought she had rebuffed him which she certainly, Betsy thought indignantly, had not.

Unfortunately at that moment the ring was found again, and when the circle broke he streaked away so rapidly that she did not have a chance to say one conciliating word. She was put out. She had liked him so much at Butternut Center, and since high school opened she had not been able to get a word from him, and now their first conversation had ended badly.

"Refreshments will be served in the Domestic Science Room," Miss Bangeter called. "Form for the Grand March."

Betsy found Tacy.

"Let's fix our hair," she said, and along with most of the other girls they crowded into the cloakroom and strove for a glance at the mirror.

They were returning to the hall, properly beautified, when Betsy clutched Tacy's arm.

"Betsy! What's the matter?"

"The T.D.S.," Betsy whispered urgently.

"Where? Where?" Tacy looked in all directions.

"Over there by the piano. See him? He *would* come just in time for refreshments!"

Tacy stared eagerly. The curly black hair, the laughing eyes, the slouching pose were just as Betsy had described them. Tacy did not feel the magic Betsy felt, but she was sympathetically enthusiastic.

"He's very nice looking. He seems older than us."

A teacher at the piano plunged into a rousing march. Herbert and Betsy, Cab and Tacy joined the line which wound around the hall and down the stairs, past Mercury, to the Domestic Science Room.

Betsy loved to march. She always went lightly on the tips of her toes, and tonight she was almost dancing. The Tall Dark Stranger had come; he was here; and she looked so pretty, wearing blue silk mull. When they reached the Domestic Science Room she looked around. He was there, and he was still alone. As at Christian Endeavor, he was surveying the scene with a superior gaze.

Betsy and Tacy, Cab and Herbert filled their plates with sandwiches, pickles, olives and Athena wafers. They received punch from Herbert's pretty mother, and perched on a table in the corner of the room. Betsy still had that glorious feeling of being successful, attractive. She waved to Alice and Winona who, with two boys, were on an adjacent table. She hardly glanced at Tony Markham and yet she knew that he was watching her. He had surveyed the whole room and his eyes had come to rest on her.

Now he helped himself generously to sandwiches and sauntered up to the table where they were perched. Betsy didn't feel frightened. She had known that he would come. He shifted the plate to his left hand and saluted with his right.

"Christian Endeavor!" he said, addressing Herbert. "Who's your girl?"

"Christian Endeavor, my eye!" said Herbert angrily. "You go way back and sit down."

"Come, come!" said Tony. "I'm a stranger here."

At that Tacy poked Betsy, her eyes brimming with fun, and Betsy laughed.

"What's so funny?" asked Tony. "What's so funny about me being a stranger?"

"It's a secret," Betsy answered, "and you might as well not ask us what it is, for we wouldn't tell you in a thousand years."

"The room is large. Vamoose! Skiddoo!" said Herbert.

But Tony leaned against the wall, his eyes on Betsy.

"Do you want the scrub team to go into action?" Cab asked Herbert, flexing his arms.

"I can handle him with one arm tied behind me," Herbert said.

"Maybe," said Betsy, "we ought to let him stay.

For hospitality's sake. The honor of Deep Valley High School."

"Do you go to high school?" asked Herbert relenting. "Or are you just horning in, like you did at Christian Endeavor?"

"I'm starting next week," said Tony. "Can't get out of it any longer. And because I've changed schools, I'm put into your pee wee freshman class."

As before, at Christian Endeavor, his smile made his rude words acceptable. Herbert grinned.

"I'll bet you flunked whatever school you went to."

"They couldn't catch me long enough to make me take the exams. So I have to start the weary grind all over."

"I give in. I'm Herbert Humphreys."

"Caleb Edwards."

"Tacy Kelly."

"Betsy Ray."

"Little Ray of Sunshine, eh?" asked Tony. Betsy blushed.

"Going out for football?" Herbert asked.

"Scrub team any good?"

"Any good? It's got Humphreys and Edwards. Need I say more?"

"Nary a word. Nary a word."

Herbert and Cab, Betsy was glad to see, were beginning to like Tony. He was a master at their form of banter. He started presently on Tacy's red hair and as soon as the boys apprised him of the fact that Betsy had manufactured curls, he teased her harder than they did. When the party broke up he joined them on the homeward walk.

Tacy had gone off with Alice. Herbert walked on one side of Betsy and Cab on the other, and Tony walked on the outside quite as though he belonged in their group, looking at her with laughing eyes.

"Aren't we asked in?" he inquired at the Ray steps.

"Not as late as this," said Betsy. "It's eleven o'clock."

"After Christian Endeavor you're asked in," said Herbert.

"And boy!" said Cab. "How her sister bangs the ivories!"

"Well! I may drop in," said Tony, quite as though he had been invited.

"I may drop in!" Betsy whispered as she went into the darkened house. She was glad that Julia was out at a dance, and for once she almost regretted her mother's sociable habit of coming into her room after parties. She wanted to think about this one instead of talking about it.

She told her mother . . . she hoped casually . . . that there was a new boy in school named Tony Markham. But she didn't say that he might drop in for Sunday night lunch. There was always room for one more, and it might be bad luck to make special preparations.

On Sunday she refused Christian Endeavor. She told Cab and Herbert they could come up afterwards if they liked. Evening approached, but she did not even change her dress. And she must have cajoled destiny properly, for when the doorbell rang Cab and Herbert were not alone on the porch. Tony was with them.

"Waiting for us here," Herbert said. "Didn't have the nerve to come in alone."

Tony laughed lazily.

"I told you before . . . I'm a stranger."

Tall and dark he certainly was, but he did not long remain a stranger. From the first step across the threshold he felt at home in the Ray house. He fell in love with the family, and they with him.

His appreciation of onion sandwiches won Mr. Ray; Mrs. Ray enjoyed his cheerful impertinence; Margaret liked him because he liked Washington, and Washington crawled up to his shoulder and licked his ear.

His rich baritone voice delighted Julia, and he was a real asset to the group around the piano. He knew all the songs The Crowd sang: "Shy Ann," "Crocodile Isle," "Cause I'm Lonesome," "My Wild Irish Rose."

Julia had a new song that evening, a waltz:

>"*Dreaming, dreaming,*
>   *Of you sweetheart, I am dreaming . . .*"

Tony threw back his head and his resonant voice rolled about the room. Fred was annoyed, but he had no need to be, for Julia's manner toward Tony was markedly sisterly. Betsy had discovered him; he was Betsy's property.

When the time came to say good night, Tony looked around the glowing music room.

"Say!" he drawled. "I'm going to just about live at this house."

"You big stiff!" said Cab. "*I* live here."

Humphreys slapped his chest.

"Where Humphreys is," he said, "there's no room for Markham. Begone now, and don't come back."

"See you tomorrow," said Tony looking at Betsy with a special look from his laughing black eyes.

"T.D.S., T.D.S.," Betsy whispered to herself.

"That Tony Markham is nice, isn't he?" said Julia as Betsy wound her hair on Magic Wavers.

"Yes, he's a cute kid," said Betsy carelessly.

After that Tony came to the Ray house almost every day. He came as faithfully as Cab and Herbert did.

14
The Trip to Murmuring Lake

ON A SUNDAY IN MID-OCTOBER, Mr. and Mrs. Ray and Margaret attended the Episcopal Church. Julia was singing a solo, and the event fell fortuitously upon the Rays' twentieth wedding anniversary. It seemed intended that they should worship that day in the church to which Julia and Betsy now gave so much of their time.

"All that kneeling down and getting up, kneeling down and getting up! But I can stand it if you can," Mr. Ray grumbled to his wife.

"I think our church is more *sensible*," said Margaret. "Don't you, Betsy?" But Betsy did not answer.

Like Julia she now loved the new church. And it was not just a matter of wearing a black robe and a black four-cornered hat, of marching down the aisle in candlelight and singing. She loved the kneeling down to pray and the standing up to praise.

"O All ye Works of the Lord, bless ye the Lord . . ." That was her favorite canticle. As she sang breathlessly, calling upon Angels, Heavens, Waters that be above the firmament, Sun and Moon, Showers and Dew, Ice and Snow, Light and Darkness, Lightnings and Clouds, Mountains and Hills, Green Things upon the Earth, Wells, Seas and Floods, Whales, Fowls of the Air, Beasts and Cattle, and the Children of Men to "praise him and magnify him forever," the panorama of the earth and the seasons seemed to wheel majestically before her eyes.

They sang this today, and glancing down she saw her father looking patient and Margaret looking polite.

"Julia's right. People just are different about the kind of churches they like," Betsy thought.

Mr. Ray perked up when Julia sang her solo at the

offertory. He and Mrs. Ray tried to hide their pride, but it was difficult, for Julia's voice soared and she looked rapt and saintly.

Larry and Herbert were in church with their father and mother. Betsy pretended not to notice them, emulating Bonnie at Christian Endeavor.

When she and Julia, having changed from vestments into fall coats and tams, came out of the church, the Humphreys were standing beside the Ray surrey. Ordinarily the Rays walked to church but today they were bound for Murmuring Lake. This had been Mrs. Ray's home as a girl; she had been married there; and the trip was in honor of the wedding anniversary.

"Going to be gone all day?" Mr. Humphreys asked.

"Yep. Anna has the day off, and the front door key's in my pocket."

"Which is funny," said Mrs. Ray, "for we never lock the back door."

"Having dinner at the Inn?"

"That's the plan. Then we're going across the lake to Jule's old home. We'll drive back late and rustle up some supper. We do it every year."

"It's a sweet idea," Mrs. Humphreys said.

"It's a bum idea," said Herbert in an undertone to Betsy. "Cab and Tony and I don't like it a little bit."

Betsy gave him a gratified smile.

Rolling down Broad Street Betsy relaxed in the back seat of the surrey between Julia and Margaret. It was delicious to hear that Tony would mind her absence. She treated him just as she treated the other boys, and not even her mother and Julia did more than suspect that she had a special feeling for him. But she had a very special feeling.

Tacy knew it, of course. To Tacy Betsy poured out all her sensations. When they did homework together, eulogies of Tony came between algebra problems. Tacy stayed all night, and they talked about Tony until long past midnight. If Tacy grew bored she never showed it. She listened with inexhaustible sympathy, always pointing out in the most heart-warming way how quickly and successfully Betsy had added Tony to her train.

It was true that Tony showed some liking for her; his teasing was affectionate. But there was something big brotherish in his attitude that Betsy did not like. She kept hoping this would change, and give place to an attitude more like Fred's to Julia, Larry's to Carney.

She did not mind being away from him today. Just thinking about him was almost more satisfactory. Besides she loved this trip to Murmuring Lake. They took it at all seasons; the Inn was a favorite vacation ground. But the October anniversary trip was the nicest.

The countryside seemed to be on fire. The maples had the red and gold of flames. Orange colored pumpkins glimmered among shocks of corn and Mr. Ray stopped and bought one for Margaret's Halloween.

Murmuring Lake was encircled by two golden rings as the trees on the shore looked down at their mates in the water.

"Just the thing for a wedding," Mr. Ray pointed out.

The Inn with its flock of cottages looked like a hen surrounded by chicks, and there was an excellent dinner in which a real hen was served with dumplings. For dessert there were two kinds of pie, ice cream and cake. You could have all four if you wished; and after they had eaten to contentment and beyond, and Mr. Ray had smoked a cigar and Old Mag had had a chance to eat and rest, they drove around the lake to Mrs. Ray's old home.

Betsy thought her mother's girlhood home extremely romantic. Its shady acres were enclosed . . . except on the lake side . . . by a white picket fence with an arched gate bearing the sign, "Pleasant Park." A twin line of evergreens led to the house, the barns and the kitchen garden. There was a rose garden, too, and a little summer house covered with vines.

"But I didn't have half the fun here that you girls have on High Street," Mrs. Ray said. "One reason I'm so easy with you is that my stepfather was so strict with us."

By "us" she meant herself and Uncle Keith. It was a family legend that Step-grandfather Newton's severity had caused Uncle Keith to run away and go on the stage. He was a boy then, and for years Mrs. Ray had not even known where he was. But they had corresponded since a joyful reunion when he came to Deep Valley playing in *Rip Van Winkle*.

With the passing of years Step-grandfather Newton had become much less prickly. Betsy was quite fond of him, in fact. But she saw him only rarely now; he and her grandmother lived in California. "Pleasant Park" had long since been sold to a farmer. The farmer's wife was hospitable and seemed to enjoy the annual October visit from the Rays.

"This is the bay window where we stood when we were married," Mrs. Ray said as usual. "There never was a happier marriage made."

"This is the oak tree she hooked me under," Mr. Ray said, leading the way across the lawn, ankle deep in leaves, to an oak with leaves the color of Mrs. Ray's hair.

"I was camping down by the lake shore," he went

on, "with a bunch of young fellows. We needed salt and knowing Jule Warrington I came up to her house after supper to borrow a cupful. That was my finish, that cup of salt. I didn't get back to the tent until midnight, and then I was hooked."

As usual Mrs. Ray put her arms around him.

"You've never regretted it, have you, darling?"

"Not for a second," Mr. Ray answered, and kissed her.

Julia, Betsy and Margaret knew all this by heart. They looked on benevolently. Strolling back to the house, Julia said to Betsy, "It's wonderful how much in love Papa and Mamma are."

"Why, of course, they're in love. They're married, aren't they?" asked Betsy.

"It isn't the same thing, you know," smiled Julia. But Betsy thought she was just being cynical as she had been about Chauncey Olcott.

"Married for twenty years! I should think they *would* be in love," Betsy muttered indignantly.

When they started home the sun was getting low, and in withdrawing it seemed to take with it all the brightness of the landscape. The girls were grateful for the warmth of their fall coats and snuggled together under the buggy robes.

Now it was Mr. Ray's turn to talk about his youth. His father and mother had come to Iowa from

Canada, he said, going as far as Chicago by train and the rest of the way behind oxen in a covered wagon. His mother had had eleven children out there on the prairies. She had been poor, and had died in her early forties. Yet she had left her mark on every child, of the ten who had lived.

She had been a school teacher in Canada, and there were always books in the little farmhouse. She had talked to her children as she washed and ironed, baked and scrubbed, about the value of an education. She had implanted in every one of them a yearning for an education, and they had not been satisfied with the little country school house. There was an academy in the town nearby and to this she and her husband had managed to send the older children in turn.

"After she died we older children tried to help the younger ones to get an education," Mr. Ray said.

There was no Protestant church out there on the prairie, although the Catholics had one.

"The Catholics have set us a good example," Grandma Ray had said. She asked her boy Bob to drive her around the neighborhood so that she might raise a fund for a church. Mr. Ray could still remember, he said, the arguments she advanced.

"You want a church here when your children marry, don't you?" "You want a funeral sermon when you die."

"You don't want your children to grow up like Indians, do you?" she'd ask the atheists. Some of the farmers really were atheists, Mr. Ray said.

Grandpa Ray had headed the list of donations with one hundred dollars. It was a great deal for him to give, Mr. Ray went on, a poor man with eleven children. Some men gave fifty, some twenty-five, some ten, five, some just a dollar.

"One man, I remember," Mr. Ray said chuckling, "said he couldn't spare even a dollar. He was one of the atheists. Mother looked at his litter of pigs.

"'How about one of those pigs, Henry Hogan,' she asked, 'so that your children can grow up in a civilized community?'

"She looked so little and spunky sitting there on the wagon seat. He gave her the pig," Mr. Ray ended.

"Do any of us look like her, Papa?" Julia asked.

"Margaret does, a little. She was small and dark— she was Welsh, you know—and she had big eyes like Margaret's."

Margaret sat straighter than ever with pride.

"Did she get the church, Papa?" asked Betsy. She knew the answer. They all knew the story, but they liked to hear it through.

"She did," said Mr. Ray. "It was the first Protestant church in that part of Iowa. It had a steeple, it was painted white, it stood under two pines out on the prairie. It's standing there still, and my mother is buried in the churchyard. We'll all go down to see it some day."

After a moment Julia asked hesitantly, "Was it a Baptist Church, Papa?"

"All the Protestant denominations worshiped there," he answered.

"Episcopalians, too?"

"They would have if there had been any around, I suppose. But there weren't any high falutin' Episcopalians out there on the prairie. My mother was a Baptist, and that's why I'm a Baptist."

Betsy swallowed hard and spoke. "Is that a good reason for being a Baptist?" she asked.

"Why, come to think of it, I don't know that it is," Mr. Ray replied. "And I don't even know that I made a true statement. Probably I'm a Baptist because I like to be a Baptist. I certainly wouldn't like to be getting up and down all the time the way the Episcopalians do."

"Neither would I," said Margaret. She volunteered, "Mrs. Wheat is a Baptist. Her husband is a deacon. I watched her wash the communion cups one day."

Julia and Betsy said nothing.

The conversation had brought them to the top of the hill overlooking Deep Valley. The valley was full of mist through which the lights of the town were shining.

"Home already," said Mr. Ray.

"The ride went quickly."

"There's nothing like a story for passing the time."

"I'm starving, I'm famished," said Mrs. Ray. "And *how* I want a good cup of coffee!"

The girls cried out that they were hungry too.

"I'll rustle up some sandwiches in a jiffy," Mr. Ray said.

"Let's build a fire in the fireplace," said Mrs. Ray. "And get the lights turned on. The house always looks so dark and cheerless when everyone's away. But perhaps Anna will have come in ahead of us."

They drove down High Street, and as the house came into sight Mr. Ray exclaimed, "By George, Anna *did* get in ahead of us! I thought her Charley kept her out late on Sunday nights."

"She's in all right," said Mrs. Ray. "Look at the lights!"

Lights were blazing all over the house.

"Doesn't she ever think of the gas bill?" grumbled Mr. Ray.

They stopped in front of the house, and instead of taking Old Mag to her barn, Mr. Ray went in with the others to see what was up.

At the front door the smell of coffee greeted them, savory and strong. The music room was empty. A fire was crackling in the dining room grate. And as the surprised Rays moved toward the dining room, a trio of voices broke into song. They were masculine voices, one deeper than the rest.

"Here comes the bride, here comes the bride . . ."

"For Heavens' sake!" cried Mrs. Ray, rushing ahead.

The table was set, not too elegantly. Tony, Cab and Herbert were dressed out in Anna's kitchen aprons. Tony was waving a knife.

"Fried egg sandwiches coming up," he said. "Do you like your eggs flopped or unflopped? Speak quick."

"Flopped," said Mr. Ray. "Two of them."

"Flopped." "Flopped." "Unflopped." "Unflopped."

Julia, without stopping to take off her tam and coat, went to the piano. Everyone sang together, "Here comes the bride."

15
Halloween

AT ONE OF THE LATE October football games Larry sprained his ankle. He was laid up for several days, and the girls went to his house after school with fudge and candy kisses.

Carney had been planning a Halloween party for The Crowd, but when she found that Larry couldn't come she decided to invite only girls. Betsy, Tacy,

Bonnie, Winona and Alice! It was to be a sheet-and-pillow-case party.

After supper on Halloween Mr. Ray and Anna brought into the kitchen the ash cans and everything movable from outside the house. Windows and doors were locked. Deep Valley boys weren't well behaved on Halloween.

Julia was going to a dance, but before she put on her own party dress she helped Betsy into the sheet and pillow case. Shouting "boo" at Margaret, Betsy started off for Carney's.

For a week the weather had been stormy. Wind and rain had stripped the trees and made sodden masses of the leaves. But tonight a white merry moon sailed in a freshly washed sky and caused the damp sidewalks to shine.

Groups of children were already roaming the streets. Feeling safe in her disguise, Betsy booed at them and waved her sheeted arms. She didn't see Cab, or anyone she knew. The boys, she had heard, were indignant at their exclusion from the party, but Betsy thought a hen party was the best kind on Halloween. Undoubtedly they would try in magic ways to peer into the future. Betsy shivered and hoped that the omens for her would point to Tony.

Not that she was anxious to get married. Far from it! She had been almost appalled, when she started going around with Carney and Bonnie, to discover how fixed and definite their ideas of marriage were. They both had cedar hope chests and took pleasure in embroidering their initials on towels to lay away. Each one had picked out a silver pattern and they were planning to give each other spoons in these patterns for Christmases and birthdays. When Betsy and Tacy and Tib talked about their future they planned to be writers, dancers, circus acrobats. Betsy certainly had no wish at all to settle down, but just the same she hoped she would see Tony's face if she walked down the cellar steps backward holding a mirror tonight.

Two sheeted figures approached the Sibley house just as she did, and at the door each one secretly showed her face to Mrs. Sibley. She was too wise to admit masked figures indiscriminately. For some time after entering, the ghosts talked in sepulchral voices, trying to conceal their true identities, but at last with uproarious laughter they threw back their pillow cases.

At the end of the Sibleys' hall were dining room and kitchen. At the right in a row were front parlor, back parlor, and a library. The rooms could be closed off with folding doors, but they were all open tonight. There was no light except from grinning jack-o'-lanterns in the corners and a fireplace blazing in the library.

The shades in all the rooms were closely drawn.

When tappings on the windows began the girls raised one shade a trifle and saw a jack-o'-lantern peering in, but later there was almost continuous tapping and they pulled the shade down.

"Probably the boys," said Bonnie.

"They're furious that they're not invited," Carney agreed. "Herbert came down before supper and teased like a baby to be allowed to come."

"He only wanted to gaze on his Bonnie," Betsy said. "He knew she would make an elegant ghost."

While they were bobbing for apples in the kitchen the front doorbell rang violently. Mrs. Sibley answered it and came back laughing.

"Three ghosts," she said, "tried to make me believe they had been invited. But they couldn't fool me. I have boys of my own."

They drenched themselves bobbing for apples; then there was an hilarious struggle to take a bite from an apple suspended in a doorway. After such routine Halloween amusements, Mrs. Sibley withdrew.

"You know where the refreshments are, Caroline. Have a good time," she said, and went upstairs to join Mr. Sibley.

"We have a freezer full of ice cream in the woodshed, so don't eat too much popcorn," Carney warned. Waving the popcorn shaker, she led the way to the library.

Betsy loved the Sibleys' library, even more than the Andrews' library although it didn't have so many books. It had the fireplace, and a window seat full of cushions and Mr. Sibley's armchair. This was a tremendous black leather-covered armchair, deep and soft with pillowy arms. It swung on a patent rocker so that it could be luxuriously tilted, and there was a footstool in front.

The girls made a rush for it, and Winona got it, and Tacy piled on top of Winona, and Betsy on top of Tacy, and Alice on top of Betsy, and Bonnie on top of Alice. But Bonnie scrambled off to help Carney with the corn.

Tapping began now on the library windows but the girls wouldn't raise the shades.

"Those ghosts had better go home," said Carney. She didn't take much interest in the prowling boys, since Larry was not among them.

When the corn was popped and buttered, more apples were brought out, and the girls started peeling them and throwing the peelings around. The peelings were supposed to make letters, and the letters were supposed to represent the initials of future husbands. Future husbands were very important that night. Betsy flung her peeling but it didn't look like a T. It was hard to get a straight letter like T out of a crooked peeling. They began the time-honored game of snapping apples.

One girl snapped another's apple while saying the name of a possible future husband. The owner ate the apple and then counted the seeds to the accompaniment of the magic rhyme:

"One I love
Two I love,
  Three I love I say;
Four I love with all my heart,
  Five I cast away.
Six he loves,
Seven she loves,
Eight they both love,
Nine he comes,
  Ten he tarries,
Eleven he courts and
  Twelve he marries."

If there were more than twelve seeds, you started over again with "One I love."

Bonnie snapped Carney's apple . . . for Larry, of course. Betsy snapped Winona's Teddy Roosevelt, which brought roars of laughter. One apple was snapped for Hank Weed, senior captain of the football team. Another was snapped John Drew, the actor.

Tacy snapped Betsy's.

"Um, let's see!" Trust Tacy not to betray Betsy's feelings. "Oh . . . Tony," she said in an offhand way.

Betsy gobbled the apple, counted the seeds fever-
ishly, chanting:

> *"One I love,*
> *Two I love . . ."*

There were sixteen seeds, so it came out, "Four I
love with all my heart."

"Hi, girls! Betsy loves Tony with all her heart."

It was the usual cry, but Winona happened to be
looking at Betsy. And Betsy blushed such a rosy red
that it could be discerned even by firelight.

"Betsy's blushing!" Winona shouted. "Betsy loves
Tony . . ."

Betsy leaned over to pommel her, and it caused an
uproar that ended the apple snapping.

"Come on now," said Carney. "We're going to
walk down the cellar steps backward and *settle* this
matter of our future husbands."

They took turns, and each girl returned to the
kitchen shrieking. When Betsy's turn came she discovered why. Carney had placed a particularly hideous
jack-o'-lantern just where it would grimace into the
mirror on the lowest step. This was fun but Betsy felt
disappointed.

Refreshments came next. Mrs. Sibley had left the dining room table all ready, the girls discovered peeking

in. It was decorated with fruit and colored leaves and in the center was a Halloween cake, frosted with orange.

"It has favors in it," Bonnie said. "A penny, a thimble, a button, a boat, a key and a ring."

"Betsy'll get the ring, I'll bet," teased Winona, dancing about.

"Don't be silly."

"Betsy loves Tony!"

"Come along and help me bring in the ice cream," Carney said. "Mamma made it herself, and I turned the freezer for absolutely hours. It's yummy."

"I hope the woodshed was locked up tight," remarked Alice.

"Don't worry. We locked and double locked it." Carney lighted a candle and led the way.

But when they opened the woodshed door, even the flickering light of the candle revealed disaster. The outside door stood open. The wind blew the candle out, but Carney was already screaming, "The ice cream's gone! The ice cream's gone!" She ran outdoors, her long white draperies fluttering behind her.

The other five followed. Like six ungainly white birds they flapped about the Sibley lawn. Soon there were nine white birds.

"I've caught Herbert," shouted Winona clutching the tallest. The rest of the girls bore down upon him.

Star of the scrub football team Herbert might be, but they forced him to the ground.

"Tell us where our ice cream is! Tell us where our ice cream is!" Six girls sat on him to enforce the demand.

"Cab! Tony!" moaned Herbert.

Two sheeted figures tried to pull six sheeted figures from Herbert's struggling body. A magnificent free-for-all fight was impeded by sheets which sent more than one tangled warrior to the ground.

"We won't tell you where the ice cream is unless we can have some!" roared Cab.

"All right," said Carney, yielding suddenly. "Come on in." And the boys dragged the ice cream freezer out from under a denuded lilac bush.

"How did you get in anyway?" Carney was asking. "I locked that door myself."

"The spirits let us in," said Tony in his deep voice.

"The strong right arm of Humphreys," Herbert said.

"And his little friend Edwards," added Cab.

They all trooped through the woodshed to the kitchen where the boys dished out ice cream while the girls put their hair to rights. Then they gathered around the dining room table where the candles had now been lighted.

Everyone was still breathless. The boys told how

they had found a crack beneath one of the shades around the window seat, and by standing on a barrel had managed to look in.

"We saw you snapping apples," Tony said.

"Betsy loves you with all her heart, Tony," Winona called down the table.

Tony turned his head and looked at Betsy.

"Can I help it if someone snaps my apple for you instead of John Drew?" asked Betsy. She spoke with commendable lightness but she felt a hot wave creeping into her face.

"Betsy's blushing!" cried Herbert. "Look at her blush!"

"Why, Betsy, I thought you loved me!" said Cab.

Tony said nothing but the expression in his eyes made Betsy tingle. She was glad when Carney distracted his attention by finding the thimble in her cake.

"You're going to be an old maid," everyone shouted.

"I am not!"

"Wait 'til Larry hears this!"

The excitement had barely died down when Bonnie created more.

"Girls! Here's a mystery. There are nine of us at the table, and nine places set, but Carney only expected to serve six."

"*O di immortales!*" cried Carney.

"Ghosts did it," said Herbert, grinning.

"I sneaked in and did it while you were snapping apples," said Cab.

"But you couldn't have!" cried Carney. "It's set so artistically. No one could have done it but mother. When you called at the front door she told you to come around to the back door later. She unlocked that woodshed door for you.

"Mother!" Carney called, jumping up and running out into the hall.

Mr. and Mrs. Sibley leaned over the banisters, laughing.

"Leave enough ice cream for your brothers," Mrs. Sibley said.

16

Hic, Haec, Hoc

By the time November was under way, homework reared its ugly head. At first Betsy had managed very well with study periods but the habit, now flourishing, of writing notes to Herbert had interfered considerably. A forty-six in an algebra test brought her up short.

And not only was her algebra teacher depressingly

uncomplimentary. Her Latin teacher was plainly not impressed. Betsy and Tacy were delighted when they were introduced to *"Hic, haec, hoc."* They took the declension for a slogan, and when Betsy called Tacy on the telephone she said *"Hic, haec, hoc,"* and Tacy answered, *"Hujus, hujus, hujus,"* and they shouted in unison, *"Huic, huic, huic."* This was undeniably very bright, but its good effects were not apparent in the classroom.

Even her English teacher did not appreciate Betsy.

"He picks on me about commas," she complained.

Joe Willard carried off first honors easily, and Betsy was a breathless second.

In Miss Clarke's ancient history class alone did she find smooth sailing, but almost everyone sailed smoothly in gentle Miss Clarke's class. From the beginning of the year to the end, Miss Clarke did not shuffle her cards.

The names of her pupils were written on cards stacked alphabetically. Miss Clarke sat down each morning with the neat pile before her, lifted a card, peered at it mildly through her eye-glasses, and asked the pupil named thereon a question. When the answer had been given, the card went to the bottom of the pile. The ancient-history textbook was so arranged that each paragraph formed a convenient subject for a question. Knowing exactly when his card would come up, a student had no difficulty in figuring out beforehand just which paragraph it was advisable to study. It was not considered sporting to study anything else.

One day in November Miss Clarke dropped her cards. They scattered widely in all directions and the consternation created in her class was quite out of proportion to the labor involved in picking them up.

"I won't take time to sort them now," said Miss Clarke, lifting the first one at hand. There were frantic mutterings among the seekers after knowledge. Books were furtively opened, pages ruffled. Almost everyone recited badly that day. Even star pupils like Betsy seemed completely in a fog.

"That little accident with my cards upset you children more than it did me," said Miss Clarke sympathetically.

Betsy saw a good deal of Miss Clarke for she was the Zetamathian faculty advisor, and Betsy was from the first an active Zetamathian. This was more or less an accident.

The two societies alternated in presenting monthly programs; Rhetoricals, they were called. Julia, who loved to perform, had long been Miss Clarke's mainstay. Seldom were there Zetamathian Rhetoricals at which Julia did not sing, recite or play the piano. Miss Clarke assumed that Betsy, being Julia's sister, was equally talented, and asked her to take part in the first program.

"Now, what would you like to do?" she asked with flattering confidence after Betsy had accepted.

"Well," said Betsy hesitantly, "Tacy and I might sing our Cat Duet."

They had sung this first in the Fourth Grade, and in every grade thereafter. The costumes had been outgrown long since, but the duet had never been abandoned. It consisted mostly of cat yowls and howls and was popular with grade school audiences. A high school audience received it hilariously at the first Zetamathian Rhetoricals.

The weather was growing wintry. Early in November Betsy looked out her window one morning to find a thin layer of white over the world. The snow was wet, and melted promptly, but a week later it came again as though it meant business. Mr. Ray had started a fire in the furnace. The rooms of the High Street house were comfortably warm as the rooms on Hill Street never had been. Betsy felt a pang when she remembered the glowing windows of the coal stove but she could not help enjoying a heated bedroom. And, of course, on Hill Street there had been no fireplace.

"The fireplace is going to be fun during the holidays," Mrs. Ray said.

"And Thanksgiving's almost here," answered Mr. Ray. "I've ordered a fifteen-pound turkey."

The Slades came for Thanksgiving dinner, bringing Tom who was home on vacation, which made the occasion eventful for Betsy. He was not only that highly desirable creature, a boy, but he was an old friend. He and Betsy and Tacy had started school together.

He was large and rugged with dark hair that always looked rough no matter how carefully he brushed it, greenish-brown eyes under glasses, and a dark skin. Not even his uniform could make him handsome but he was an original and interesting boy. He was musical; he played the violin; well, too, Julia said. His violin joined Julia's piano at all The Crowd parties.

Cox Military hadn't changed him, except that he now said "Hully Gee!" all the time. The Crowd had never even heard, "Hully Gee!" before. But everyone started to say it. Deep Valley rang with "Hully Gees!" after Tom went back to school.

December came in. The snow was still white and fresh but it was growing ominously deep. When the walks were shoveled, after a snowfall, the drifts were as high as a man's head. Betsy kept warm in a grey coat and a grey fur piece, and sometimes replaced her grey hat, which was topped by a red plaid bow, with a stocking cap or tam-o'-shanter, also red.

Clubs were in full swing; Mrs. Ray was frenziedly preparing a paper for her Study Club. The lodges were giving dances. Julia and Fred went with Mr. and Mrs. Ray to the Knights of Pythias dances sometimes. Starting off in their party dresses, Mrs. Ray and Julia looked like sisters.

The Opera House began to have its visitations of plays. The best one was a musical comedy called *The District Leader*, with a Joe Howard in it. Winona took the girls in The Crowd, and the following day she and Betsy and Tacy went up and down Front Street gathering up the advertising pictures of Joe Howard. They had cases on him, they said. Fred brought Julia the songs from the show, and The Crowd sang them around the piano.

"What's the Use of Dreaming?" Tony sang that one better than Joe Howard, everyone agreed.

The Crowd stood with locked arms to sing and often Tony's arm was locked in Betsy's. "My Wild Irish Rose," "Crocodile Isle," "The Moon Has His Eyes on You," "Dreaming." The songs they sang came to hold in their melodies the very essence of what Betsy felt for Tony, the magical sweetness.

For a few days after the Halloween party she had felt distressingly self conscious with him. His teasing eyes seemed to be searching her face to see if what Winona had said was true. But this had worn off; it was bound to; he was at the Ray house so much.

Yet there was a difference now. It was small; he was far too brotherly still; but Betsy was almost sure she saw a difference. He asked her to go with him to some of The Crowd parties; he didn't just go along. He paid for her when they went to the Majestic. He stayed later than the others did when The Crowd came to her house.

Going to and from classes in school he always hailed her. "Hi, Ray of Sunshine!" Sometimes he stopped to talk. Sometimes he wrote her a note, but only when he had something to tell her. He didn't write notes just for fun as Herbert did. Betsy kept these careless scrawls in her handkerchief box under her handkerchiefs and the sachet bag.

Occasionally after school Betsy walked home with Tacy. She liked to visit the Kellys who all loved and petted her. She liked to call on the neighbors . . . the Riverses, Mrs. Benson, and the rest. It was satisfying to appear in the haunts of her childhood with the aura of high school about her. The hills were white now; she and Tacy couldn't go up to their bench. Betsy's old house was rented, and about the time she left Kellys, the lights would go on in the windows.

At this hour, often, the sky was the color of a dove's breast. The snow which all day long had sparkled in the sunshine looked pale. Walking homeward, looking up at the sky, and around her at the wan landscape, she felt an inexplicable yearning. It was mixed up with Tony, but it was more than Tony. It was growing up; it was leaving Hill Street and having someone else light a lamp in the beloved yellow cottage. She felt like crying, and yet there was nothing to cry about.

She made up poems as she tramped homeward, the snow squeaking under her feet. Sometimes when she reached home she wrote them down and put them with Tony's notes deep in the handkerchief box. But she did this secretly.

"What has become of your writing, Betsy?" her mother asked. "Are you sure you don't want Uncle Keith's trunk down in your bedroom?"

Betsy was sure; she didn't want it, although she still climbed to the third floor and visited it sometimes.

Writing didn't seem to fit in with the life she was living now. Carney didn't write; Bonnie didn't write. Betsy felt almost ashamed of her ambition. The boys teased her about being a Little Poetess. She felt that she would die if anyone discovered those poems in the handkerchief box, and the bits of stories she still wrote sometimes when she was supposed to be doing algebra.

She told more stories than she wrote. She told them to Margaret. They were about Margaret herself and a girl named Ethel Brown who lived in Detroit and was gloriously beautiful and led Margaret off on enchanting adventures.

Anna liked to listen to them too.

"That Ethel Brown," she'd say. "She reminds me of the McCloskey girl. What was she wearing, Betsy?"

And Betsy would produce pale blue dresses and blue hats, or pale pink dresses and pink hats, or yellow dresses and yellow hats quite as she used to produce them for Tacy and Tib.

She told these stories mostly on evenings when her father, mother and Julia were out. Ethel Brown was a secret among Betsy, Margaret and Anna. When Betsy ran out of stories, Anna would tell some . . . not about Ethel Brown, of course. Hers concerned dragon flies who sewed up people's eyes, about horse hairs that turned into snakes.

One day after an evening of story telling in the kitchen, Margaret plotted to secure a hair from Old Mag's tail. She secured it, and put it in a bottle, and waited quiveringly to see it turn into a snake. It never turned but her faith in Anna was quite undiminished. Horse hairs had turned into snakes for Anna, as surely as Ethel Brown lived in Detroit.

At church now they were practising the Christmas music. Some of it was familiar and caused to ring in Betsy's head the bells of childhood Christmases. Some of it was unfamiliar, for Episcopalian hymns were different from Baptist hymns. All of it was beautiful. It filled the empty chilly church with a glory like golden light.

Julia, who never cared what people thought, often went down into the nave and knelt and said a prayer. Sometimes Betsy went with her. She even went alone when Julia was practising a solo, and the nave was unlighted, and no one would see.

When she prayed alone like that, it seemed to her that she could hardly bear the painful sweetness of life. She prayed that she might grow prettier, that Tony might come to love her, that she might be a writer some day. It was amazing how light and free she felt, after she prayed.

Walking home on the rare occasions when they didn't have masculine company, she and Julia talked about the Episcopal Church. Betsy had definitely decided that she too wished to join it.

"There's a confirmation class beginning after Christmas," Julia said. "The Bishop comes to confirm people in the spring. Oh, Bettina, I wish we could go into that class together!"

"So do I," said Betsy. "Of course I'll have to be baptized. Papa asked me if I didn't want to be baptized this year but I put it off. I'd rather be baptized in the Episcopal Church if I'm going to be an Episcopalian."

She pondered. "We have to talk it out with Papa before that confirmation class begins."

"Shall we do it right now?"

"No, we want to be able to tell him we've thought it over thoroughly. Let's wait until after Christmas."

"You're so practical, Bettina! You have so much sense!" Julia cried.

She often said this, and Betsy did have sense. When Julia appealed to her for advice Betsy seemed to shuck off her romanticism as though it were an actor's dress and become in an instant a balanced capable person.

But Julia had more courage. She never, Betsy felt, would have put Uncle Keith's trunk in the attic and buried her poems in a handkerchief box.

Often Betsy strengthened herself with Julia's courage. And she valued her sister, too, for a gift she had of widening horizons. Betsy lived more intensely in the moment than Julia did. She loved some things more ardently. Her home, the Sunday night lunches, The Crowd, holidays, Hill Street, meant more to her than they did to Julia. The hills that shut in the town of Deep Valley shut Betsy into her own dearly loved world.

Julia loved the Great World. She longed to sing, to act, to study, out in the Great World. The Great World was more real and much more important to Julia than the Deep Valley High School.

17

The Brass Bowl

Christmas was definitely in the air now, not only in the churches. In school both literary societies were preparing Christmas programs, and teachers were growing indulgent under the influence of the approaching holidays. Anna was involved with Christmas cookies, plum pudding, mince meat, and two kinds of fruit cake. Mrs. Ray had thought one kind enough, but Anna had said firmly that the McCloskeys always had two. And when Anna quoted the McCloskeys, the Rays were silent. More and more they bowed to this legendary family.

Mrs. Ray was busy with Christmas shopping, and one night at supper she announced:

"I hope you haven't bought my Christmas present, Bob, for today I saw just what I want."

"I thought you were Christmas shopping for the rest of us, not yourself," jibed Mr. Ray, as he served Anna's excellent corned beef hash with poached eggs, a favorite winter supper.

"I've bought plenty for the rest of you," said Mrs. Ray, "and you'll think so after New Year's when the bills come in. But I can save you a great deal of shopping around by telling you exactly what I want!"

"What is it?" asked Margaret who had saved fifty cents.

Mrs. Ray was not ready to tell yet.

"It's expensive," she warned. "You can all go in together to get it. You don't need to buy me another thing. I'll be perfectly contented with just this."

"But what *is* it?" cried Julia and Betsy.

"It's in Dodd and Storer's window. Just what I want for the front parlor window. A big brass bowl!"

"A brass bowl!" said Mr. Ray disgustedly. "I will not give you a brass bowl!"

"It's perfectly stunning, Bob," Mrs. Ray said. "I just have to have it. It looks just like me."

"If a brass bowl looks just like you I'm sorry for your husband," Mr. Ray said. "I always thought you had a pretty shape."

"Don't be silly," said Mrs. Ray. "It looks just like our big front window, like our parlor, like our home."

"Well, you might as well forget it," Mr. Ray answered. "I like to give you presents for yourself, not the house."

"I'd rather have that brass bowl than a mink fur piece."

"Bosh!" said Mr. Ray.

A few days later at supper Mrs. Ray mentioned the bowl again.

"I was shopping today," she said. "That brass bowl is still in Dodd and Storer's window. How does it happen you haven't bought it?"

"I have no intention of buying it," Mr. Ray answered. "I'm going to give you a personal present, not a house present."

"I love this new house so much that it's practically me."

"Bosh!" said Mr. Ray again.

Every day that Mrs. Ray went shopping she went to Dodd and Storer's to see whether the brass bowl was still in the window. It always was. And since she went Christmas shopping almost every day she mentioned the bowl at supper almost every night."

"Haven't you even seen it yet?" she demanded of Mr. Ray.

"I can't help seeing it," said Mr. Ray. "I pass Dodd and Storer's every day on my way to the store."

"I've seen it too," said Julia. "I went to look at it on my way to Mrs. Poppy's for a lesson. It's a beauty."

"Bob," said Mrs. Ray. "Do you hear what Julia says?"

"I hear," answered Mr. Ray, "but your present is all bought and paid for. It's in the safe at the store. And it *isn't* a brass bowl."

"Then you have to buy me two presents," Mrs. Ray said.

A night or two afterwards at the supper table, Anna, passing gingerbread, remarked: "Charley and I walked past Dodd and Storer's last night to see Mrs. Ray's brass bowl."

"Mrs. Ray's brass bowl!" repeated Mr. Ray. "What do you mean, Mrs. Ray's brass bowl?"

"The one you're going to buy for her," Anna replied.

"He certainly is," chimed in Mrs. Ray. "What did Charley think of it?"

"He thought it was lovely," said Anna. "And so did I. The McCloskeys used to have one just like it in their big bay window."

"Do you hear that, Bob?" Mrs. Ray asked. "We can't let the McCloskeys get ahead of us."

Betsy and Tacy went down town on their Christmas shopping expedition. This was a tradition with them. They went every year, visiting every store in town, and buying, at the end, one Christmas tree ornament. When Tib lived in Deep Valley she used to go with them, and sometimes Winona went. This year they went alone.

It was joyful, as always, to walk with locked arms along a snowy Front Street, gay with its decorations of evergreen and holly boughs, and the merry jingle of sleigh bells. Betsy drew Tacy to a stop before Dodd and Storer's window.

"Mamma has set her heart on that brass bowl," she said.

"It looks just like Mrs. Ray," said Tacy.

"That's what she says," answered Betsy. "I don't believe Papa's going to buy it for her, though. He hasn't told us, but I believe he's bought the mink fur piece she was teasing for before she saw the bowl."

Even Margaret made a trip down to Dodd and Storer's to see the brass bowl, and Margaret brought up the matter of buying it. Mrs. Ray was in the kitchen with Anna, and Mr. Ray and the girls were in the parlor.

"Aren't we going to buy Mamma her brass bowl?" Margaret asked. "I saw it today, and I thought it was very nice. I'll put in my fifty cents."

"We certainly won't buy it," Mr. Ray answered. "No sirree Bob. She's so sure I'm going to buy it that it wouldn't be any surprise. I've bought her something she's wanted a long time, and it's for herself, not the house." He lowered his voice to a whisper. "A mink fur piece."

"Then I'll buy her some violet perfume," said Margaret. "She always likes that."

"The fur piece will be wonderful, Papa," Julia assured him. "She's been wanting one for ages."

"She'll be thrilled with it," Betsy said.

But Julia, Betsy and Margaret were secretly a little worried about the brass bowl as Christmas drew near. Mrs. Ray seemed so buoyantly satisfied that she was going to get it.

"Here's where I'm going to put the brass bowl I'm expecting for Christmas," she remarked to Tony when he came in and found her studying the front parlor window.

"What kind of a plant shall I put in my brass bowl?" she asked Tacy the very day before the day before Christmas. "A palm? Or one of those new poinsettias?"

The Ray house by this time was almost bursting with Christmas. Holly wreaths were up in all the windows. Mr. Ray had brought home candy canes; Washington had a red and green bow on his collar. And everyone had been warned by everyone else not to look in this or that drawer, or this or that closet.

"I don't dare to speak," Margaret said. "I'm so afraid I'll give something away."

"Don't worry, if you mention that I'm getting the brass bowl," said Mrs. Ray. "To be sure, it's still in Dodd and Storer's window, but I think Papa asked Miss Dodd to keep it there just to fool me. Didn't you, Bob?"

"Once and for all," said Mr. Ray, "you are not going to get that brass bowl."

But on the morning of the day before Christmas he weakened. Before he started off for the store he called the three girls into the kitchen.

"I'll be darned," he said, "if I'm not going to buy Jule her brass bowl. I believe she really wants it so much that she's going to be disappointed if she doesn't get it, in spite of the mink fur piece."

Julia, Betsy and Margaret heaved a triple sigh of relief. Then Julia had an anxious thought.

"But perhaps it's sold by now. This is so near Christmas."

"No, it's still in the window. I looked yesterday, and Miss Dodd wouldn't keep it there if it were sold."

Julia gave her father an ecstatic hug, and she and Betsy and Margaret hugged each other and jumped softly up and down.

"What is it? What's up?" Anna asked in a stage whisper.

"The brass bowl," Betsy whispered. "Papa's buying it for Mamma. Won't it be fun when she sees it Christmas morning?"

Mr. Ray beamed all over his face.

When he came home that night, however, the beam was absent. He was smiling, but it was the fixed determined smile he wore when he was worried or unhappy about something. At the first opportunity he drew the girls aside.

"The bowl's gone," he said.

It was as though a door had opened, admitting a draft of wintry cold.

"Who bought it?" Margaret asked, her lips trembling a little.

"An out-of-town customer, Miss Dodd said. It's gone from the window."

"It doesn't matter at all, Papa," Julia said. "Mamma is going to be so delighted with her fur piece."

"And she doesn't expect the bowl really," Betsy declared.

"I'm going to tell her," said Mr. Ray, "that I tried to get it and it was gone. I'll tell her tonight."

Anna's head with its knob of hair on top poked in at the door.

"Did you get that brass bowl, Mr. Ray?" she whispered. "Do you want to hide it up in my room? Where is it?"

"I couldn't get it, Anna," Mr. Ray answered. "It was sold."

"Oh, my poor lovey!" said Anna. "No brass bowl!" She slammed the door.

"Mr. McCloskey," Mr. Ray said ruefully, "would have bought it in time."

They all laughed because they felt like crying.

At Christmas Eve supper, which was oyster stew, Mr. Ray told Mrs. Ray that she wasn't getting the brass bowl. He told her it was sold to someone else. He made a joke of it, but something in his tone made it plain that he was telling the truth.

"Darn it all, Jule," he said, "I gave in and tried to get that silly bowl for you, but I was too late."

Mrs. Ray acted as though it didn't matter at all.

"I was only fooling about the whole thing," she said. "There are other brass bowls in the world."

"Not as puny as that one, lovey," said Anna

lugubriously, clearing the soup plates to make way for chocolate cake.

"Just exactly as puny," Mrs. Ray insisted. "Maybe I'll get one for my birthday."

There was the usual Christmas Eve ritual. They decorated the tree. Betsy put on the golden harp from this year's shopping expedition with Tacy. She hung the red ball she had bought last year, the angel from the year before.

The tree stood in the dining room, and its candlelight mingled with the soft light from the fire in the grate as Julia went out to the piano and they all sang, "O Little Town of Bethlehem," "It Came Upon the Midnight Clear," "Hark, the Herald Angels Sing," and "Silent Night."

Then they gathered around the fire with Margaret in the circle of her father's arm, and Betsy read from Dickens' "Christmas Carol," the story of the Cratchits' Christmas Dinner. Margaret recited "'Twas the Night Before Christmas," and Julia read the story of Jesus' birth out of the Book of Luke. Later they turned out the lights to fill one another's stockings which were hung around the fireplace. They all forgot about the brass bowl.

But next morning they remembered it. It was still dark and cold when Margaret clamored to see her presents. Mr. Ray went down to open the drafts in the furnace and rebuild the fire in the grate. Mrs. Ray went down to light the candles on the tree, and Anna started coffee to boiling and sausages to frying.

"I wish Mamma was getting her bowl," Betsy whispered to Julia as they hurried into their clothes. Margaret didn't dress. She only put her bathrobe on over her outing flannel gown.

Mr. Ray came back upstairs to say that the dining room was warm now. Laughing and excited, they pelted down the stairs. Anna pushed through from the kitchen, intent upon her stocking. They all reached the fireplace at about the same time.

And almost all together they gave unbelieving exclamations. For on the floor in front of the fireplace, catching on its polished surface every gleam of every dancing flame, stood the brass bowl!

"Stars in the sky! Stars in the sky!" cried Anna.

"Santa Claus must have brought it," shouted Margaret, dancing about.

"Papa! You fooled us!" Julia and Betsy fell upon him.

Mr. Ray, however, looked completely mystified. He stared from the bowl around the circle, and his eyes came to rest at last upon his wife.

Then he began to laugh. He laughed until his face grew crimson. He laughed until he shook. He laughed so hard that all the rest laughed with him even before they knew what the joke was.

"You—you—" he said to Mrs. Ray, and went over to shake her. "She bought it herself," he announced to the rest. "*She's* the out-of-town customer!"

"That's right," said Mrs. Ray. "That brass bowl and I were meant for one another."

"She bought it herself!" cried Anna, rocking with laughter. "Stars in the sky, wait 'til Charley hears this!" She looked at Mrs. Ray, now snug in her husband's embrace. "It's just what Mrs. McCloskey would have done!" said Anna approvingly.

18

What the Ouija Board Said

THE REST OF CHRISTMAS went like a glorified Sunday. It was Tuesday, actually. The family went to church in two different parties, and at the Episcopal Church Julia and Betsy in black vestments and four-cornered hats sang with all their hearts:

"O come, all ye faithful, joyful and triumphant . . ."

The church was rich with the fragrance of ever-green boughs brought into candlelit warmth from a snowy world.

There was plenty of snow, but it was old snow. The weather was mild; not Christmassy, everyone said. Dinner was Christmassy enough to make amends. The Rays ate to repletion, and afterwards Mr. and Mrs. Ray took naps while Julia, Betsy and Margaret on the hearth beside the tree read Christmas books, played with Margaret's toys and ran the Ouija Board which was one of Betsy's presents.

For a time the small three-legged table refused to budge. It sat stubbornly motionless upon its polished board with Julia's and Betsy's fingers poised on top, not stirring even after the five minutes of reverent si-lence recommended by the printed directions. At last, however, it began to move, at first hesitantly, then more and more briskly until it was sliding about the board with perfect confidence. It not only went to "Yes" and "No" but spelled out answers to all sorts of questions. This was later, after company had come in.

There was a great deal of company. Herbert and Larry came with their parents; Tom Slade . . . home for the Christmas holidays . . . came with his. Fred, Cab and Tony dropped in. Katie and Tacy made the long walk from Hill Street. Betsy and Tacy planned to exchange their gifts at The Crowds' Christmas tree at

Bonnie's, the next night, but they had to see each other on Christmas Day, of course.

All the visitors had a fling at the Ouija Board and the little table on its padded legs flew about tirelessly spelling out messages for everyone.

"What lies ahead for me during the coming week?" Betsy asked in theatrical tones, her fingers on the table. She and Tacy were running it at the moment with Fred, Cab, Tony and Herbert looking on.

Promptly the table moved. Betsy watched with delighted intensity. In a business-like fashion, as though it knew exactly what it was doing, it slid from letter to letter. The boys chanted the letters aloud:

"T-R-O-U-B-L-E"

"Trouble!" everyone shouted together.

Betsy was aghast. If she had been running the table with anyone but Tacy she would have thought her partner had pushed it for a joke. But if Tacy had pushed, she would have made it spell Happiness, or a Lot of Parties, or Fun. And certainly Betsy herself would not have pushed it to spell Trouble. Trouble was the last thing she had in her mind at the beginning of this party-spangled holiday week.

There was general laughter, but Tacy understood the look on Betsy's face.

"I don't believe in a silly old Ouija Board," she said.

"But what made the table spell that out, I wonder?" Betsy asked.

"Some thought in your mind," explained Julia over Fred's shoulder. "You pushed it unconsciously."

"But I wasn't thinking of trouble."

"Oh, probably you were. You're so dramatic, Bettina. Some impulse deep down inside you suggested that it would be dramatic to have the table spell out trouble."

Betsy pretended to be satisfied, but a tiny worry pricked her.

About twilight it started snowing. Soon there were rims of white on the dark branches of the trees, deep swathings of white on the bare young shrubs around the house. Everyone had gone except the Humphreys and the Slades, who had stayed for turkey sandwiches. By the time they left, lawns, roads and walks were one billowing drift.

"We should have had this last night," everyone said as Mr. Ray went out to sweep the soft snow off the steps before his guests descended. Parting cries of "Merry Christmas!" were muffled by the snow, still coming silently, steadily downwards.

It snowed during most of the following day, providing a shut-in time ideal for enjoying Christmas presents. But it cleared by evening. The stars were out, looking fresh and surprised, the moon was rising when Tony, Cab and Herbert stamped in to accompany Betsy to Bonnie's Christmas Tree party.

This was a real party, and although the weather was too cold for the blue silk mull, Betsy wore a festive dress of bright red velveteen. She had put a sprig of holly in her definitely curly hair, and she was well sprinkled with perfume . . . her own. Having announced far and wide her wish for perfume for Christmas, she had received several bottles. They were still under the tree and the boys doused her some more, for good measure. Julia was giving a party, and Herbert went to the kitchen to call on his friend Anna and sample the refreshments. At last Betsy tied on her party scarf, Tony held her coat, Herbert and Cab put on an overshoe apiece. She brought out the box in which she had packed her tissue-wrapped, ribbon-tied gifts for The Crowd. Tony took possession of it, and they started out gaily.

"I hope all the walks have been shoveled," said Mr. Ray following them to the porch.

"They have, Mr. Ray," Herbert assured him. "Of course there are plenty of nice big drifts in case Betsy needs her face washed."

"Don't you dare!" cried Betsy, thinking of her fragile curls.

"The Ouija Board said she was in for trouble, you remember," Tony called.

"Now see here! This is a *party*. And I'm wearing my new dress."

Perhaps because of the new dress, the boys were very circumspect. They pushed one another freely into the drifts which rose fresh and soft on either side of the walk, but Betsy was spared. They took great scoops of snow in their hands and threatened to put it down her neck, but they didn't, and when they threw snowballs they managed to miss her.

Taking off her party scarf in Bonnie's bedroom, Betsy was delighted to find her hair still wavy. She ran happily down the stairs.

Entering the stately front parlor where a Christmas tree was shining, she received a surprise. It came in the form of two smacks, one on each cheek, one from Cab and one from Herbert who had bounced out from either side of the doorway.

"Why . . . why . . ." sputtered Betsy.

"There's mistletoe over the door," Herbert yelled.

Betsy looked up, forgetting to move away, and Tony dashed over and kissed her.

"Well, for Heaven's sake!" cried Betsy, blushing and rushing away through an uproar of laughter.

"Tacy's coming in next. Gosh, she'll be mad!" said Cab in a stage whisper as he and Herbert stationed themselves beside the door again.

Dr. and Mrs. Andrews enjoyed the fun as much as anyone, especially Mrs. Andrews. Betsy wondered sometimes whether it was the Paris influence that made them so different from other ministers and other ministers' wives.

When everyone had arrived except Larry, who would be late, Herbert said, and all the presents had been placed around the tree, Mrs. Andrews stood up, smiling. Earrings glittered in her ears beneath her crisp dark hair.

"We shan't wait for dear Larry," she said in her clipped speech. "He'll have to forgive us for going ahead. St. Nick's here." She clapped her hands, and a burly, red-jacketed, white-whiskered Santa came in from the hall. He crossed to the tree and it was three minutes, or anyway two, before anyone except Carney knew that he was Larry.

"I knew the second you came into the room. I knew from the way you walked with one shoulder higher than the other," Carney insisted later.

He began to distribute the presents, and through the noise and laughter Betsy kept thinking that Tony had kissed her.

She wished that he had kissed her before Cab and Herbert. Then his kiss would have been the first she had ever received from a boy, and that would have been fitting. She tried to forget that Cab and Herbert had kissed her first.

"My first kiss!" she thought romantically, referring of course to Tony's kiss and ignoring the others. She wished she could remember exactly what it was like, but unfortunately she couldn't. It had come so quickly and unexpectedly; it was as nondescript as the other smacks.

She glanced once or twice in Tony's direction. He was wearing his best dark suit, and a most becoming red tie. His black eyes shone with laughter but his lips wore the indulgent smile that was his usual reaction to Crowd parties. He always seemed a little aloof, more worldly than the rest.

Without intending to, she looked at him so hard and long that she drew his eyes to her. He winked.

It was a merry party. After the gift giving, they played charades. They were called to the dining room for a Christmas punch, and cakes, and little individual mince pies that Mrs. Andrews had made in November and had kept in crocks in the cellar ever since. English mince pies, she said.

When they left the house the weather was turning cold.

"I'll let Cab and Tony escort you home alone and unaided," Herbert said; and to Larry, he added, "I'll wait for you here. It won't take you long to say good night tonight."

"It never does. But that isn't my fault," Larry muttered, and Carney flashed her dimple.

So only Cab and Tony walked with Betsy up the Plum Street hill, and Cab dropped off at his own house as they passed it.

It happened that just as Cab left them Tony took Betsy's arm protectively. She felt her heart gyrate a little. Tony often accompanied her to and from parties but always with two or three other boys. They weren't often alone. And he was different, alone; he was more serious; he was never serious with the other boys around.

There were millions and millions of stars; big ones and little ones; and high above them glowed a great full moon. They walked slowly, the snow crunching under their feet, looking up at the moon. They tried to find the man in it, the lady in it. Betsy couldn't find the lady in it, and they stopped, Tony holding her arm while he pointed it out. They walked slowly on.

"This is beautiful," Betsy thought to herself. "I'll remember it always. Oh, I wish it was a mile to our house!"

But it was only half a block, and the music from Julia's party came out to meet them along with lights streaming from every window.

"Won't you come in?" Betsy asked. "We ought to be just about in time for refreshments."

"I certainly will," Tony replied.

The rugs had been rolled up in the music room and parlor. Mrs. Ray was at the piano, and four couples were dancing. Mrs. Ray knew how to play two dance tunes; a waltz and a two-step. She was playing the two-step now. Tony and Betsy took off their overshoes, and Tony swung Betsy into the dance.

Betsy had never been to a dance. But she had danced all her life. The rugs in the Ray house were often rolled up for an impromptu waltz or two-step to one of Mrs. Ray's two tunes.

"Gosh, Betsy! You can dance," said Tony.

"You've learned somewhere yourself," Betsy replied. And indeed he had. None of the other boys in The Crowd danced much, but Tony danced with the feeling for rhythm that made his ragtime singing so exceptional. He danced with subtlety, inventing steps as he went and Betsy followed him perfectly without missing a beat.

By mutual accord, when the music paused, they dropped their wraps on the nearest chair, and when the music resumed they started dancing again.

It was a waltz this time, but not Mrs. Ray's waltz. Looking around Betsy saw that her mother was dancing with Fred. Julia had sat down at the piano and she was playing, as only Julia could, the new hit waltz song, "Dreaming."

"Dreaming, dreaming,
Of you sweetheart I am dreaming,
Dreaming of days when you loved me best,
Dreaming of hours that have gone to rest . . ."

Tony hummed a few bars in his rich deep voice.

Julia's crowd, after calling out greetings, paid little attention to them. As for Tony and Betsy they forgot that the others were there. They did not speak to each other; they were too intent upon their dancing. Betsy danced on the tips of her toes. Standing so, she was just about Tony's height, and they moved like one person.

"I believe I like dancing better than anything else in the world," Betsy thought.

The music stopped, but to Betsy's amazement Tony's arms didn't fall away. Instead they tightened, and she felt a kiss on her cheek. She looked, confused, into Tony's laughing eyes.

"Wasn't it smart of me to stop under the mistletoe?" he asked.

They were in the doorway between music room and parlor, and there was indeed a mischievous white-berried spray hanging above them. Blushing, Betsy pulled herself away.

This was different from the kiss she had had at Bonnie's. No one had seen what had happened. No one was noticing them at all.

"It wasn't fair. I'm mad at you," said Betsy.

"Aw, come on! You're not really mad. Are you?" He still held her hand. It was delicious.

"I am too," said Betsy. "I'm not speaking to you."

The Crowd was moving into the dining room where Anna had brought in the lighted chafing dish. Tony and Betsy followed; their hands parted.

After that, Betsy admitted reluctantly in thinking about it later, Tony acted exactly like himself. He joked with her mother, he joked with Julia, who tied on a ruffled apron and took charge of the chafing dish. And without ever quickening his gait, he managed to be extremely helpful which was always Tony's way. He brought in the coffee, toasted wafers, passed plates filled with shrimp a la Newburg.

After refreshments there was a little more dancing and Tony danced with Katie and Dorothy, and Leo and Fred danced with Betsy. When the party broke up, Tony waved at her over a number of intervening heads.

"Swell time, Betsy!"

He seemed to have forgotten all about the moment under the mistletoe, but she couldn't believe that. It must have been important to him since it was so world-shaking to her.

When she and Julia and her mother had at last

211

finished discussing the party, and Betsy was ready for bed, she turned out the gas and went to the window. She looked out at the millions of stars; the smallest ones were only shining dust; she looked at the big calm moon that she and Tony had studied. She thought about Christmas night and the Ouija Board.

"Trouble!" she said. "Trouble!" Her tone was scornful. And yet the questioning joy that filled her, looking at the moon, was a little like trouble, at that.

19

The Winter Picnic

THE NEXT NIGHT THERE was another party. Parties came thick and fast in Deep Valley during holiday week. This one was a hen party. The boys not only were not invited, they were warned that the wood-shed would be locked. There would be no stealing of refreshments tonight, Alice said.

The party was at Alice's house, which was near Tacy's but not on Hill Street. Her house nestled against a different fold of the hill. It was a long way from High Street, and Betsy was to stay all night with Bonnie in order to avoid the late walk home.

By request Betsy brought her Ouija Board, and after they had played games and admired Alice's tree the girls took turns asking the Ouija Board highly personal questions.

"What is the name of Carney's future husband?" laughed Bonnie, her soft plump fingers atop the magic table.

"Bonnie, stop!" cried Carney. But the table was already speeding about the board, spelling out "L-A-W-R-E-N-C-E."

"Why doesn't Tacy like boys?" asked Alice.

"But I do like them," protested Tacy. "I just don't think they are little tin gods."

"All right, table," said Alice. "What boy in The Crowd does Tacy like best?"

The table did not move.

"See?" said Tacy, but they waited.

At last, laggardly, it spelled out, "T-O-M."

"Tom!" everyone shouted.

"Oh, well!" said Tacy unruffled. "It had to say something."

Betsy and Tacy were running the table now.

"What does this week have in store for me?"

"Don't ask that silly question, Betsy."

"But I want to see what the board will say tonight."

The table did not hesitate. Promptly it set about spelling out a word.

"T-R-O-U-B-L-E."

"Well of all things!" cried Bonnie, while Betsy and Tacy looked with real perplexity into each other's eyes. "Maybe you're going to freeze your nose at the picnic tomorrow."

"Or sprain your ankle when we go skating Saturday night," said Alice.

That was the more likely mishap. Betsy had weak ankles; she was a miserable skater; she hated skating although she didn't admit it any more. Since she had started going around with a Crowd, she always pretended radiantly to like whatever the others liked, and the others . . . Carney and Bonnie especially . . . adored skating.

Betsy barely listened to these clever conjectures. She thought about Tony and the kiss beneath the mistletoe, and her heart turned over. She hadn't told anyone about that kiss. Not even Tacy.

Before she and Bonnie went to sleep that night, Bonnie grew confidential. In spite of Alice's elaborate and delicious refreshments an hour earlier, Bonnie and Betsy had raided the Andrews' icebox and brought to the bedroom cheese, apples, olives, cookies, cold ham, and some of Mrs. Andrews' famous little mince pies. They sat on Bonnie's bed in dressing gowns, their feet tucked under them, munching.

"Don't you wish you could be crazy about someone, Betsy?" Bonnie asked. "Like Carney is about Larry, I mean? It must be wonderful."

"Yes, it might be interesting," said Betsy carelessly, thankful that Bonnie didn't suspect her feeling for Tony.

"You don't . . . do you, Betsy . . . have a crush on anyone?"

"Heavens, no!"

"Are you sure?" Bonnie's tone was pressing.

"Positive. I don't know why it is, but all the boys are alike to me."

"Me, too. Pin is swell but I just can't get thrilled about him."

Bonnie nibbled mince pie thoughtfully.

"I heard something about Tony," she said. Betsy waited, hardly breathing, and Bonnie went on. "I don't believe it, though. I heard that he smokes cigarettes."

"I don't believe it either," said Betsy. "Not for a minute."

"I *hope* he doesn't," said Bonnie, looking worried. "He really is just about our age, though he seems so much older. He does seem older; don't you think so, Betsy?"

Betsy agreed.

"It really worries me," Bonnie said. And then they talked about the picnic planned for the next day.

As soon as they woke up they looked out the window to take stock of the weather. It was pleasant. Sunshine glittered on the drifts covering Bonnie's lawn.

"It's a curious idea, a picnic in December," said Mrs. Andrews at breakfast. It was a very English breakfast, Betsy thought with satisfaction . . . ham, poached eggs, muffins, jam and tea.

"Don't walk too far," Dr. Andrews cautioned. "Remember the Christian Endeavor Christmas tree tonight."

"I won't forget, Papa. How could I? I'm on the decorating committee."

After breakfast Bonnie remarked to Betsy, "I wish I could make Tony come to Christian Endeavor regularly. I think it would do him good."

"Why . . . I suppose it would," said Betsy.

"That smoking business!" A little line of worry appeared again between Bonnie's wide calm brows. "Christian Endeavor would put a stop to that . . . if it's true. Christian Endeavor has such a good influence on the boys."

Betsy agreed that it had.

She hurried home to pack a picnic lunch and dress. She wore her heaviest dress, folded a red woollen muffler inside her coat and pulled on a red stocking cap, leaving a few curls outside to frame her face. She wore red mittens too.

Cab and Tony appeared with gunny sacks full of kindling over their shoulders. With Betsy they tramped to the Sibleys' to meet Carney, Bonnie, Tom and the Humphreys boys. They joined the rest of the crowd at Alice's house.

The sun shone benevolently causing the snow to glisten as though strewn with diamond dust. They went down Pleasant Street and up a little hill leaving the last house of Deep Valley proper behind. On the other side of the hill, lying in the wide white valley was the cluster of small houses known as Little Syria. In childhood Betsy and Tacy had reached it by another route for by some trick of geography it was also over their own Big Hill. It had been a favorite haunt with them, and Tacy drew near to Betsy now, and took her arm and squeezed it.

"Remember Naifi?" she asked.

"I wonder what's become of her."

"They left Deep Valley a long time ago."

Betsy turned to Herbert who was swinging along beside them.

"Tacy and I once got to know the Syrians quite well."

"How did that happen?" he asked, and Betsy and Tacy, laughing, told him of a long ago contest between

Julia and Tib for the honor of being Queen of Summer, and of how it had ended with the coronation on Betsy's lawn of a little Syrian girl named Naifi who was actually a princess.

"You're fooling."

"No, really. She was a Syrian *emeera* . . . that means princess."

"Which house did she live in?" Herbert asked. They were now passing the settlement. The little houses were banked with snow; their roofs were laden with it. Woodsheds and chicken houses were almost submerged, and the only signs of life came from children building snow men on the lawns.

"She lived right here," said Tacy pausing before a small house.

She squeezed Betsy's arm again, and Betsy squeezed back as they walked on. It had been fun telling Herbert the story of that childhood adventure, such fun that she had not even thought of Tony. Usually she was conscious of his presence even when he was not near her, and as a matter of fact he was seldom far away. She looked about to see where he was.

Tramping through snow at the head of the party were Larry and Carney, hand in hand. Behind them Alice and Winona were accompanied by Pin, Cab and Tom. They had left Little Syria behind now but, turning around, Betsy saw Tony and Bonnie just passing Naifi's house. They were walking very slowly.

"She must be talking to him about Christian Endeavor," Betsy thought.

Larry and Carney paused and hailed The Crowd. Waving their arms to the east where a ridge of hill came down to meet the path and a frozen stream crossed it, they signified that they were turning off. Halfway up the glen a flat rock was soon swept clean of snow. The kindling brought from home was sufficient to start flames among piled branches.

At first the fire was a thing of bright beauty, leaping like a dancer. But it was allowed to burn down to a more serviceable glow. Sticks were sharpened, and wiener-wursts thrust upon them. The fragrant juices dripped into the embers.

"Gee, it smells good!" Winona said.

Alice put a pail of cocoa to heat. Carney and Bonnie were emptying the baskets, arranging buttered rolls, cookies, olives, and several cans of beans. Betsy and Tacy roasted their wienies with their arms about each other. It was good to be back picnicking beyond the Big Hill.

"After we eat," said Tacy, "let's follow this frozen brook up the glen. We'll find a waterfall, I think."

"Let's," said Betsy examining her wienie, cramming it into a roll and beginning to eat.

No one talked much and in fifteen minutes only a very small bird could have found a worthwhile tidbit.

Then came snowballing and face washing and hilarious chases.

While Pin and Herbert washed Winona's face, those natural housewives Carney and Bonnie replaced cups and spoons and napkins in the baskets. Betsy and Tacy with Tom and Cab went off to find the waterfall.

Tony, Betsy observed, was helping Bonnie with the unexpected efficiency she had observed so many times. Bonnie was talking earnestly, but he wore his most superior expression.

"She certainly is having a time," Betsy thought, "getting him to promise to come to Christian Endeavor." She didn't exactly like these prolonged conferences. But she was happy to be exploring with Tacy. They found the frozen waterfall . . . icicles of every length made an iridescent drapery. They saw a cardinal flash against the snow. They found a bush with red berries and broke off a branch.

"You always take a bouquet home from a picnic," Tacy said.

Betsy was happy and yet there was a prick of unhappiness underneath. Walking back to the rock she wondered whether Tony and Bonnie were still talking.

"Probably by now he's fooling around with Winona," she thought. "And Herbert and Pin are with Bonnie."

But when they reached the picnic site neither Tony

nor Bonnie were to be seen. Pin, Herbert and Winona were climbing trees; Larry and Carney were putting out the fire.

"Where are the rest of the kids?" Betsy asked casually, pretending that she wasn't sure who was missing.

"Tony and Bonnie went on ahead," Carney answered.

They had gone on ahead! Well, why shouldn't they? Bonnie, Betsy remembered, had to help decorate the Christian Endeavor tree. It was early for that, though. Probably Bonnie had gotten cold? But Bonnie never got cold.

Betsy suddenly felt very cold indeed. The sun had disappeared. The world was pearl-colored from hill to hill upward and from hill to hill downward. Two saucers of pearl met around the horizon.

Betsy wound her red muffler more tightly and pulled down her stocking cap. She didn't care how far she pulled it down now; she was willing to poke all her curls out of sight if Tony was not there to see.

"That cross country tramp *did* tire you," her mother said at supper.

"No, it didn't, Mamma."

"You seem awfully tired."

"I'm not tired, really."

"I don't think you ought to go to the Christian Endeavor party tonight."

"Now you're talking sense," Mr. Ray put in. "She's been to parties two nights running and she's going to one or two more this week, if my ears haven't deceived me."

"Oh, no, Papa," said Betsy. "Tomorrow night we're going skating, that's all. And coming up here for Welsh rarebit afterwards."

"And you don't call that a party? Well, it's too much. Why do you want to go to a Presbyterian Christian Endeavor party, anyway? You're a Baptist."

"And an Episcopalian. She seems almost more Episcopalian than Baptist to me," Margaret said innocently.

Betsy and Julia both squirmed.

"Oh, please let me go!" said Betsy. To her annoyance tears rushed into her eyes. "Maybe I am a little tired," she added, wiping them quickly. "But I do want especially to go."

"Well," said her mother, weakening. "If you go upstairs and rest until time to dress it might be all right. Don't you think so, Bob?"

"I suppose so," said Mr. Ray. "And tomorrow night's the skating, but the night after that you stay home. Do you hear?"

"Yes, Papa," said Betsy readily. That night was the one night of the week for which there was no party planned.

Up in her own room she didn't light the gas; she went to the window and looked out. The snow had the brilliant almost unearthly glow it often had at twilight.

"I must be tired," she thought, taking off her dress and shoes and getting into her bathrobe. "Otherwise I wouldn't feel so blue. There's nothing to feel blue about."

But she couldn't get out of her mind the memory of Tony and Bonnie, lagging behind on the walk to the glen, and deep in conversation on the picnic rock. What had they done when they reached home, she wondered? Had Bonnie made him tea, as she did for the girls sometimes? Real English tea. It would have tasted good after their cold walk. Cold was becoming to Bonnie, too. It made her cheeks like roses.

"It makes my nose red," Betsy thought, and tears came into her eyes.

She crawled into bed and buried her face in the pillow. The pillow was quite damp presently.

Julia came into the room.

"Do you feel all right, Bettina?"

"Just tired. Don't light the gas."

"I won't. But when you're ready to dress, I'll do your hair. I want to try it in a pompadour."

"Do you?" Betsy asked. Furtively she dried her cheeks on the blankets. She turned face up as Julia sat down beside her, smelling of her sweet cologne.

"What are you going to wear?" Julia asked.

"My white waist over pink, I guess. With a pink hair ribbon. And my pleated skirt."

"Wear it over blue, and a blue hair ribbon. Blue is so becoming to you, Bettina. You look divine in it."

Julia leaned over and kissed her sister lightly.

"You rest now," she said. "I'll be back in half an hour."

"I wonder if Julia suspects," Betsy thought, as the door closed.

The possibility that Julia suspected was comforting somehow. Betsy stopped crying and rested hard. Afterwards Julia did her hair in a lofty pompadour, and the blue underwaist peeping through eyelet embroidery, the blue hair ribbon, were becoming indeed.

Cab called for her before she was dressed, and as she was coming down stairs the bell rang again. As usual Anna rushed to answer it.

"What did you have for dessert tonight, Anna?" Betsy heard in a familiar teasing tone. Then, "For gosh sake, look at Betsy in a pompadour!"

Cab took up the cry.

"A poetess in a pompadour!"

"Come, Ray of Sunshine," Tony said, "and give us a look. It's stunning. It's altogether too stunning for Christian Endeavor."

"Are you going to Christian Endeavor?" Betsy asked. She asked it quite naturally for already she felt all right. Tony was just the same.

"Might as well," he answered lazily. "Bonnie asked me to. She thinks I'm going to the dogs." He stretched his arms and added in a gratified tone. "Yes sir, Bonnie thinks I'm going to the dogs."

Julia, who had seated herself at the piano, whirled around sharply.

"*Bonnie* thinks so?" she asked. "Bonnie's trying to reform you or convert you or something?"

"I guess so," Tony answered. "Why?"

"Nothing," answered Julia. "I just wondered."

"Now she knows," Betsy thought.

Julia's glance was shrewd but her tone, as she turned back to the piano, was light.

"Well, go get religion if you must," she said. "But come back here afterwards. I got all the songs from 'The Time, the Place and the Girl' for Christmas. I thought we could try them out tonight."

"That sounds like fun," said Tony. "I'll be back all right."

With this expert sisterly backing, Betsy felt her last qualm vanish. As Tony helped her into her coat, she even forgot that the Ouija Board had spelled out T-R-O-U-B-L-E.

20

T-R-O-U-B-L-E?

SHE REMEMBERED AT THE Christian Endeavor party.
There was no religious service tonight, just Christmas
carols, the tree, games, and refreshments. But Bonnie,
as hostess, was as poised and gracious as when she
presided over a meeting.

Tony sauntered over to her at once. Betsy, watching
out of a corner of her eye, saw Bonnie's welcoming

smile. They did not spend much time together, but it wasn't Tony's fault. She made it clear that as President of the Christian Endeavor she must scatter her attention over the entire group. This she did with tactful kindness, drawing awkward and bashful members into the circle, making sure there was a candy cane on the tree for everyone, serving cider and doughnuts.

Tony gave up after the second try. He did not relish rebuffs. He joined Cab, Herbert and Betsy and they sat together, played together, ate together. He was in high spirits, and Betsy had fun, but the pricking was back.

As the party was breaking up, Bonnie came over to Tony.

"I'm sorry I couldn't pay much attention to you, Tony. You know, it's a big responsibility, being President of Christian Endeavor."

"Sure, sure!" said Tony. "I had a good time. I don't aim to associate with Presidents anyway. Or with Vice Presidents, or Secretaries, or Treasurers, or even Sergeants at Arms."

Bonnie looked troubled.

"You're angry," she said. "I'm so sorry. I'm sure I could make you understand if I had more time. You know I want you to come to Christian Endeavor regularly, not just for parties."

"Not a chance!" said Tony scornfully. "How do you like Betsy's pompadour?"

"I love it." Bonnie smiled at Betsy. "*You* think he ought to come. Don't you, Betsy?" she asked.

"I certainly do," Betsy replied.

"If I could just talk with you!" Bonnie repeated. But Tony answered cryptically:

"Sorry. I have a date with 'The Time, the Place and the Girl.'"

Betsy inwardly blessed Julia.

"Well, *I* have a date to walk home with Pin," said Bonnie, sounding annoyed. "I was going to suggest your stopping off at my house before we go skating tomorrow night, but I withdraw the suggestion."

"You can't withdraw it," said Tony triumphantly. "You never made it."

"Well, don't come!" said Bonnie sharply, forgetting she was President of Christian Endeavor, "because I'll be busy."

"Certainly I won't come," replied Tony. "I'm busy myself. But I'll bet a nickel that if I did come you'd open the door with a bright and smiling face."

"I would not!"

"You would too!"

"I would not!"

"Children, children!" said Cab. "Remember this is Christian Endeavor. Remember this is the Christmas season of peace and good will." He began to laugh and Betsy joined in. She laughed almost too hard.

"Come on," said Tony, taking Betsy's arm. "Let's go."

Betsy didn't enjoy the walk home as she had enjoyed another walk just two days before, although the same moon was shining and Cab again dropped off at his own home.

"My family's fit to be tied," he said. "They don't see why I go to Christian Endeavor anyway when I'm Welsh Reformed. But I wouldn't have missed that brawl you and Bonnie had tonight for a farm, Tony."

"Bonnie," said Tony, "gives me a pain."

"Are you going to call for her tomorrow night?"

"I am not! What's more, I'm going to smoke a cigarette as soon as we get to the pond."

"Tony! You wouldn't!" cried Betsy.

Tony laughed. "Wait and see," he said.

After that he and Betsy went to the Ray house, and with Julia and Fred they sang all the songs from "The Time, the Place and the Girl." They popped corn and made fudge. They had a marvelous time.

"How did Bonnie's reforming Tony come out?" Julia asked casually as she and Betsy were preparing for bed.

"Ran into a snag," said Betsy. "I think he likes her though."

"That reforming," said Julia, "is one of the oldest lines in the world, and one of the best."

"But she's really and truly interested in getting Tony to join," Betsy said soberly.

"And she really and truly likes him," Julia answered tartly.

"Yes, I think she does," said Betsy. She remembered the midnight confab she and Bonnie had had after Alice's party. Bonnie had been trying to find out then whether Betsy liked Tony. Perhaps she should have confided?

"They had a quarrel tonight," Betsy said slowly. "And Tony says he's going to smoke a cigarette at the pond tomorrow night just to make her mad."

"Hmm!" said Julia. She looked worried. "But you don't really care for Tony, do you, Bettina?" she asked. "Not seriously, I mean."

"No," answered Betsy, glad to salvage her pride. "All the boys are alike to me. I think I like Cab the best. But in a *very* unromantic way."

"That's good," said Julia, and kissed her, and went off to bed.

Betsy wound her hair on the Magic Wavers so tightly that it hurt. She had a terrible feeling inside. She felt as though her mother were sick, or as though she had been flunked out of school, or as though the end of the world were drawing near. She wound her hair on the Wavers so tightly that tears came into her eyes.

The weather turned cold that night. The thermometer dropped like a bucket into a deep well.

"I think it's too cold for skating," Mrs. Ray said the next afternoon, and Betsy's hopes rose. "Maybe the boys and girls would just as soon come here for the rarebit and forget about skating."

"Oh, I don't think so, Mamma," Betsy answered vivaciously, for if there was going to be a skating party she wanted to be allowed to go. "But I'll telephone Carney and Bonnie and see what they think."

How wonderful, she thought on the way to the phone, how marvelous it would be if the skating party were called off! It seemed to her that the threat implicit in Tony's cigarette would melt into nothingness if The Crowd were assembled around her own fire.

"I'll try to make them call it off," she said over her shoulder.

But Carney scoffed at the idea.

"Why, this is grand skating weather," she replied. "The pond is swept and the boys are out there now laying a bonfire. I just love a cold night for skating, don't you?"

"The colder the better for me," Betsy answered. "It was Mamma's idea to call it off. I was going to telephone Bonnie and ask her opinion but I won't bother now."

"She's right here," Carney answered. "We're sitting by the fire doing shadow embroidery on our new waists. Come on down and I'll make some fudge."

"No, thanks. My family thinks I'm going out too much."

"Where have I heard that before?" laughed Carney. "Wait, then! I'll call Bonnie."

"Hello, Betsy?" came Bonnie's soft voice.

"Hello," said Betsy. "My mother had some insane idea that it was too cold for the skating. But Carney and I have decided to forget it."

"Oh, yes!" said Bonnie. "It isn't a bit too cold. Unless your mother is really worried, Betsy?" It was like Bonnie to add that.

"No. It was just a suggestion."

"What did you think of the fracas Tony and I got into last night?"

"I think he's smitten with you," said Betsy, laughing heartily.

"Oh, Betsy!" said Bonnie. "You're the one Tony's always hanging around."

"He's just part of my long voluminous train," answered Betsy. "It's so long I have to measure it every night."

"Do you use a yardstick?" giggled Bonnie.

"I use algebra," said Betsy. "X plus X plus Y plus Z. Wouldn't O'Rourke be pleased if she could hear me spouting algebra?"

"Betsy, you're killing!" Bonnie dissolved in mirth. "Carney wants to know what the joke is. She says, why don't you change your mind and come on down."

"No," said Betsy. "Tell her I'm sitting by my own fire doing algebra problems about how many boys are smitten with me. Good-by, Bonnie. Don't forget what I said. Tony has a case on you."

"You're killing. Good-by," Bonnie replied.

Betsy felt better when she came away from the phone. She felt rather shaky; there was something upsetting in the air. But she no longer felt like crying.

"Tony has a case on Bonnie," she said gaily to her mother.

"I don't wonder," Mrs. Ray replied. "Bonnie's a very attractive girl. And she'd be good for Tony; don't you think so?"

"Oh, yes," said Betsy. "And the skating party is definitely on, just as I thought it would be."

21

T-R-O-U-B-L-E!

CAB, HERBERT AND TONY arrived together that evening to walk to the pond with Betsy.

"I thought you were stopping by for Bonnie," Betsy said jokingly to Tony.

"Like fun!" he answered. "Too much Christian Endeavor around that house for me!"

"Bonnie's going with Larry and Carney," Herbert

remarked. "When I heard of that set-up I telephoned and volunteered my invaluable services. But she turned me down."

"You see?" said Betsy. "She's expecting you, Tony."

"What about Pin?" Tony inquired.

"He's taking Winona."

"How does that happen?" Julia asked.

"Bonnie turned him down too," said Herbert. "What ails the girl?"

Betsy glanced at Tony.

"Pin sort of likes Winona," he said. "They're both tall, and they're both thin, and they're both crazy."

Betsy felt dazed.

She put on the red stocking cap, determinedly pulling out her curls, tucked the red muffler at its most becoming angle, picked up her skates and swung them.

"Who wants the great and supreme honor?"

"Humphreys," said Herbert, and grabbed them. But when he had them in his hands he regarded them disapprovingly.

"They look dull," he said.

They did look dull. Betsy had not skated that season. She hated skating so much that even the sight of skates was abhorrent to her, and she had dug these out of the basement cupboard only that afternoon.

She had dressed warmly, but as soon as she went out of doors she realized that she hadn't dressed warmly enough. The air went down her throat like an icy drink. Inside her coat and dress and the extra warm underwear she shivered.

"You'll warm up when we get to skating," said Tony, who was holding her elbow.

"I'm not a very good skater," Betsy said.

"If you skate half as well as you dance I'll be satisfied."

"Maybe I *have* improved since last year," Betsy thought, meaning that she hoped she had. But her spirits were low.

Even the sight of the pond did not lift them although the bonfire was beautiful. Branches had been piled higher then her head and their wild glow reddened the snow.

"Gosh, we're going to have fun!" said Herbert. "Sit down, Betsy, and let me get your skates on."

"I'll do it," Tony said. That should have made her feel better but it didn't. Her qualms mounted as she sat down on the bench while Tony expertly buckled on her skates.

Carney and Bonnie hailed her. They had shed their coats but they didn't look cold. They wore heavy turtle neck sweaters and stocking caps, pulled efficiently down.

"You'd better pull that cap down around your ears," said Tony, and even helped to stuff her curls back underneath it. Betsy felt that she looked hideous with no hair showing and her big clumsy coat. She struggled to her feet.

Tony was kind about her poor skating. He said her ankles must be weak, and gave a long dissertation about how to strengthen weak ankles. After a turn or two around they came back to the bench beside the fire. About that time Tacy, Alice and Tom arrived. Cab asked Betsy to skate, and Tony skated off to take Carney away from Larry.

Cab, too, was kind about Betsy's deficiencies. Herbert, however, who skated with her next, was brutally frank.

"Gosh darn it, Betsy!" he said, "Skating's so easy. Why haven't you learned?"

"I just don't like to skate," said Betsy crossly.

"Well anybody born in Minnesota ought to like to skate," said Herbert. "And ought to know how."

Betsy's ankles wobbled. She lurched and leaned on Herbert heavily. Larry and Carney flashed past her, together. Cab and Bonnie came behind. Pin and Winona were skating separately. Both were skillful. Tall and thin, Pin looked like a dragon fly as one long leg after another swung easily through the air.

"I think I'll go back to the bonfire," Betsy said.

"Heck!" answered Herbert. "If you want to skate I'll drag you around."

"I don't want to skate," said Betsy. "You have enough to do, dragging yourself."

"Well for Pete's sake!" said Herbert, breaking off the spat with an exclamation so sincerely startled that Betsy said, "Who? What? Where?"

"There," said Herbert. "Tony! What do you think of that?"

Tony was standing beside the fire, one foot on the bench in a nonchalant attitude. Between two fingers he held a cigarette at which he took an occasional careless puff.

"Some of the fellows smoke of course," said Herbert hastily. "But just behind the barn, as it were. Not at a party with girls around. What's got into Tony?"

Betsy did not answer.

Carney had seen him. Betsy saw Carney tug at Larry's arm. Larry turned to look and then Larry and Carney skated rapidly toward Bonnie, and tugged at Bonnie's arm.

Tony blew smoke thoughtfully upward, threw the cigarette down and mashed it out, took a pack from his pocket and selected another.

"For Pete's sake!" Herbert said again.

Betsy saw Bonnie speak to Cab, then leave him alone on the ice. Skating expertly, looking round and cute in her big sweater, she went rapidly toward Tony.

"Hello," said Tony, when Bonnie reached him, and with ostentatious politeness threw his cigarette into the fire.

"Tony," said Bonnie, "will you skate with me?"

"Isn't it customary," asked Tony, "for the boy to ask the girl?"

"Maybe," said Bonnie. "But I'm asking you. Please, Tony."

"Do you want to skate or preach?" he asked.

Bonnie smiled. After all, she was not at Christian Endeavor now. She smiled and put out a mittened hand.

"Skate," she said.

Pin and Winona started clowning on the ice. Winona sat down with a bang and laughed. Cab was trying to skate backward with Tacy. Tom was with Alice. Betsy told Herbert that she had twisted her ankle, and insisted that she liked to sit by the fire alone. He skated off, and she sat by the fire alone.

Tony and Bonnie skated slowly, in perfect harmony, their arms crossed in front, their hands clasped. Betsy tried not to look at them. She looked at the fire. She looked up at the cold disinterested moon and off at the pale unfriendly landscape.

She watched the other skaters, and laughed at their mishaps, and waved when they waved to her. Now and again one or another skated over to sit with her and talk. But Tony didn't come, nor Bonnie.

By and by Tacy noticed that Tony and Bonnie had skated together for a long, long time. She and Cab skated over to Betsy.

"I'm cold," said Tacy. "Can I keep company with you?"

"I'm hungry," said Cab. "When do we start back to the Ray house?"

"Any time," said Betsy. "But people still seem to be having an awfully good time."

"Tony and Bonnie especially," said Cab. "He's smitten and smitten hard. She'll make a Presbyterian out of him yet. Bet a nickel."

"I'll bet you haven't got a nickel," said Tacy.

"And I wouldn't bet even if you had," added Betsy, refusing Tacy's offer to change the subject. "It looks to me like a perfectly awful case."

"Maybe the big bum will stop hanging around your place, getting under my feet," said Cab.

"I'm going to round the others up," said Tacy quickly, "and tell them that we're starting on."

It was very cold, going home. Betsy's hands ached, and her feet ached, and she knew that her nose was as red as a beet. But she laughed at Cab's jokes even harder than usual, and at Tacy's jokes too, for Tacy was full of jokes. Tacy kept her arm twined through

Betsy's, and thought of very silly things to say about Betsy's crippled condition.

Betsy's ankle felt all right now; as a matter of fact, it had felt all right all along. But she was glad that Julia, after they reached home, offered to make the rarebit.

"Keep off your ankle, Betsy. You know my rarebit is perfect."

Betsy took off the stocking cap and resurrected her curls. She sat by the fire and her nose was its normal color by the time the rest came in. But it didn't matter, for Tony paid no attention to her. He was teasing Bonnie.

"She pulled me out of the gutter practically," he said to Julia who received his joke coldly. She sent him to the kitchen to make toast, but it only made things worse.

"Come along and help me, Bonnie. I'll go to the dogs out here in the kitchen all alone."

Bonnie went along and helped him. They were a long time making toast, and they burned it.

Betsy laughed continuously, even at Herbert's jokes about her terrible skating. Now that they were at home, Herbert relented about her sad showing on the ice. He offered to take her out the next day and teach her to skate.

"And get my head snapped off?" asked Betsy. "I'm afraid of you when you get near ice, Herbie. I wouldn't even let you go to the ice box with me."

"Aw, I wasn't that bad!" Herbert said.

For the first time he looked at Betsy with a faintly romantic eye. His adoration of Bonnie had died for lack of nourishment, and he hadn't even noticed now that she was burning toast in the kitchen in Tony's company.

"Gosh, you have red cheeks tonight, Betsy," he said. "Do you paint?"

He took out his handkerchief and rubbed her face to find out. Cab helped him until Betsy cried for mercy. Tony and Bonnie were back from the kitchen then, but Tony didn't join in the fun.

He joined, of course, in the singing that followed the rarebit. Arms locked, The Crowd circled about the piano, and sang until the room quivered.

> *"Dreaming, Dreaming,*
> *Of you sweetheart, I am dreaming,*
> *Dreaming of hours when you loved me best,*
> *Dreaming of days that have gone to rest . . ."*

Tony's arm was locked in Bonnie's, and now and then she looked up at him to smile. Betsy didn't sing much. She was laughing with Herbert.

She was still full of laughter when she and Julia went up to bed.

"That reforming line worked all right," she said. "Bonnie didn't know it was a line, though."

"I notice that Herbert looks at you with new eyes. And he's so handsome! Much handsomer than Tony."

"Tony, the dear departed," Betsy said.

It was all very well until the lights were out, the slit in the storm window opened, and Betsy beneath the blankets. Then the tears she had been holding back gushed out in a relieving flood. She cried and cried, holding the pillow tight in her arms for comfort.

T-R-O-U-B-L-E, her Ouija Board had spelled.

This was trouble, all right.

22

New Year's Eve

BETSY SUNK THAT NIGHT into a well of grief, and in the morning she did not propose to climb out. Her father knocked on her door as usual but she did not budge. Margaret, on her way downstairs, put her head in.

"Time to get up, Betsy."

Still Betsy did not budge.

When Mr. Ray called Julia from the foot of the stairs, he called Betsy too. Betsy did not even answer.

Julia came in, tying the violet ribbons of a most becoming dressing sacque.

"What's the matter, darling?"

"I just don't want to get up," said Betsy.

"It must be your ankle," Julia said quickly. Of course! Her ankle! Julia was wonderful. She closed the window, adjusted the shades, and plumped up Betsy's pillows. She went to the bathroom and returned with a wet washcloth and a towel. She handed Betsy a comb.

"I'll explain to Papa about your ankle," she said, departing, "and bring you some breakfast."

Betsy didn't even say "Thanks." She just burrowed deeper into the pillow. With her eyes shut and her face half smothered she could keep out the picture of Tony smiling down at Bonnie, but she could not keep out an ominous feeling of something bad and sad waiting for her if she stirred.

Her father brought her tray himself.

"Sit up and wash your face," he said cheerily. "I'll have a look at that ankle."

Betsy sat up reluctantly. She scrubbed her face with the cold washcloth, poked her foot out of bed beyond the hem of her outing flannel night gown.

"No swelling," Mr. Ray observed.

Drawing up a chair he poked the ankle. "Hurt?"

"No," said Betsy.

He poked it again. "Hurt?"

"No."

When he poked it a third time, Betsy said, "Ouch!"

"It hurts *there?*" asked Mr. Ray, sounding surprised. He poked it again.

"Ouch!" said Betsy, pulling the foot away.

Mr. Ray looked perplexed.

"Must be a strained ligament. You can get up after breakfast, but no skating or rampaging today," he announced.

"I'd just as soon stay in bed," said Betsy. "I don't feel very good. Not *too* bad," she added hastily, remembering Tacy's party the following night. Mrs. Ray had come into the room.

"A day in bed wouldn't do Betsy any harm," she remarked.

"If the ankle isn't better tonight I'll put a strap on it," Mr. Ray said and patted her head, and departed, his wife following.

Betsy took the tray on her knees.

"I'm not a bit hungry," she thought, looking morosely at the sausages and fried potatoes, the hot buttered toast, the jam, the steaming cocoa. But when Anna came up to get the tray, it was empty.

"I'm glad your ankle didn't go to your stomach,

lovey," she said. "As long as a person can eat, he can put up with anything. That's what Mrs. McCloskey used to say."

"Did the McCloskey girl ever sprain her ankle?" Betsy asked listlessly.

"Both of them," answered Anna. "I made her apple dumplings for dinner that day. How'd you like some apple dumplings, lovey?"

"Oh, Anna, I'd love them! That is," Betsy added, "if I don't get to feeling worse. If I move my ankle I feel terrible. But if I stay in bed I think I could eat some apple dumplings."

"Sure you could," Anna replied.

When the tray was gone Betsy had the feeling that the time had come to face her sorrow, but somehow she couldn't get around to it. Margaret came in with one of her Christmas books and suggested hopefully that Betsy might feel better if she read aloud for a while.

"It's a very appropriate book," Margaret said. "It's about a little lame prince, and you're lame, Julia says."

Betsy read out loud and grew so interested that she almost forgot to say, "Ouch! That hurts!" when her mother helped her into a chair in order to freshen the bed. While her mother dusted the room, they gossiped cheerfully. Julia came in next.

"I'm going to beautify you," said Julia. "There's no reason why you shouldn't look like an interesting invalid."

"I don't care how I look," said Betsy, feeling suddenly completely wretched.

"You know how I love to fix people up," Julia answered. "Where do you keep your best dressing sacque?"

"In the bottom drawer," said Betsy.

It was made of pale blue silk and embroidered with little pink rosebuds. It tied with pink ribbons and was very becoming. Before Betsy put it on Julia brushed her hair and dressed it in a pompadour with two pink ribbons. She went into her mother's room and came back with a chamois skin dipped in powder and ran this over Betsy's face.

"Now lick your lips and wet your eyebrows," Julia commanded. "And you'll look pale and interesting enough for anybody."

Betsy licked with rising interest.

Julia helped her into the dressing sacque, tied the ribbons, and put a small beribboned pillow in back of her head. Betsy enjoyed having Julia work about her. She liked the touch of her small white hands, and the smell of that cologne she used.

"Now," said Julia, "I'm going to manicure your nails."

They often manicured each other's nails. Betsy was clumsy at it but Julia was skillful. She filed and clipped and buffed until Betsy's nails looked like pink pearls.

"You have beautiful nails. I never saw such half moons," Julia said.

In the midst of all this Cab and Herbert arrived.

"Come on up," Julia called.

"Betsy's sick, but it isn't contagious," Margaret explained gravely at the top step.

The boys tiptoed in clumsy solicitude into the blue and white freshness of Betsy's room.

"You don't look sick," said Cab.

"Gosh, you look pretty!" exclaimed Herbert. The admiration which had dawned in his eyes the night before was brighter now. He looked at Betsy much as he had been wont to look at Bonnie.

Betsy languished on the pillow.

"It's my ankle. Any time I go skating again!" she said, looking at Herbert reproachfully.

"Gosh, I'm sorry," said Herbert. The boys sat down to watch the manicure. The doorbell rang again, for Tom and Pin.

"Hully gee!" exclaimed Tom looking at Betsy.

"What's the matter?" asked Pin.

"Ankle. I twisted it last night. I was skating with a big brute who doesn't know what it's like to have weak ankles."

"Help! Betsy! Go easy," begged Herbert.

"Yes, you're the brute," said Betsy.

Flirting while my heart is breaking, she thought to herself. She was doing a good job of it too. Herbert straddled a frail chair, grasped the top of it with strong brown fingers, and stared in enchantment.

"You're Anna's favorite," said Betsy. "But you're not mine. I'm going to put a stop to that piece of pie business."

"I would too," said Julia, buffing.

"Make Anna give it to me," said Cab.

"Or me," said Tom.

"I never even tasted Anna's pie," said Pin.

"You ought to come to see me oftener," said Betsy, giving him a radiant smile. Dog that I am, she thought. Pin had veered to Winona. He didn't belong to Bonnie any longer. He wasn't Betsy's rightful prey. But she was too reckless to care.

"There's an idea," said Pin. "Just what nights do you have pie?"

"Betsy's beaux," said Julia, "are eating us out of house and home."

Everything was going beautifully when the doorbell rang again. Betsy heard Tony's voice speaking to Anna. She heard his lazy steps on the stairs. He lounged in the doorway.

"What do I see before me?" he asked. "Betsy or Madame DuBarry?"

"We all know you're taking sophomore history."

But it was Julia who said it, not Betsy. At the sight of his curly thatch, his laughing black eyes, Betsy's high spirits vanished. She leaned back and didn't say a word.

Someone explained about the ankle. Someone else explained that Herbert was in bad. And anyone could see what Herbert's condition was. He was staring at Betsy, rapt and tongue-tied. Anyone could see who looked, that is, or cared. Tony did neither. He seemed sorry about Betsy's ankle, but having expressed himself in his usual offhand way, he lapsed into an abstracted silence. The banter went on but Tony didn't join in, any more than Herbert did, or Betsy, who felt misery invading her again. He was so charming, so casual, so incomparably superior to all the other boys. How could she give him up? But she had given him up. She didn't feel old enough or wise enough even to try to take him back from Bonnie.

"I'm tired," said Betsy suddenly.

"And the manicure is finished," Julia said, getting up. "I think Betsy had better rest now."

"Clear out, all you kids," said Herbert.

There was a scraping of chairs and pushing toward the doorway. Herbert was the last to go out.

"Going to be able to go to Tacy's tomorrow night?" he asked.

"I hope so," said Betsy, closing her eyes. Wretched

as she was, she gave thought to the picture she must make, lying pale and exhausted on the lacy pillow.

"I wish my eyelashes were thick and curly like Margaret's," she thought. "I'm thankful that they're dark at least."

She hoped they looked startlingly dark, and that her fingers, helplessly curled, looked startlingly white against the blue counterpane.

Julia glanced at her approvingly, tiptoed out, and closed the door.

The boys stayed downstairs to sing a while. Tears slipped through Betsy's fortunately dark lashes as she listened to the dear familiar tunes. She heard the boys departing one by one. Then Anna brought up her dinner.

The afternoon was punctuated with callers, female callers now. Tacy sat on the bed beside Betsy, holding her hand. Carney and Bonnie came, laughing, bringing the winter in on pink cheeks and snowy furs.

Betsy bestirred herself out of listlessness for them.

"Didn't I tell you, Bonnie," she asked, "that Tony was smitten? He's simply crazy about you. He was in here this morning and just mooned around."

"He 'phoned her three times this morning," Carney chuckled.

Three times! Three dull blows at Betsy's heart. He must have 'phoned her twice before he came over to the Rays, and probably once after he left. She couldn't remember that Tony had ever 'phoned her. He wasn't a telephone addict as some of the boys and most of the girls were.

"Did he call up just to talk?" Betsy asked.

"Oh, he called up the first time to ask me to go to your party with him, Tacy," Bonnie said. She sounded amused. "And the second time he asked me not to forget that I had promised. And the third time he asked me not to let anybody else come along. But nobody would be apt to come anyway. Pin has gone over to Winona."

"And Herbert," said Tacy, "as you all may have noticed last night, has transferred his affections with a bang to Betsy."

"Good!" said Bonnie. Her sincerity knocked Betsy's triumph over like a house of cards.

During supper and the early evening Betsy was alone in her room. Sad as she was, she enjoyed lying in bed, warm, petted, while familiar household sounds floated up from below. This was only an interlude. Tomorrow she would be up on her two feet, facing the world and her trouble.

"No visitors for Betsy tonight," Betsy heard her mother say after a ring of the bell. Then Margaret came upstairs.

"Herbert sent you this," she said, holding out a

small box of candy. "He says he's sorry about your ankle. He wants to know, will you let him take you to Tacy's party tomorrow night?"

"I'll go with him if I'm able to go," said Betsy. "You can have the candy, Margaret. Oh, I might take just a piece or two," she added, thinking better of this gesture.

Julia went out that evening on a sleigh ride. Mr. and Mrs. Ray went out too. Betsy and Margaret and Anna ate Herbert's candy to the last stale chocolate drop, and Betsy told them Ethel Brown stories. It wasn't an unhappy evening. But when the gas was turned out and the snowy world was quiet, her grief came back, seeking a little attention. Betsy gave it the tenderest attention. She thought of Tony, his charms and falseness, until she fell asleep.

The Crowd saw the old year out at Tacy's. Betsy's father, fearing for her ankle, drove her up in the sleigh but Cab and Herbert went along. Tony and Bonnie arrived late.

The rambling white house at the end of Hill Street was full of greens and Christmas cheer. The Crowd played games, and the refreshments—as always at the Kelly house—were superabundant. These were served about half past eleven, and the company was still eating when the bells and whistles of downtown Deep Valley sounded faintly. Everyone jumped up and began to cry "Happy New Year!" Betsy and Tacy kissed each other.

Breaking away from the rest they ran out of doors. The winter stars were icily bright. Snow gleamed on the hills where for so many years, winter and summer, they had played together.

In the little yellow cottage which had once been the Ray house, lights were shining. It could almost have been home still. Betsy and Tacy could almost have been children again.

"I wish I still lived there," said Betsy, hugging Tacy, partly from love and partly from cold. "It's such trouble to grow up."

"I hope you have a very happy new year," Tacy said.

23
The Talk with Mr. Ray

IT WAS ARRANGED that Betsy . . . the ankle had to be treated tenderly . . . was to stay all night with Tacy. The Kellys would drop her at home on their way to church New Year's morning. She enjoyed sleeping in the slant-roofed bedroom with Tacy and Katie and eating breakfast with the large merry Kelly family.

The Kellys were full of anecdotes about her child-hood and Tacy's, and it was comforting somehow.

Later Betsy and Tacy had a serious hour alone. They made their New Year's resolutions, and when she got home Betsy wrote them down. Never had she made such serious, such sobering resolutions. She resolved to work harder at school, to read improving literature, to brush her hair a hundred strokes every night, not to think about boys . . . especially not about Tony . . . and to have the talk with her father about joining the Episcopal Church. After the holiday dinner when Mr. and Mrs. Ray went to take naps and Margaret departed with her Christmas sled for a little sedate coasting, Betsy broached the matter to Julia.

"It's almost time to talk to Papa about this church business."

"I know it," said Julia looking troubled.

"The confirmation class begins in February; along about Lent."

"And that's another thing, Betsy. We'll want to keep Lent this year."

Julia was incredibly bold at times. Betsy had thought, of course, about keeping Lent after she became an Episcopalian. She had dreamed about giving up something for Lent, as Tacy did. It had seemed delightfully romantic. But she had played with these ideas only in reveries. Julia was actually proposing to carry them out.

"Do Episcopalians eat fish on Friday?" Betsy asked weakly.

"I'm not sure," said Julia. "There's High Church and Low Church. I think we're Low Church here in Deep Valley. But Anna wouldn't mind cooking fish for us."

"Julia!" cried Betsy, shuddering. "Can you imagine Papa?"

"It's pretty awful," Julia agreed. "What shall we do, Bettina?"

After some thought Betsy asked, "Do you suppose Papa would think we knew our minds by now?"

"We've been singing in the choir all winter."

"We go back to school a week from tomorrow. Let's talk to him a week from today."

"That's a good plan," Julia said.

The second week of vacation was outwardly much like the first. Boys and girls dropped in, and there were parties. But Betsy ploughed through the parties as though they were ordeals comparable to the examinations looming ahead in school. Tony and Bonnie came to everything together, late usually, looking moon-struck. Tony dropped in at the Ray house, but in the flesh only; his thoughts were plainly on Broad Street.

It helped, Betsy found, to adhere to her resolutions as though they were laws laid down. No matter how tired she was at night she brushed her hair a hundred strokes before rolling it up on Magic Wavers. She banished Robert W. Chambers from her room and brought in Longfellow, Whittier and Poe. She ruled Tony sternly from her thoughts. And the Sunday before school resumed, in the robing room at church, she said to Julia: "Today is the day we talk to Papa."

Julia looked grave and beautiful in her black robe and the black four-cornered hat.

"How do you feel?" she asked.

"Queer in my stomach. And why do we always say, 'talk to Papa'? We have to talk to Mamma, too."

"We know Mamma will understand," said Julia. "She's a very Episcopalian type. But Papa is such a Baptist!"

"And you remember all he told us about his mother. It's going to be hard," Betsy said gloomily.

"Bettina," said Julia. "When you pray in church this morning, pray about it, and so will I. Maybe we can find a chance to pray alone after everyone is gone."

That was the sort of thing that Betsy thought of doing, and Julia boldly did.

Organ music sounded, and the girls formed into a line, two abreast, for the processional. They marched and sang:

"Clear before us through the darkness,
Gleams and burns the guiding light,
Brother clasps the hand of brother,
Stepping fearless through the night."

When she came to "Brother clasps the hand of brother," Betsy glanced at Julia. Julia wasn't looking at her, of course. Nothing ever disturbed Julia's rapt expression when she was singing. Betsy doubted that it would alter if the church burned down. But surely, Betsy thought, she must see the significance of the hymn. Change that "Brother clasps the hand of brother," to "Sister clasps the hand of sister," and how perfectly it fitted!

"Let us pray," the Reverend Mr. Lewis said.

The Reverend Mr. Lewis as usual prayed for a number of things, for remission of sins, for peace, for grace, for the President of the United States, for the Clergy and People, and for all conditions of men. But whenever the ritual permitted a personal supplication, Betsy made only one prayer.

"Please help us to tell Papa," she prayed, digging her forehead into her curved arm, forgetting even to try to look pretty.

After the service Julia with calm authority told Fred and Herbert not to wait for them. She and Betsy went down into the body of the church and said their special prayer.

Walking home through the bleak cold, Betsy said, "Now after dinner today, we'll do it."

"After his nap," Julia added.

After dinner and his nap their father, as usual on Sundays, settled down in the parlor with the Sunday paper. He liked best to sit in a curved leather chair that his Lodge had given him after he was Grand Master and to cross his feet on an ottoman in front. With a cigar in his mouth and the paper folded neatly, he read with absorption.

Today Mrs. Ray was reading, too. And Margaret and Washington were looking at the funnies. Julia and Betsy came down the stairs together, as though still marching two abreast in a procession.

"Papa," said Julia, "Betsy and I want to have a talk with you."

Mr. Ray looked up, and he must have seen from their faces that they had a serious matter on their minds, for he put the paper down, and placed his cigar carefully across an ash tray.

"Do Mamma and Margaret get in on this?" he asked them.

"Yes," said Julia. "They might as well."

"Sit down, then," said Mr. Ray, and they sat down gingerly on the edges of their chairs. Mr. Ray took his feet off the ottoman, crossed his legs and leaned back calmly, tucking a thumb into his striped Sunday vest.

"Go ahead," he said, looking from Julia whose pointed face was pale under her pompadour to Betsy whose cheeks were red as fire.

"Papa," said Julia, "Betsy and I want to join the Episcopal Church."

Mr. Ray continued to lean back, but no longer calmly. Julia's announcement had really startled him.

"You do, eh?" he said. He kept his tone offhand, but he sounded as startled as he looked. "What do you think of this, Jule?" he asked, playing for time.

"I've seen it coming," Mrs. Ray answered.

"Do you mean," he said to Julia and Betsy, "that you like all that kneeling down and getting up, kneeling down and getting up?"

He was talking fast, half jokingly. He was . . . Betsy knew . . . trying to adjust himself to their bewildering idea.

"Papa," said Betsy, "don't joke. Julia and I know that you'll feel terrible. In the first place it will be so embarrassing to you; you're a prominent Baptist. People will think it strange of you to let us join the Episcopal Church. They'll criticize you, and we can't stand the thought of that. And yet we both want to be Episcopalians. That's why we thought we'd ask you to . . . sort of . . . talk it over."

Mr. Ray grew serious then. Still with a thumb in

his vest he looked at them out of wise, kindly eyes.

"Let me set you right on one thing first of all," he said. "We aren't going to decide this on the basis of what people will say. You might as well learn right now, you two, that the poorest guide you can have in life is what people will say. What the Baptists in Deep Valley will think of mother and me if our girls go off and join the Episcopal Church has nothing to do with the matter."

Margaret got to her feet, standing straight like her father. Crossing the room she rubbed against his knee and he made a place for her in his chair. He kept his arm around her while he talked, and Margaret stared at her sisters with black-lashed disapproving eyes.

"Don't you agree with me, Jule?" Mr. Ray asked.

"Yes, I do," said Mrs. Ray. "I've done lots in my life the Baptists didn't approve of. Papa has too. We belong to a dancing club; we play whist; we go on picnics sometimes on Sundays. But we don't do anything we think is wrong, and the Baptists respect us. They even asked Papa to be a deacon."

"But there's another thing," said Betsy. "We know how much the Baptist Church means to Papa. We know about Grandma Ray starting the church down in Iowa. It makes Julia and me feel bad to stop being Baptists." Her eyes filled with tears. "It makes us feel terrible," she said.

Julia's eyes filled with tears too, although she didn't cry as easily as Betsy did. She winked violently, and then took out a handkerchief. But since Betsy was groping vainly for a handkerchief and needed one even more, Julia passed hers along and kept on winking. Betsy wiped her eyes and blew her nose.

"See here," said Mr. Ray. "Anybody would think from the way you talk that *I* was the one who had a problem about what church to join. You are the two who have the problem. What makes you think you want to be Episcopalians, anyway?"

But now Betsy was tongue-tied. Not because she was afraid she would cry, although that entered in, but because she was shy of putting into words deeply felt emotions. She didn't mind putting them into written words. She could have written her father an essay on her feeling for the Episcopal Church, but she couldn't tell it to him.

Julia spoke eloquently. "It's the beauty of the service, Papa," she said. "Betsy and I both respond to it. The music lifts us up, and the ritual is like a poem. We were just made to be Episcopalians."

"You've thought this over? It isn't just a whim?"

"We've thought it over for weeks and months," said Julia, glad to be able to say so. "We're sure of everything except whether or not we ought to hurt you and . . ."

"Julia," said Mr. Ray. "You'd never make a lawyer. I repeat that mother and I don't enter into this. You're seventeen years old, and Betsy's past fourteen. Both of you are almost women, and personally I'm glad to discover that you've given some thought to religion. It's a right thing to do when you begin to grow up. It's what I did, and what your mother did, and what . . . I am sure . . . your Grandmother Ray would approve if she were here. The important thing isn't what church you want to join but whether you want to join a church at all.

"Certainly you can be Episcopalians. I'm sure mother agrees. Don't you, Jule?"

Mrs. Ray nodded and reached for the handkerchief Julia had given Betsy.

"And I hope," Mr. Ray continued, "I hope very much that if you're going to be Episcopalians, you'll be good Episcopalians."

"We'll try to be," Julia said quickly.

"But that isn't what I hope most," Mr. Ray added. He knotted thoughtful fingers around his chin.

"Yes, I hope you'll be good Episcopalians," he repeated. "I hope you'll go to church as regularly as mother and I do. We miss a Sunday now and then, when it's fine picnicking weather. We know that God made the out-of-doors, too. But year in, year out, we go to church pretty regularly.

"And we support the church. You have to think of that. Churches need an income just as a family does; and it is your duty to support your church if you join one. With more than money, too. A church needs members who take an active part in the church work. Mother and I don't do as much as some, and some folks overdo it, in my opinion, but we try to carry our load. My point is that if you're going to join a church, you want to be prepared to support it, both with money and time."

"Yes, Papa," Julia and Betsy said.

"But that's just the beginning," Mr. Ray went on, and sat straight in his chair. "It isn't enough to go to church, and to support the church. The most important part of religion isn't in any church. It's down in your own heart. Religion is in your thoughts, and in the way you act from day to day, in the way you treat other people. It's honesty, and unselfishness, and kindness. Especially kindness."

He paused.

"Well, that's that," he ended, his face breaking into a smile. "You two go and be Episcopalians, if you can stand that everlasting kneeling down and getting up. I never could. Everything's settled now, until Margaret here comes and tells us that she wants to be a Mormon."

"I won't," said Margaret, sitting very straight. "I

don't know what a Mormon is, but I want to be a Baptist. I'm always going to be a Baptist." And she turned and buried her face in her father's striped Sunday vest.

Mr. Ray hugged her. He got up. And everyone got up, Mrs. Ray, and Julia, and Betsy, and Margaret. They all embraced in a big family hug, tighter and tighter.

"Now," said Mr. Ray. "I'd better go put the coffee pot on." For that was what the family always did in moments of stress. Margaret didn't drink coffee of course, and Betsy's Sunday cup was mostly cream and sugar. Yet they understood what their father meant when he moved with a competent tread toward the kitchen.

24

An Adventure on Puget Sound

THE NEXT DAY they went back to school, and it was an excellent time for being religious, for being serious-minded, for being heart-broken. The thermometer was far below zero and examinations were looming ahead. Stiffly wrapped, Betsy and Tacy hurried along High Street muttering Latin conjugations. When boys and girls dropped into the Ray house after school, they all studied. Tacy, Alice and Winona came to stay all night and study.

"Why do you have to study *together?*" Mr. Ray asked. "When I was a boy we didn't study in droves. And what help is all the fudge?"

"Nourishment, Papa, nourishment," Betsy explained. "We need strength. Composition is a cinch, of course; and history won't be bad, Clarke is such a darling. But Latin and algebra! Wow!"

Julia too was ferociously intent upon study. She was going to no dances; she quarreled with Fred and refused to make up.

"I'm tired of him anyway," she confided to Betsy. "And it's a very convenient time to be between beaux . . . examination week."

When Fred telephoned Julia was out. When he came Julia was busy. She wouldn't make up. Fred grew haggard. His eyes showed sleepless nights.

"This is pretty hard on Fred," said Betsy indignantly. "He's going to flunk everything, because he's worrying about you."

"Very foolish of him," said Julia, settling down to her Cicero.

The last examination came on Friday, and after school The Crowd surged into the Ray house not only to make fudge but to sing and to ask the Ouija Board who had passed and who had not. Saturday night The Crowd went sleighing. Bells jingling on the frosty air tried to compete with harmonizing from the boys and girls tucked under robes in the big sleigh. Tony and Bonnie sat side by side, his arm draped along the back of the seat. It was a horrible party for Betsy who remarked at frequent intervals that she never had had so much fun in her life.

Monday, the new term began and Betsy found that she had passed in everything. She squeezed through algebra by a breath, through Latin by a hair. Her history mark was fair, but gentle Miss Clarke was disappointed that students who were so brilliant in class made such a poor showing on examination papers.

"You must have been nervous," she said consolingly to Betsy.

Mr. Gaston, although he had seemed so unappreciative of Betsy all term, gave her a high mark . . . ninety-six. It was topped in the class only by Joe Willard's ninety-seven. And shortly Betsy was given another proof of her composition teacher's good opinion.

Miss Clarke approached her after school.

"I've been talking with Mr. Gaston," she said, "and he and I both think that, although you are only a freshman, you can write an essay good enough to be read at Rhetoricals."

"Really?" cried Betsy. Her modest surprise was

assumed, but her pleasure was genuine.

"Aren't you proud?" Miss Clarke asked, patting her shoulder. "We are planning an All-American program, and we want you to write a paper on Puget Sound."

"Puget Sound?" Betsy echoed vaguely.

"Just go to the library," Miss Clarke said, "and read all you can find on Puget Sound. Then write an interesting essay about it."

"Yes, ma'am," said Betsy.

She was delighted with the assignment. It not only provided a highly creditable excuse for absenting herself from the gatherings of The Crowd and the presence of Tony and Bonnie, but it poulticed her sore heart. An essay for Rhetoricals on Puget Sound!

She told the family about it at supper, and they were pleased and impressed.

"Your Aunt Flora lives on Puget Sound," Mr. Ray observed. "You might write her for some material."

"Where is Puget Sound?" asked Margaret, and Betsy, who had not yet looked it up, was relieved when her father answered for her.

"It's an arm of the Pacific extending into Washington state. Seattle where your Aunt Flora lives is built on Puget Sound."

"Papa and I once took a trip on the Sound," Mrs. Ray added. "We went from Seattle to Olympia on the Steamer Princess Victoria."

They talked about the trip throughout supper.

After supper Betsy collected all the pencils she could find. She took them to the kitchen and sharpened them while Anna looked on admiringly. She hunted up a notebook and wrote on the first page, "Puget Sound." The next day after school she ignored the social advances of her friends and turned toward the library.

There was a driving north wind. The cold air stung her cheeks above the grey fur piece and numbed her hands. Her feet were numb too, inside her overshoes, as she crunched along the snowy walk. But she was happier than she had been for days. She felt a fierce proud satisfaction. It was an adventure to be going to the library to learn about a strange new place called Puget Sound.

"I think I'll name my essay that," she planned. "'An Adventure on Puget Sound.' I don't believe Clarke would mind if I worked a little story in."

Miss Sparrow, the small twinkling-eyed librarian, was glad to see Betsy. They were old friends.

"You haven't been down for a long time," she said. She unearthed endless fat and fascinating volumes on the state of Washington and the Pacific Northwest and Puget Sound.

Betsy walked home through a cold even sharper

than she had faced coming down, but she didn't mind. She was thinking of pines standing ruggedly above green water, of Mt. Rainier rising white and fair, or colored like candle flame by sunset. She didn't think once of Tony and Bonnie.

At the supper table, she was bursting with the glories of Puget Sound, but she had to divide talking time with Julia.

Julia had had a singing lesson that day, and *she* was bursting with news of some new records Mrs. Poppy had played on the gramophone.

"They're Caruso records. Enrico Caruso. When you hear him sing that 'Laugh, Pagliaccio,' you absolutely have to cry."

"Who is Enrico Caruso?" Margaret wanted to know.

"Just a fat little fellow who likes his spaghetti," Mr. Ray joked.

"Just the greatest singer in the world," Julia said, giving her father a crushing look.

"Not so great as Chauncey Olcott, I'll bet," said Betsy.

"Chauncey Olcott! You can't mention him in the same breath. You'd better stick to Puget Sound, Bettina."

Steamers on Puget Sound, Mt. Rainier, spaghetti and Caruso surged through Betsy's dreams that night. The next day after history class she spoke to Miss Clarke.

"Miss Clarke, you wouldn't mind, would you, if I put some characters into my essay? Took them on a trip through Puget Sound, maybe?"

"I think it would be a nice idea," Miss Clarke answered, beaming. "It would put a little color, a little life, into the paper."

"That's what I thought," Betsy said.

She went to the library every day after school and at home, in front of the fire, wrote industriously in her notebook. Cab was disgusted and Herbert's budding romantic interest died. Betsy didn't mind. She had given herself heart and soul to Puget Sound.

Her father was much interested in the essay. He talked about Puget Sound every night at supper, and when he paused for breath Julia chimed in about Enrico Caruso. She went often to Mrs. Poppy's to listen to his records.

"I'd give ten years of my life to hear him utter one note," she cried dramatically.

Betsy grew almost as absorbed in Enrico Caruso as she was in Puget Sound. She asked questions about him. He was an Italian she discovered, stout and dark, with a tenor voice so divine that his stoutness and darkness didn't matter at all.

The essay was finished at last and the day for Rhetoricals arrived. At noon Betsy changed from her school waist and skirt into the red velveteen. Mrs. Ray dressed up too. She was going to hear the program as parents often did when their children performed.

"I wish I could go," Mr. Ray said. "I'll have to wait until supper to hear all about it. Will you let me read the essay tonight, Betsy?"

"Of course," said Betsy. Up to now no one in the family had read it; and this worried Mr. Ray a little.

"Has one of the teachers read it?" he asked now. "Somebody ought to check your facts. I suppose you covered the salmon fisheries?"

"Miss Clarke read it," Betsy answered evasively, "last night after school."

"Did she like it?" Mr. Ray inquired.

"She liked it all right," Betsy said.

As a matter of fact Miss Clarke had seemed surprised by the essay. She had changed color two or three times while she was reading. She had coughed and gone out for a glass of water. She had taken off her eyeglasses and polished them and put them on again.

"It's not exactly what I expected, Betsy," she had said. "But perhaps it will do our Rhetoricals good."

This was such a queer compliment that Betsy did not repeat it to her father, and she thought about it with some trepidation when, sitting on the platform with the others taking part in the program, she watched Miss Bangeter, tall, dark and majestic, walk to the front of the platform. After a few words Miss Bangeter turned the meeting over to Miss Clarke.

Miss Clarke explained that the program was to cover all parts of the United States. She announced the opening number, a contribution from the chorus. Since Betsy sang in the chorus she had a chance to stand on her shaky legs and get accustomed to the audience. It was vast and frightening.

The chorus sang "Dixie," and that covered the South. A girl read one of Brett Harte's stories, and that covered California. A boy recited from Whittier's "Snow Bound" and that covered New England. Betsy sat on the platform with her hands clutching her essay, copied out on foolscap paper in her best handwriting. Her legs were still shaky, her hands were like ice, and her mouth felt as dry as a piece of carpet.

Miss Clarke announced that the next contribution would cover the Pacific Northwest. It was an essay on Puget Sound, written and read by Betsy Ray.

Betsy rose and walked to the front of the platform.

There was a burst of the hearty applause that high school students love to give as a welcome change from being quiet. She saw Herbert's wide grin, Cab's twinkling eyes, Tacy's pale face. Julia too looked anxious but her mother was calm and confident, a little stern, as she was when Julia sang.

"An Adventure on Puget Sound," Betsy said.

She started to read to the accompaniment of the fidgeting, whispering and paper rustling that usually keep pace with the reading of an essay to a high school audience. But after a moment you could have heard a pin drop. For Betsy's essay wasn't an essay, exactly. It was an account of a trip which half a dozen girls in stiffly starched sailor suits and breezy sailor hats were taking on the Steamer Princess Victoria on Puget Sound. The girls were named Betsy, Tacy, Julia, Katie, Carney and Bonnie.

Betsy—in the story—was afraid the sea air would straighten out her home made curls. This brought a gust of laughter from the audience. Bonnie quoted the guide book, trying to make the trip educational. Carney flashed a lone dimple and cried, *"O di immortales!"* Katie talked with an Irish brogue, and Tacy was seasick.

The gust of laughter became a wind. Miss Bangeter rapped for order.

Betsy's essay had a plot. Julia burst into the luxurious salon, richly upholstered in brown leather, where the ship's orchestra was playing and a gay throng was assembled, to tell her companions that Enrico Caruso was on board. She was determined to have a look at him, and the girls searched the faces of their shipmates but saw no one who looked godlike enough to be Enrico Caruso. They saw, however, a short fat swarthy Italian; he seemed, indeed, to be eyeing them.

In the dining room, hung in palest green, full of women in ball gowns, flowers and candlelight, with the orchestra now playing behind potted palms, they continued to search for Caruso. Failing to find him, they watched the stout Italian who consumed five spring chickens and vast quantities of spaghetti. It was at this point that Tacy grew seasick.

They went out on deck and noted the panorama of wooded hill and fertile plain. Bonnie told them that Puget Sound was the Mediterranean of America. When not searching for Enrico Caruso they watched the sun set on Mt. Rainier, the color of candle flame.

"How Caruso must be enjoying this!" sighed Julia. The Italian who was in the next deck chair, seemed interested in her remark. "I'd give ten years of my life to hear him utter one note," Julia remarked dramatically.

The moon rose, and someone suggested singing.

"Girls!" rebuked Julia. "We couldn't sing with Enrico Caruso on board!" But they talked her down, the moonlight called for singing so strongly. They began to sing.

They sang "Shy Ann, Shy Ann, Hop on My Pony," and "What's the Use of Dreaming" and "Crocodile Isle" and "Cause I'm Lonesome." Then Katie suggested "My Wild Irish Rose."

"We need a tenor. Fake one, Katie," Julia said.

But Katie didn't need to fake one, for at that point the Italian joined in their song in a tenor voice so golden that the stars above Puget Sound swam in glory as they listened. At the end the little man rose and bowed to Julia.

"The lady might like to know me. I am Enrico Caruso," he said.

"And he ate five spring chickens!" breathed Julia.

That was the final line.

The auditorium of the Deep Valley High School rocked and roared applause. Miss Clarke looked timidly toward Miss Bangeter. Miss Bangeter was laughing and clapping her hands. She wiped her eyes too before she rose and rapped for order and walked to the front of the platform.

"Betsy certainly surprised us," she said. "She left out a few important facts about the Sound, I must admit. And I think she should turn in a report on the Salmon Fisheries, just to show that she knows about them, as I have no doubt she does. But she certainly made us all want to take that trip. Didn't she?"

Uproarious applause was the answer.

Betsy's knees that stopped shaking now. Her mouth felt natural again. She was happy. She was proud. Let Bonnie have Tony if she wanted him!

"The pen is mightier than the sword," she thought. Sword wasn't the word, exactly. But it was the best she could find with the Deep Valley High School whistling and stamping its feet.

25
Change in the Air

"When the days begin to lengthen,
Then the cold begins to strengthen."

MR. RAY QUOTED THE OLD saw every February and every February it was true. The weather was mercilessly cold. Good black coal rattled steadily into the furnace. Bluejays took refuge under the eaves of the house, ruffling their feathers.

"You can put molasses on the end of a stick and catch one," Anna said. Margaret tried. She didn't succeed, but it helped to defeat February.

Mrs. Ray defeated it with a thimble bee; Betsy and Tacy wore their best dresses and served. Julia defeated it by writing to the music store in Minneapolis and ordering another opera score; *Aïda* this time. She also acquired a new beau named Hugh. The examination papers were barely dry when she started throwing bright glances at this slender studious youth who soon was completely at home in the Ray house. Only Washington now served as a reminder of the hapless Fred.

Julia and Betsy were busy too with confirmation classes. They observed Lent rigorously for a time. Julia gave up dancing, a sacrifice Betsy could not very well make since The Crowd had not started going to dances. She equaled it, however; she gave up candy; she gave up fudge.

"What shall we do with the money we save on the grocery bill?" Mr. Ray asked. "Would you like a trip to California, Jule? How about an auto?"

In the after school gatherings at the Ray house there was a great emptiness, most imperfectly satisfied with cookies. When The Crowd gathered elsewhere and fudge was offered, Betsy accepted her portion, took it home and put it in a box.

"I'm going to eat it Easter Sunday," she explained.

Before Easter she and Julia would be confirmed, and even sooner Betsy would be baptized. She had asked Mr. and Mrs. Humphreys to be her godparents.

"Doesn't that make us practically related?" Herbert asked, walking home from confirmation class.

"I'd be glad if it would," Betsy answered. "I never had a brother."

"You don't seem like a sister exactly," Herbert said. "I'll tell you what you are; you're my Confidential Friend."

After that Herbert and Betsy, writing notes to each other in school, put C.F. after their names.

But Betsy did not confide in Herbert. She was not much of a confider, except to Tacy. Herbert, however, poured into Betsy's ear his infatuation for a round-cheeked girl named Irma. This was not very flattering but it was good experience for a writer, Betsy thought. Since her triumph with Puget Sound she was very much the writer.

"That affair with Tony helped my writing," she told Tacy. "I mean, it will when I get around to write. It's good for writers to suffer."

Tony dropped in often, teasing and affectionate as ever, and quite unaware of having improved her art.

The girls in The Crowd were making friendship pillows. Carney and Bonnie had started the fad. They asked friends to write their names, nicknames and pet jokes on pillows, and then they embroidered over the penciled scrawls. Betsy was as poor at embroidery as she was at algebra but she started a friendship pillow. After school she often went down to the Sibleys' to work on it with Carney and Bonnie.

Usually there was a fire in the library grate, and beyond the windows stretched the snowy side lawn. Betsy's thread tangled and knotted, the work bored her unspeakably. So shortly she took to reading aloud while the others sewed. Curled in Mr. Sibley's chair she read "Helen's Babies," and they laughed until they cried into their friendship pillows. Carney finished Betsy's pillow for her.

When they fell to talking she was always surprised anew by how different Carney and Bonnie were from herself. They actually enjoyed embroidering and sewing; they were interested in learning to cook and keep house. They expected to marry and settle down, right here in Deep Valley, perhaps.

A contrast to these domestic chats was provided by her bedtime talks with Julia.

"When we're out in the Great World" . . . Julia would begin. She spoke freely of New York, London, Berlin and Paris and expected to know them all intimately some day.

March and St. Patrick's Day brought the annual

supper in the basement of the Catholic Church. Katie and Tacy with shamrocks on their shirt waists, green bows in their hair, waited on the Rays.

"Who do you think I just waited on?" Tacy asked Betsy. She went on without waiting for an answer. "O'Rourke and Clarke. I was scared to death. I couldn't get over the idea that O'Rourke was going to ask me to work an algebra problem."

"I suppose you chatted with Clarke about the Ancient Romans," said Betsy.

"No, we talked about you. That is, they asked me whether this supper was as good as the one we ate on Puget Sound. And Clarke said you were a very talented girl."

"Did she, really?"

"Yes. And then she said something funny. She said you were going to have a chance to prove it. What do you suppose she meant by that?"

Betsy found out the next day after school. Miss Clarke called her into the empty classroom, and it was plain that something important was in the wind. Miss Clarke was smiling tremulously; her soft cheeks were flushed. She took off her eyeglasses, polished them, and put them back.

"I'm sure you know," she began at last, "about the Essay Contest. The Philomathians and Zetamathians compete every year for the essay cup. Each society chooses one senior, one junior, one sophomore and one freshman to make up a team. A subject is assigned, and the two teams are excused from all homework in English in order to have time for library study.

"Then on a Saturday morning in May, they are locked into a classroom with Miss O'Rourke and myself. They are not allowed to bring any notes, and they are given three hours in which to write. The essays are graded on the point system, and the society whose team piles up the most points, wins. The awarding of the cup, as Julia may have told you, is an event of Commencement Week.

"Since the Philomathians have won the cup for debating," Miss Clarke went on, "and we hold the athletics cup, the contest this year is extremely important. Naturally we are very anxious to win. I have selected with great care the students for the Zetamathian team. You will be interested to hear who our freshman representative will be." She smiled at Betsy, and her eyes gleamed through her glasses. "After a conference with the English teachers," she continued, "I have selected Betsy Ray."

Betsy blushed vividly. Her heart pounded with joy.

"I am sure," Miss Clarke said, "that the freshman points, at least, will go to the Zetamathians."

Betsy tried to look modest but she was sure of it too. She could almost hear her name read out when the winning contestants were announced. All eight contestants sat on the platform. The four who had won the higher ratings rose when the cup was presented.

"What is the subject?" she asked.

"'The Philippines: Their Present and Future Value.' And Betsy, there's one thing Miss Bangeter advised me to mention. You mustn't mind. I thought your story about Puget Sound was delightful. In fact, it led to your being chosen now. But on the Essay Contest you have to be serious. Your paper has to be a sound piece of work, well fortified by facts. Do you think you can write that sort of thing?"

"Oh, yes," said Betsy. In her thoughts she added airily, "Just give me a pencil." There was nothing she would have hesitated to write from an epic poem to an advertisement. "And I love to work at the library," she added.

"I know." Miss Clarke smiled. "I always talk with Miss Sparrow before selecting students for the Essay Contest. She knows who is capable of study, and who is not. You haven't asked," Miss Clarke added mischievously, "who your Philomathian freshman rival is."

"Who is it?" asked Betsy politely.

"Joe Willard," Miss Clarke replied, "and he is an excellent English student. You'll have to work to keep up with him."

"I certainly will," laughed Betsy, but she was only saying what she thought was expected of her. True, Joe Willard wrote well, and he topped her grade in Composition. But had Joe Willard, or anyone else in high school, been writing poems, stories and novels all his life? Had Joe Willard written a paper on Puget Sound that was the sensation of the year? Betsy considered the freshman points as good as won.

"The Zetamathians are relying on you, Betsy," Miss Clarke said.

Betsy was very, very pleased, and Tacy, waiting for her outside, was overjoyed.

"Of course you'll win," she said. "Oh, Betsy, I'm so proud of you!"

"Shucks!" said Betsy, but she was proud of herself.

They burst into the house and told Mrs. Ray. She was busy with Miss Mix who was making her disturbing spring visit, but for a moment Mrs. Ray forgot about her checked brown and white suit, and Julia's pink silk, and Betsy's canary-colored silk, and Margaret's plaid. She ran downstairs to tell Anna and to telephone Mr. Ray.

Miss Mix gave Betsy one of her rare smiles.

"I hope you'll win," she said.

"Oh, she's sure to win, Miss Mix," said Tacy.

"I have to do a lot of work between now and the middle of May," Betsy said, feeling important.

After Tacy left she hunted up a notebook and some

pencils. She went to the kitchen to sharpen the pencils and enjoy Anna's admiration.

"I think I'll go down to the library and start studying now," she announced.

But when she had put on her grey coat and fur piece and the hat with the plaid ribbon, it seemed too bad not to go down to the Sibleys' and share her exciting news with Carney and Bonnie.

"I'll start work at the library tomorrow," she decided.

She burst into the Broad Street house breathless, but before she had taken off her overshoes, she saw that Carney had news of her own.

"What's the matter?" she asked.

"Matter enough," said Carney darkly. "Come on in. Bonnie will tell you herself."

In the library Bonnie looked up from her friendship pillow, but she didn't smile.

"Has Carney told you?" she asked.

"Told me what? Whose funeral is this, anyway?"

Bonnie's big blue eyes filled with tears.

"It's mine, I guess," she said. "I'm going back to Paris."

"To Paris!" cried Betsy. "Aren't you glad?"

"Glad!" echoed Bonnie. "Why should I be glad? If you think Paris is half as nice as Deep Valley, Minnesota, you're mistaken, that's all."

She threw her arms around Carney, and they

buried tearful faces in each other's shoulders.

Betsy felt ashamed. "I know just how you feel," she said. "It was like that with Tacy and Tib and me when Tib went to Milwaukee. And of course Milwaukee isn't half as far away as Paris. But we have lots of fun writing letters. We'll write you dozens of letters, Bonnie."

"That will be g-r-r-and," wept Bonnie. "But when I hear about all your parties it will only make me feel bad."

"They won't be half so much fun without you," Carney said, sniffing.

"We'll miss you terribly," Betsy said. She began to feel a little weepy herself.

Bonnie straightened up and wiped her eyes.

"This is very silly of me," she said. "But oh, I've enjoyed this winter! We've had such wonderful times!"

"When are you going?" Betsy asked.

"Right away. That's what's so awful about it. Papa's been called back to that American church in Paris, and we're sailing from New York the last of the month."

Sailing from New York! Bonnie said it as carelessly as though she were saying, "Going to the Majestic."

"I'm going to give a big party for her," Carney said. "And Mrs. Humphreys is going to give one too, Larry says."

"And I'll give one too," said Betsy. "And I'm sure that Tacy will, and probably Alice and Winona. There will be party after party, Bonnie."

"That will be grand," said Bonnie, cheering up.

Not until she was out in the twilight did it occur to Betsy that this round of parties might interfere with her study for the Essay Contest.

"But it doesn't matter," she thought. "I'll have plenty of time to study after Bonnie goes. Anyway I can win that contest with one arm tied behind me. I'm almost sorry for Joe."

In her mind's eye she had a sudden picture of him. Blond, bright-eyed, with that determined smile.

"I wish I knew him better," she thought unexpectedly. "But I don't think he likes me. And then, he's so busy, working every day after school. He won't be able to go to the library much. So it's really more fair if I don't."

This reasoning led her back to parties and thence to Bonnie's departure. Not until that moment, which caught her at the corner of High Street and Plum, did it occur to her that Bonnie's going left Tony free again. She was glad to note that she felt no pleasure in this disloyal thought, although the quick memory of Tony and Bonnie made the winter twilight deepen, made her feel homesick on the very steps of home.

26

Of Church and Library

As CARNEY AND BONNIE had prophesied, Bonnie's impending departure brought a most unlentenlike round of parties. Except for the fact that she was saving candy in a box instead of eating it, Betsy would have forgotten that it was Lent. Parents were indulgent because they too regretted Bonnie's going. To The Crowd it was a real sorrow which must be drowned in endless high jinks.

The girls went down to the Photographic Gallery and had their pictures taken with Bonnie. Boys and girls together went to the jewelry store and bought her a locket and chain. And on an afternoon toward the end of March she left on the four-forty-five which went to the Twin Cities where she would change for Chicago and New York.

The Crowd saw her off, and she wept when they gave her the locket.

Dr. and Mrs. Andrews, after saying their goodbys, retired to the parlor car but Bonnie stayed out on the observation platform until the train pulled away. She wore a green suit and hat and a big corsage of flowers . . . from Tony, who looked far too nonchalant. Her blue eyes kept brimming, and she dabbed at them with a very clean white handkerchief. Carney looked grimly determined not to cry, and Larry kept a protective hand on her arm.

The train moved away, and Bonnie waved the white handkerchief. Everyone waved back as the little green figure grew smaller and smaller, and blurred, and disappeared.

Tony took Betsy's arm.

"Come on," he said. "Let's go raise the roof." But Betsy felt no triumph in this return. She knew that his heart was on the four-forty-five speeding toward St. Paul.

Cards came from Chicago and New York, and at last a letter from Paris. Still Bonnie's soft laugh was missed at The Crowd gatherings, and interest in Christian Endeavor . . . especially among the boys . . . dwindled regrettably.

Yet the spring held important matters for them all despite Bonnie's going. It was important to watch the giant snowdrifts melt, to hear joyful rivers rushing in the gutters and to see brown patches of last year's grass. And early in April Betsy was baptized. It had been planned that this event would take place just before her confirmation, but Mr. Humphreys had to go to California on sudden mysterious business, so they hurried it up.

It occurred during Evening prayer just after the Second Lesson. Betsy was impressed when she noticed that the Reverend Mr. Lewis used the rites prescribed for Baptism to Such as Are of Riper Years. "Riper Years" had a solemn sound. And it was a solemn occasion. Mr. Humphreys looked grave, and so did pretty, fluttery Mrs. Humphreys. But there was a mischievous gleam in the blue eyes of the irrepressible Herbert as Betsy passed him on her way to the font.

She was wearing her vestments, for she came down from the choir for the ceremony. Candles were glowing, and to Betsy the simple church looked like a cathedral.

A chill ran down her spine when the Reverend Mr. Lewis asked "Dost thou renounce the devil and all his works, the vain pomp and glory of the world . . . ?" She renounced them according to the prayer book but the "vain pomp and glory of the world" rang accusingly in her ears. She was not entirely sure that she renounced them; she hadn't even seen them yet.

In a moment Mr. and Mrs. Humphreys had spoken her name, "Elizabeth Warrington Ray," and she was being sprinkled.

She was a little disappointed when it was over to find that she felt exactly as she had felt before. She wondered how she had looked during the ceremony. She had forgotten to look the way she planned to look, which was just the way Julia had looked when she was baptized. It served her right for thinking of the "vain pomp and glory of the world!"

The Humphreys came for Sunday night lunch and gave her a gold cross on a chain. Betsy felt self-conscious. It didn't seem right to exchange quips with Larry and Herbert when she had just been baptized.

The following Sunday was even more momentous. With Julia and Herbert and Herbert's new love, Irma, and many more boys and girls, she was confirmed.

While she waited for her turn to kneel before the white-haired Bishop, Betsy watched Julia kneel, her face exalted. She heard the Bishop say:

"Defend, O Lord, this Thy child with Thy heavenly grace; that she may continue Thine forever; and daily increase in Thy Holy Spirit more and more until she comes unto Thy everlasting kingdom."

Presently the Bishop said the same thing to Betsy. His words sank into her heart as gently as the kind old hands touched her head.

Out in the robing room Julia, still with an exalted face, took Betsy's hand and pressed it.

"We're Episcopalians now."

Mrs. Ray and the three girls bought new Easter hats. And Betsy and Tacy helped Margaret dye eggs. They put on a patronizing manner but they enjoyed it as much as Margaret did. They told her how they used to color eggs, and save the dyes and later color sand and have sand stores. Margaret loved to hear about when Betsy and Tacy were little girls.

"I can even *remember* when you were little girls," she boasted.

On Easter morning, Julia and Betsy went to early communion. No doubt about it, they were Episcopalians now! At eleven o'clock they started off again, and Mr. and Mrs. Ray and Margaret started off for the Baptist Church, and Anna, in a huge hat laden with flowers, stiff bows of ribbon and a bluebird, started off for the Lutheran Church.

"It's too bad there isn't a Mormon in the family," Mr. Ray said.

That afternoon Betsy opened the candy box she had filled during Lent.

"You're going to pass it around, aren't you?" asked Hugh. "It's only Christian to do that."

"It looks awfully stale," said Tony, "especially that peanut fudge."

"It tastes delicious," said Betsy, but since it was, decidedly, stale she passed it generously.

Tony had come to the Rays every day since Bonnie left. One day during Easter vacation he came seven times. Betsy had planned to devote vacation to study for the Essay Contest. But it was difficult with Tony dropping in and out.

One day when she knew he was going to the Majestic, she went to the library but she told him what time she planned to leave. Oddly this coincided with the time he would be leaving the Majestic.

"I may come around and pick you up," he said.

Betsy made sure that her hair was in curl. She put on a crisp hair ribbon and a white ruffled shirt waist, fresh from Anna's iron. Then she hunted up the still empty notebook, her still unblunted pencils and went to the library.

"I've been looking for you," Miss Sparrow said.

"Miss Clarke told me you had been chosen for the Essay Contest team. Congratulations, Betsy!"

"I'm awfully pleased about it," Betsy said, smiling.

"You'll have to work hard," Miss Sparrow warned. "The others have a head start. They have been coming almost every day for a couple of weeks now."

"I can catch up," Betsy said.

"You can't take any books on the Philippines out of the library," Miss Sparrow explained. "They are all assembled on a special shelf and there is a table where the contestants may read and take notes. Come, I'll show you." She led Betsy through the stalls to a table at the back of the library where a senior girl and Joe Willard were reading. They looked up briefly and smiled as she approached. Miss Sparrow nodded toward the table, toward a shelf, and withdrew.

Betsy loved the library; especially she loved the open stalls where she had often wandered happily. But there was to be no wandering now. The volumes dealing with the Philippines confronted her, looking ponderous and more than a little dull. Filled with zest for her new enterprise, she chose three of the heaviest and sat down at the table.

"The Philippines: Their Present and Future Value," she wrote in her notebook, and opened a book importantly. She started to read it and she liked the descriptions of the scenery, the natives. But she knew this could be no Adventure on Puget Sound. She must grapple with facts, with figures, with statistics. She began the long hard pull.

After a while the senior girl got up, replaced her volume on the shelf, nodded and departed. Joe and Betsy read with absorbed concentration until they discovered themselves in the dusk. Elsewhere in the library, lights had come on and Joe snapped on the green-shaded light over their table.

Betsy smiled at him.

"I'm surprised," she said, "that they allow Philomathians and Zetamathians to study at the same table."

Joe returned her smile.

"The Zetamathians don't come very often," he said. "I'm worried about them. I don't want to take an unfair advantage."

"They can look out for themselves. They're good," Betsy said. She said it with a blush that ran down to the collar of her fresh white shirt waist.

"Yes, but look what they're up against. Terrific competition," Joe returned.

He was, Betsy thought, as she had often thought before, very good looking. His yellow hair gleamed in the light of the overhanging lamp. He had thick eyebrows of a somewhat darker shade, with eyelashes to match. His eyes were as blue as Herbert's but their expression was different.

He almost always wore the same red tie and the

same blue serge suit, carefully brushed and pressed, but in spite of this obvious shortage of clothing and the well-known fact that he worked after school and Saturdays, there was nothing humble about him. He held his head at a cocky angle, and there was a swing in his walk. He was touchy; Betsy knew that; but people liked him just the same although no one knew him very well. He had no time for the athletics which drew the boys together, and he ignored the girls . . . perhaps because of a lack of pocket money.

"I have an idea," he announced now. His eyes shone as though he were pleased with himself. The defiant lower lip was outthrust. "Want to hear it?"

"Yes. Of course I do."

"The Philomathians have a head start on the Zetamathians," he said, "and they don't like it at all. They are men of honor, the Philomathians are. The Philomathians have been coming down here every Sunday and every day during vacation. They can't come in the evening for they work in the evening, they toil for their daily bread. But they are unusually bright, and they've learned practically all there is to know about The Philippines: Their Present and Future Value. They are darned worried about the Zetamathians. Especially," he added, "since the Zetamathians are just a poor weak girl."

Betsy blushed again.

"Now, here's the idea," said Joe Willard. "The Philomathians might walk home with the Zetamathians, and on the way they could tell them the whole sad story of the Philippines. What do you say?"

Betsy didn't know what to say. She wished to Heaven that she had not thrown out that suggestion to Tony. Tony was wonderful, of course. And he had broken her heart. And she couldn't hear the song, "Dreaming," without wanting to cry. And it was all very romantic. But there was something about Joe Willard . . . any girl in high school would like to have him walk home with her.

"It's a grand plan," said Betsy. "But . . ." She was groping for the casual significant words which would indicate that although she had an engagement tonight, she would not have one on another night. "I'm sorry . . ." she began, and faltered, for at just that moment Tony came swaggering through the stalls. He barely glanced at Joe Willard.

"Ready?" he asked possessively.

"Not quite," Betsy said. "Won't you wait for me outside? I'll be with you in a minute."

"That's a bum idea," said Tony. "Where's your coat?" He found it and held it up. "I'll tell you all you want to know about the Philippines walking home," he said.

It was a most unfortunate remark. Betsy turned to

Joe Willard but his blond head was bent over his book. His ears were red and when he said good night his manner was icy.

Betsy was exasperated, all the more so when she reached the library steps. Tony wasn't even alone; Herbert and Cab were waiting. This was no romantic saunter through the melting spring twilight, but just the usual impersonal bantering and pushing about.

Joe Willard didn't ask Betsy again to let him walk home from the library with her. He didn't pay any attention to her beyond civil hellos and good-bys. Once, most unethically, in an attempt to draw him into conversation again, she asked him where to find a certain piece of information. He told her, but bent over his books before she could manage more than "thank you."

And Betsy's visits to the library were few and far apart. For April was bringing true spring. Buds were swelling, bold bright robins were back. The Crowd had no trouble beguiling Betsy out on expeditions behind Old Mag or Dandy. She went on picnics with Tacy, too, building fires, drinking smoky cocoa, searching in matted leaves for violets and Dutchmen's breeches.

In the ecstasy of the season she almost stopped suffering, she took no interest in school, and telling herself that May eleventh was a very long way off, she quite forgot about the Essay Contest.

27

The Essay Contest

HER FATHER REMINDED HER of it on the morning after her birthday. She had become fifteen with all due ceremony of claps on the back, birthday cake and gifts, and at breakfast Mr. Ray remarked pointedly:

"'The Philippines: Their Present and Future Value' is a mighty big subject. A *mighty* big subject."

"I know, Papa," said Betsy penitently, and during

the next few days she really did study for the Essay Contest. She went to the library and delved into the fat dull books. They depressed her by revealing the magnitude of her task.

"Dear me!" she said to Tacy. "In May I must buckle right down."

But early in May a blow descended. The heavens, so to speak, fell.

The trees along High Street wore pale green chiffon now. Plum trees were in heady bloom. Birds were flying about with bits of straw in their bills, or sitting on eggs, or at least singing madly. Human beings were almost as busy, uncovering flower beds and raking last autumn's leaves.

Carney passed Betsy a note. "Bonfire at our house tonight. Can you come? Herbert will call for you."

"Assisted by the amiable Herbert," wrote Betsy, "I will wend my way to your residence as requested."

Carney received this sparkling reply without a smile, which was odd, and the note that Betsy presently received from Herbert was also strangely sober.

"I'll call for you early tonight. Something to tell you. H. Humphreys."

"I wonder what's up?" Betsy thought.

When Herbert arrived, Mr. Ray was out rolling his newly seeded lawn. And Betsy coming down the steps, hatless, her hands thrust into the pockets of her light spring coat, was deeply startled by what she heard.

"Yes, I saw your father," Mr. Ray was saying. "He told me about the move to California."

"California!" Betsy ran down the walk.

"It's true," Herbert said. "We're clearing out, just as soon as school is over. We're going out to San Diego to live."

Betsy was aghast. First Bonnie, now Larry and Herbert! The Crowd could not survive this second blow.

"How perfectly awful!" she cried.

"Isn't it?" asked Herbert. Yet there was discernible in his bright blue eyes the stirrings of adventurous interest. "Dad says California's fine, though. No winter, which is tough, but there's swimming in the Pacific Ocean."

"Betsy's grandparents live in San Diego," Mr. Ray said.

"Gee, Betsy, come out to visit them and I'll show you around."

They developed this idea as they walked through the spring twilight to Carney's. Betsy was quite intoxicated with the notion of seeing orange trees, poinsettias, the mountains and the Pacific in Herbert's company.

"It won't be for a couple of years, probably. We'll be so grown up we'll hardly know each other."

"I'll bet you'll still blush when I call you Little Poetess," Herbert said. "Do you know, Betsy, I was in love with you in fifth grade?"

"You were?" Betsy was amazed. "Why all the girls were crazy about you."

"Well, you certainly had me going. You wore a locket and you used to swing it when you studied."

Betsy started to say, "I guess I'll buy myself another locket." But her sidelong glance showed his eyes brimming with mischief. She remembered how much more fun he was when he wasn't in love, and changed her mind.

"Now you're my C.F.," she said. "And I want lots of letters. All about the California girls."

They were having such a good time that their "hellos" at the Sibleys' side lawn were completely cheerful. Herbert went to the giant pile of leaves already burning in the driveway and Carney came to meet Betsy.

"I see that Herbert hasn't told you," she said looking at Betsy's smiling face. Betsy felt a disloyal pang.

"Yes, he has," she said sobering. "Isn't it awful?"

"Awful," repeated Carney, not a trace of dimple showing. "Awful doesn't describe it. I think it's cruel of Mr. Humphreys, absolutely cruel. What does he have to go to California for? Isn't Minnesota all right?"

Larry joined them, his face a thunder cloud. Here was no glimmer of the adventurous zest Herbert had shown. He took Carney's hand, which startled Betsy for a moment. Larry and Carney "went together" and had since seventh grade but they weren't spoony. Carney detested spoony girls.

Now, however, her hand closed around Larry's. Without speaking they went back to the fire.

If it were Tony going away, I'd feel like that too, thought Betsy, and glanced toward his lounging figure.

Carney's small brothers were bringing wheelbarrows full of leaves to feed the flames. The fire crackled briskly and threw out a brazen heat. The smell of the smoke brought back to Betsy bygone Hill Street springs.

"I must be getting very old," she thought, "the way things remind me of things."

When the fire had burned low the boys piled on branches from trees Mr. Sibley had been trimming, and when these in turn were reduced to embers they toasted marshmallows on pointed sticks. Spreading coats and blankets, they sat down around the fire and now it was the time for singing. They came at last to "Dreaming."

"Dreaming, dreaming,
Of you sweetheart I am dreaming,
Dreaming of days when you loved me best . . ."

Tony was sitting near Betsy singing in his deep rich voice. She expected the melody to flood her heart as usual with melancholy memories, but it didn't somehow. She glanced toward Larry and Carney.

Boldly Larry held Carney's hand in his, and they didn't even try to sing. Carney sat stiff and straight, like a hurt child.

The imminent departure of the Humphreys for California was very, very sad. But at least it meant another rash of parties. One day it was suddenly, alarmingly, the tenth of May and the following day would bring the Essay Contest.

"Are you well prepared, Betsy?" asked Miss Clarke after school, looking a little anxious.

"Oh, yes," said Betsy. "I'm going down to the library though to check on a few facts."

Miss Sparrow looked anxious too.

"You haven't done much reading, Betsy. Do you have some books on the Philippines at home?"

"No," said Betsy. "But I've talked with my father. And I'm going to work a while right now."

She went through the stalls to the table reserved for the contestants. Seniors, juniors and sophomores were there, reading with frenzied concentration. But not Joe Willard.

"He knows all there is to know about the Philippines," thought Betsy with a sinking heart. She skimmed through the big books aimlessly. "Oh, well," she thought. "I'll get by on my writing." But Joe Willard, she remembered, wrote very well indeed.

Tacy who called for her cheered her as they walked homeward.

"You can write circles around Joe Willard," she said.

"Oh, sure, sure," said Betsy. "I ought to know a few more facts though."

"Just skim lightly over the facts," Tacy advised. "Your essay will be so interesting that the judges can't put it down."

Julia at the supper table took the same attitude. Mr. Ray had asked Betsy some questions about the Philippines, receiving evasive answers.

"Betsy writes so well, Papa. She doesn't need to know those dull old dates."

"Betsy," said Mrs. Ray, "has been writing since she could hold a pencil. I remember her when she was five years old asking me how to spell 'going down the street.'"

"Ja, Betsy will win all right," remarked Anna, clearing the plates. "Maybe you'd better take coffee with your breakfast, lovey, like on Sunday mornings?"

"I believe some coffee *would* be a good idea," said Betsy importantly, "but I don't have a qualm about the contest. Not a qualm." She spent the evening going over her notes. There were gaps, alarming gaps in her information.

Cab came over, but she did not see him. Herbert telephoned but she did not talk. Tony arrived but she did not even go downstairs.

Tony . . . she could hear from upstairs . . . wanted to sing.

"I'm afraid we'd disturb Betsy," she heard Julia say. "She's concentrating on the Philippines. It can't really be necessary, though. She's sure to win."

Tony laughed. "I told Joe Willard today he might as well be buying some black crepe for his hat band."

"What did he say?" asked Julia.

"He only grinned."

Betsy didn't like the sound of that. She slapped her notebook shut, wound her hair on Magic Wavers, and went to bed.

"Sleep is what I need," she thought. "With a good night's sleep I can write better than anyone in Deep Valley High School."

And she had a fair night's sleep although, she told the family at breakfast, she dreamed about Aguinaldo.

Her father said he was glad to hear that she knew there was such a person but the rest of the family was impressed. When Margaret asked Betsy to help with her hair ribbon, Mrs. Ray told her not to bother Betsy; Betsy had something important on her mind. Anna brought her coffee, and although Betsy always combined it with so much sugar and cream that its stimulus was diluted, it did her good to drink it.

"Here I go," said Betsy. "Joe Willard, watch out!"

She snatched up a hat and a pen, and ran outdoors.

It seemed strange to be going to school on Saturday morning. Children were playing on all the lilac-scented lawns. It had rained last night, but today the sun was out, and the air was filled with moist sweetness.

The high school, of course, was deserted. But Miss Clarke and Miss O'Rourke were waiting in the upper hall, behind a small table.

"All notes and books must be left here," Miss Clarke said.

"I haven't any with me," Betsy answered smiling.

"That's right," Miss Clarke beamed. "Go into the algebra classroom. You will find paper on the desk, but don't start to write until the bell rings."

Betsy found two seniors, two juniors and two sophomores in the classroom.

"I wonder where Joe Willard is," she said to herself.

"I should think he'd like to get here in time to collect his thoughts a little."

But it was exactly one minute to nine when Joe Willard sauntered in. He walked up to the desk and helped himself liberally to foolscap, then walked back to a desk in the corner and ran his fingers over his yellow hair.

Miss Clarke and Miss O'Rourke came in and closed the door.

"When the bell rings," said Miss O'Rourke, "you may start to write. And you must stop at twelve o'clock. If you finish sooner, put your essay on the desk and go out quietly. The subject, as you all know, is 'The Philippines: Their Present and Future Value.'"

As she spoke the last word, a gong sounded. Eight boys and girls dipped their pens in ink.

First Betsy wrote the title, "The Philippines: Their Present and Future Value." She puzzled a moment about what to write next. Miss Clarke had advised that she think out her opening paragraph in advance but she had not done this, being a great believer in the inspiration of the moment.

And inspiration did not betray her. As always when she took a pen or pencil in her hand, inspiration cast a golden light. A flowery opening paragraph soon found its way to paper, the final sentence leading, just as it should, into a second paragraph.

But unfortunately today she could not write entirely by the light of inspiration. Her essay was supposed to have a solid core of knowledge based on six weeks' study. Instead of going happily where her fancy led, she was obliged in every paragraph to conceal the absence of facts. History was padded with legends that happened to stick in her mind. For exports and imports she substituted descriptions of orchids and volcanoes and sunsets on Manila Bay. It took ingenuity. It took thought. It took time.

At eleven o'clock Joe Willard rose, strolled to the front of the room and laid his paper on Miss O'Rourke's desk. There was a slight swagger in his walk. Closing the door he looked back over his still struggling colleagues. Betsy felt sure that he had not intended it so, but his gaze met hers.

"He is positive, sure, he's going to win," she thought. "Well, so am I." And in desperation she put in some snappy conversation between Aguinaldo and Commodore Dewey. It livened up the essay a good bit.

Except for Joe Willard, everyone wrote until twelve o'clock. The gong rang then and somewhat soberly the contestants took their papers up to the desk and filed out. Two weeks would pass before it was known which society had won. The cup would be awarded and the winners of the class points announced at the term's last assembly.

"Satisfied, Betsy?" Miss Clarke asked.

Betsy nodded brightly.

"We certainly are lucky that you are a Zetamathian," Miss Clarke said. But Betsy's homeward walk was slower than usual and considerably more subdued.

28

Results

BUT SHE RAN UP the steps of home smiling.

"Fine! Fine!" she replied to all family queries about how the Essay Contest had gone. At dinner she described the events of the morning dramatically.

"So this Willard boy ran out of things to write about at eleven o'clock, did he?" her mother asked.

"It really wasn't fair," said Julia, "to put anyone up against Betsy."

"Hail the conquering heroine!" said Tony when he dropped in that afternoon.

In a little while Betsy forgot the misgivings which had filled her at Joe Willard's departing gaze. Everyone from Miss Clarke to Margaret was convinced that she had safely won the freshman points; she began to believe it herself.

There was little time to think of the matter, however, for again examinations were upon her. Betsy and Cab took up the greeting she and Tacy had originally evolved.

"*Hic, haec, hoc,*" he would cry from the front door every morning.

"*Hujus, hujus, hujus,*" Betsy would respond from within.

"*Huic, huic, huic,*" they chorused together. "Who says Latin isn't spoken familiarly now?"

"I'd like to get hold of the fiend who invented algebra," Betsy groaned to Tacy as, well fortified with fudge, they studied after school.

Composition did not worry her, but she read the ancient history from cover to cover.

"It's extremely interesting," she remarked in surprise. Studying, as she had done all year, only the paragraph she expected to be called on to discuss, she had missed the immense, moving sweep of the narrative.

Julia was even more desperate then Betsy. She was

not only faced with examinations. She was singing a solo for Commencement. "An Open Secret," it was called, and she practised it from morning until night.

"*Pussy willow has a secret,*" Julia warbled, and in Betsy's mind Pussy Willow's secret was mixed up with Latin conjugations, algebraic equations and the Punic Wars. It added to her confusion on all these topics.

The chorus, in which Betsy and Tacy sang, was also preparing a number for Commencement:

> "*My heart's in the highlands,*
> *My heart is not here.*
> *My heart's in the highlands,*
> *Achasing the deer.*"

Betsy and Tacy had their private version.

> "*My heart's in the high school,*
> *My heart is not here.*
> *My heart's in the high school,*
> *Achasing my dear.*"

This was supposed to refer to Betsy's infatuation for Tony, and Betsy and Tacy considered it gloriously funny. When they had studied until they were groggy, and Betsy was walking halfway home with Tacy through the late afternoon, they sang it:

"My heart's in the hi-i-i-i-gh school
My heart is not he-e-e-re . . ."

The light green world of May echoed to delirious laughter.

Examinations began. These were followed by daily indignation meetings at the Ray house.

"How could Morse be so beastly?"

"How can O'Rourke look so pretty and give such hideous exams?"

Larry and Carney alone were not concerned about exams. They did not even seem to care whether they passed.

"The Time, the Place and the Girl" came to Deep Valley. Carney was allowed to go with Larry . . . in the evening . . . alone. Sympathetic parents hoped this would afford a measure of consolation. The Humphreys were leaving for California on the day after the day after Commencement.

The first event of Commencement week was the joint evening meeting of Philomathians and Zetamathians at which the essay cup would be awarded.

Which society had won the cup was still unknown to all except the judges. There was no doubt, however, in the minds of those around Betsy about the freshman points, and by this time there was no doubt in Betsy's mind either. That feeling she had had was crazy. Of course she would win.

The eight contestants were to sit on the platform along with Miss Bangeter, Miss Clarke, Miss O'Rourke and the presidents of the two societies. The four who had received the most points would rise when the cup was awarded.

"I'm glad you have your canary-colored silk to wear tonight, Betsy," Mrs. Ray said. "Since you have to stand up and bow."

"Let me do your hair," said Julia. They hurried upstairs after supper, and Margaret looked on while Julia worked.

Katie, Tacy and Alice called for them.

"See these new gloves? I wore them just so I could split them clapping for you," Tacy said. "Gee, you look nice!"

Betsy's cheeks were burning. The canary-colored dress fitted to perfection, and her pompadour stood up like a fan.

The assembly room was divided between Philomathians and Zetamathians, and the Zetamathians this year had the alcove side. This was most desirable, for on these evening meetings boys and girls were allowed to perch on the bookcases.

The Crowd, parting from Betsy, rushed for them. Betsy hurried to the platform. Four Philomathians, their president and Miss O'Rourke, four Zetamathians, their president and Miss Clarke, flanked Miss Bangeter's tall table. Betsy sat opposite Joe Willard. They smiled at each other.

The crowded assembly room looked gayer than usual, for the Zetamathians wore streamers of turquoise blue; the Philomathians were decked with orange. Defiant chants were hurled first from one side of the room and then the other.

"Zet! Zet! Zetamathian!"

"Philo! Philo! Philomathian!"

Tony sat with Winona, Pin and the Humphreys on the Philomathian side. Tacy sat on a bookcase with the crowd of Zetamathians; all of them were eating peanuts. First one and then another waved to Betsy, or threw kisses, or clapped hands softly high in the air. Betsy did not respond except by smiling. She sat with her hands folded, her ankles crossed.

Tall and benign, Miss Bangeter called the meeting to order. The high school song was sung, and the opening ceremonies, minutes of previous meeting, announcements and reports ran their usual course.

"And now," said Miss Bangeter, "we come to the main event of the evening, the awarding of the Essay Cup." She indicated a table on which three silver cups were prominently displayed. One was tied with an orange bow, one with turquoise blue. The Essay cup stood in the center, unmarked.

"As you know," she continued, "eight students

have competed, two from each high school year. Freshmen are judged together, sophomores are judged together, and juniors, and seniors. That is our attempt to make the Contest perfectly fair. We *think* you increase in knowledge and ability as you go on through high school." (Laughter.)

"I will announce the class awards in turn, and at the end the total number of points piled up for each society. First, the freshmen." She paused, and Betsy blushed. She glanced swiftly at Joe Willard's cocky blond head, his handsome determined-looking profile.

"The freshmen contestants, as you all know, are Joe Willard and Betsy Ray. Both are excellent English students. The one who gained the freshman points is . . ." She paused and smiled while a wave of subdued laughter and exclamations of anxiety swept across the hall. A whispered chant came from the alcove:

"Betsy, Betsy, Betsy."

A similar chant rolled from the opposite wall:

"Joe, Joe, Joe."

"The winner of the freshman points," Miss Bangeter repeated, "is Joe Willard."

Betsy was stunned. So for a moment were the Zetamathians. Automatically she found herself smiling. She found herself applauding frenziedly as Joe Willard, looking both poised and abashed, rose and sat down again. The Philomathians cheered and applauded so enthusiastically that he had to stand up a second time. Betsy applauded too and even turned her radiant smile toward the alcove.

Tacy was not applauding. She was shaking her fist at Joe Willard. She was joking, of course; and yet she meant it too. Cab and Tony had taken out big white handkerchiefs and were pretending to be weeping.

Betsy felt as though she were in a dream. Her ears were ringing, and the events that went forward on the stage seemed unreal. The other winners were named in turn. The final scores were announced. The Philomathians won the cup. It was presented to the Philomathian president.

Before joining her surprised indignant Crowd, Betsy sought out Joe Willard.

"Congratulations," she said, putting out her hand. "I'm sure your essay was wonderful."

For once Joe's blue eyes were friendly.

"Got just what you deserved," he said. "You should have let me walk home with you that night."

Of course, as usual, Betsy blushed.

Betsy did not sleep very well that night. The next morning she woke up so early that even Anna was not about. She dressed and went softly out of the house. If she had still lived on Hill Street, she would have gone up on the hill. As it was, she sat on the porch steps, but it was nice there. The dawn colors were still in the sky above the German Catholic College. The lawn was brushed with silver, and the birds were so bold, so abundant . . . it seemed as though they knew that for this hour they owned the world.

Betsy was ashamed of herself. She was deeply and thoroughly ashamed. This feeling had nothing to do with her hurt pride. And its deepest cause was not the disappointment of her family, her friends, Miss Clarke. That had been loyally masked with assertions that "it doesn't matter anyway," "you'll show them next year," "the judges were crazy." Her mother especially was sure that the judges had taken leave of their senses. But in her father's eyes Betsy had seen the opinion that the judges had shown excellent judgment. It was this view, shared by Betsy herself, which troubled her now.

"Maybe, of course," she thought, "Joe Willard writes better than I do. And if he does, that's all right. The world is probably full of people who write better than I do." (She doubted it.) "What makes me feel bad is that I didn't give myself a chance."

When Julia had a part in a home talent play, her social life went by the board. If she had a solo to sing, she practised it, even though she neglected everything else.

"That's the way my writing ought to be treated," Betsy thought.

She looked back over the crowded winter. She did not regret it. But she should not have let its fun, its troubles, its excitements squeeze her writing out.

"If I treat my writing like that," she told herself, "it may go away entirely."

The thought appalled her. What would life be like without her writing? Writing filled her life with beauty and mystery, gave it purpose . . . and promise.

"Everyone has something, probably. With Julia it's singing, with Anna, it's cooking, with Carney and Bonnie, it's keeping house and having families . . . something that's most important of all because it's theirs to do."

She jumped up and went down the steps and started walking.

She walked down High Street, past the high school, and on and on, trying to beat out on the sidewalk her angry self reproach.

"Help me to straighten this thing out!" she said to God. "Please, please, help me to straighten this thing out!"

Presently she found herself tired, hungry, happy and knowing exactly what to do. She turned and hurried toward home.

The house smelled of coffee now. Anna was in the kitchen. Betsy burst in smiling.

"You're out early, lovey. Hungry?"

"Starved! What's for breakfast?"

"Bacon and eggs."

"Bacon and eggs! They're just what I want," Betsy

cried. "Anna," she said, "will you do something for me after breakfast?"

"Sure, lovey! What is it?"

"That old trunk in the attic, that big square trunk of my Uncle Keith's. I want you to help me bring it down."

"Where you going to put it?"

"In my bedroom," Betsy said.

"In your pretty blue bedroom?" Anna demanded. "It won't look nice there, lovey. There's plenty in that room already."

"That trunk's going in," said Betsy, "if everything else goes out." She walked around the kitchen smiling. "Gee, I'm hungry! I could eat nails."

"Strike the gong," said Anna. "And as soon as the dishes are done, we'll move that trunk."

No one in the Ray family made any comment when Uncle Keith's trunk came back to Betsy's room. Her mother found a shawl with which to cover it when it wasn't being used as a desk . . . the very same shawl that had covered it on Hill Street. Margaret came in to sit on it, looking pleased. Betsy brought her Bible and prayer book, a dictionary and the volume of Poe, a pile of freshly sharpened pencils and what notebooks she could lay her hands on.

"Stand up, Margaret," she said. "I'm going to arrange the tray. And I'm going to buy a whole pile of new notebooks as soon as Commencement is over."

29
The Hill

AND NOW COMMENCEMENT week was in full swing, along with a burst of Minnesota heat. Betsy had trouble keeping her hair in curl for the class play, Class Day and all the other festivities.

The chorus was rehearsing daily in the Opera House where Commencement exercises would be held. Betsy and Tacy wandered behind the scenes, reminding each other of the time they had played in *Rip Van Winkle* and discovered Uncle Keith.

Commencement night came, and Julia in the pink silk dress sang, "An Open Secret."

"Pussy willow has a secret," she sang, leaning toward her audience, almost acting the words out.

Betsy in the canary-colored silk, Tacy in pale green mull sang that their hearts were in the highlands.

"I almost sang 'My heart's in the high school'" Tacy giggled, walking home.

"So did I. I started to, even. Let's sing it now."

They sang it, arms entwined, walking home along the dark streets. *"My heart's in the hi-i-igh school . . ."*

"There's no one I can be so silly with as I can with you," said Tacy.

Report cards were issued next day, and they both passed. Betsy Ray: algebra, 75; Latin 78; ancient history, 91; composition, 92.

Mr. Gaston infuriated the class by telling them that they must read *Ivanhoe* over the summer. Betsy had read it, but she didn't say so. She acted as cross as everyone else.

That night, the night before the Humphreys left, The Crowd was invited to the Ray house.

"I want to make it like all the other parties we've had this year," Betsy planned.

But she couldn't. It was far too warm for a fire in

the grate. Doors and windows were open, and the porch was hung with baskets full of daisies and geraniums and long trailing vines. A hammock swung there too.

They sang the old songs, though. Julia played the piano as usual and The Crowd, with arms locked, stood behind her. They sang "My Wild Irish Rose," and "Crocodile Isle," and "Cause I'm Lonesome," and "Dreaming." Julia made Welsh rarebit in the chafing dish.

Herbert and Cab disappeared from the party, and soon Margaret came running into the dining room to say that everyone should come to the music room to see a show.

"I'm to say that it's for Larry and Carney," she announced.

Herbert in Mrs. Ray's best silk dress and Anna's big feathered hat leaned over the stairs pretending to be Juliet, while Cab, wearing Julia's new cape and strumming on a pot cover was Romeo, serenading. They were very funny, and it did everyone good, especially Larry and Carney.

"Anna wouldn't have loaned that hat to anyone but you," Betsy told Herbert. "Her heart is broken because you're going away."

"Maybe I'll get a little of her cooking now," said Cab.

"No," interposed Tony, "I'm stepping into Humphreys' shoes."

When The Crowd left Tony stayed behind. Mr. and Mrs. Ray had already retired.

"Betsy and I are going to do the dishes," Tony said. "My first step toward getting in with Anna."

"I can take a hint. Good night," said Julia. She blew them a kiss and went upstairs.

Tony washed and Betsy wiped. Tony was good at washing. He scraped and rinsed and stacked the dishes before he began, and kept a kettle of hot water boiling.

"You're the most efficient lazy person I ever knew," said Betsy.

They talked about the Humphreys' going, and about how sad it was to see The Crowd break up, and about what they would do next year with Bonnie and Larry and Herbert all gone.

"So long as the Ray family doesn't move away, I'll do all right," Tony said.

The dishes finished, they went into the dining room, the parlor, the music room. They put them all in order. It was strange to be alone with Tony in the deserted downstairs with the family asleep above. Not asleep, exactly. Her mother would come into her room to talk the party over. But there wasn't a sound anywhere in the house.

Betsy and Tony went out on the porch and sat down in the hammock.

The night was very warm and soft; stars spangled the sky behind the German Catholic College. The air was sweet with the smell of syringa bushes from the house next door. Tony's rough sleeve touched Betsy's arm. She was wearing the short-sleeved canary-colored silk. They pushed the swing and rocked slowly back and forth.

And suddenly it came to Betsy with electric force that she wasn't in love with Tony any more. She liked him, she liked him enormously, but if Cab, or Herbert, or Pin had been sitting in the swing beside her, she would have felt no differently.

Thinking back she realized that this had been true for some time. Not for weeks had there been any magic in the sight of that curly thatch, those bold black eyes, that lazy sauntering walk. The feeling she had had was gone; it had vanished; it just wasn't, any more.

"Tony," said Betsy. "I'm so happy."

"So am I," said Tony. His tone was caressing and he moved his arm slightly as though with a little encouragement he might become sentimental. Betsy jumped up.

"Will you come over in the morning to help me make fudge? I promised Herbie a box for the train."

"Sure," said Tony. "It will give me a chance to see my new inamorata, Anna."

Betsy laughed.

"I'm glad you have an inamorata, Tony. But as far as I'm concerned, I'm fancy free."

The Humphreys left for California the next day, and half of Deep Valley was at the station. Mr. and Mrs. Ray and all the High Fly Whist Club were there to say good-by to Mr. and Mrs. Humphreys. Larry's and Herbert's crowd was there, and the football crowd, and some of the teachers, and a delegation of business men.

"Everything but the band," Tony remarked.

"And a band wouldn't do. We're too sad," Betsy said.

"Remember to write to me, all you kids," said Herbert.

Larry held Carney by the arm. They didn't talk or joke. And when the four-forty-five moved out of the station with the Humphreys on the observation platform, Betsy slipped her arm through one of Carney's arms, and Tacy took the other.

This, thought Betsy impressively, closes a chapter in our lives.

She didn't say it, for it sounded sad, and she wanted to comfort Carney.

For several days she devoted herself to comforting

Carney. Bonnie, she knew, could have done it better. But Betsy did her best. She went to the Sibleys' every afternoon and Carney played the piano, classical pieces, while Betsy listened. Curled in Mr. Sibley's chair, Betsy read out loud while Carney sewed.

Letters from Larry came from St. Paul, from Omaha, from Santa Fe. There were picture postals from Herbert, too, for Betsy. Indians, the Grand Canyon, and at last the orange trees and poinsettias of California.

"I really must go out to visit Grandma," Betsy thought, sticking these alluring post cards into her mirror.

One afternoon Tacy telephoned.

"Mamma's baking cake for supper. That kind you like, without any frosting on it."

"I get your point," said Betsy. "I'll be there. Walk down to meet me; will you?"

"I'll meet you at Lincoln Park."

It was mid-June now, and very hot. Betsy wore her pink lawn jumper, the one she had worn, she remembered, when she went to the Majestic and saw Cab chopping wood, the day Anna came, almost a year ago. She carried the same pink parasol and walked slowly through the heat.

Tacy met her, and they locked their damp arms.

"Gee, I'm glad to see you," Tacy said. "I've missed you since school ended."

"I've missed you too," said Betsy. "I'm going to come up to Hill Street lots this summer."

"Are you going out to that farm again?"

"The Taggarts? I don't know." She had a sudden smothering memory of her homesickness. "I wonder whether I'd be homesick if I went again? Probably not. I'm so much older."

She did feel unbelievably older.

And Hill Street emphasized the change. They stopped at almost every house, to talk with the old neighbors, pat familiar dogs, exclaim over children who had put on inches and acquired big front teeth. All the neighbors exclaimed that Betsy was a real young lady.

Mr. and Mrs. Kelly said they couldn't get over how she had changed.

"I haven't changed inside," said Betsy. "I'd like to eat supper up on our bench."

"Oh, let's!" cried Tacy. "May we, Mamma?"

"Papa," Mrs. Kelly said. "Fix a plate for each of them."

So Mr. Kelly filled Tacy's plate, and Betsy's. And they each took a glass of milk and a piece of Mrs. Kelly's cake, still warm from the oven. Laughed at by the family and laughing at each other, they walked carefully out of the house and up the road to the bench at the top of Hill Street.

Hill Street looked very green and fresh with

sprinklers running and roses in bloom. The sun was setting behind Tacy's house.

"Just where it ought to set," said Betsy. "It hasn't set in the right place since I left Hill Street. Oh, Tacy, it's wonderful to be back!"

And yet, even as she spoke, she knew that she did not wish to come back, not to stay, not to live. She loved the little yellow cottage more than she loved any place on earth, but she was through with it except in her memories.

She thought of the High Street house which had looked so bare at first on its windy corner. It was still a little bare, although now the vines Mr. Ray had transplanted from Hill Street covered it with their familiar pattern, and baskets full of flowers hung around the porch and shrubs were set out. It was bare, but it was full of the things that make a house, a home.

How many songs the music room had echoed to! How many onion sandwiches had been eaten on Sunday nights around the fireplace! The brass bowl in the big front window looked like High Street, not Hill Street. Uncle Keith's trunk still seemed out of place in her bedroom, but it was a challenge there.

In the High Street house she had fallen in love and out of it again. She would never forget Tony kissing her under the mistletoe even though now, to her continued amazement, he was just like anyone else . . . all the magic gone.

On the steps of the High Street house she had met her disappointment after the Essay Contest. She thought suddenly about Joe Willard. He had never been inside her house . . . yet.

She and Tacy sat looking down Hill Street while the clouds in the sky behind Tacy's house turned pink. Their hands met and as always, unfailingly, joined in a loyal clasp.

For
ROSEMOND *and* ROMIE LUNDQUIST

Contents

This above all: to thine own self be true,
And it must follow, as the night the day,
Thou canst not then be false to any man.

—WM. SHAKESPEARE

1

The Winding Hall of Fate

"JUST A FEW LINES to open the record of my sophomore year. Isn't it mysterious to begin a new journal
like this? I can run my fingers through the fresh clean
pages but I cannot guess what the writing on them
will be. It is almost as though I were ushered into the
Winding Hall of Fate, but next day's destiny was hid-
den behind a turning."

Betsy paused, and read what she had written with a dreamy self-satisfied smile.

She was curled up on a pillow beside her Uncle Keith's trunk which she used as a desk. It stood in her bedroom, a large blue and white room with two windows in which white curtains were blowing. The time was September, 1907, and next day she would be a sophomore in the Deep Valley, Minnesota, High School.

"My ambition," she continued, *"is to be an author some day, and therefore I'll describe myself and some of my friends. My name is Elizabeth Warrington Ray but most people call me Betsy. My sister Julia always calls me Bettina.*

"I am tall, and thin as a willow sapling with a droop which my mother calls a stoop but I hope isn't too homely. Some benighted people, boys mostly, even think it is pretty. I have dark brown hair, put up in a pompadour over a rat, perfectly beautiful skin but just ordinary hazel eyes, and my teeth are parted in the middle.

"My hair is wavy most of the time, but to manage that I have to put it up on Wavers at night, which I despise, because what am I going to do when I get married? But on the other

*hand if I don't put it up on Wavers, I probably
never will get married. That's the way I look at
it. Not that I care about getting married. But I
certainly want to be asked.*

"*I don't see why Edison and these people
who go around inventing autos and things
can't concentrate on something important like
how to make a girl's hair stay curled without
Wavers. Of course, I adore autos, though.*

"*And speaking of autos . . .*" Betsy paused,
and gave her diary a look. "*Speaking of autos,
we are just back from two months at the lake
and the whole town is agog, simply agog,
about a new boy with a bright red auto. He's
the grandson of the rich old Brandish who
lives across the slough. His name is Phil . . .*"

"Hoo, hoo, Betsy," came a masculine voice outside
the house. Betsy slammed her journal shut, crammed
it into her trunk and ran to the window.

In the street below, a black-haired boy with a
bright humorous face sat on a bare-backed brown
nag. Cab Edwards was riding the family horse down
to the watering trough at the foot of High Street.

"Hello," called Betsy.

"Hello. Heard you got back last night. Have a
good time?"

"Swell. Any fun around here?"

"Dead as a doornail. Seen anyone yet?"

"Just talked on the 'phone to a few of the kids."

"What are you doing today?"

"Picnic with Tacy."

"Well, I'll be in tonight." He slapped the horse's rump, then changed his mind and "whoa'ed" her to a stop. "Say: Read *Ivanhoe*?"

"Sure," said Betsy. "Why?"

"Don't you remember? Gaston told us to read it over the summer. We have to pass a test on it, second day of school."

"I remember. Just like one of Gaston's ideas! It doesn't bother me, though. I read *Ivanhoe* in the cradle practically."

"Gosh, I wish I had," said Cab, and slapped his horse again, and rode on down the hill.

Betsy looked after him, and up the hill beyond where trees made a thick green fringe against the sky. High Street itself ran horizontally, halfway up a hill which was criss-crossed by streets and had a German Catholic College on the crest. Off at another angle rose the cluster of hills where she had lived as a child, where Tacy still lived, and where they would picnic today. All were bathed in an early morning freshness.

Betsy went back to her trunk and the journal.

"Where was I? Oh yes, Phil."

"It's a good thing there's a new boy on the scene for last year's Crowd is shattered, simply shattered. Larry and Herbert Humphreys have gone to California to live. Their going was tragic because they're boys. Two perfectly good boys snatched by Fate out of Deep Valley High School.

"There's a new girl named Irma coming into our Crowd, but there always seem to be plenty of girls. I wonder why that is???? She's nice; she's very sweet, with a figure like Lillian Russell's. The boys are crazy about her . . . none of us can see why exactly. She and Winona are thick as thieves.

"Winona is tall and thin with black eyes that are positively snapping. She's full of the D. . . . Carney, (Caroline Sibley), is very pretty, neat as a pin, with eye glasses perched on her nose, and one dimple. The boys like her, girls like her, too. She always says just what she thinks, and she wouldn't know how to be catty. It's hard to describe Carney without making her sound sissy. But she isn't. Not a bit. She's full of the D . . . too.

"The other girls in our Crowd are Alice, who lives up near Tacy and is very full of fun, but her parents are strict. And Tacy who is . . .

well, there's nobody like Tacy. She's been my chum since we were five years old, and you couldn't have a better one. Tacy's bashful but full of the D . . . She likes to imagine things the same as I do and make adventurous plans about when we grow up. Most of the girls just plan on getting married but Tacy and I want to see the Taj Mahal by moonlight, and go to the Passion Play, and live in Paris with French maids to draw our baths. The funny thing about Tacy is that she's perfectly indifferent to boys. She's the only girl I know who doesn't think that Boys are the Center of the Universe.

"Tib is my chum, too, but she moved to Milwaukee. She's little and blonde and very pretty. At least she used to be. I wonder whether she's changed as much as I have in the last two years? I've certainly changed.

"As for boys, the most interesting boy in school isn't in our Crowd. He isn't in any crowd. His name is Joe Willard, and he's blond and terribly handsome. He hasn't any family, but lives in a room somewhere and works at the Creamery afternoons and Saturdays. Last year he won the Freshman points in the Essay Contest. Away from Elizabeth Warrington Ray! The aforementioned Miss Ray is

going to have REE—VENGE *this year. (There's an Essay Contest every year.)*

"Cab just about lives at our house, and so does Tony. I used to be in love with Tony last year. Doesn't that seem funny? Tom comes here a lot when he's in town. He goes away to school though. Cox Military!

"These boys are nice. They're perfectly dandy. But they're just neighbors. There's nothing romantic about them. Where is Romance, anyway, I wonder? Is it in these unwritten pages?"

Betsy flipped them thoughtfully through her fingers. A gong sounded downstairs, and she put her journal away a second time. Going to the mirror she turned her self-styled willowy figure slowly for inspection. Her blue sailor suit was old, chosen because of the planned picnic, but the belt encircled a waist gratifyingly slim. Betsy's face, however, was anxious. She usually gave a mirror an anxious face.

The door opened, and her mother's red head ducked in.

"Dressed? I'm glad. Get Julia up; will you?"

"I'll try," said Betsy. She crossed the hall to her older sister's room.

Getting Julia up was harder than it looked to be

when one saw her. Slender, almost fragile, in a thin white nightgown, she was flung lightly across the bed, face down, her dark hair fanning out.

Betsy shook her vigorously. "Julia! The gong! There it goes again!"

"Let it go gallager."

"But breakfast's on the table." Betsy shook her again.

Julia sat upright, her violet eyes flashing.

"But *why* do I have to get up? Just because Papa was born on a farm and all ten children always came to meals on time . . ."

The door swung open and Margaret, the nine-year-old sister, came in, her hair ribbon spreading white wings above her shining English bob. Her black-lashed eyes, always large and serious, widened in surprise.

"Why, that's *just* what Papa was saying. All *ten* of them used to be on time, and he sent me up to . . ."

"I know. I know. Well, *I* don't live on a farm. And I'm going to be an opera singer." But Julia was good natured now. She jumped out of bed, smiling. "Opera singers," she continued, dressing under her night-gown, "have sense enough to work at night and sleep all morning. They *invariably* sleep until noon. And that's what I'm going to do . . ."

"Come on, Margaret," said Betsy and they ran downstairs.

Sunshine was pouring into the dining room which was papered with pears and grapes above a plate rail full of Mrs. Ray's best china. Here, too, the curtains were blowing, full of autumnal zest. Mr. and Mrs. Ray were already seated, and Mr. Ray looked up sternly as Betsy and Margaret slipped quietly into their chairs. Tall, large, dark-haired and hazel-eyed like Betsy, his usual expression was one of calm benevolence, but he lost it when the girls were late to breakfast.

Mrs. Ray had already poured a soothing first cup of coffee, and now Anna, the hired girl, brought in eggs and bacon, raw fried potatoes, buttered toast, and cocoa for the children. Mrs. Ray made conversation briskly. "The girls go back to school tomorrow."

"If Julia gets up in time." Mr. Ray turned to look through the music room, up the still empty stairs.

"Cab came by this morning, Papa," Betsy said talking very fast. "He's having a fit because he hasn't read *Ivanhoe*, and Gaston said we had to read it over the summer vacation. Do you think that's fair, Papa?"

"Reading *Ivanhoe* isn't exactly punishment," Mr. Ray replied.

"Of course not. But it's the principle of the thing."

Julia slid into her chair, shook out her napkin. "It's the principle of the thing, Papa," she repeated.

Mr. Ray gave her a look to show she hadn't fooled him.

"There's a principle involved in getting down to breakfast, too," he said. But as his gaze swept the now completed circle, his brow cleared. "Reading *Ivanhoe* won't kill any of you," he decided cheerfully. "How about another cup of coffee, Jule?"

When the coffee was drunk, he walked around the table, kissing his womenfolk. Mrs. Ray jumped up, ran her arm through his and walked with him out to the porch.

"It's good to be going back to the store," Mr. Ray said. "The lake's fine, but it isn't like 400 High Street."

"This house is a year old, and I love it as much as I ever did. I'm going to have fun cleaning it," Mrs. Ray replied.

The morning was busy. Anna started scrubbing while Mrs. Ray at the telephone ordered meat and groceries. Then Mrs. Ray wound her red head in a towel and started scrubbing, too. Julia and Betsy unpacked the trunk, settled drawers and closets. Margaret went out to pick greens for the fireplace and a bouquet of nasturtiums.

After noon dinner Tony, without knocking, poked his head in at the door.

"Hello, folks! Glad you're back."

The girls hailed him joyfully, and accompanied him

to the kitchen to greet Anna. He persuaded Mrs. Ray to come down from a step ladder, picked up Washington, the cat, and they all sat down to talk.

Tony's black hair stood up in a curly bush. He had black eyes, bold and laughing, and a lazy teasing air.

"Last year I was in love with him. Now he's almost like a brother. Life is strange," thought Betsy.

"What did you do at the lake?" Tony was asking.

"I learned to swim," said Margaret.

"Julia forgot about Hugh, got a new beau, and then bounced him before we came home. Not a nice thing to do," Betsy said.

"I didn't have any piano," Julia explained plaintively. "And Bettina wrote all summer . . . a novel, I guess."

"Speaking of novels," said Tony, "what about this *Ivanhoe* Gaston said we had to read?"

"I read it years ago. But I think it was beastly of him to assign it. Have you read it?"

"How could I? I've been delivering groceries all summer. And by the way, I'm supposed to be doing it now." He lounged to his feet. "I'm late, but I'll be a little later if Julia will pound the ivories just to prove you're home."

So Julia went to the piano and started one of last year's songs. Mrs. Ray and Margaret, Betsy and Tony stood behind her and sang:

"Dreaming, dreaming,
Of you sweetheart I am dreaming,
Dreaming of days when you loved me best,
Dreaming of hours that have gone to rest . . ."

Then Tony hurried off to his delivery wagon and Mrs. Ray to her step ladder, and Margaret went out to play. Julia stayed at the piano.

"I'm going to have a lesson today. Better warm up," she said, opening an opera score.

Julia spent all her allowance on opera scores; spent it before she received it, usually, for she had an ill-advised charge account with a music store in St. Paul. She got her money's worth, though. She sang the operas from cover to cover, all the parts and all the choruses. The newest one was called *La Boheme*: it was about Bohemians.

Bohemians, like Tib's grandparents? Betsy had asked. No, Julia had explained, artists and writers. The poet, Rudolph, was writing when a little seamstress came to his door asking a light for her candle. She told him her name, and then came the aria which Julia started now. *"Mi chiamano Mimi,"* it began, and it meant, Julia said, that people called her Mimi, although her name was Lucia; and it went on to say that the flowers she embroidered in her work made her think of distant flowery fields.

"Mi chiamano Mimi," Betsy hummed softly and found a shoe box and went to pack a picnic lunch.

A Betsy-Tacy picnic, she thought as she foraged, was just about the nicest thing in the world.

When the box was packed and firmly tied with a string, she put on her hat and set off for Hill Street, up side streets that climbed gently at first, then more and more steeply. Children were playing in the streets, but tomorrow they would be in school.

"Tomorrow," thought Betsy, "I start down the Winding Hall of Fate."

And just at that moment, with what seemed prophetic timing, an automobile horn wailed behind her. Turning, she saw a red automobile. It was passing with almost meteorlike swiftness, fifteen or twenty miles an hour. Yet Betsy had a good view of a large boy, wearing a visored tan cap and a brown linen dust coat, behind the steering wheel.

<h1 style="text-align:center">2</h1>

<h1 style="text-align:center">Dree-eee-eaming</h1>

WHEN SHE ENTERED the familiar block in which she
had lived for the first fourteen years of her life, Tacy
came running to meet her. Tacy was tall, with red hair
bound in Grecian braids, blue eyes that were both shy
and merry, tender red lips, a slender freckled face. She
and Betsy embraced and kissed.

Tacy carried a copy of *Ivanhoe*.

"That fiend of a Gaston!" Betsy said.

Tacy groaned. "I only started it yesterday. Gee, it's long!"

"Take it along on the picnic."

"Not much! I'm not going to mix up any old crusades with Mamma's devil's food cake."

"Devil's food cake?" cried Betsy. "Really?"

"This is a celebration," Tacy said, "because you're home."

At the Kellys' white house, Betsy lingered to talk to Tacy's large gentle mother, with rosy efficient Katie, the sister Julia's age, and the other sisters and brothers. It was midafternoon when she and Tacy at last started up the Big Hill. This rose behind the former Ray cottage, across the street from Tacy's, a slope which Betsy and Tacy had climbed uncounted times.

They climbed contentedly now with the shoe box, a wicker basket spread with a red and white cloth, newspapers with which to start a fire and the tin pail in which they proposed to make cocoa. Sumac was reddening on either side of the rough rutted road.

At the top of the hill they paused to look out over the town. Then they turned right and entered a double line of beech trees which in their childhood they had called the Secret Lane. Leaving that deep shade behind, they came out on another crest of hill where low trees were widely spaced and there was a sweeping valley view. But this valley was empty except for the clustered rooftops of Little Syria. Beyond that settlement stretched the slough, and the wooded river bluffs.

"We can see almost to Page Park," Betsy said.

"Let's take a picnic out there sometime," Tacy suggested. "Maybe the whole Crowd will go."

"What's left of it," Betsy amended. "It isn't much of a Crowd with the Humphreys gone."

"Have you heard from Herbert?" asked Tacy as they sank into the grass.

"A letter every week. He loves to write letters, and so do I. So we're still Confidential Friends."

It was warm in the grass. The sunshine hit the hill full on, glittering over the goldenrod which rolled in a green-gold flood to the depths of the valley. The sky hung like a painting full of clouds.

"Those clouds make steps," said Tacy staring upward.

"I wish we could climb them," Betsy answered dreamily. "Walk up and up, and out into the air."

"Just keep on going. See where we got to."

"The clouds were beautiful out at the lake."

They talked about Murmuring Lake. Tacy and Katie had visited at the cottage which stood with its feet in the water not far from Pleasant Park, Mrs. Ray's girlhood home.

"I used to go out alone in the boat," said Betsy. "Row over to the bay where the water lilies are, take along a notebook and pencil, and write."

"What did you write?"

"Poems. And I worked on that novel you said reminded you of *Graustark*. I'm not going to neglect my writing the way I did last year. Joe Willard isn't going to win the Essay Contest again."

"I should say he isn't," Tacy answered indignantly. "Lightning doesn't strike twice."

"It wasn't lightning," Betsy answered slowly. "He's good. Do you know, Tacy, I wish he was in our Crowd."

"I remember you liked him," said Tacy, "when you met him at Butternut Center."

That had been in summer, a year ago. Betsy was returning from a visit with the Taggarts, farm friends of her father's. Waiting for her train in the hamlet of Butternut Center, she had gone into the general store . . . Willard's Emporium . . . to buy presents for the family.

Joe had waited on her. He was a nephew of the Emporium Willards. He had helped her pick out the presents, and they had had fun. But they hadn't hit it off at school, somehow.

The sun slipped behind Tacy's cloud-built stairs, and at once the air took on a premonitory chill.

"Better get our fire going," Tacy said briskly. She always took charge of the fire, being better at it than Betsy which didn't, however, signify much.

She twisted the papers into a heap on the rock

while Betsy brought twigs and branches. Smoke billowed generously, blackening the pail which was set precariously atop a nest of branches. It filled the air with its smell so fraught with promise, and Betsy and Tacy grinned at each other across the checkered cloth.

"I wish Tib was here," Betsy said.

"Have you heard from her?" asked Tacy somewhat later when the cocoa had thumped in its pail, and she had poured a cup for each of them.

"Yes," answered Betsy, spooning beans. "She's taking dancing lessons from a very good teacher."

"Is she going to that Browner Seminary again?"

"Yes. I wonder what a girls' school is like? It must be peaceful. No boys around."

"I thought you liked boys," said Tacy, surprised.

"I do. But they're an awful worry. At the lake, there weren't any boys my age living near us and it made life so peaceful. When there are boys you have to worry about how you look, and whether they like you, and why they like another girl better, and whether they're going to ask you to something or other. It's a strain."

"That's why I don't bother with them," said Tacy. She leaned back on her arms and looked up at the sky where her stairs had dissolved into glistening gold-rimmed clouds. "I'm peaceful all the time like you were at the lake."

"I'm not in love this year at least."

"You soon will be," Tacy prophesied.

Betsy too leaned on her arms, and they both stared upward while color flooded up behind the clouds as though from a geyser gushing rose. The clouds were tinged with pink, as the sky behind them paled. At last scattered clouds were pink all over the bowl of the sky.

"I saw that Phil Brandish on my way up to your house today," Betsy volunteered at last. "How does it happen he's coming here to school?"

"Kicked out of Cox Military."

"How thrilling!" Betsy sat upright. "What did he do?"

"He just wouldn't toe the mark, Tom says."

"I remember when he and his sister used to come visiting. Don't you? Aren't they twins?"

"Yes. Phyllis is in a girls' school somewhere. They sent Phil here to see if Grandpa Brandish couldn't straighten him out. But you might as well not feel romantic about Phil Brandish, Betsy."

"Why not? Has Irma got him?"

"No. But he's older than we are."

"Oh, fudge!"

"He's going with a senior crowd," said Tacy contentedly.

"Well, we can dream about him anyway," said Betsy. And beginning to feel silly, as she usually did at the end of a picnic with Tacy, she started to warble "Dreaming," inventing suitable words.

> "*Dreaming, dreaming,*
> *Of your red auto I'm dreaming.*"

Tacy chimed in, inventing too.

> "*Dreaming of days when we went to ride,*
> *Dreaming of hours spent by your side.*"

They composed joyfully.

> "*Dreaming, dreaming,*
> *Of your red auto I'm dreaming,*
> *Love will not change,*
> *While the auto ree-mains,*
> *Dree-ee-eaming.*"

"You fake an alto," said Betsy, and they sang their masterpiece again. They fell into the grass and laughed until echoes rolled over the hill.

But the grass was wet. It was drenched with dew.

"Golly!" said Betsy. "It's getting late. And cold!"

They put out their fire, which wasn't difficult and piled the empty plates and cups hurriedly into the basket. The tender pink was suddenly gone from the sky. It was gray with a star or two, and the crickets were singing.

The Secret Lane was already broodingly dim.

"This lane reminds me," said Betsy, "of something

I wrote in my journal this morning."

"What?"

"That starting a new journal, and our sophomore year was like being ushered into the Winding Hall of Fate. This lane doesn't wind, but it's certainly like a hall."

"What do I see ahead?" asked Tacy dramatically. "Methinks I see Betsy Ray in a bright red auto!" And that was a signal for them to burst again into song. Arms bound around each other's waists, for it was both scarily dark and frostily cold by now, they began to sing. They sang all the way through the Secret Lane, and when they came out to a light-sprinkled view of the town, and down the rough bumpy road that led to Tacy's house.

> *"Dreaming, dreaming,*
> *Of your red auto I'm dreaming. . . ."*

At the end Tacy changed from alto to tenor with a stunning dramatic effect:

> *"Love will not change,*
> *While the auto REE-mains,*
> *DREE-EE-EAMING."*

3
Ivanhoe

When Betsy and Tacy reached the Kelly house they saw Old Mag hitched out in front and Julia, Hugh, Tom and Cab sitting with Katie and Leo in the front parlor.

"They drove up to get you," Tacy hazarded. "It got so dark."

"Let's go in the back way; we look like frights," Betsy said. They stole up to Tacy's room, washed their faces, brushed and braided their hair. Betsy borrowed a little powder from one of Tacy's grown-up sisters, and they entered the parlor with good effect.

"We're discussing the noble work of *Ivanhoe*," said Cab. He was short but springy and vigorous with a dark Welsh face full of fun and sparkle. His suits were always meticulously pressed, his shoes well polished. Tom, on the other hand, was burly and carelessly dressed.

"I'm about halfway through," said Tacy.

"I haven't started it," said Cab. "Don't ask me in when we get home, Betsy. Don't suggest fudge or singing or anything else. I have to read *Ivanhoe*."

"Hully gee, I'm glad I go to Cox!" said Tom. "They never heard of the thing."

"Did we read *Ivanhoe* when we were young?" Julia asked Katie.

"I have a faint recollection of it," Katie answered. "Isn't there a tea kettle boiling in the first chapter?"

"That's *Cricket on the Hearth*," said Hugh who was studious and serious.

When the Rays started home Tom wanted to stay, but Tacy would have none of him.

"I have to read *Ivanhoe*. GOOD NIGHT."

Back on High Street, Betsy did not mention fudge but when Cab saw Tony and Carney in the lighted parlor, he went in.

"I can't stay, I can't stay," he kept repeating. "I

have to read the noble work of *Ivanhoe*."

"You can't read it on an empty stomach," Tony said.

"Cab told me not to mention fudge," said Betsy. "But there's chocolate and sugar in the kitchen."

So they all went to the kitchen, except for Julia and Hugh who remained in the parlor, and Tony put on an apron. Just as the fudge reached a boil, Winona and Irma, and Pin, a senior boy, dropped in.

Winona inquired at once, "Say, who's read *Ivanhoe*?"

"What's *Ivanhoe*? Sounds like a cigar," said Tony, stirring.

"It's a noble work which I propose to read as soon as Betsy will let me go home," said Cab.

"I'm simply struggling with it," said Irma, and at once all the boys looked sympathetic and as though they wished they could be helpful.

"What *is* it about Irma?" Betsy thought.

She had, as Betsy had told her journal, a beautiful figure, and round soft eyes and a round soft mouth. And she was sweet. The girls liked her usually, but when boys were around she was exasperating.

"Betsy's read it," Cab remarked.

"But not this summer," Betsy hastened to explain. "I just happened to read it when I was a child. Had a sore throat, or something."

"Well, gosh! When are we going to read it?" asked

Winona who was perched on the kitchen table swinging her long legs.

Tony poured the rich dark mass he had been stirring into a buttered pan. "While the fudge cools?"

"Here! Let me lick that spoon!" Winona hopped off the table.

"Not much! I lick the spoons around here."

The long sticky spoon waved wildly above wildly bobbing heads.

As soon as Winona arrived at any gathering, a scuffle ensued. Winona loved scuffles. Her black eyes and white teeth gleamed, her long black braids came loose, fudge streaked her face as she scuffled with Cab and Tony. Pin watched her, grinning, and Irma giggled, a soft alluring giggle.

"It makes me lonesome for the Humphreys to have the Crowd together," Carney said to Betsy. She meant "for Larry," Betsy knew.

It made Betsy wish for Herbert too, although she and Herbert had not "gone together" as Carney and Larry had. But it would have been nice to have Herbert around. Especially since Cab now looked at Irma with such admiring eyes.

"What's going on out here?" Julia demanded, appearing in the doorway.

She wanted to get away from Hugh, Betsy suspected. Julia was growing bored with Hugh, as she did with all her beaus. She cast off beaus with the utmost callousness, and kept Betsy busy comforting them.

"Come on in and sing while the fudge cools," Julia suggested now.

"I can't stay, I can't stay," Cab kept murmuring, but he stayed. Arms locked, the Crowd sang around the piano. When Julia started "Waltz Me Around Again, Willie," Tony flipped back the rug and asked Betsy to dance. Mrs. Ray's curly head popped over the banisters.

"Pardon me for mentioning it, but isn't tomorrow a school day?"

"We'll go home," Tony said. "But it isn't a school day, really. We just go over to register. Cab can read *Ivanhoe* all afternoon."

"The noble work!" said Cab. "We've made fudge, Mrs. Ray. May we stay to eat it?"

"Eat it in a hurry, and go home," said Mrs. Ray, and smiled, and disappeared.

The fudge was brought out hastily and cut.

"Darn your *Ivanhoe*!" said Carney who was a junior. "I thought we could go to the Majestic tomorrow afternoon."

"It's a grand idea," Betsy cried.

"Why, we can read *Ivanhoe* in the evening, can't we, Cab?" Tony asked.

Cab looked gloomy. "There are five hundred and thirty-four pages in the noble work," he said.

"I wish that Gaston was boiling in oil," remarked Winona, munching fudge.

As Tony had said, there were to be no classes the following day, but it was officially the first day of school so Anna made muffins for breakfast.

"The McCloskeys always had muffins for breakfast on the first day of school," she said when she brought them to the table around which, to Mr. Ray's satisfaction, the entire family was gathered . . . Mrs. Ray tall and slim in a starched yellow morning dress, Julia and Betsy in new shirt waists and skirts, Margaret in a new striped gingham with a big striped bow atop her head. Tacy, too, was present, having called for Betsy early.

The McCloskeys were a family for which Anna had worked in a legendary past. She never told where the McCloskeys had lived nor whither they had gone, but she held them over the Rays' heads. New members of the family turned up in her talk whenever she needed them to make a point. The Rays found it hard sometimes to live up to the McCloskeys. But again, as now, they were true friends.

"Why did the McCloskeys have muffins on the first day of school, Anna?" Betsy asked.

"Maybe the little McCloskey girl didn't like new

teachers," offered Margaret. She looked sober.

"Why, Button," said her father. "You wouldn't like to stay in Miss Parry's room forever."

"Yes, I would. After a while I could help her teach."

"Have some plum jam on your muffin, lovey," Anna said. "I bet you'll have a puny teacher." Puny, which Anna thought meant handsome, was her word of highest praise.

"*I* certainly need muffins," Mrs. Ray remarked. "This is the last fall Julia will be starting off to high school. Isn't that perfectly awful, Bob? Did you dream when she started kindergarten that such a day would ever come?"

"I suspected it," said Mr. Ray.

"And Betsy and Tacy are sophomores!"

"Just think," said Betsy, "how old we'll seem to the freshies. Remember how old the sophomores seemed to us last year?"

"Old and know-it-all," said Tacy.

"Remember how we hurried over early to get those back seats? This year we're not in any hurry at all. Have another muffin, Tacy."

"This year," said Tacy, "I'm positively nonchalant."

"I'll stifle a yawn as I stroll in."

"Ho hum! High school! What a bore!"

"Aren't they bright, Papa?" Julia asked.

"Teachers are underpaid," said Mr. Ray. "I'm going to speak to a friend on the school board and get raises for the lot."

"Not for Gaston, Mr. Ray!" cried Tacy. "Not after he made us read *Ivanhoe* this summer!"

"That Gaston!" said Betsy. "He doesn't appreciate my flowery style of writing!"

"No wonder!" said Julia scornfully. "He came to Deep Valley to teach science. He's a science teacher, really."

"Maybe he won't be teaching English this year. Maybe he'll be teaching his beloved biology, and we'll have a new English teacher. Oh, wouldn't that be wonderful?" Tacy cried.

She made this heartening suggestion to Cab who joined them on High Street. High school–bound boys and girls crowded the sidewalk, filling the golden morning with noise and excitement. But Cab was still gloomy.

"Naw, we'd have heard. And I'm in a heck of a spot. My father asked me if I'd finished *Ivanhoe*, and I said I had. I'm not a liar. I read the last page. But what about the other five hundred and thirty-three?"

The wide-flung doors of the turreted red-brick high school sucked them all in. On the landing as they clattered upstairs, Mercury welcomed them with up-flung arm. In the large upper hall they separated,

Betsy and Tacy going to the girls' cloak room to hang up their hats and look in the mirror. For all their boasted unconcern Tacy's cheeks were scarlet, and Betsy's pink.

They passed on into the assembly room, which was large, with a turret-alcove. Betsy and Tacy found adjoining seats about halfway along the second of the sophomore rows. Leaving tablets and pencils to prove ownership of their desks, they strolled back to the hall.

Here they paused before a glass-covered case in which three silver trophy cups were displayed. These were the cups . . . for athletics, debating and essay writing . . . for which the two high school societies annually competed. The athletics cup bore the turquoise blue of the Zetamathian Society to which Betsy and Tacy belonged. The bows on the other two cups were Philomathian orange.

Betsy stared at the Essay Cup and something of the self-condemnation she had felt last spring when she lost the freshmen points flooded into her heart. Tacy read her thoughts.

"Not this year, Joe Willard!" she said, shaking her fist at the cup.

Betsy laughed. "Let's go into the Social Room. Impress the freshies."

No written law barred freshmen from the Social Room. It was merely a classroom, designated as a gathering place during school intermissions. But sophomores, juniors and seniors claimed it as their own. Betsy and Tacy, sailing in, threw condescending glances at the freshmen in the hall.

Betsy looked for Joe Willard, but she did not see him. Carney approached with junior sangfroid.

"Just think!" she said to Betsy. "The Humphreys are registering out in San Diego."

"It must seem funny," Betsy said.

She tried to imagine not living in Deep Valley. She tried to imagine graduating as Julia would do this year . . . not coming back to the high school when September touched the leaves with gold. Julia, she knew, was longing to be free of it. She didn't even want to go to the state university. She wanted to be studying acting and singing out in the Great World. That was what she always called it, "the Great World." Betsy planned to see the Great World too, of course. Oh, yes, she and Tacy planned to circle the globe. But they weren't in a hurry to start.

"I love it here," Betsy said abruptly. "I just love it."

Carney flashed the lone dimple which changed her face from demure reserve to mischief. "There's Phil Brandish, the red auto boy."

Betsy looked around. He was in a corner with a noisy crowd. He stood out from the rest both because he was better dressed and because he was taller. He had straight light brown hair that fell down over his forehead.

"Tacy says he's in with a senior crowd."

"Yes, he's just a junior, though. But he doesn't interest me. He's too sophisticated. I don't like sophisticated boys."

The first gong clanged, and out in the hall freshmen scrambled. The sophomores in the Social Room smiled tolerantly. They strolled into the assembly room just as the second gong sounded.

Up on the platform Carney, who played the piano, was already at her place. Miss Bangeter, the principal, rose from her arm chair and walked to the reading desk. She was a tall, queenly woman with a mass of slippery black hair, and piercing eyes. Speaking with a Boston accent she announced the opening hymn.

The school rose, and boys and girls released pent-up excitement in song that shook the rafters.

> "*Mine eyes have seen the glory,*
> *Of the coming of the lord . . .*"

The school sat, and Miss Bangeter read a Psalm. She read from the Bible every morning, and Betsy looked forward to this moment, to Miss Bangeter's grave voice intoning the majestic poetry. Today's psalm was one she liked especially, because it had hills in it:

"I will lift up mine eyes unto the hills."

The school joined in repeating the Lord's Prayer.

After opening exercises Betsy and Tacy made the rounds of the classrooms to register for Latin, geometry, modern history and rhetoric and find out what books they were to buy.

Mr. Morse who taught Latin was impassive; he seemed never to have seen them before although he had taught them Latin grammar last year . . . or hoped he had. He told them to buy the *Commentaries of Caesar*.

Miss O'Rourke who had suffered them through algebra welcomed them to geometry with breezy friendliness. She was curly-haired, merry-eyed, pretty, but strict. Betsy and Tacy, well aware of their deficiencies, shuddered under her genial gaze.

Miss Clarke who taught history was anything but strict. The students hailed her with affectionate condescension. She was Zetamathian faculty adviser, and relied on Betsy a great deal in society affairs. If Mr. Gaston, as Betsy had claimed, did not appreciate her talents, Miss Clarke more than made up for the lack. Even Mrs. Ray, even Tacy, was no more generous with praise.

They passed on to Mr. Gaston's room. He had not yet come in, but shortly Joe Willard came in. He held his head at a challenging angle which matched the swing of his walk and the confident almost defiant slant of his red lower lip.

Joe Willard was the only boy in high school without a home. He was different from the other boys, but he didn't seem to mind it. He was even dressed differently, Betsy noticed. All last year he had worn a blue serge suit. This year he wore blue serge trousers, but his coat was light brown. No boys wore coats and pants that did not match, but Joe Willard did, today.

And they looked all right. Perhaps because they were so carefully pressed, or perhaps because he was so handsome. His summer tan made his blond pompadour look even blonder, and his blue eyes bluer below his thick light brows.

He did not glance at Betsy, but when she went over to him he smiled.

"How come you didn't show up in Butternut Center?" he asked.

"I didn't visit the Taggarts this year. We went to the lake."

"You shouldn't have missed Butternut Center," he said. "There was a runaway on the Fourth of July and a funeral on August the second."

"Wasn't there a church social?"

"Come to think of it, there was. Cocoanut cake. If you'd been there I'd have bought you a piece."

To her annoyance Betsy blushed. She was given to

blushing, especially with Joe Willard. The pink ran down to her high, white, lace-edged collar.

"Read *Ivanhoe*?" she asked hastily.

"Of course. Why?" He sounded puzzled.

"Don't you remember? Gaston told us to read it over the summer. None of the kids have read it. They're having fits."

"You've read it, haven't you?"

"Yes. But I'm not admitting it."

He looked at her keenly.

"You wouldn't!" he said.

Now what did he mean by that? Betsy wondered, blushing again. Did he know she was so dissatisfied with herself that she was always pretending to be different? Probably he did, and despised her for it. More than anyone she knew, Joe Willard was always, fearlessly, himself.

Tacy interrupted, hissing tragically. "There he comes, the brute."

Mr. Gaston entered and strode to his desk. He was a dark, sardonic-looking young man with thick, unrimmed glasses. He took the roll call briskly, announced the list of books to buy. Then he looked around and grinned.

"You remember, of course, that tomorrow you take a test on *Ivanhoe*?"

Cab and Tony conferred in whispers, with more

and frantic whispers interjected by Tacy, Alice, Irma and Winona. Then Cab rose. He took a jaunty stance, his hands in his pockets.

"You're joking, aren't you, Mr. Gaston. You didn't seriously mean that we were to read five hundred and thirty-four pages . . . over *vacation*?"

Mr. Gaston looked more sardonic than ever.

"Why, Cab, reading *Ivanhoe*'s a pleasure."

"Yes, sir, but don't you think it might be a good idea to give the test next week? In case some of us haven't had time to finish the book?"

Mr. Gaston gazed at him coldly.

"I'm teaching this class, young man. The test will be given tomorrow. I hope *you've* finished it?"

"I read page five hundred and thirty-four last night," said Cab, and winked at Betsy and sat down.

"Class dismissed. *Ivanhoe* tomorrow." Mr. Gaston said.

4
More Ivanhoe

IVANHOE AND MR. GASTON notwithstanding, the
Crowd went to the Majestic that afternoon.

Alice had finished the novel, and Tacy had only a hundred pages left. Winona was cheerfully resigned to flunk-
ing. "I'll flunk plenty of tests before the year's over."

"I've read parts of it," said Irma. She didn't seem too
worried. Perhaps she thought that even Mr. Gaston
was not impervious to her soft-eyed charm.

Tony didn't seem too worried either, but Cab's air was reckless. It troubled Betsy.

"Really, Cab, I think you'd better stay at home and read."

"Can't. My father thinks I've finished the noble work."

"Then come over to our house and read."

"While the rest of you see *Raffles*? Not much!"

So after dinner the Crowd went together to Cook's Book Store to buy books and then proceeded to that other store which, not many years before, by means of red and yellow paint and a flamboyant sign had become the Majestic Theatre, a High Class Place of Amusement, with Up to Date Moving Picture Entertainment, Especially for Ladies and Children. Admission 10¢.

In the afternoon, to the satisfaction of the Crowd, admission was only five cents. Paying their nickels they filed in to one of the rows of hard seats. On the screen up front, flickering, silent figures acted out the adventures of *Raffles, the Amateur Cracksman*. Afterwards a girl played the piano and sang. The verses were illustrated by garishly colored slides.

> *"Shine, little glow worm, glimmer,*
> *Shine, little glow worm, glimmer . . ."*

The Crowd hummed under its collective breath.

Repairing to Heinz's, to the small mirror-walled room in back of the bakery which was labelled Ice Cream Parlor, it did more than hum. It sang, banged, whistled, shouted from one small table to another as though across a football field. Mr. Heinz was indulgent. He appreciated the devotion . . . and the nickels . . . of high school boys and girls. *Ivanhoe* was forgotten in Banana Splits and Deep Valley Specials, and at parting Cab said to Betsy:

"See you tonight."

"You will not see me tonight. You read *Ivanhoe* tonight."

"I'll read it after I get home. Midnight oil, you know. The family will be in bed, and I'll pore over the noble work beside my shaded lamp . . ."

He was fooling, but he was anxious. Betsy knew it; Cab's father could be stern.

She wanted to turn him out when he came that evening, but Hugh had dropped in, and Tony, and Tom with his violin. And they all had to leave at ten o'clock sharp. Mrs. Ray said so.

Julia kept them all around the piano, somewhat to Hugh's annoyance. He could see that her feeling for him had cooled and wanted to find out why, but Julia couldn't tell him, not knowing herself, and so she avoided a tête-a-tête.

"Now go home and read *Ivanhoe*," Betsy hissed to Cab at ten o'clock.

"Maybe," put in Tony, "he'd do better in the morning not knowing a lick of *Ivanhoe* but having his wits about him."

"Maybe in the morning I'll have an inspired idea."

"You're dippy," Betsy said, shutting the door.

She dreamed about *Ivanhoe* that night. She woke dreaming about it, and went to the bookcase for her well-worn copy and brought it back to bed. She had not admitted it, but she loved the book. She had read it countless times.

She grew so interested now that she read past the breakfast gong. She dressed like a flash then, but when she reached the table even Julia was there and Mr. Ray was almost ready to leave for the store.

"I'm sorry, Papa. I was looking over *Ivanhoe*."

"*Ivanhoe! Ivanhoe!*" said Mr. Ray. "The way the Deep Valley High School treats the classics!" He went around the table stiffly, kissing good-by.

But he unbent before departing for Tacy came in and her opening cry made him smile.

"I've finished *Ivanhoe*!"

"Tacy," said Mr. Ray, "how is your father bearing up under this?"

"He says he wishes Sir Walter Scott had never been born," Tacy replied.

A burst of song sounded from the porch. Tony and Cab were ascending, their arms across each other's shoulders, singing in harmony to the tune of "Tammany."

> "*Ivanhoe,*
> *Ivanhoe . . .*"

"Let me out of here," said Mr. Ray, and made a dash for the street.

Tony and Cab came in smiling.

"Nothing like a good night's sleep," said Cab, rubbing his hands.

"We had that inspired idea," Tony said. "Both of us. Same idea."

"What is it, for goodness' sake?"

Tony searched though his pockets for a pad of paper and a pencil, and Cab too brought out writing materials with a businesslike air.

"We thought," Cab explained, "we might sit here and take notes. We thought that while you were finishing breakfast you might chat a little about the noble work."

"Just give us the high points," Tony said.

Betsy stared at them and began to laugh. Everyone laughed.

"Stars in the sky!" cried Anna. "This *Ivanhoe*! What is it, anyway?"

"It's a story, Anna. Betsy's going to tell it to us in a few well chosen words."

"Well, I'm going to listen," said Anna, and sat down, dish towel in hand.

Betsy gulped her cocoa and put the cup aside. She folded her hands on the table then, and Cab and Tony took chairs opposite and stared hard, as though by looking at that curly beribboned head they could absorb its precious knowledge of Scott's masterpiece.

"Well," began Betsy, and paused. She thought of Joe Willard and took a deep breath and started again. "I have to say something that will shock you. It's a perfectly grand book."

"What?" Cab and Tony cried together.

"Perfectly grand. If you don't say so, Gaston will know you haven't read it, because you couldn't read it without liking it."

Tony looked at her sharply. "You're not fooling?"

Cab wrote down on his pad of paper, "Perfectly grand."

Betsy decided to begin where Scott had.

"It begins," she said, "in that pleasant district of merry England which is watered by the River Don."

Tony put down his pencil. "You *are* fooling!"

"No really. That's the first sentence. It opens in a forest with a swineherd named Gurth, and Wamba, son of Witless. . . ."

"See here, Betsy! In ten minutes we can only hit the high spots."

"All right," said Betsy, yielding. It saddened her that Cab and Tony should not know about Gurth and Wamba, and the meeting with the Pryor. She felt she was cheating them, but it couldn't be helped.

"The important characters," she said, "are Wilfred of Ivanhoe, a knight, returned from the Crusades; Rowena, the girl he's in love with; Cedric, her guardian, who disapproves; Rebecca, a girl who's in love with Ivanhoe; and some assorted villains."

"Fine!" said Tony. "Now we're getting somewhere."

"King Richard's in it, too. He went to the Crusades, and left England in charge of his brother Prince John, who's a crook. Richard comes back to see what's going on, disguised as the Black Knight. He comes to the tournament and on the second day when Ivanhoe is fighting three men at once. . . ."

"A good fight?" asked Cab, leaning forward.

"Just the best one ever written, that's all." Betsy's cheeks flamed. She told the story of the tournament and told it so well that Anna leaned across the table, breathing hard, Tacy's eyes sparkled and the boys forgot to scribble notes.

"Betsy," said her mother. "You'll be late for school."

They went out to an almost empty High Street with Betsy still talking, Tacy, Cab, and Tony now hanging on every word.

"Does Prince John give in, and admit that Ivanhoe won?"

"Yes, and Ivanhoe chooses Rowena to be Queen of Beauty."

"Do they live happily ever after, then?"

"Heavens, no! She's kidnapped, and so is Rebecca. They're held captive in a castle, with Ivanhoe, and the Black Knight storms it."

They dropped down on the school steps, and Betsy kept on talking. The first gong rang and they moved slowly toward the upper hall where Betsy continued to talk until the second gong clanged.

"Anything else?"

"Remember the bad feeling between the Normans and Saxons."

"What happens to Rebecca?"

"She goes into a convent."

"Sounds like quite a tale," drawled Tony, returning his notes to his pocket.

"Wilfred of Ivanhoe, Rowena, Cedric, Rebecca . . ." muttered Cab.

Tacy took Betsy's arm. "It was wonderful the way you told it, Betsy." And then Tacy too started muttering, "Wilfred of Ivanhoe, Rowena, Cedric, Rebecca . . ."

All through the morning, whenever Betsy looked toward Tacy, Tony or Cab she saw them muttering.

Mr. Gaston greeted the rhetoric class with a glance derisively bland. He gave the next day's assignment, ignored the frantic whispering going on all over the room, and said casually: "Now I want each one of you to write me an essay on *Ivanhoe*."

He leaned back in his chair and unfolded a scientific journal.

Betsy swept a glance around the room. Tony, Cab and Tacy were all muttering. Joe Willard looked as he had looked before he set to work on the Essay Contest last year. His paper, ink, and pen were ready and he was brushing his fingers thoughtfully over his yellow hair.

Betsy smiled at her paper. What a delightful assignment! What fun to write an essay on her beloved *Ivanhoe*! She dipped her pen in ink.

She began where she had tried to begin before, and now there were no Tony or Cab to cry, "Just give us the high spots, Betsy!" She told all about Gurth and Wamba and descibed the Lady Rowena's beauty and Ivanhoe's mysterious coming and the arrival of Rebecca and her father.

The clock said that half the allotted time was gone, so she hurried on to the tournament. She tried to make spears ring in her prose as they rang in Sir Walter's.

Now and then she almost thought she succeeded.

Looking up dreamily, she saw that Tony and Cab had already finished. Joe Willard still had his pen in his hand, but he was reading what he had written. Mr. Gaston had closed his magazine. He was tapping the desk and looking at the clock, obviously impatient.

Betsy rushed for the finish, scattering blots. But Rowena and Rebecca were still captive, the story hung in the air like a bright banner, when the gong sounded and Mr. Gaston said:

"You may leave your papers on my desk as you go out."

Betsy was sorry she had not finished, but after all, she reflected, panting and warm from her attempt, Mr. Gaston would certainly see that she knew her *Ivanhoe*. It was nice what she had said about those silvery spears: and the part about Rowena's hair. Even Sir Walter Scott hadn't thought to compare it to maple syrup.

"How did you get along?" she asked Cab anxiously.

"I think I did the noble work justice."

"Mine was a masterpiece," said Tony.

"Mine was all right, too," said Tacy.

Betsy sighed in proud relief.

It was two days before Mr. Gaston returned the

papers. And during those two days *Ivanhoe* continued to possess the Ray household.

"If Washington should have kittens . . . but he won't, because he's a boy . . . I'd name one Ivanhoe and one Rowena," Margaret said.

Mr. Ray heard about Betsy's fifteen-minute condensation of the masterpiece with a chuckle.

"I wonder how Cab and Tony will come out?"

"I think they will get Fair at least," Betsy said. Mr. Gaston marked his papers Excellent, Good, Fair and Poor.

When the class filed in on the third morning the papers were piled on his desk. After roll call he tapped them condescendingly.

"These essays on *Ivanhoe* weren't bad," he said. "Really, they weren't bad at all! Three of them are marked 'Excellent,' and from a class of the mentality of this one, that's pretty good." Mr. Gaston liked to make that sort of joke.

Three "Excellents!" Betsy, without thinking, flashed Joe Willard a glance. She intercepted one from him, and they both smiled. Both felt sure where two Excellents had gone, but what about the third one?

"None of you," Mr. Gaston continued, "will be surprised to hear that one 'Excellent' went to Joe. But the other two may startle you. They did me."

He smiled mockingly.

"Tony and Cab," he said, "drew 'Excellents,' too."

To say that the class was startled was putting it mildly. Tony and Cab grinned from ear to ear. Tacy threw up her hands in pantomime to Betsy.

"Tony and Cab," Mr. Gaston continued, "turned in essays that showed they had read the book. I must admit, Cab, that when you told me you had finished it, I had my doubts. But you and Tony obviously had not only read *Ivanhoe*. You had digested it. Therefore, your papers are brief, concise. You just . . ." Mr. Gaston's smile for once was genuinely approving, "you just hit the high spots."

Tony slipped down until the desk almost hid his face. Cab's ears were red.

"Your admirably organized papers," Mr. Gaston went on, "were in contrast to some I received. Some writers who, perhaps, had not even finished the book tried to show off their so-called literary skill at Scott's expense."

At that Betsy turned crimson. Mr. Gaston had spoken in the plural, but no one in the class would doubt that he meant her alone. For just a moment she was appalled. Then the joke in the situation struck her, and she smiled around at Cab, Tony and Tacy. Joe Willard was looking at her with a puzzled expression.

Tony and Cab after football practise, headed for the Ray house. They paused on the hill to pick a bouquet of sumac, goldenrod, asters and prickly thistles, and presented it to Betsy with sweeping bows. There was much joking and when Mr. Ray heard the story, he laughed until he shook.

But saying good-by to Betsy, Cab turned serious. He was, after all, Welsh Calvinistic Methodist.

"Betsy!" he said. He looked around to make sure that no one was listening. "Betsy, I just want you to know. . . . I'm going to read the noble work. The whole five hundred and thirty-four pages. Darned if I don't!"

And he did.

5
Septemberish

SEPTEMBER WAS VERY Septemberish that year. It was
Septemberish in the excitement of the opening days of
school. These were so busy that soon the quiet summer at the lake seemed like a remote and peaceful
dream. But a dream ... Betsy thought ... it was good
to have had. She liked to remember the faintly rocking boat, the smell of water lilies, and her novel.

School was demanding. It came at her from all sides.

During the first week sophomores, juniors, and seniors, with ostentatious politeness invited the freshmen into the Social Room. There they talked up the merits of the two school societies. The freshmen must choose their societies, and rivalry was keen.

"Just look at the trophy cups. You'll find orange bows on two of them," Betsy heard Philos everywhere saying, and every time she heard it, she writhed. If she had not lost the freshmen points to Joe Willard, the Zetamathians might have had the Essay Cup.

Teaming up with Tacy, she worked frantically, telling freshmen boys that the Zets had all the pretty girls; freshmen girls that the Zets had all the nicest boys. It seemed to work.

They saw Phil Brandish surrounded by Philo girls. As a newcomer, he too would join a society today.

"*Dreaming, dreaming,*" hummed Tacy mischievously. "You'll never have a better chance."

"I'll think of the red auto and plunge," Betsy said.

But she didn't, and Tacy had known that she wouldn't speak to Phil Brandish. He was too old, too big, too worldly. They continued to court the freshmen.

At the afternoon assembly Miss Bangeter and the presidents of the two societies spoke.

"Philo, Philo, Philo!" "Zet! Zet! Zet!" shrieked the

opposing clans. Lists were passed, and after the signing Phil Brandish wore an orange bow.

Early in September, also, came class elections. Betsy felt a thrill when she was elected secretary of her class. The family at supper was pleased, too.

"I'm not a bit surprised, though," her mother said.

"Na, neither am I," said Anna, passing biscuits. "The McCloskey girl was secretary."

"Bettina is a natural leader," said Julia, whose opinion of Betsy was so good that it kept Betsy busy living up to it. Margaret's eyes were awed.

Mr. Ray always laughed at Mrs. Ray for being proud of their daughters, but his face had a special look when one brought home news like this. He was anxious that Betsy should be a good secretary.

"Go to every meeting, Betsy. And write up the minutes carefully in a notebook you keep for that purpose."

"I'll buy one tomorrow," Betsy said, happily. She had a weakness for fresh new notebooks and finely sharpened pencils.

September brought plenty of these, along with new books, and the impact of new studies. Some of these jarred all too heavily.

"Geometry is awful, simply awful," Betsy wailed.

Julia couldn't understand this. "I love geometry. It's like music."

"Like *music*?"

"Yes. It's exact, like music."

"Stop! Stop! I've always liked music. Don't you go comparing it with something hideous. . . ."

"Poor Bettina!" said Julia, and that night she tried to help. She placed the ruler carefully with her slender white fingers, drew lines with fastidious precision, and explained that when two straight lines intersected, the vertical angles formed were equal. She spoke with such a glowing face that Betsy tried not to scowl.

"Do you understand now, Bettina? Isn't it fascinating?"

"I'd never call it fascinating. But perhaps I begin to see . . ."

She didn't. When she was called to the blackboard next day she went on dragging feet. Chalk in an icy hand, she turned to look pleadingly at Tacy who was suffering with her, just as Betsy suffered when Tacy was called to the board.

"Don't look at Tacy. Look at the blackboard," said Miss O'Rourke, good naturedly but crisply.

Betsy looked. She tried despairingly to remember what Julia had said. What was that about vertical angles? It had all fled.

"Betsy," said Miss O'Rourke. "I think you've made up your mind that you can't understand geometry. Well, you'll have to unmake it. You understood algebra, and you can understand geometry."

She marked Betsy's card with a firm unmistakable zero, and Betsy went back to her seat.

It was good to escape from school after such a session, to pile into the surrey behind Old Mag or the Sibleys' Dandy, and roam country roads in the lazy sunshine. The woods were still green except, here and there, for an old tree turning yellow. But September was in the smoky air.

Only girls went on these expeditions, for the boys were busy with football practise. Joe Willard didn't play. Betsy saw him sometimes after school streaking toward the Creamery while the other boys streaked toward the field. Tom had left for Cox, and on these feminine rambles the shortage of boys in the Crowd was a favorite topic.

"There are plenty of boys in school. They just have to be lured into our Crowd."

"Irma could lure a few," someone would say if Irma happened not to be along.

"Yes, but when Irma lures them, she keeps them. What good would that do us?"

"What about that good looking Joe Willard?"

"He's a woman hater," said Winona who had tried vainly to inveigle him.

"I think we get along fine without boys. I love hen parties," Tacy said. But no one thought this even worth answering.

"Why the heck the Humphreys had to go to California!" someone always groaned, and Carney always looked sober.

Everyone in the Crowd missed the Humphreys but not as Carney did. The letters which passed steadily between Deep Valley and San Diego did not fill Larry's place. Neither did any of the many boys who were attentive to her.

As happened every September Chauncey Olcott came to the Opera House and Mr. Ray took the family to hear him. Anna went with Charley, her beau. They sat in the balcony, and between acts she came to the railing to wave to the Rays sitting below. She wore such a big hat, such a fluffy boa, so much perfume and jewelry of every sort that she attracted considerable attention. There was much craning of necks. But the Rays waved loyally back.

This year's play was called *O'Neill of Derry*. But the name didn't matter much. The play was always like last year's play, and probably next year's too. They were all laid in Ireland, they were full of plumed hats, high boots, laced bodices; and the Irish tenor, still handsome although stoutish, always sang the ballad he had earlier made famous:

> *"My wild Irish rose,*
> *The sweetest flower that grows . . ."*

When he began Mr. Ray always took Mrs. Ray's hand, and the girls sat very still, not to miss a note or quaver. Even Julia enjoyed it, although she infuriated Betsy later with condescending remarks.

"Chauncey Olcott," she said, "should really have done something with his voice."

"*Done* something!" Betsy repeated. "*Done* something! He's made himself famous with it. What do you call *doing* something?"

"He might have sung real music. Oh, Bettina, you must hear Mrs. Poppy's records! You must hear the really great ones . . . Caruso, Scotti, Melba, Geraldine Farrar. . . ."

"Chauncey Olcott," said Betsy stubbornly, "is good enough for me."

When not irritated by slurs on Chauncey Olcott, however, she was a sympathetic repository for Julia's talk of the Great World.

Julia took singing lessons from Mrs. Poppy, a large blond former actress whose husband managed the Melborn Hotel. They lived at the Hotel. Julia had been studying for a long time now, but she still came home from every lesson with burning cheeks and a faraway look in her eyes. She went straight to the piano, usually, and started to sing one of her opera scores. And after supper she often called Betsy into her room. She would talk and talk about pitch and resonance and breath control, illustrating with a *"Ni-po-tu-la-he,"* followed by another *"Ni-po-tu-la-he"* which to Betsy sounded just the same.

"Do you hear the difference?" Julia would demand, and rush on without waiting for an answer. "Isn't it marvelous?"

She would dart across to Betsy, comfortably ensconced in the window seat, grasp Betsy's hand and press it over her own diaphragm while she sang the *"Ni-po-tu-la-he"* again.

"Do you feel that? Here! That's the way to produce a tone."

Betsy felt as bewildered as she did by geometry, but she pretended to understand.

Above Julia's dressing table was a large picture cut from a magazine of Miss Geraldine Farrar, the American singer who was scoring such triumphs in Europe and New York. Her long glittering train coiled about her feet; her head was high; her smile, triumphant. Julia used to gaze at this picture thoughtfully.

"I think I look like her."

"You do."

"She seems taller. But it's just that train."

Julia, standing on tiptoe, pushed down her slender hips.

Julia was soloist in the girls' vested choir at St. John's Episcopal Church. The choir too started in

September after a summer recess. Betsy also was a member and she liked marching down the aisle and singing, in a long black robe and a black four-cornered hat. But she liked even better going alone to the early Sunday morning service.

She could usually waken herself by planning to do so. She slipped out of the house while the rest of the family was sleeping. The world was misty, cool, the lawns frosted with dew and filled with great numbers of blackbirds feeding busily.

The attendance at this service was small. There were usually just a few old ladies and Betsy. The Rev. Mr. Lewis knelt and rose, read the prayers, moved about the snowy candlelit altar, in a sort of reverent abstraction which Betsy shared.

"Ye who do truly and earnestly repent you of your sins . . . and intend to lead a new life . . ."

Every Sunday morning Betsy resolved dreamily to lead a new life.

She always got back for breakfast very hungry and as for the new life . . . usually it didn't last very long. But every Sunday morning she could start one again.

As September moved on there was a fire in the grate for Sunday night lunch. It was cozy; it was remindful of last winter to have a fire again. Mr. Ray made the sandwiches as usual. He was famous for his Sunday evening sandwiches. And after these were eaten, along with coffee, and cocoa, and a big layer cake, the family and the ever-present guests sat around the fire and sang.

But the grand climax of the month was, of course, Julia's birthday. She was eighteen this year. Mrs. Ray gave her a party for eighteen girls, including some of Betsy's friends. And Betsy and Carney, assigned to serve the refreshments, were hilariously inspired to wear their fathers' dress suits. The black trousers were turned up, the waistcoats were padded out with pillows. Both girls painted on mustaches and goatees of burnt cork. They were, someone said, good enough to serve at a fashionable wedding.

And that gave Winona an inspiration of her own.

"Girls! Girls! Let's have a mock wedding!"

Mock weddings were a favorite diversion in Deep Valley.

"I'll be the groom," cried Carney. "I'll act like a typical male and pick Irma for my bride." She fell to her knees at Irma's feet.

"I'll be the minister," shouted Betsy.

They all scurried about, pushing palms into a half circle in the Rays' front window, pinning a lace curtain on the giggling Irma and giving her a cabbage bouquet. Winona, in Mrs. Ray's bathrobe, acted as bridesmaid and Tacy in Mr. Ray's smoking jacket played the Best Man. Julia sang "O Promise Me" with many high falsetto trills and Mrs. Ray banged out the wedding march.

Breathless from laughter Betsy rushed to the dining room table for the remnants of birthday cake.

"We must each take a piece home and sleep on it. That's what you always do after a wedding."

"Yes," said Julia's friend Dorothy. "You put it in a box along with the names of seven boys. Every morning for seven mornings you draw out a name, and the last one will be your future husband."

"Carney will make all seven 'Larry.'"

"No, you have to name seven different boys."

"But what if you haven't met your future husband yet? I hope I haven't," Tacy said.

"Write 'A Stranger' on one of the slips."

Julia ran upstairs for pencils; paper was hurriedly torn into strips, and the girls set to work.

"Is there anyone here who isn't beginning with Phil Brandish?" Betsy asked. But everyone was too busy to answer. She wrote "Phil Brandish" with a flourish and picked up the second slip of paper. On that she wrote without hesitation "A Stranger."

Herbert had acquired a romantic aura since going to California. She licked her pencil and wrote "Herbert." Cab ought to be put down. Of course he had a crush on Irma, but everyone couldn't go with Irma. She put down "Cab." She put down "Tony" for old times' sake, and "Tom" because she had known him longer than any other boy.

"I have one slip left," she announced.

"I have five," groaned Tacy.

Everyone else was either thinking or writing.

Betsy put the end of her pencil in her teeth, and her mind's eye roved over Deep Valley High School. It paused at a challenging blond head.

"Girls!" shouted Winona. "I've put down 'Gaston.' If I draw that last I invite you to my suicide."

"I'm putting down 'Chauncey Olcott,'" said Tacy. "There's a Mrs. Olcott, I believe, but Chauncey will just have to get rid of her."

"I haven't a local boy in my list," said Julia loftily.

That caused a sensation among the seniors.

"Why, Julia! What about Hugh?"

"I'll auction off Hugh."

"Really?" "May I have him?" "I think he's cute."

Through the clatter of voices, Betsy pondered over her seventh slip.

"See here," she called out suddenly. "I'm thinking of the general good. I'm thinking of someone we could use in our Crowd."

"Who?"

"Joe Willard."

"I've told you before, and I'll tell you again, he's a woman hater," Winona declared.

"Oh, fudge!"

"If you think you can get him into the Crowd, why don't you try?"

"Ask him to a party or something?"

"I will, maybe," Betsy said. She wrote "Joe Willard" firmly on her seventh slip.

Tacy and Katie stayed all night after the wedding, and there was more hilarity about putting the wedding cake, and the names, under their pillows.

In the morning Betsy drew out Cab, and the following morning, Tony, and after that Herbert and Tom. At last she was down to A Stranger, Phil Brandish, and Joe.

But alas and alack, that morning she did not make her own bed! She was late, and left it for Anna who knew nothing about the great enterprise. Anna found some crumbs of cake and soiled papers and threw them all out. She even changed the sheets for good measure, and Betsy's plight was pitiful. She was stranded by Fate not knowing whom she would marry . . . A Stranger, Phil Brandish, or Joe.

6
The Moorish Café

THE MOCK WEDDING WAS followed shortly by a wedding anniversary, a real one . . . Mr. and Mrs. Ray's.

It came in mid-October and every year, or almost every year, the family celebrated in the same way. They went out to Murmuring Lake, had dinner at the Inn, and then visited Pleasant Park. Mr. and Mrs. Ray showed the three girls the oak tree they had been sitting under when Mr. Ray proposed; they pointed out the big bay window in which they had been married. The trip usually came at a glittering autumnal moment when Minnesota was a paradise of blue skies and lakes, with red and gold leaves overhead and underfoot.

On the year Betsy was a sophomore, however, the fifteenth of October was a rainy day.

The rain began the night before, but lazily.

"It'll clear. We won't be starting until after school," Mr. Ray said optimistically. Mr. Ray was always optimistic. He never expected things to go wrong, but if they did he was not daunted. If a plan upset he could always make another one, so pleasant that everyone was almost glad the first one could not be carried out.

In the morning it was plain that he would have to plan, and plan fast. The rain was a torrent, and the wind was lashing the shrubs to and fro.

Whistling, as he always did when troubled, Mr. Ray went to the basement and started the furnace. Heat crept comfortingly through the registers, but no one cheered up. Anna made popovers, which helped any situation. Still the breakfast table was subdued, until Mr. Ray, with his second cup of coffee, remarked:

"I have a snoggestion." "Snoggestion" was what

he always called a particularly good suggestion. Faces brightened all around the table.

"What is it, Papa?" Margaret asked eagerly.

"We'll put off the trip. But just so your mother won't think I'm sorry she hooked me twenty-one years ago today, here's what I'm going to do."

"What?" Everyone waited radiantly.

"Take her out to supper tonight. Take her down to the Melborn Hotel. Poppy has put in a new café. The Moorish Café, he calls it. Oriental decorations, lights so low you can hardly see your nose, an orchestra making hoochy koochy music. All the fellows are taking their best girls there, and I'm going to take mine . . . tonight!"

"Bob!" cried Mrs. Ray. "How dear of you!" She tried not to show that she was disappointed because their daughters weren't included.

Of the three girls, Julia rallied first.

"That's a lovely snoggestion. It's the proper thing for a bride and groom to go off all alone."

"Um-hum," said Betsy and Margaret.

"And the new café is wonderful. Just like the Twin Cities, Mrs. Poppy says. Maybe Anna will make us beef birds," added Julia, glancing at Margaret who was especially fond of beef birds.

"But Anna has the evening off," objected Mr. Ray.

Anna, replenishing popovers, spoke hastily. "Na,

I'll stay home. It does that Charley good to get left once in a while. Margaret and I'll have fun making the beef birds. Won't we, Margaret?"

"No," said Mr. Ray. "It wouldn't be right to disappoint Charley. I don't like to see anybody disappointed." He seemed not to notice the crestfallen faces around him.

"Well, I can't make beef birds, but I can make pancakes . . . Margaret can help flop them," Julia volunteered.

"Pancakes and maple syrup! You won't have anything that good at the Moorish Café." For Margaret's benefit, Betsy smacked her lips in simulated delight.

"I like pancakes," said Margaret sitting very straight. She even smiled, although glassily.

Mrs. Ray looked troubled, but she wanted Mr. Ray to know that she was appreciative so she said gaily, "I'm going to dress up. I'll wear my new tan satin dress. And you have to put on your dress suit, Bob Ray, whether you want to or not."

"It isn't back from the dry cleaners, after Julia's party."

"Yes it is. It came yesterday."

"But I haven't a clean collar."

"You have plenty of clean collars."

"I've lost my studs!" Mr. Ray wailed.

He always pretended that he didn't like to put on

his dress suit. It was a family joke, and Margaret's eyes began to shine.

"Your studs are right in my jewel case where they always are," Mrs. Ray scolded. "If we're going to the Moorish Café, we're going to do it *right*."

"Go late, Mamma," urged Julia, laughing. "Twin City people eat very late, Mrs. Poppy says."

"Of course we'll go late. Seven o'clock."

"I can't wait until seven o'clock for my supper," Mr. Ray groaned.

"Not supper. *Dinner, Dinner!*"

All the girls were laughing now.

"See how she picks on me, Anna?" Mr. Ray asked. "Don't you think I'm a wonder to have stood it for twenty-one years?" He went around the table, kissing. And when he came to Mrs. Ray he kissed her twice. "I'm even willing to stand it for twenty-one more," he said.

Julia, Betsy and Margaret in waterproof coats and rubbers braved the storm to go to school. They swam there and back, they reported at noon.

By late afternoon it had cleared a little. There were layers of turquoise between the gray clouds along the western sky.

"We could almost have gone to the lake. But I'm glad we didn't. Because Mamma is going to the Moorish Café," Margaret said.

"Let's start to make our pancakes, shall we?" Betsy asked. Anna had left. The kitchen was clean and empty.

"Wait until after we're gone," Mr. Ray suggested. "Mamma will need you to hook her dress up, probably. And Julia always ties my tie."

"All right. We'll see you off in style before we eat," said Julia.

So Mr. Ray went to the bathroom to shave, and the girls went to help their mother dress.

She was sitting at her dressing table, wearing a lacy corset cover and a bell-shaped taffeta petticoat, bright green. Her red hair was dressed in its high pompadour. She was powdered, and had darkened her reddish brows with the charred end of a match. She looked pretty, but she gazed at the mirror critically.

"I wish, I wish ladies could wear rouge, like actresses do," she said.

Betsy laughed, but Julia was sympathetic. "I like your face pale, Mamma. Your hair is so red, your eyes so blue. Just remember to bite your lips going into the Moorish Café."

She helped her mother into the tan satin dress, which was heavy with buckram lining, elaborate with high boned collar, lace-covered yoke, *soutache* braid on sleeves and flowing skirts. While Betsy hooked it, Julia went off to tie her father's tie, and Margaret sprinkled violet perfume on a fine embroidered hand-kerchief. Mrs. Ray was buttoning white kid gloves, when Mr. Ray came in.

Mr. Ray looked handsome in his dress suit. In spite of his jokes he really liked to wear it. He was tall and very erect; he almost bent backwards, in fact. He was beginning to get stout around his middle. But it only made him look more dignified, Mrs. Ray said. His black hair lay flat and shining on his head. He had a big nose, fresh cheeks, and hazel eyes which were full of mischief now.

"Come on. Hurry up," he said as Mrs. Ray stroked down the fingers of her gloves.

"Why, Bob! It's only six o'clock."

"I know. But I want to go for a ride before dinner, a long romantic ride in the twilight. Haven't you any sentiment?"

"I have plenty of sentiment," said Mrs. Ray and kissed him.

She turned for his inspection gaily. Mr. Ray shook his head at his daughters.

"Not one of you girls," he said, "is as good-looking as your mother."

Then he put on his top coat and got his silk hat and his gold-headed cane. He held Mrs. Ray's wrap and they all went downstairs.

Betsy whispered to Margaret who ran into the

kitchen and returned with one fist clenched.

"Good-by, darlings!" Mrs. Ray bestowed fragrant rustling kisses.

"Good-by! Have a good time."

"It's so nice for you two to go off *alone*," said Julia, and her father turned and winked at her.

"Now!" Betsy hissed in Margaret's ear.

Margaret ran through the doorway and threw a handful of rice.

"Margaret!" "You little rascal!" Mr. and Mrs. Ray shouted and dodged. The girls laughed and Julia banged the door and leaned against it.

"Bettina! Margaret! I know the most wonderful secret."

"What?"

"Are they out of sight?"

"Not yet. They're climbing into the surrey."

"Well, wait! I won't tell 'til they're gone."

After a breathless moment the sound of Old Mag's clopping hoofs died out down the street.

"It's a good thing I can act," said Julia then. "I've known for the last ten minutes. Ever since I went to fix Papa's tie."

"Known what?"

"We're going to the Moorish Café."

"*We're* going?"

"Me, too?" asked Margaret stupefied.

"Yes, baby. You, too. Mr. Thumbler's hack is calling for us at a quarter to seven. We're going to surprise Mamma. It's Papa's idea."

Betsy leaped and squealed. Margaret was sedate as always, but her eyes almost swallowed her face. Julia flung her arms around them both.

"We've got to *hurry*! For once I can't be late. Papa wants us sitting at the table when he brings Mamma in, and in our very best dresses."

"I can button everything except the middle button," Margaret said, and they made a rush for the stairs.

Julia was ready last, of course. But before beginning on herself she had dressed Betsy's pompadour and tied Margaret's hair ribbon into sculptured beauty. They kept Mr. Thumbler waiting only five minutes.

In the hack Margaret sat erect and tense. Autumn fog circled the street lamps. Lighted parlors looked cozy in the dusk.

"Most people are doing their dishes. We're going to the Moorish Café," Margaret said.

Julia squeezed her hand. "Aren't we glad we're us?"

"If we weren't us, who would we be?"

"Let's see," said Betsy. "If Mamma had married somebody else, we'd be just half ourselves."

"And if Papa had married someone else, too, there'd be another half of us goodness knows where."

"How exciting! I could pass myself on the street."

"Half of yourself could say to the other half, 'Miss Ray, your petticoat hangs.'"

Julia and Betsy were having fun but Margaret said, "Oh, dear!"

"Don't worry!" said Julia. "It couldn't possibly have happened. Papa and Mamma were meant for each other, and we were meant for them."

Mr. Thumbler deposited them grandly at the Melborn's limestone entrance, and Julia led the way inside. The Café was on the ground floor. One could enter it from the street or from the lobby. Mr. Ray had told Julia to enter from the lobby; Mr. Poppy would be waiting for them. And he was. Three hundred pounds of suave sophistication.

"Good evening, Mr. Poppy. Here are the three bears," Julia said breezily. She was as poised as though she came to the Moorish Café every day. Betsy was fervently admiring. She assumed her Ethel Barrymore droop, and attempted a bored smile, but her own smile kept coming through, excited and eager.

"Three bears indeed!" said Mr. Poppy. "Three beautiful young ladies! You're coming up to the apartment after dinner, Mamma says." He always called Mrs. Poppy, "Mamma."

Taking Margaret's hand he led them into the Moorish Café.

Music swam out to greet them, seductive and soft. The long narrow room was mysteriously dim, lighted only by small brass lamps studded with red and green and purple glass. When she grew accustomed to this colored dusk, Betsy saw rich rugs and hangings, a turbaned orchestra.

They came to a table for five bearing a sign Reserved, and a large tissue-wrapped package.

"I've had my instructions," Mr. Poppy said, and placed the three girls in a row facing the door which led to the street.

They were barely seated when the door opened. Mrs. Ray, looking tall and lovely, her red head rising above her velvet wrap, came in, followed by Mr. Ray. He gave his hat, coat, and stick to a girl who came forward to get them, and Mrs. Ray looked around graciously. She didn't look to see anything. She looked as a woman looks who knows she is being inspected . . . head high, face proud and smiling.

Julia, Betsy and Margaret squeezed hands under the table.

"Table for two, sir?"

"It's ordered. Ray is the name."

The oriental waiter almost scampered down the room.

He paused before the three girls but for an instant Mrs. Ray did not even glance down. Then she looked to see what was causing the delay, and her company expression melted into amazement and delight.

"Girls! Girls! What are you doing here?"

"Papa invited us." Margaret was almost bursting.

"Happy anniversary, Mamma!"

"Congratulations, Mamma!"

Mrs. Ray turned to Mr. Ray who smiled broadly.

"Bob," she said, "this is perfect! Absolutely perfect!"

And it was!

The Moorish Café was even more Twin Cityish than Mrs. Poppy had said. The music was very hoochy koochy, and for dinner they had oyster cocktails, and then soup, and then fish, and then turkey, and then salad, and then dessert . . . pie, ice cream or Delmonico pudding. The coffee came in small long-handled brass pots.

"Just like they have in Little Syria," Betsy cried.

Everyone had coffee, dark and very sweet, in cups the size of thimbles.

Mrs. Ray opened the tissue-wrapped package. It held a dish, gold-rimmed, hand-painted with sprays of green leaves and reddish colored berries.

"I thought it looked like October," Mr. Ray said.

The orchestra stopped its hoochy koochy music, and played "O Promise Me," which Julia had sung at the Mock Wedding. All the other diners smiled at the Rays, and Margaret sat straight and acted very dignified, as though she couldn't imagine why they were smiling.

Even when the music ended the party wasn't over, for the family went up in the elevator to the Poppys' apartment overlooking the river. In her pink and gold parlor, large, pink and gold Mrs. Poppy passed candy and grape juice and cigars and played while Julia sang.

Standing like Geraldine Farrar in the picture . . . although she lacked the glittering train . . . Julia trilled through a waltz song by Arditi. Mr. Ray listened with crossed legs, looking grave. He didn't understand much about music. Mrs. Ray looked stern, as she always did when her children performed. Betsy thought about the Moorish Café, and Margaret tried not to act sleepy.

Mrs. Poppy put her arm around Julia.

"You have a very talented little girl," she said. "I wish she could hear some grand opera. She's my star pupil—absolutely."

And that was a nice thing for parents to hear on a wedding anniversary.

Leaving the Poppys, they went down in the elevator to the big, warm, brightly lighted lobby.

"You wait here," Mr. Ray said. "I'll go out and bring around Old Mag. . . ."

He was interrupted by Margaret, still erect although very drowsy now.

"Oh, Papa! I almost forgot."

"What, dear?"

From the pocket of her dress Margaret drew out a dollar and handed it to him.

"What's this?" asked Mr. Ray looking mystified.

"It's yours," said Margaret, trying not to yawn. "You forgot and left it on the table down in the Moorish Café. I saw it just as we were leaving. I've been meaning to give it to you."

"Oh, thank you, Button," Mr. Ray said.

His lips twitched a little, and Mrs. Ray and Julia smiled at each other, but Betsy didn't see anything funny in Papa forgetting a dollar and Margaret rescuing it.

"Wasn't that killing about Margaret?" asked Julia at home, undressing while Betsy wound her hair on Magic Wavers.

"What about Margaret?"

"Her picking up the tip."

"Tip?"

"The tip Papa left for the waiter."

"Oh . . . oh . . . yes, of course. Perfectly killing," said Betsy. She laughed heartily but her expression was puzzled. A tip! A tip! What, she wondered, was a tip?

7
The Man of Mystery

WINONA DID NOT ALLOW Betsy to forget that she was going to ask Joe Willard into the Crowd.

"When are you going to do it?" she prodded.

"Whenever I give a party."

"Well, when are you going to give one?"

"Not until Papa forgets the fifty-four I got in my geometry test. Joe Willard will keep. Don't worry."

Yet she herself felt a little worried, and she couldn't see why. It was certainly all right to invite Joe into the Crowd. It was the grandest Crowd in school and he belonged in it. She looked for a chance to speak with him alone but this was not easy to find.

He was elusive around school. He went from one class to another as though shot from a gun. If a girl wanted to talk to him she had to stop him; he never waylaid anyone. He swung through the halls confidently, a little brashly, and he was fun in class. He liked to say things that would startle people . . . teachers or pupils. At such times he had an infectious grin which swept the group into his mirthful mood.

He was popular, but very little known.

"He's practically a Man of Mystery," Betsy thought. She began to look for him outside of school.

Every Saturday now there was a football game. Some were played in neighboring towns, and Julia's friends made up parties and went off on the train with the team, and Stewie, the coach. Betsy's crowd was content to meet the train when it returned with the conquering or defeated heroes.

But they attended the home games in a body. Wearing streamers of maroon and gold, they drove out behind Old Mag or Dandy, who waited patiently on the outskirts of the field.

This year there was an auto at the games, Phil

Brandish's bright red auto. When they saw it, Betsy and Tacy used to hum, "Dreaming, Dreaming." But Phil Brandish didn't know they were on earth. Big, obstreperous, noisy, he was usually with a crowd of boys. Once he brought a senior girl, alone. They sat in the auto with a big box of candy, watching the game from afar.

"The big stiff ought to go out for football," Cab said. "He doesn't care for a thing but that darn auto, takes it to pieces and puts it together again and crawls underneath it and lies there by the hour."

Cab himself was still on the scrub team, but he practised ardently.

It was the custom for spectators to watch the games from the sidelines, walking up and down the field to follow the play. They saw it as it is never seen from grandstands . . . the mud on the heroes' faces, the tears in the eyes of the boy sent out of the game, the grim concentration of the quarterback, calling signals hoarsely, the bottle of arnica, gore now and then.

Football was still puzzling to Betsy, but she enjoyed the excitement, the crisp air, the trees on the far horizon which, as the season progressed, changed from ruddy gold to russet and dry brown.

Betsy looked for Joe, but she never saw him. He worked every Saturday, football or no football. She remarked on this to Cab.

"Needs the filthy lucre, I suppose," Cab replied. "I know he likes football. Sometimes when we practise late, he drops by the field. Stewie lets him take a fling, and he's good. Darned good. Stewie'd give a lot to have him on the team. He told him so, the other night, and I thought Joe would be pleased. But he acted sort of superior about it. He said, 'Oh, I'll play in college!' And got away as quickly as he could."

"College!" said Betsy. "He's going to college!"

"Some people are gluttons for punishment," Cab replied.

This conversation proved so enlightening that Betsy sounded out Tony.

"Where does Joe Willard live?"

"With Mrs. Blair, a widow, at the north end of town. You know that little gray house, sort of under Agency Hill? My mother knows her, and she says Joe's all right. He doesn't want any mothering, though. He eats around at restaurants and he won't let Mrs. Blair give him a home-cooked meal, unless she'll let him pay her."

"I wonder why that is?"

"He's independent! But Mrs. Blair likes him. He pays his rent and keeps his room neat . . . except for books. It's all over apples and books, she says."

"He was eating an apple and reading a book the first I saw him," Betsy remarked.

"He loads up with books every night coming home from the Creamery. He just about lives at the library," Tony replied.

Betsy's heart warmed. She loved the library, too . . . the quiet, the smell of books, the fireplace in the Children's Room with a painting called "The Isle of Delos" over the mantle. And she loved Miss Sparrow, the small winsome librarian, with her curly untidy hair and merry eyes.

When Hallowe'en drew near Mrs. Ray told Betsy she might give a party, a costume party for boys and girls, and that same afternoon, after school, Betsy got out her library card.

"Isn't it late to be going to the library?" her mother asked.

"Oh, I just remembered something," Betsy replied off-handedly.

"Well, wear your heavy coat. It's turning cold."

"I will," said Betsy. She put on her red tam and mittens with her gray winter coat.

The warm well-lighted rooms were almost empty, and Miss Sparrow helped Betsy choose some books. She had known for years that Betsy planned to be a writer; they often talked about it. Tonight she suggested books by women writers . . . Jane Austen's *Pride and Prejudice*, *Wuthering Heights* by Emily Brontë.

"It will give you confidence to read them," Miss Sparrow said.

"I wish you'd give me a list of novels to read, Miss Sparrow."

"I'd love to."

"Novels that would help me learn to write."

"And you ought to read poetry, too. In fact, the poetry is more important now, in my opinion. You're at the age when poetry sinks in. . . ."

Joe Willard didn't come but Betsy didn't care. The trip had been well worth while. Smiling and full of plans, she swung out into a chilly twilight . . . and met Joe on the library steps.

Unceremoniously he seized her books and looked at the titles.

"I'm surprised," he said grinning. "I thought you'd be reading Robert W. Chambers."

"I read women writers. I think they're the best," Betsy said.

"Especially Elizabeth Warrington Ray, I suppose."

"Oh! Do you know her work? I thought it would be beyond you."

"I wade through it now and then." His blue eyes were gay above a blue woolen muffler tucked inside his coat. He handed back her books.

"Have you read these?" Betsy asked.

"Naturally. I've read everything."

"I'll bet you haven't read . . . *Hamlet*."

"Shakespeare in one volume. Take it off the parlor table and try it some time."

They were getting on famously when Betsy said with an abrupt change of tone, "Joe, I want to talk to you."

"No charge. Can I advise you about Gaston's peculiar methods?" He was still joking, but his tone had changed, too. He sounded wary.

"It's about our Crowd. We think you ought to . . . ought to . . . I mean, I want you to come to a party."

His friendly look faded.

"Thanks very much. I'm afraid I can't."

"But you don't even know when it is!" Betsy cried. "How do you know you can't come when I haven't even told you when it is?"

"I know. Thanks just the same."

"It's a Hallowe'en costume party."

"Fine, fine! Have a good time."

"Joe," said Betsy. "I think you belong with our Crowd. Everyone thinks so. And we do have the best times. We play around at each other's houses, and go to the Majestic and Heinz's together. . . ." She stopped, because his expression grew more and more hostile.

"Thanks a lot. Mind if I go now?"

"But why, why, don't you want to go with our Crowd?"

He looked trapped. After a brief pause he said, "It would just bore me, that's all."

Bore him! Betsy could hardly believe her ears. Imagine her beloved Crowd boring anyone!

Betsy didn't get angry easily; she almost never got angry. But she felt a hot flare of anger now.

"I see. I'm sorry I mentioned it."

Her tone was as cold as the wind which came sweeping down Broad Street across the library steps. It whipped at the blue muffler and pulled it loose. The muffler was so becoming, and Joe wore it with such a jaunty air, that Betsy wondered with irritation if he was going without an overcoat just to call attention to his muffler. Or maybe overcoats bored him, too.

"See you in Gaston's hangout," he said, and swaggered into the library, quickly, as though it were a refuge.

Betsy stood on the steps, and tears came into her eyes. Her feelings were mixed up. She felt hurt, humiliated, angry, and yet she was almost sorry for him . . . or would be, except that you just couldn't be sorry for Joe. He was so proud, so confident . . . it would be ridiculous.

"Bore him!" said Betsy, trying to whip up her anger, but it was fading fast.

That night she telephoned the Crowd about the

party. She told the girls that Joe Willard wouldn't come but she didn't tell anyone what he had said. She didn't want to make trouble for him . . . rude as he had been.

To Winona she said airily, "He *must* be a woman hater. He even hates me."

She couldn't settle down to study, and finally she went into Julia's room. Betsy wasn't much of a confider, but Julia's advice was invaluable sometimes.

Julia, who was buffing her nails, listened thoughtfully. After Betsy had finished she said, "I think you went at the thing wrong."

"But why? I was perfectly honest."

"Too honest."

"You can't be too honest."

Julia put down her buffer. She spoke slowly.

"Of course not. But it wouldn't have been dishonest, exactly, to have kept on talking, having fun. He'd have asked to walk home with you . . . it was getting dark. And maybe . . . who knows . . . Mamma would have kept him to supper? We had apple pie. And then we'd have asked him to Sunday night lunch, and he'd have fallen for Papa's sandwiches. And we'd have told him about the party, and started planning costumes. You could have asked him to plan one for you. The first thing he knew he'd *be* at your party, and smack in the midst of your Crowd."

"Julia," said Betsy. "You're wonderful. Why don't I know how to wangle things?"

"You'll learn."

"You didn't learn. You were born knowing how."

"Yes," said Julia, glancing up at Geraldine Farrar. "But even if you wouldn't do a thing like that instinctively as I would, you could figure it out. You're a writer. You could plan it out and do it."

Betsy was silent.

"About Joe! Wait a few days and try again, using a little finesse."

"No," Betsy interrupted firmly. "We bore him. He said so."

"Maybe he didn't mean that. Maybe he just can't afford to go with a crowd."

"Oh, fudge! We're not millionaires. Cab delivers papers; doesn't he? Tony drives a grocery wagon every summer! All of us have a terrible time managing on our allowances. No, we just bore him, like he said."

Julia didn't answer. She knew that tone . . . and look. There was no use trying to change Betsy when she was feeling stubborn.

Before Hallowe'en a curly-headed Irish boy named Dennis started going around with Cab. Cab brought him to the Ray house, and Betsy asked him to her party. And she asked a football hero named Al who had started going with Carney, and a boy nicknamed

Squirrelly who had a case on Irma.

The party was a great success, and soon the Crowd had plenty of boys.

But not one, Betsy thought sometimes, feeling hurt inside, was so nice as Joe Willard, who went his solitary way.

8

Rosy Apple Blossoms

BETSY ALWAYS HAD had the gift of getting along with people. She was like her father in that. Bob Ray had friends all up and down Front Street; he had friends all over the county. And everyone in high school liked Betsy . . . or had last year. Now, however, there was this new coolness between her and Joe Willard. She hated it, but she didn't know how to end it. Presently something even more antagonistic arose between Betsy and another person. And the person was no one less than Mr. Gaston, the rhetoric teacher.

He had liked her well enough last year. His recommendation had helped to give her the coveted chance to compete on the Essay Contest. But this year, he liked her less and less.

Mr. Gaston, as Julia had said, wished to be a science teacher. He did not enjoy teaching English. The only part of the subject that interested him was punctuation, paragraphing, spelling. He liked neat, factual papers.

Betsy punctuated and paragraphed better than most; her spelling was good, and her papers were neat. But alas, they were almost never factual! Betsy liked to invent, to create. She could not write even about Our System of Taxation without coloring it up a bit.

When at rare intervals . . . very rare, for Mr. Gaston, the scientist, disliked fiction . . . an original story was given as a class assignment, Betsy went into a delirium. She wrote and wrote, evolving hair raising plots, conjuring up romantic characters, describing Paris, Vienna, and other cities she had never seen. The class liked Betsy's stories, but the general approval only deepened Mr. Gaston's exasperation.

"Betsy, you have this miser hoarding a twenty-five

dollar gold piece and there is no such coin."

"Oh, well . . . I'll make it twenty dollars then."

But Mr. Gaston would not allow her to toss off the mistake. The story was returned with a red F for Fair, when Betsy felt fiercely sure that it was the best submitted. (Except for Joe Willard's, perhaps. He wrote good stories, too, and his gold pieces were always of a proper denomination.)

Seething, she mentioned the affair at supper.

"Really, Bob," exploded Mrs. Ray, "you ought to speak to the school board."

"Now, now, Jule! Remember you have red hair!"

"I am remembering. That's why I suggest something temperate like speaking to the school board." Mrs. Ray's blue eyes were snapping. "The very idea! Bothering Betsy about twenty-five dollar gold pieces. . . ."

"And commas," put in Margaret, remembering Betsy's most frequent complaint.

"It won't do Betsy any harm to learn about commas," Mr. Ray said. "I've noticed myself that she scatters them like grass seed."

"Who reads Shakespeare for the commas?"

"Maybe . . ." Mr. Ray's eyes twinkled. "I duck when I say it. You hold the carving knife, Margaret. . . . Maybe Betsy isn't quite in Shakespeare's class?"

That drew Julia into the fray.

"How do you know she isn't? Maybe this generation

is going to produce another Shakespeare, and maybe it's Betsy."

"It wouldn't surprise me a bit," interjected Mrs. Ray.

"What do you think, Margaret?"

Margaret looked grave. "Just who is Shakespeare, exactly?"

"*Ja,* who is this Shakespeare?" Anna burst through the swinging door. The argument had penetrated to the kitchen only faintly, but Anna knew that Betsy was being attacked.

"Who is he anyway?" she demanded, squaring her plump shoulders. "Does he ever come here? Well, he'd better not."

"He's dead," Julia said.

Anna was dashed, but only for a moment.

"Small loss, probably. If anyone picks on you, Betsy, lovey, you know who to come to. I always said the same to the McCloskey girls." She returned to the kitchen, breathing heavily.

Everyone laughed, and Julia began to tell about Miss Bangeter's Shakespeare class.

This was an institution at Deep Valley High School. It was a class of which the whole school spoke with reverence. It was open only to seniors, and was almost of college level, other teachers said. They eavesdropped when they could, on Miss Bangeter's reading of the plays.

"You'll adore it, Bettina," Julia said. "Just now we're studying *As You Like It*. How I'd love to play Rosalind!"

She read the play to Betsy that evening, and after that Betsy read all the plays right along with Julia. Julia passed on Miss Bangeter's explanations, her comments, her enthusiasm, and Betsy took to experiments in blank verse. Tacy thought they were wonderful.

"Better not show them to Gaston though," she added cautiously.

"I know. He'd think I was conceited. But I'm not. Am I, Tacy?"

"Of course not!"

"I just happen to be able to write, like Julia can sing, and Carney can sew, and Gaston . . . probably . . . can cut up frogs."

"Cutting up frogs is all he's good for."

"If there's anything I'm not, it's conceited," Betsy declared. But Mr. Gaston continued to think that she was. He thought it all the more after November Rhetoricals.

Rhetoricals were programs which the two literary societies presented in alternate months. In November it was the Zetamathians' turn, and early in the month Miss Clarke asked Julia and Betsy to drop into her room after school. Miss Clarke had long leaned on Julia in preparing the Zetamathian Rhetoricals. Julia loved to oblige with a solo, or to play the piano, or to act in a skit. And Betsy last year had sung the "Cat Duet" with Tacy . . . and had read an original paper.

"My two Rays!" Miss Clarke said happily when Julia and Betsy came in. She was a pretty woman with soft dark hair, soft white skin, and soft eyes behind round glasses which emphasized her gentle guilelessness. Her manner in class was timid and appealing, but out of class she had an innocent girlish gaiety which beamed in her eyes now.

"I've been thinking," she said, "how sad it is that Julia is going to graduate! Of course, I have Betsy coming along, but this is the last year I'll have you both. I've been wondering what you could do for Rhetoricals *together*."

"A duet?" asked Julia hopefully.

Miss Clarke shook her head.

"Betsy's going to repeat that 'Cat Duet' with Tacy on one of the programs this year. No, I have a better idea. A really marvelous one. I want Betsy to write a song which you can sing."

"Not the music!" cried Betsy, alarmed.

"Oh, no, dear! We'll take the music of some popular song. I'd thought of that 'Same Old Story' everybody's singing."

"Just new words? That's a cinch!"

"Listen to her!" Miss Clarke turned to Julia. "I suppose she could do it overnight?"

"Why, yes," said Betsy. She was surprised at such a to-do about something so easy. Julia was delighted with the plan, so Betsy went home and wrote new words for "Same Old Story."

When November Rhetoricals came, Miss Clarke introduced the number with a little speech about the Rays. She told about Betsy's writing the words and the school began to clap. Mr. Gaston, sitting on the platform, folded his arms and looked sardonic. Then Carney sat down at the piano, Julia came to the platform, and everyone clapped again.

Julia had dressed her hair with a long curl over her shoulder. And since this song definitely wasn't grand opera, she dropped all her grand opera airs. She sang like a musical comedy soubrette, sauntering along the platform, with a special smile or toss of her head to end each verse.

There were verses about the Freshman Girl, the Sophomore Girl, the Junior Girl and the Senior Girl, and after each verse the same refrain:

> "Same old story,
> Same old High,
> Same old bunch of gigglers
> As the years pass by.

She's a hummer,
A shining light,
For she's Deep Valley's High School Girl
And she's all right."

At the end of the last chorus there was such a clamor of applause that Carney began to repeat. Julia, with true instinct, opened her arms.

"Everybody sing!" she cried, and everybody sang, even Miss Bangeter. Everybody, that is, except Mr. Gaston. He kept his arms folded and looked unpleasant while the assembly room rang.

"Same old story,
Same old High,
Same old bunch of gigglers
As the years pass by . . ."

It was sung over and over. After school it was hummed in the cloak rooms, in the halls, and along High Street. Miss Clarke was triumphant, and Julia and Betsy were decidedly pleased with themselves.

But Betsy stopped being pleased next morning in rhetoric class.

When she came into the room, Mr. Gaston looked up with a smile dangerously bland. It followed her while she went to her desk and sat down.

"We feel fortunate to have a poetess in our midst," Mr. Gaston said, and Betsy blushed. Everyone laughed, but almost no one laughed at his next joke.

"When we come to the study of poetry, perhaps I'd better step down and let Betsy take the chair."

He stacked the attendance cards and grinned maliciously.

"It was reassuring to hear that the Deep Valley High School girl is such a fine specimen," he said.

Betsy was furious, but not so furious as Tacy who fixed him with indignant bright blue eyes. Cab and Tony scowled, Dennie, the new boy in the Crowd, pulled at his curly hair and looked uneasy. Joe Willard, Betsy saw, was gazing out of the window.

Betsy did not enliven the supper table with this encounter. She had decided, wisely, to keep her troubles to herself. But she argued mentally with Mr. Gaston all through the evening, and after she had gone to bed.

"I never claimed it was great poetry." "It was meant to be *funny*." "I'd like to hear what kind of verses *you'd* write!" And so on, into the night.

The next day, however, Mr. Gaston was unusually affable. "Ashamed of himself, probably," Tacy whispered. Betsy struggled faithfully to keep her rhetoric papers as dull as possible and things went smoothly for a while. But then Mr. Gaston assigned another short story. That was her downfall.

He assigned it, of course, only because the schedule required it.

"Any subject . . . any subject you like," he said, waving his hands to express contempt. "Try not to be too flowery."

This, Betsy realized, was probably aimed at her, but she was too pleased to worry. She planned out her story walking home.

It was a sunless afternoon. The look of the world spelled the word November.

"I'm going to put my story in the spring," she thought. "That's what's so nice about writing. You can go into any season you want to."

Her story was about a band of gypsies who stole a child, and before she began Betsy closed her eyes a minute and thought about spring. She thought about the apple orchard behind the Hill Street house, and saw blossoms swaying against a vivid sky. Then she wrote her opening sentence.

"Under a tree hung with rosy apple blossoms, an infant boy was sleeping."

The stories were collected next day. The following day, before returning them, Mr. Gaston faced the class.

"I asked you," he said, "as a special favor, not to be too flowery. But our poetess . . ." Betsy squirmed and blushed . . . "is not only flowery. Her flowers are the wrong color. I haven't read your story, Betsy, and

441

I don't intend to. The opening sentence is enough for me." He read aloud scornfully:

"Under a tree hung with rosy apple blossoms . . ."

He laid down the paper.

"Rosy apple blossoms! Rosy apple blossoms! Whoever heard of rosy apple blossoms? Apple blossoms, my dear young lady, aren't pink. They are white."

Betsy's blushes receded. She turned, in fact, a little pale.

"I think they are pink, Mr. Gaston."

"You *think* they are pink?" Mr. Gaston glared at her through his thick glasses. "But I *know* they are white."

"It's the under part of the petals," Betsy said falteringly. "They're pinkish, sort of."

"Pinkish, sort of!" Mr. Gaston mocked.

Betsy looked around, a little wildly. Joe Willard was staring out of the window. She brought her gaze back to Mr. Gaston stubbornly.

"We had lots of apple trees when we lived up on Hill Street. I always liked to look at them in May."

"You should have examined them accurately. You would have found that they are white."

"But they weren't white." Betsy was near to tears, but it was from anger.

"They must have been peach trees," Mr. Gaston said.

"They were apples. I've eaten the apples."

"Betsy," said Mr. Gaston, with a maddening, condescending smile. "If you were a little younger, I'd ask you to write a hundred times, 'Apple blossoms are white.' As it is I merely ask you to rewrite your story, and eliminate any inaccuracies."

He picked up another paper.

But the subject was not quite done with. Joe Willard turned from his study of the trees beyond the window and raised his hand.

"Yes, Joe?" Mr. Gaston said, changing his tone.

"It is my opinion sir, that apple blossoms are pink."

Mr. Gaston was silent, stunned.

"Pinkish, rather," Joe continued. "I think Betsy's word 'rosy' is excellent. They're colored just enough to make the effect rosy."

The silence in the room had width, height, depth, mass and substance.

Then Mr. Gaston found his voice, a particularly acid voice.

"Very interesting. But we can't let this turn into a botany class. Tacy, your story is mediocre, but it is at least short, blessedly short."

After class Betsy brushed past marching pupils to go up to Joe. He was wearing the odd coat and trousers and a distant triumphant smile.

"Joe," said Betsy. It was the first time she had addressed him since he told her that her Crowd bored him. "Joe, that was nice of you to speak up about the apple blossoms. I . . . I appreciate it."

The smile left his face.

"It was just simple justice. Nothing personal in it. I'd have done it for anyone," he replied coldly, looking her coldly in the eye.

9

Washington, Lincoln, and Jefferson

THE FIRST SNOW CAME, dramatic as always. One day, unexpectedly, it appeared in the air. Children all over Deep Valley held up their hands to catch the flakes on their mittens, and shouted and raced with delight.

Presently the gray-brown world was covered with feathery white. Boys and girls, walking home from high school, pelted one another with snowballs. Margaret came out with her sled.

She slid with dignity, small skirts spread tidily, her back straight as a ramrod, down to the watering trough. Hugh joined her, and pulled her up the slope so that she could slide down again. He was morose. He had dropped in on Julia, who had said she was busy, giving a lesson to Tacy. Hugh thought it was just another excuse for getting rid of him. But as a matter of fact Julia actually was giving Tacy singing lessons.

Tacy's voice was true and sweet. It was like an Irish harp with plaintive questioning and joy and sadness in it. And Tacy loved to sing. She was so shy that she could not imagine singing in front of the whole school, alone, as Julia did. But standing beside the Ray piano, with Julia whom she had known all her life, she poured out her heart in song.

Julia passed on to Tacy readily all Mrs. Poppy had taught her. "I use Mrs. Poppy's method," Julia liked to say importantly. She was all seriousness during the lesson, and even Betsy was barred from the room.

Julia was busy with the many and lofty activities of seniors, with the choir, and her singing lessons. But presently she grew busier still, for the Episcopalian ladies, wanting to raise money for new hymnals, decided to put on a home talent play. *Wonderland* was its name. It was to be given in the Opera House, and Julia was asked to play the leading part, the princess.

Betsy's crowd of girls was in the chorus. They were to dance a Scarf Dance. Through November the entries in Betsy's journal were all about *Wonderland*: "Rehearsal for *Wonderland*." "Homework and *Wonderland*." "Practised the Scarf Dance for hours. My feet are killing me." Then they began to read, "*Wonderland* and Harry." The references to Harry which followed almost every night thereafter indicated, however, only Betsy's interest in her sister's affairs. It was Julia's life into which Harry had entered.

Harry was playing the part of the prince, and he was not a high school boy. He had been graduated from the High School some years since, had attended the state university for a year, and had now returned to work in his father's bank. He was old. He was so old that he wore a mustache. He was a large self-assured young man, a trifle condescending to the town girls.

He was graciously condescending to Julia at the first rehearsal, where it was discovered that they shared a duet and several love scenes. But they walked home from the second rehearsal, and after that he wasn't condescending any more.

"Same old story," Betsy hummed mischievously when, after the third rehearsal Harry and Julia broke away from the group saying that they were going downtown for a snack. Harry had taken Julia's arm

possessively, and in his eyes was a look her sister knew well.

He started coming to the Rays' regularly. He brought Julia flowers and candy. He brought her the score of *The Red Mill*, and he and Julia sang a duet from it:

> "Not *that you are fair, dear*
> Not *that you are true . . ."*

He lifted his eyebrows and puffed out his chest. He quite eclipsed poor Hugh.

But Hugh did not give up easily. In the show window of a hardware store on Front Street some Spitz puppies were being exhibited. Julia took Margaret down to see them and Hugh, making one of his forlorn unwanted calls, heard their enthusiastic descriptions. Late the next afternoon he appeared with one of the puppies under his coat, and presented it to Margaret . . . a delightful little fellow with soft white fur hanging almost to the floor, and a shiny black nose like patent leather.

This gift seemed at first a masterstroke. Julia went into ecstasies more extravagant even than Margaret's. Although the puppy was as white as snow, she gave him a bath and dried him in towels before the dining room fire. She rummaged through her ribbon box for blue and cherry-colored ribbons which she tied into his collar.

"I'll name him Lincoln. It goes so well with Washington. Don't you think so?" Margaret asked.

"Lincoln's sort of hard to say. We could call him Abie, though," Betsy volunteered.

"You're our sweet precious little Abie," Julia cooed, and Hugh looked sheepishly triumphant.

Harry dropped in that night and he wasn't too pleased with Abie. He said that Spitz dogs shed their long white hairs in a most annoying way.

"You won't like it, Mrs. Ray. They have bad dispositions, too, I understand."

After Harry was gone, Mr. Ray looked down at Washington which Julia's last year's beau had given to Margaret, and at Hugh's gift of Abraham Lincoln. They were sleeping peacefully, one on Margaret's lap and one on Julia's. Mr. Ray shook his head and chuckled.

"When will Jefferson appear, and what will he be? White mice? A canary? We'll have a menagerie, Julia, if this keeps up."

Julia's soft white fingers rubbed Abie between the ears. She merely smiled.

Hugh soon discovered that although Julia was so fond of Abie she was no fonder of him than she ever had been. And Harry had an enormous advantage.

Because of the *Wonderland* rehearsals he was with Julia almost daily, and they joked about their love scenes, but they worked hard on the duets. Julia saw to that.

There was a dress rehearsal in which everything that could possibly go wrong went wrong, but by the next evening all had miraculously straightened itself out. The house was packed even to the boxes. The boys in Betsy's Crowd sat in the topmost gallery . . . the peanut gallery it was called . . . and they cheered and whooped when the Scarf Dance was executed flawlessly.

Julia's solo was a glorious success, and at its conclusion the usher presented her with two bouquets: pink roses from Hugh and red ones from Harry. Julia cradled them impartially, one in each arm, while she smiled and bowed. But when she appeared in the next scene she had a red rose in her hair.

Soon after this the evening paper announced that an actress named Rose Stahl would come to Deep Valley in a Broadway success called *The Chorus Lady*. Immediately after supper the telephone rang. It was Anna's night out and Julia, Betsy, and Margaret were doing the dishes, Julia washing, Betsy wiping, Margaret putting the dishes away.

Margaret answered the telephone.

"It's for you, Julia," she said. "It's Hugh."

Julia dried her hands and sat down at the phone in a niche beside the cellar door. In a big checked cover-all apron of Anna's, she looked absurdly small. But the poise of her dark head on her slender smooth white neck was alert and resolute.

Listening with interest, Betsy and Margaret heard her say:

"Umm . . . I can't hear you, Hugh." She touched the receiver hook gently and pushed it up and down. "I hear such a queer sound. What *can* be the matter?"

In a moment she said, "The phone must be out of order. You'd better call me back." And she put the receiver into the hook and began to laugh.

"Hugh said there was nothing wrong with this phone except that I was wiggling the hook."

"Well," replied Betsy, "you were."

"Of course I was." Julia was busy cranking to make a call of her own. "He was asking me to go to *The Chorus Lady*. I don't want to accept if Harry is planning to ask me."

"What under the sun are you doing?" Betsy cried. "You can't *ask* Harry whether he's going to ask you."

"No," agreed Julia. "But I can give him a chance."

And in a moment Betsy and Margaret, watching with fascinated eyes, heard her say sweetly, "Harry, what was that song you wanted me to learn? Was it 'Rose in the Garden'? I'm ordering some music and

I just wasn't sure . . ."

There was a silence followed by some unrevealing murmurs. Then Julia cried with a rising inflection, "Really? Why, I'd love to!" There were more unrevealing murmurs, and she said good-by.

But before she could rise from her chair the phone rang again, angrily. Betsy and Margaret stood transfixed. Julia's voice was sweet as honey.

"Yes, Hugh, I hear you perfectly now. What *could* have been the matter? Rose Stahl in *The Chorus Lady?* I'm so sorry. I've accepted another invitation."

She put the receiver on the hook once more and came briskly back to the dishpan.

"Julia," said Betsy. "I don't see how you can be so mean to poor Hugh."

"When he gave us Abie, too!" cried Margaret. She straightened into what Julia and Betsy called her Persian princess air. "I wish I was older. *I'd* go with Hugh to see the show," she said and walked haughtily out of the kitchen.

Betsy too saw *The Chorus Lady.* She went with Winona, Irma, Carney, Alice, and Tacy. Winona could not get passes for so many so they sat in the peanut gallery taking plenty of peanuts and Miss Clarke as chaperone. The boys in the Crowd appeared in a body and after the play they all went to Heinz's, and Miss Clarke had more chaperoning to do than she had bargained for. She took off her glasses and polished them until she almost wore them out.

Harry didn't bring Julia to Heinz's. He scorned this resort of the high school crowd. He took her instead to the Moorish Café, for an oyster stew, an expedition which had two unfortunate results.

In the first place Mr. Ray was displeased.

"She's only a school girl," he protested to Mrs. Ray.

"But it's such a lovely place. And he is such a fine young man," Mrs. Ray replied. "And he asked Mrs. Poppy to join them, so Julia would have a chaperone."

Mr. Ray grumbled, unconvinced. "No judgment! Just what you'd expect from a Democrat!" Mr. Ray was a Republican.

Julia, however, was so dazzled by oyster stew at the Moorish Café, that she broke off with Hugh completely. When he dropped in the next day she remarked that she thought Rose Stahl was as great as Sarah Bernhardt. Hugh protested mildly, and Julia retorted with such provocative fire that before Hugh knew exactly what had happened he was out on the steps going home. He and Julia had quarreled, irrevocably.

"And I don't give two cents for Sarah Bernhardt! I never saw the woman!" he wailed to Betsy, who was full of pity as she always was for Julia's discarded beaus. Margaret was cross with Julia. She wore her Persian princess manner steadily for a week.

Harry was aware that Margaret did not like him. He started bringing her gum drops and picture books.

"How would you like some gold fish?" he asked her one night, and Mr. Ray choked over his cigar so violently that he had to go out to the porch and cough. He returned with dewy, twinkling eyes.

"Harry," he remarked soberly, "I know that you're a rising young Democrat. I wonder whether you've given any thought to Thomas Jefferson."

"Why, sir," said Harry, flattered, "I can't say I ever did."

"I advise you to," said Mr. Ray. "I advise you to consider him seriously."

"Papa," said Julia next morning at breakfast, "that was really too bad of you. He might have caught on."

"I wish he had, the store window dummy!" Mr. Ray said. "Moorish Café, indeed!"

The days slipped along to Thanksgiving. Tom came home, and that meant parties. Carney, Irma, and Winona all gave parties, and Tony took Betsy to Winona's, while both he and Cab accompanied her to Irma's. But Betsy wasn't satisfied. With Julia's great conquest so fresh in her mind, she was very dissatisfied indeed.

"Tony's just . . . Tony," she said to Tacy. "And Cab . . .

well, Cab couldn't very well take Irma to her own party. I wish I were more popular with boys."

"Why, Betsy!" cried Tacy. "Your house is always full of boys."

"We feed them," said Betsy glumly.

"It isn't that. They like you."

"Exactly." Betsy was bitter. "They like me so well they slap me on the back. I wish I could be different, suddenly. I wish I could change overnight. Walk into the high school tomorrow just utterly different, so that the boys would be struck dumb . . . even Phil Brandish."

"*Drea-ee-eaming,*" trilled Tacy, and she and Betsy began to laugh. But Betsy grew gloomy again.

"Just wait," she said, "I'll go away some day, and come back all changed like that girl in *The Conquest of Canaan*, languid sort of, and wearing a slinky Paris gown."

"You won't be half so nice as you are right now," said Tacy, who didn't like to hear Betsy criticized even by Betsy herself.

The Rays had Thanksgiving dinner with the Slades this year. The families entertained each other at Thanksgiving, turn and turn about. The dinner was magnificent, as usual, and after it was finished, the grown people napped, Margaret went roller skating, Harry took Julia to the Majestic, and Tom and Betsy went for a walk. Betsy was pleased to go walking with Tom who looked distinguished in his Cox School uniform. They set off across the slough.

They had reached a street which curved up toward the rambling Brandish mansion when a deep horn boomed, and a bright red automobile slowed to a stop beside them.

"Hello," Phil Brandish said.

Betsy was so excited that she almost choked.

"Ah," said Tom. "Greetings and salutations!" This was an expression he had brought home from Cox.

"Want a lift?" Phil Brandish asked.

"No, thanks," said Tom to Betsy's disappointment.

She hoped frantically that her hat was on straight, that her nose was not red from the wind. But Phil Brandish was not looking at her. He was looking at Tom's uniform.

"Still in jail, I see," he said.

It seemed to Betsy that he was trying in a heavy inept way to make a joke. But Tom did not take it so.

"Jail, heck!" said Tom. "It's the finest school in the country. And it isn't mourning your departure either."

He scowled and took Betsy's arm.

Phil Brandish looked at her then, but absently. His eyes were yellowish brown. He was big, bigger than Tom, and notably well dressed. His felt hat had a crease down the middle; his overcoat was of rich dark wool, well cut; a checked muffler was folded with care.

"What's biting you?" he said to Tom. "I didn't mean anything."

"Neither did I. So long," said Tom. He and Betsy moved away, and the red auto whizzed away too like an angry hornet.

"He gets my goat," confided Tom. "He means all right, I guess, but he didn't fit in at Cox."

"He doesn't here either, exactly," Betsy said.

"I don't believe he knows how." Tom sounded puzzled. "He's always had too much money. He's traveled with his folks all around the world, gone to one school after another, had things handed to him on a platter."

"Cab says all he cares about is that auto."

"He was nuts about machinery at Cox," Tom replied.

They walked all the way to Page Park, and when they returned it was growing dark. Young and old gathered cozily around the Slade fire, where apples and cider were set out, and Tom's grandmother told stories. She was a very old lady, wizened and small, with thin white hair and sunken lips. She could remember Indians going on the warpath in the valley.

Betsy loved to listen to Grandma Slade's stories, but when the Rays were walking home her thoughts returned to Phil. She was irritated that he had paid so little attention to her. He would have paid attention to Julia.

"I wish I could go away," thought Betsy, harking back to her talk with Tacy. "It isn't practical just to wake up in the morning different. But if I could go away I'd come back so fascinating, so mysterious, Phil Brandish would *have* to look at me."

She planned all the way home and while she wound her hair on Magic Wavers, and after she went to bed, about going away and coming back different, a sirenlike woman of the world.

10

A Letter from Mrs. Muller

BETSY DREAMED ABOUT going away from Deep Valley, but she didn't for a moment suspect that around a bend in her Winding Hall of Fate a journey was actually waiting.

The day she reached that noteworthy bend everything began just as usual. She brought Tacy in after school, which was entirely usual. As usual she dropped her books on the music room table while she shouted for her mother . . . not that she wanted her for anything in particular . . . and when Mrs. Ray answered from upstairs, Betsy and Tacy went out to the kitchen to see what there was to eat.

"Fresh molasses cookies, lovey," Anna said. They heard Mrs. Ray's high heels on the stairs and just as they dipped their hands in the cookie jar Mrs. Ray came into the kitchen.

"Betsy," she said, "you have a letter from Mrs. Muller. I hope it doesn't mean that Tib is sick."

Betsy took the letter quickly, and while she tore it open Mrs. Ray and Tacy waited without speaking. Both of them were very fond of Tib, who for so many years had made the team of Betsy and Tacy a threesome. Betsy unfolded the sheet of creamy white stationery and her face was swept by a smile so amazed and delighted that Mrs. Ray and Tacy were as mystified as they were relieved.

"Mamma!" Betsy cried, "Mrs. Muller wants me to come to Milwaukee for Christmas!"

"Why . . . why . . . what an idea!"

"Do you think I can go?"

"You'll have to ask Papa. What does she say?"

Betsy handed the letter to her mother and threw her arms around Tacy. They danced and squealed.

"Don't get too excited," Mrs. Ray advised, "until you know whether you can go. It's a long trip for you to make all alone. Expensive, too."

Betsy and Tacy took their cookies into the front parlor, where they studied Mrs. Muller's letter. It was brief and concise but it produced an hour or more of uninterrupted conversation.

"Imagine," cried Tacy, "seeing Tib again!"

"And Tacy, I'll see Aunt Dolly!" Tib's Aunt Dolly had visited the Mullers in Deep Valley. She was a doll-like blonde, and Betsy and Tacy had always thought her the most beautiful creature in the world.

"I wonder whether she's as pretty as she used to be."

"Prettier, probably. She's engaged, you know."

"Do you remember her lovely clothes?"

"Do I!"

Julia came in and Betsy and Tacy fell upon her with the magnificent news. Margaret came in and was staggered by it. At last Tacy had to go home, but Betsy promised to telephone her the first thing after supper. She accompanied her out to the porch, and paused there in the twilight, shivering.

"Tacy," she said, "do you realize what this is? It's the chance I've been waiting for."

"Piffle!" said Tacy, and shook her.

"I'll come back completely changed."

"You won't be half as nice."

"Won't you have some tea, Lady Glexter-Glexton?" Betsy drawled in a languid voice. "Celeste, my smelling salts, please!"

Tacy tried to throw her off the porch into the wait-ing drifts. Betsy struggled, shrieking. She freed herself and ran into the house. There she embraced her mother.

"Oh, I hope . . . I hope . . . I hope I can go!"

"Don't get your heart too set on it, Betsy," Mrs. Ray warned. "You know what big expenses Papa has. Three girls, and this big house. You'd need some new clothes, too."

"I know. If I can't go, it's all right," Betsy said.

She went upstairs and tried to do homework, but her head was whirling. She turned out the gas and went to the window, looked out over the purpling snow. She imagined the lighted train, like a glittering serpent, winding its way to far-off Milwaukee.

"I'd have to eat on the diner!" she thought.

It was a family custom not to broach any new im-portant matter to Mr. Ray until he had had his supper.

"No man, not even an angel like your father, likes to decide things on an empty stomach," Mrs. Ray of-ten said.

But by the time Anna had brought in warm apple sauce and the fresh molasses cookies, Mr. Ray no-ticed the excitement in Betsy's face.

"What have you got up your sleeve, Betsy?" he asked. "I can see there's something."

"It's not up my sleeve," said Betsy, reaching into

the "V" of her dress and drawing out Mrs. Muller's letter. Smiling broadly she handed it to him.

Mr. Ray read it very slowly. In fact he read it over twice. But that, Betsy felt sure, was only to give him time to turn the matter over in his mind.

"Do you want to go?" he asked then, looking up.

Betsy tried to restrain her smile. She tried to draw it in, to look sober.

"I'd love to go," she said, "if you think we can afford it. But if we can't, it's perfectly all right."

"I wasn't thinking about that," Mr. Ray answered. "I was thinking about your being away from home on Christmas. We have a pretty good time right here."

"I know," said Betsy. But she locked out of her mind the picture of her family on Christmas Eve, trimming the tree, filling the stockings, singing carols and reading from *The Night Before Christmas* and Dickens' *Christmas Carol* and the Gospel according to St. Luke. If she let herself think about this she might not go . . . she might miss the ecstatic experience of visiting Tib in Milwaukee. "I don't think I'd be homesick though," she went on, hastily.

"It would seem pretty funny . . ." Mr. Ray began, and then he stopped and thought awhile. "It would be quite an experience, Betsy," he went on, "to have Christmas in a city like Milwaukee. I've been in Milwaukee. It's so German that it's like a foreign city, and the Germans make a lot of Christmas." He looked across the table at Mrs. Ray and his brow furrowed slightly. "Really, Jule," he said, "for a girl who wants to be a writer, it might be educational to spend Christmas in Milwaukee."

"But can we afford it, Bob?" Mrs. Ray asked. "I think Betsy is quite old enough and responsible enough to make the trip alone. But she'd need some new clothes, and we all know how many expenses you have."

"Never mind about that," said Mr. Ray. "I think she ought to go. Julia went with you to California to visit your mother. It's Betsy's turn to have a trip. Next, we'll send Margaret to Timbucktoo."

The worried look left his face and he began to act happy.

"I want you to get a lot out of this trip, Betsy," he said. "I think it would be a good idea to learn a little about Milwaukee before you go. It was built by Germans, mostly . . . Germans and Austrians and Bohemians and Poles . . . who didn't like old country ways. They had the good sense to come to America.

"The Germans brought a lot of Germany with them, but it was mostly the good part. Singing societies, and coffee cake, and Christmas trees." He got up and went around the table to squeeze Betsy's shoulders.

"Well, well, just imagine!" he said, "Betsy's going off to leave us! She's going to spend Christmas in Milwaukee."

Anna came into the doorway to say that the McCloskeys often went to Milwaukee. It was a tony city, she said.

Mrs. Ray said she would try to get Miss Mix, the dressmaker; they would start sewing at once.

Betsy ran to telephone Tacy, and the Ray family sat in the parlor and talked excitedly about Milwaukee for a long time.

Betsy was exultantly, rapturously happy, and when Betsy was happy, Mrs. Ray often said, she was happier than anyone else in the world. But after she went upstairs to study she began to feel a little queer inside. She remembered how homesick she had been when she visited the Taggarts.

"Tib's different from the Taggarts though, and I'm more than a year older."

Christmas thoughts tried to push their way into her mind. Every year since they were small children she and Tacy had gone Christmas shopping together. They always visited every store in town and each of them always bought just one thing, the same thing every year, a Christmas tree ornament.

"We can go shopping this year, of course. I won't be here though to see the new ornament on the tree."

But Betsy forced back these thoughts with that stubbornness she had in her nature.

"I'm going to go! This is my chance. Maybe I can't change much in two weeks, but I can change a little. Anyway I won't miss a wonderful thing like this, having Christmas with Tib in Milwaukee."

She put on her night gown, and wound her hair on Wavers and rubbed into her face a wonderful new cream she had seen advertised in the magazines. It was supposed to make one's skin as radiant as rose petals.

"I hope it will work by the time I go to Milwaukee," she thought, looking into the mirror wistfully.

Betsy used more creams, lotions, and curlers than most of her friends. Carney and Tacy never used them at all and were very scornful of them. Betsy joked about her beauty aids, but in private she didn't think them funny.

She longed with her whole heart to be pretty, and if . . . as Julia and Tacy insisted . . . she was pretty already, she longed to be prettier still. The heroines in her stories were always beautiful. Some author's heroines were plain but attractive; they had tip-tilted noses, or freckles, or other flaws. Betsy's heroines were perfect, golden-haired and rosy or raven-haired with white magnolia skin. Betsy always made them look just as she wished to look herself.

The rest of December went by on wings. Word of Betsy Ray's holiday visit to Milwaukee spread through the school, and Betsy found herself flatteringly marked out for attention.

Her father bought the tickets. She would leave at eight o'clock in the morning and arrive in Milwaukee at nine twenty-five that night. She would ride in a parlor car, and have two meals in the diner. She would leave on the twenty-first of December.

"I know," said Cab, "you're trying to get away from mistletoe, but you can't do it, Miss Ray."

"Not much," said Tony, looking wicked. "Just when does that train leave?"

"Heaven preserve us!!!" Betsy wrote in her journal. "The boys are coming down to see me off and bring mistletoe to kiss me good-by. Horror of horrors!!!"

The days grew busier and busier. Miss Mix was in the house making a new party dress for Betsy. It was a pink silk with white daisies in it, and with it Betsy would wear a wreath of daisies in her hair. And Miss Mix was making a red and green sailor suit for traveling. Betsy and her mother went downtown and bought a red hat. It was big with a stiff wired bow across the back.

"It will match your red velveteen dress, as well as this one," Mrs. Ray planned.

Mrs. Ray acted like the general of an army. She

shopped, mended, pressed. And Anna, a loyal lieu-
tenant, washed and ironed until all Betsy's clothes
were the pink of perfection.

"If only I could put Julia in my trunk and take her
along to do my hair," Betsy said.

The trunk stood open in Betsy's room, and slowly
it was being filled . . . not only with clothes. The
Crowd brought tissue-wrapped bundles to put in it.
And Betsy had to buy or make Christmas presents to
take along, as well as to leave behind.

It was strange to see home preparations for Christmas going forward. Anna was making fruit cake,
plum pudding and mince meat. Betsy would not be
there to eat them. Her mother was dressing a doll for
Margaret. It was a yellow-haired doll with a red silk
dress trimmed with black lace and insertion. Betsy
would not be there to see Margaret's delight.

Holly wreaths went up in the windows. Washington and Abie received red and green bows. The house
was ready for holiday parties. Betsy would not be
there to share in the fun.

Closets and drawers were full of packages at which
other people were warned not to look. These would
be stuffed in the stockings on Christmas Eve. But
Betsy's stocking would be hung in Milwaukee, if it
were hung at all.

"I don't believe the Mullers hang stockings. They

just have a Christmas tree," Betsy remembered.

The choir was busy rehearsing Christmas music. Betsy would not be there on Christmas morning to sing in a joyful, pine-scented church.

But she took part in the school Christmas program. It was given on Friday, the day before she left. She and Julia and Tacy sang a trio, a musical setting of Tennyson's poem:

> "Ring out, wild bells, to the wild sky,
> The flying clouds, the frosty light:
> The year is dying in the night;
> Ring out wild bells, and let him die.
>
> Ring out the old, ring in the new . . ."

Betsy was proud of Tacy that afternoon. Standing between the two Rays she was not frightened, and her voice rang out so sweetly that people spoke of it afterwards.

"You must sing a solo at Rhetoricals, sometime," Miss Clarke said.

"Oh, no," Tacy began, but Julia cut in,

"Certainly she will. In the Spring, Miss Clarke. I'll help her get it ready."

That afternoon Betsy and Tacy delivered Betsy's Christmas presents. It was a pleasant day with sunshine sparkling on the snow and afterward they went on their annual Christmas-shopping expedition.

"We're not going to be cheated out of that," Tacy had said, and Betsy had laughingly agreed.

But now she didn't have the proper feeling. Not the decorated windows, nor the tinkling sleighbells, nor Tacy's arm hooked happily into hers bred the giddy mood in which one could shop gaily for everything from diamonds to bon bons and finally buy only a Christmas tree ornament.

The nearer she came to the moment of departure for Milwaukee the nearer Betsy came to homesickness. She still wanted to go more than she wanted not to go, but she wanted to go less and less.

Tacy sensed that Betsy's spirits were low and tried to cheer her up by acting nonsensical. She drew her to a stop before a toyshop window. It was such a window as they used to gaze at entranced, with jacks-in-the-box, teddy bears, and dolls of every description.

"Now let's choose," Tacy said, speaking in a childish sing-song. "Which one do you want Santa Claus to bring you? I want that big one in the pink dress."

Footsteps behind them stopped and Betsy knew that someone had paused. But she followed Tacy's lead.

"Let me see," she said in baby talk, pointing. "I think I'd like *that* one, and a buggy to take her riding in."

"Oh, no!" cried Tacy. "*I* want that one."

"You can't have it. I saw it first."

"You did not."

"I did so."

As they wrangled Betsy turned her head, and saw a tall boy directly behind them. She looked into the puzzled yellow brown eyes of Phil Brandish.

Aghast, Betsy squeezed Tacy's hand, but Tacy thought it came only from affection and kept on talking. Betsy extended her foot in its sturdy overshoe and brought it down on Tacy's foot, hard.

"Ouch! What the dickens . . ." Tacy exclaimed. She usually caught on quickly but now she had to be nudged in the ribs before she, too, looked around. Phil Brandish, averting his eyes, walked on.

"Tacy!" Betsy wailed. "How perfectly awful!"

"And I got you into it!"

"I'll never get a ride in that red auto now."

They were between laughing and crying. So they went to Heinz's for the consolation of hot chocolate. There laughter triumphed. They laughed so hard thinking what idiots they must have seemed to Phil . . . Philip the Great, Tacy called him . . . that Betsy forgot all her lonesome feelings.

Numbers of boys and girls dropped in at the Ray house that night. Almost the whole Crowd came. Someone wanted to sing Christmas carols but Julia tactfully refrained. She knew what sort of thing made people homesick. Instead she played the newest popular songs.

> *"Baby dear, listen here,*
> *I'm afraid to go home in the dark . . ."*

Tony and Winona clowned through that one. And Carney and Irma, the newly weds, sang in harmony:

> *"I would, if I could, but I can't,*
> *Because I'm ma-a-a-r-r-ied now."*

Again Betsy's laughter kept away tears.

There was something eerie and unnatural about the next morning. The Rays were up and about while it was still dark. Even Julia was up. Mr. Ray went down early to open the drafts in the furnace. Anna followed, and the rich fragrance of coffee floated though the house. They ate breakfast by gaslight, and everyone talked very fast.

Then Julia dressed Betsy's hair, and Margaret polished her shoes, and Anna pressed the tie of the new sailor suit, although it didn't really need pressing. Mr. Ray went out to hitch up Old Mag. He brought her around, sleighbells chiming, while the east was still stained with red. Betsy embraced Anna, and the family went out to the surrey, Julia and Margaret carrying Betsy's grip. Her trunk had been sent on the day before.

The whole Crowd was at the station. Tony looked sleepy, but he was there. Dennie came tardily at a run. Some brought train letters which Betsy stuffed into her purse.

The waiting room was crowded and gay, and brilliant jokes were bandied. The boys had, indeed, brought mistletoe, and Tony held some over Betsy's head.

"All Gaul is divided in three parts, and you have two of them," said Betsy, ducking.

There was a scuffle but she wasn't kissed.

The train whistled far down the track, and everyone poured out into the frosty morning. It was daylight now, but still cold. There was more laughing and joking.

"Don't flirt with the Milwaukee boys," Cab called, as the great black giant of an engine rushed into the station, sending out clouds of steam which froze in the air. Its bell was swinging madly back and forth.

"*Ring out, wild bells,*" Betsy whispered to Tacy, "*Ring out the old, ring in the new* . . . Betsy."

"Piffle!" Tacy said.

Betsy kissed her. She kissed Margaret whose small arms clung tightly, and Julia who smelled sweetly of cologne, and her mother who smelled of violets, and her father who smelled of cigars. His face was ruddy with cold, and wore a determined smile.

"Have a good time, Betsy." "Remember us to the Mullers." "Don't drink too much of the beer that made Milwaukee famous."

Followed by these mingled cries and witticisms, Betsy ascended to the parlor car. Her father gave her grip to the porter, and all four Rays went inside for a minute. When they were gone, Betsy rushed to the window. She rapped on the glass and threw kisses and screamed, "What did you say?" at the frantically moving mouths outside. The boys were yelling through cupped hands.

Then the big bell started to ring again. The whistle blew, aloof and melancholy. The train moved, and slowly the group dropped out of sight . . . the bright tams of the girls, the caps of the boys pulled down against the cold, Margaret's excited, almost anxious face, Julia's smile, her mother's stern look, her father's benevolent one.

They all passed out of sight, and Betsy turned around to the warmth and luxury of the parlor car. She settled herself in the green plush seat. She was on her way to Milwaukee.

11

Tib

THE GRINDING WHEELS of a train are apt to sing a
song. The song they sang for Betsy ran like this:

"There's a place named Milwaukee, Milwaukee,
Milwaukee, Milwauk, MilwaukEE,
There's a place named Milwaukee, Milwaukee,
A beautiful place to be . . ."

There was a story behind that song.

One summer afternoon when Betsy and Tacy were five years old, they dressed up in their mothers' clothes, took Mrs. Ray's card case and went to call at a strange, chocolate-colored house which was their particular admiration. No one answered their ring and a neighbor shouted out that the people who lived there were visiting in Milwaukee. Betsy and Tacy were charmed by the word. Walking home, after leaving two of Mrs. Ray's cards in the mail box, they made up a song about Milwaukee.

Later, Mrs. Muller found the cards. Thinking that Mrs. Ray had called she returned the courtesy, and that had begun the friendship of Betsy and Tacy and Tib. They had taught Tib the song and had all sung it together, and now from that distant roseate past, it came back to Betsy as she rolled along toward the city of those dreams.

"There's a place named Milwaukee, Milwaukee,
Milwaukee, Milwauk, MilwaukEE . . ."

There was a second verse. It had something to do with Tacy, Betsy remembered. Something about going to Milwaukee with Tacy "ahold of her hand." She wished Tacy were with her now. Not that Betsy, at the moment, felt the need of anyone's hand. She felt poised and confident, and at least thirty years old. But she wished that Tacy were going, just for the fun of the thing.

She rummaged in her pocket book, and found Tacy's train letter, and read it. It was full of love and joy in Betsy's good fortune. Tacy didn't say in the letter . . . she had never once said . . . "I wish I were going." She was never envious, no matter how many nice things happened to Betsy.

This struck Betsy suddenly. She wondered for the first time how she would feel if Tacy were going to visit Tib and she were staying at home. It could just as well have happened that way if the Rays instead of the Kellys had had ten children. Frosting has to be spread thinly over a large cake.

"Tacy," Betsy thought, "is a wonderful person." It was the first time she had ever consciously estimated her friend.

The porter, a colored man in a white jacket, took her hat and put it in a paper bag, which he tucked into the rack over her head. She folded her coat neatly, and put that there too, and looked around the parlor car, which was impressive with wide windows. There were only two or three other passengers, not especially interesting. So she just sank deeply into the soft chair and looked out the window.

The countryside was spread thickly with snow,

against which bare trees showed purplish brown. They were in planted groves mostly, except for scattered oaks in the fields and yellow willows along the frozen streams. The farm houses were small, the red barns big with advertisements for Peruna painted on them. Fences and telegraph poles, horses, sheep and cattle and black and white pigs rushed past.

It was prairie country at first. But near the Mississippi the bluffs began. After leaving Winona, named for the same Indian maiden from whom Winona Root took her name, Betsy gazed with her own eyes on the fabled Mississippi. Her train crossed the river. She was in Wisconsin.

"I've left my native state," she remarked in a jubilant half whisper.

She could hardly wait for noon, having heard about dining cars from Julia after the California trip. When the bluffs flattened out into rolling prairie again, a waiter came through the train calling, "Dinner served in the dining car! First call for dinner!" Betsy was the second person in. She was second only because she waited for someone else to lead the way, and she followed close on the heels of this experienced traveler.

The diner surpassed all expectations. It was pure romance to sit at a table spread with glossy linen and eat a delicious meal while looking out at a flying white landscape. She began to think about her great project of changing herself.

"Two weeks is an awfully short time," she thought. "But two weeks away from home is longer than two ordinary weeks. How shall I change? Shall I change my hair-do? I'm not good at that. Shall I change the way I talk? Make my voice low and musical, and my laugh sort of mocking? That would be good!"

She tried it out softly, but the waiter heard her.

"Is anything wrong, miss?" he asked, looking startled.

"Nothing, thanks," murmured Betsy, blushing. She went on planning.

"Maybe I can copy Aunt Dolly. But she's a different type. I think I'll just try to act worldly and a little bored. The trouble is I never get bored."

She paid for her dinner and left a tip, as her father had done at the Moorish Café.

She had been cautioned in the most urgent terms against talking with strangers . . . indiscriminately, that is. "Probably a woman with small children would be all right," her mother had said. She was delighted on returning to the parlor car to find a woman with a baby. Betsy offered to hold the baby, and soon was in conversation.

Mrs. Gulbertson had been visiting her sister in Baraboo and she told Betsy all about her sister's troubles with her husband. Betsy reciprocated by telling all about Tib, and after Mrs. Gulbertson had left the train, Betsy kept on thinking about Tib.

"I wonder what she'll be like now. She's fifteen, the same as I am. Freddy must be about thirteen and Hobbie is Margaret's age." Frederick and Hobson were Tib's brothers.

Twilight descended and night came on with a rush. The porter pulled down the shades and turned on the lights. Betsy began to feel strange, speeding away through darkness to a big and unknown city. She started to wonder what the family was doing at home, then decided she had better not think about that. She read the last of her train letters, and was glad when the waiter came again calling, "Supper served in the dining car!"

This time Betsy was first into the diner.

She began to think about Milwaukee. She had tried to learn a little about it, and she knew that it had been founded almost a hundred years before by a French Canadian named Solomon Juneau. Before his arrival there was only an Indian village and a fur trading post on the bay where the Milwaukee River emptied into Lake Michigan. Juneau married the half-Indian daughter of the trader, and their seventeen children gave the new town a flying start.

In Europe, through those years, a great hope had

swelled that the people could rid themselves of despotic rulers. Starting in France in 1848, a series of revolutions had gone off like a string of firecrackers. But in Germany and Austria the revolts had been quickly crushed, and many of the brave men who had started them had fled to the new world, to Milwaukee in Wisconsin. Forty-eighters, they were called.

More men followed from Germany, and Austria (including Bohemia, an unwilling part of Austria), and other European countries. They were very industrious, skilled in many trades; and they made Milwaukee a prosperous, well-governed city. But more than most immigrants they had clung to homeland ways. Milwaukee was truly like a foreign city, Betsy's father had said. She could hardly wait now for her first sight of it.

After supper the time dragged. Although not due at Milwaukee until almost half past nine, Betsy went into the washroom at eight o'clock. She washed and shook pink powder into a chamois skin and rubbed it over her nose. She combed her hair and redid her pompadour, very high and stiff.

Back in the parlor car she made friends with a spinsterish lady and told her all about Tib. A married couple from Waukesha made overtures and she talked about Tib to them, too. At last the man pulled up the shade and said, "I believe we are coming into

Milwaukee." And the porter came in and started brushing people.

Betsy watched closely and when her turn came she didn't make any mistakes. He took her new red hat out of the bag and brushed it and she put it on. She stood up while he brushed the red and green sailor suit and wiped off her shoes. When he had helped her into her coat and furpiece, she gave him fifty cents and he said, "Thank you, miss. I hope you have a good time in Milwaukee with your friend Tib."

With her grip close beside her feet, she sat down and waited tensely. The train was running through lighted streets now, and it seemed to Betsy she could not endure the few remaining moments. Then the passengers rose and formed a line and the train entered the station.

"Milwaukee!" shouted the porter, and suddenly she felt very young, nervous, and inadequate. She found herself out on the platform with her grip at her feet.

"Red cap? Want a red cap?" Her father had told her a red cap was a boy who would carry her grip. One was standing beside her now, smiling. She nodded.

"Where to, Miss?" Where to, indeed! Other passengers were scurrying away. If the Mullers did not meet her . . .

"Betsy, darling!" Betsy heard a familiar, high sweet

voice. She turned to see a slight figure running toward her, a girl in a purple coat with yellow hair shining beneath a flowered hat. Betsy threw her arms around Tib.

She had forgotten how tiny Tib was. They hugged and kissed, and Mr. Muller, looking just as he had always looked, large, blond, stoutish, watched them smilingly.

"The little Betsy!" he said, shaking hands. "But she is a young lady now, *nicht wahr*, Tib?"

"*Ja*, Papa," said Tib, "*und sie ist sehr schön.*"

"Tib!" cried Betsy, "You're talking German."

"*Natürlich,*" Mr. Muller said.

Laughing they swept down the platform.

Betsy felt self-possessed again. She heard herself talking like Julia, very grown-up.

"Yes, I had a pleasant trip. The meals on the diner were delicious."

"Before we start home," Tib said, "we thought we'd take you up Grand Avenue to see the Christmas crowds."

"What fun!" Betsy cried.

She had never seen a big city at night, or at any other time for that matter . . . and she found it breathlessly exhilarating. The streets were as bright as day, but the brightness had a different quality. There were trolley cars with glittering windows and a press of horses and carriages, and autos with clamoring horns. The store windows were full of beautiful things to buy.

She and Tib and Mr. Muller pushed merrily through the crowds. Soon, however, they reached a hackstand and Mr. Muller helped them into a horse-drawn hack.

"We must get home," he said. "Mamma and the children, too, are anxious to see Betsy."

They rode for a long time, leaving the business district behind. They didn't talk very much, and whenever they passed an arc light Betsy stole a look at Tib. Usually Tib was looking at her. She seemed younger than Betsy and not only because she was small. She was still wearing a hair ribbon.

"You have your hairs up, haven't you?" she asked suddenly. She said "hairs," Betsy noticed, and not "hair."

"Yes," said Betsy. "I started last year."

"I put mine up for parties."

"Have I changed much?" Betsy asked.

"Have you changed!" Tib gave her little fluttery laugh. "I should say you have changed."

"*Jawohl, Jawohl,*" said Mr. Muller.

They paused at last before a square redbrick house which had lights in every window and a wide entrance door.

"This is our house. It's a duplex," Tib said. "I

guess I told you about it in my letters." She had, but Betsy had not been able to visualize a duplex. There were no duplexes in Deep Valley. "The first floor is our house. The second belongs to someone else," Tib explained.

Betsy was fascinated. "Why, it's like living in a sandwich."

Mr. Muller laughed. "A sandwich, *ja*? Well, we're going to live in this sandwich only until we decide a few things." Betsy wondered what he meant by that.

Inside she seemed to be back in the Muller home in Deep Valley. For Mrs. Muller, who kissed her affectionately, looked just the same. She was still short and square with yellow hair like Tib's and she wore diamond ear rings. The boys were taller, but Fred was still slender and artistic, while Hobbie's face was dimpled and full of mischief. Matilda still wore her hair in braids around her head, and spectacles, and a stiffly starched apron. The lines in her forehead made her look cross, but she smiled when she greeted Betsy.

"This is good!" she said in broken English. "This remembers me of Deep Valley."

The duplex was very spacious. In the big front parlor were a sofa and chairs covered with blue velvet, which Betsy remembered. The dining room had the remembered display of heavy silver and cut glass. Matilda's kitchen, as always, shone like a polished pan.

Betsy was still looking furtively at Tib. Although she was so small she had a rounded bust above a very slender waist. She was feathery-light in her movements as Tib always had been. She was still Tiblike.

She wore a shirt waist and skirt, but it didn't look tailored like other peoples' shirt waists and skirts. There was a fluffy collar on the waist and the skirt was draped up with a velvet bow. She had a new foreign accent. Betsy thought it was cute.

They sat down in the back parlor and Matilda brought Mr. and Mrs. Muller steins of foamy beer, milk and cookies for the children. They were Christmas cookies, kuchen, they were called, some with colored sugar on them.

"I remember these from Deep Valley, Mrs. Muller," Betsy said in Julia's tones, nibbling.

At last Betsy and Tib went down the hall to Tib's room which was fancifully gay.

"I'll bet we'll talk all night," Betsy said as Tib turned back a white organdy spread lined with blue silk.

But they didn't. They weren't well enough acquainted yet. Betsy was still using her company manners and Tib was a little formal herself bringing out towels and wash cloth for Betsy with a perfect hostess air.

Tib put on a thin night gown trimmed with pink

rosettes. She tied up her hair with a pink ribbon. Betsy wound hers on Magic Wavers. She hated to, but she wanted curls next day. She was glad that although her night gown was of flannel it was new and pretty with sprigs of blue flowers in it.

They knelt down to say their prayers on opposite sides of the bed.

"I wrote you, didn't I," said Betsy, rising, "that I'm an Episcopalian now?"

"Yes. Would you like to go to church tomorrow?" Tib asked politely.

"I'd love to," Betsy said. And she added as they climbed into bed, "Now we mustn't talk too late!" But they didn't talk at all. They kissed each other good night and Betsy lay in the dark thinking how strange, how almost fantastic it was that she was here in Milwaukee of which she had heard so much for so many years.

"There's a place named Milwaukee, Milwaukee,
A beautiful place to be . . ."

The words sang in her ears just as though the wheels of the train were still turning. They sang themselves over and over until she fell asleep.

12

Sunday in Milwaukee

THE FOLLOWING MORNING, as agreed, Betsy and Tib
went to church. Prayer books in their kid-gloved
hands, they started off decorously beneath a dull sky.

They went by trolley, an exciting experience for
Betsy, although she tried not to show it. Tib, however,
did not act superior because she was a city girl.

Betsy was still talking like Julia, and Tib's elegant

manner was, Betsy suspected, not quite her own. Even so, they drew closer and closer to the old loving intimacy as they talked about Tib's school. The Sem, she called it.

"It's closed for the holidays. But I'm going to take you to see it. Grosspapa Muller sends me there. All his daughters and granddaughters have gone to Browner."

"Do you like it?"

"Very much. I like to play basketball and act in the plays. And the girls are nice. They're rich," said Tib, "but you'd never know it. We all have to dress conservatively."

Tib, Betsy thought, looked far from conservative. True she wore her fair hair in a braid, turned up with a ribbon, and only a very little, girlish jewelry. But Tib could not look conservative any more than a gold-finch could. Her hair ribbon was lilac color, and she wore a lilac silk dress beneath the purple coat. Mrs. Muller made Tib's clothes, and they were charming, but unusual. People called them "Frenchy." The style was really Viennese. Mrs. Muller's parents were Bohemians and came from the city of Vienna.

"Do many girls board at the school?" Betsy asked, as the trolley hummed along through streets full of large, comfortable homes set in spacious lawns.

"Yes. There are lots of us day girls, though."

"I should think it would be fun to board there."

"It is. I stay overnight with my friends sometimes. The lights blink at nine forty-five and they are called 'first winks.' They go off at ten and that's 'second winks.' At 'first winks' a tray of crackers and milk is put out on the landing in the dorm for anyone who is hungry, but when I stay we have spreads in the gym, very secret and scary."

"I can't imagine your being scared."

"That's part of the fun." Tib laughed. "The boarding pupils, if they are caught, are 'campused' for a while . . . no walks, or trips to town. I'm glad I'm a day girl because I have more freedom. And I certainly need freedom because of Grossmama Hornik."

"Grossmama Hornik?"

"She has her own ideas about my education. The Horniks and the Mullers," Tib continued, "are very different. Grosspapa Muller manufactures beer kegs. He is rich and everyone is a little afraid of him. Grossmama Hornik is strict, too, but no one is afraid of her, except Grosspapa Hornik, perhaps. He is a tailor, and they live up over the shop. I don't know whether it's because they're Viennese or what, but they're gayer. They like dancing and singing and beautiful clothes."

"I remember Aunt Dolly's beautiful clothes."

"Grossmama Hornik wants me to have dancing lessons," Tib continued, "so I have them from the best teacher in Milwaukee. And Uncle Rudy . . . he's Mamma's brother and Aunt Dolly's . . . takes me to concerts and plays. That reminds me, we have tickets for the theatre tonight, you and I."

"How perfectly thrilling!" cried Betsy. "What are we going to see?"

"*Reiterattacke*. That's German. Something about the cavalry. It's very funny."

"Will it all be in German?"

"Yes. There's a German stock company at the Pabst. Uncle Rudy didn't remember that you don't understand German, I guess. But I'll tell you what's going on."

"I love the theatre so much," said Betsy, "that I wouldn't care if the play was in Chinese. But Tib!" She grasped Tib's arm suddenly. "It can't be tonight we are going."

"Why not?"

Betsy laughed merrily at Tib's mistake. "It's Sunday!"

"Yes," answered Tib, "that's the night Uncle Rudy got the tickets for, Sunday, the twenty-second."

Betsy was silent, astonished. She could hardly believe her ears. They were going to the theatre on Sunday. It was certainly Sunday, for they were on their way to church.

Nobody Betsy knew ever went to the theatre on Sunday. The Rays were not straight-laced, but they wouldn't have dreamed of doing such a thing . . . any more than they would have danced on that night, or played a game of cards.

For a moment Betsy wondered wildly whether she should refuse to go. Elsie Dinsmore, she remembered, had refused to play the piano on Sunday; she had fallen off the piano stool instead. But Betsy had never thought much of Elsie Dinsmore.

"I'm almost sure," Betsy thought, "that Papa would say, 'When in Rome, do as the Romans do!'"

Tib lifted a gloved finger and rang a bell.

"Here's where we get off," she said.

The church with its tall spires was impressive, and they walked up the broad stairs in silence. Inside it was lighted by candles and drenched with color from the stained glass windows. It seemed to be full of prayers, and as Betsy and Tib knelt to add two more, an organ started playing.

Betsy was carried away by the beauty of the service. The voices of the boy sopranos were like angel voices . . . so high, sweet, and unearthly.

"I wish Julia could hear them," she thought.

As though in a dream she went through the familiar service, kneeling and rising and making the proper responses. Her heart seemed to open up into one great wish . . . to be good.

Outdoors again, they found that it had been snowing. Fresh soft snow covered the steps, walks and lawns. It lay in mounds on the lacy branches of the evergreens. Still uplifted by the service, Betsy looked around.

"It seems like a miracle!" she cried.

"We should have worn overshoes." Tib took off her kid gloves and put them into her pocket. "You'd better do the same," she advised. "Dampness isn't good for kid."

"When the choir sang, I felt as though the heavens were opening," said Betsy.

"Did you?" asked Tib, looking puzzled but impressed.

She hadn't really changed, Betsy thought.

Back at home Tib put on a ruffled apron trimmed with pink bows which made her look like a valentine. But she helped Matilda with brisk efficiency. This, too, seemed natural. Tib had known how to cook, sew and bake before either Betsy or Tacy could boil water.

Betsy offered to help, but Tib pushed her out of the kitchen, just as she used to do.

"You . . . you . . . *Dummkopf*," she said affectionately. "Go away until you are called."

Feeling agreeably incompetent, Betsy withdrew to their bedroom. She was glad to have a few minutes in which to bring her journal up to date. She wrote a letter home, too, and one to Tacy. Then she was called to the table, and it was a table worth drawing a chair to.

Dinner began with noodle soup and ended with *Schaumtorte*, piled high with whipped cream. In between were *Sauerbraten*, with red cabbage and potato dumplings, hot raised biscuits and several kinds of jam.

Mr. Muller had beer. He gave sips to Fred and Hobbie and offered one to Betsy.

"It's bitter," Tib warned.

"No thanks," said Betsy, smiling. Going to the theatre on Sunday was, she thought, concession enough to the Romans.

Mrs. Muller said that since they were going to the theatre that night they had better rest. So after dinner they went to their room and while Mr. and Mrs. Muller napped, and Fred and Hobbie looked at the funny papers, Betsy and Tib stretched out on the bed and talked.

Now, for the first time, the bars of strangeness came completely down. Betsy was not acting like anyone else any more, and neither was Tib. They were Betsy and Tib again, mutually adoring. As of old Betsy talked and Tib listened, her blue eyes flatteringly round.

Betsy talked about the Crowd. She showed Tib snapshots of the various boys and girls. Tib knew Tacy, Winona and Tom but almost none of the others.

Tib had not yet started going out with boys.

"That's odd," said Betsy, feeling very worldly. "You're so pretty and cute."

"Oh, they like me," said Tib . . . not boasting, just telling the truth. "But I don't know many boys. I take my cousin Heinrich to school dances."

She was enthralled by Betsy's picture of Deep Valley gaieties, and Betsy painted with a lavish brush.

She told about Tony with his bushy black hair, his bold eyes and laughing mouth. She told about being in love with him last year, and how strange it was that she had stopped. She described Cab, Dennie, Pin.

"Betsy, you sound terribly popular."

"Oh, no," said Betsy with elaborate carelessness. "They just like to come to our house."

"Oh, that's it!" Tib replied matter-of-factly, which was not at all the thing to say. But Betsy understood Tib.

She described Joe Willard and told about their feud. She even went up to Olympian heights and described Phil Brandish.

"Brandish?" Tib repeated. "A Phyllis Brandish goes to the Sem."

"Why, she's Phil's twin sister. I knew she went to a boarding school. Do you like her?"

"I don't know her very well. She's a junior and she's . . . well . . . different."

"I know what you mean. So is Phil," said Betsy.

She kicked her heels reflectively in air. "I think Phil Brandish is the most thrilling person in school. I'm not in love with him, but I'd die with joy if he ever paid any attention to me."

"If you wanted him to, you could make him," said Tib with utter confidence.

"I wonder," said Betsy. "I wonder whether I could."

Mrs. Muller, who had waked from her nap, called in just then to remind the girls to rest. So they stopped talking, and Betsy closed her eyes but her thoughts continued in the path where Tib had set them.

It led, of course, directly into her plan for changing herself.

"I haven't changed a bit so far," she admitted. "In fact I'm getting more like myself all the time."

Yet here in Milwaukee with the aura of Tib's adulation about her, the idea seemed more practicable than ever. She dreamed about going back to Deep Valley completely, stunningly different, until Mrs. Muller called them to coffee.

The Mullers, like most Milwaukee families, had coffee every afternoon. On Sunday, because of the big dinner, coffee came later and combined itself with supper. The table was spread with cold meats and *Kartoffel salat*, sweet rolls and cakes and, of course, kuchen.

Before they had finished Uncle Rudy came in. He was tall and slim in impeccably tailored clothes. He had a yellow pompadour, and yellow mustaches, waxed and twisted upward.

Betsy promptly fell in love with Uncle Rudy. She was madly in love, for at least a week.

He was accustomed to it; many women were in love with him. He was a jaunty, carefree young man. He could play the piano, Tib told Betsy, better than Paderewski. He joked with Betsy about not liking the beer that made Milwaukee famous. He sold it on the road. He was the uncle who had sent Tib Schlitz beer calendars, long ago, in Deep Valley.

He drove them to the Pabst in a dashing cutter behind a high stepping horse whose harness was strewn with bells. His auto, he said, was put up for the winter. It was a Steamer, and it took him thirty minutes to get up a head of steam.

"But then it goes like blazes. If you were here in the spring, I'd give you a spin," he declared, giving Betsy a smile which turned her head completely.

He left them at the Pabst. Betsy was so excited by the festive crowd that she felt almost helpless, but Tib with her usual calm got them safely to their seats. The audience was very well dressed. The women rustled in silk or satin dresses and sparkled with jewels. Everyone seemed to know everyone else.

The orchestra played Christmas airs.

"*Reiterattacke,*" Tib explained, was a military farce. It was full of handsome officers (but not so handsome as Uncle Rudy), clanking swords and sabers, and pink-cheeked girls. The audience laughed uproariously and Betsy laughed, too, even before Tib had a chance to explain the jokes. Tib understood almost all the German, and when her knowledge failed, their neighbors helped them out. During intermission the talk was all in German.

"It doesn't seem as though we were in America," Betsy said, looking around.

"Papa," observed Tib, "thinks Milwaukee isn't American enough. He and Mamma like it better in Deep Valley. He argues with Grosspapa Muller about it. That is," Tib added, laughing, "as much as one *can* argue with Grosspapa Muller."

"Why can't one argue with Grosspapa Muller?"

"You'll see on Christmas Eve."

13
The Seven Dwarfs

BETSY AND TIB, FRED and Hobbie were busy on Monday stringing cranberries for the tree. Mr. Muller was away at his office. He was an architect, and Fred wanted to be an architect, too. He was always sketching town halls and cathedrals on a drawing board like his father's. Mrs. Muller was doing last minute shopping, and Matilda was busy in the kitchen. The heavenly aroma emanating therefrom was in contrast to her temper.

"She'd better be careful," Hobbie murmured resentfully, after he had been refused a sixteenth cookie. "The *Christkindel* comes tonight."

"The *Christkindel*?" repeated Betsy, puzzled.

"The fairy Christ child," Tib explained. "He comes on the twenty-third of December to see whether children have been good. See that you behave today, Betsy *Liebchen*."

"He comes again on Christmas Eve to Grosspapa Muller's," Hobbie said, fitting a cranberry on his needle with stubby fingers.

"He brings the presents," Tib explained again.

"But what about Santa Claus?" Betsy demanded.

"He's called the Christmas Man," said Tib. "He's not so important in Milwaukee as he used to be in Deep Valley."

That night Mr. Muller brought home a Christmas tree. Even though the Mullers were to spend Christmas Eve at Grosspapa Muller's and Christmas Day at Grosspapa Hornik's there had to be a tree in their own home. Unlike Santa Claus, Christmas trees seemed to be very important in Milwaukee. The older people were as excited as the children when Mr. Muller carried in his huge fragrant bundle.

The next afternoon, which was Christmas Eve day,

all of them trimmed it. They put on candles, and carved wooden toys, and cookies hung on ribbons, and little socks with candies in them, as well as the usual bright balls. They draped the strings of cranberries around the spiraling branches and placed a star angel on the top.

Tib and Fred were very artistic and it was a beautiful tree. They had fun trimming it, too; but it seemed strange to Betsy to be hanging the Mullers' balls and angels and to think that at home a tree was being trimmed with the dear familiar ornaments . . . some that she and Tacy had bought on their Christmas shopping trips.

As early twilight gathered outside the windows she thought of the Christmas Eve ritual at home going on without her. She remembered the doll her mother was dressing for Margaret and was swept by homesickness almost as acute as she had suffered at the Taggarts.

But no one suspected it, and it didn't last. Hobbie made her laugh by shouting, "We must get gedressed for Grosspapa Muller's."

"Yes," said Mrs. Muller. "We are expected there at half past five. Dress, and make quick."

So Betsy brought out her new party dress, the pink silk with daisies in it, and the daisy wreath.

"I'll fix your hairs for you," Tib offered.

"Hair, hair, beautiful Dutchman!" Betsy teased,

but she was glad to have Tib dress her pompadour and pin on the wreath. Tib was almost as clever as Julia was with Betsy's silky, hard-to-manage hair.

Tib put her own hair up because this was a party. Her pompadour made a pale golden cloud. She wore a wreath too, and her filmy white dress was trimmed with loops of rosebuds.

"You look just like a fairy tale princess, and you always did," said Betsy.

Tib lifted her skirts and waltzed about.

Mr. Muller wore his best waistcoat. Mrs. Muller wore a rich, dark silk. The boys were dressed in their Sunday suits, with white shirts and carefully knotted ties. They had scrubbed their faces until they were pink, and brushed their blond heads until they shone. Mr. Muller's face looked like Hobbie's tonight, full of fun and mischief, all care gone.

Matilda had left to spend the evening with relatives. The hack was waiting in front. Mr. Muller shooed them all out and they drove off to Grosspapa Muller's. It was a long ride through the spectral winter evening, a ride Betsy was never to forget.

It was memorable just to be outdoors, instead of indoors, on Christmas Eve. And the city was so given over to Christmas that it seemed as though the *Christkindel* really was abroad. Lighted trees shone through many windows and there were roving groups of singers in the streets. *"Stille Nacht, heilige Nacht."* Their voices came plaintively over the snow.

They passed a small band, four shabby men with trumpets, horn and drums, who were playing raucously, *"Du bist wie eine Blume."* Mr. Muller sang with them. He asked the hack driver to stop, and put out his head and cried, *"Fröhliche Weihnachten!"* which meant "Merry Christmas." The leader came running, pulling off his cap, and Mr. Muller tossed a coin.

They crossed the frozen river, and went on toward Lake Michigan. The houses grew bigger. Betsy felt as though she were in a dream.

Grosspapa Muller's house sat on a corner. It was a large gray stone house with wrought iron balconies. There was a carriage house in back. Old Johann lived over that and took care of the horses, Tib explained. All the windows were full of light.

There was a wide lawn, now buried deep in snow.

"In the summer Grosspapa Muller has a row of seven dwarfs on his lawn," Tib said.

"Each one," Hobbie added, "has a different colored hat."

"They are in the basement now. Johann repaints them every winter. I'll take you down to see them," Tib promised squeezing Betsy's hand.

Betsy felt more dream-bound than ever, listening to this talk of seven dwarfs.

The hack drove up to the porte-cochere. It was the first time Betsy had ever alighted at a porte-cochere. A massive carved door hung with a holly wreath was flung open by a smiling servant and the Mullers trooped into a crowded hall.

The house seemed bursting with Mullers, old and young. Betsy and Tib laid off their wraps in the Yellow Room upstairs and when they descended the wide, deeply carpeted stairs, they found themselves surrounded by uncles, aunts and cousins. The great hall, the front and back parlors, richly furnished and hung with mistletoe and holly, were swarming with them.

All the uncles were large and stout, and so were the aunts whom Tib called *Tante*. They wore diamond ear rings, such as Mrs. Muller wore. Grosspapa Muller had given all his daughters-in-law diamond ear rings, Tib said. Their dresses were rich and elaborate, but none of them looked stylish, somehow. Tib's mother, Betsy thought, was the only stylish looking woman there. She seemed more American, too, than the others, and so did Mr. Muller.

The children ranged from pig-tailed twin girls Hobbie's age to the tall cousin Heinrich whom Tib took to the Seminary dances. He was nice looking, with curly brown hair, but not half so fascinating, Betsy thought, as Uncle Rudy. Men and boys alike, when introduced to Betsy, bowed stiffly from the waist. Some said "How do you do?" but others said, *"Guten Abend, Fräulein."*

"Come," said Tib. "I want you to meet Grosspapa."

"And Grossmama?" asked Betsy mischievously. It was funny the way all the Mullers referred only to Grosspapa Muller.

"Grossmama, too, of course," said Tib, not knowing that she was being teased.

Grosspapa was larger and stouter than any of his sons. He had a gleaming bald head which seemed to begin at his black overhanging eyebrows. His black beard, speckled with white, almost concealed his snowy waist-coat. He addressed Betsy in German, and she found herself answering, *"Guten Abend, Herr Grosspapa,"* and curtseying, as Tib did.

Grossmama Muller was small and timid. Her graying hair, which had once been fair was drawn back into a tight bun. She too wore diamond ear rings.

The double doors leading to the library were closed. The children kept trying to look through the cracks and were pulled away by their elders. At last a bell was heard.

"There's the *Christkindel*'s bell," Tib whispered to Betsy. But the company was not yet ready to answer the summons.

One of the young lady cousins went to the piano,

and it developed that the pig-tailed twins had prepared a surprise for their Grosspapa. Why not for
Grossmama, too, Betsy wondered? They played a
Mozart duet, somewhat shakily, with violin and flute
and Grosspapa was pleased.

After that everybody sang Christmas songs. From
Grosspapa to Hobbie they sang with a will, and Betsy
joined in, although she was the only one singing in
English.

But in the library the bell became imperative. The
great doors slid back, and Betsy saw a Christmas tree
so tall and majestic that it seemed to fill the large,
high-ceilinged room. It was twinkling with lighted
candles, sparkling with ornaments, and it threw off
a delicious woodsy fragrance. After a long-drawn
breath the company joined hands and marched
around the tree singing . . . but in German . . .

> "O, Christmas tree, O, Christmas tree,
>   How lovely are thy branches . . ."

Betsy wanted to pinch herself, to make sure she
was awake, but she couldn't manage it very well with
Tib holding one hand and a pig-tailed twin swinging
from the other.

All around the room were tables covered with sheets.
The smiling servant girl hurried about taking off the
sheets, and there were tables for everyone . . . the

servant girl, the cook who came in from the kitchen, and old Johann, wrinkled and nut-like. There was even a table for Betsy laden with boxes of candy and cakes, hair ribbons, pin cushions, pen wipers, and sachet bags.

The children were mad with excitement. They were throwing paper to the floor, and the aunts were picking it up and folding it neatly. Everyone was kissing and thanking everyone else.

Then Betsy was swept on the tide of Mullers into the dining room for a delicious cold supper . . . roast fowl and ham, potato salad, pickled herring, pickles of many kinds and little curly anchovies; cream filled horns, cakes glazed with sugar and others decked out with peaches and cherries. There was hot chocolate for the children, and the men and women had wine. They toasted Grosspapa and Grossmama, and the President of the United States and Kaiser Wilhelm.

"Grosspapa Hornik," Tib whispered, "won't toast Kaiser Wilhelm nor Kaiser Franz Josef either. He doesn't like Kaisers. He and Grosspapa Muller don't get on very well."

The children went back to the tree to play with their dolls and toys. Soon the younger ones began to grow sleepy. At last with mingled cries of *"Fröhliche Weihnachten"* and "Merry Christmas," oldsters began to put on coats and furs.

"Tib!" said Betsy. "I haven't seen the dwarfs!"

"Come quick!" cried Tib, catching her hand.

She pulled Betsy toward the dining room and Fred and Hobbie and Cousin Heinrich followed. They ran through the pantry and kitchen, down spotless stairs, into the largest cleanest basement Betsy had ever beheld.

There, indeed, were the seven dwarfs standing in a row. The biggest one didn't come to Betsy's shoulder. The smallest was about a foot high. They were made of cast iron and wore short Alpine jackets and little Alpine hats with feathers in them. Each hat was a different color . . . red, green, purple, yellow, pink, blue and brown.

"Every winter," said Tib, "Grosspapa has them repainted. And every spring, as soon as the snow melts, he puts them out on the lawn. Since he has retired from business he takes more interest in his dwarfs than in anything else, Papa says. Every year he puts them out differently. Some years they head north, and some south, and some east, and some west. But always the big dwarf leads."

"Grossmama Muller," said Fred, "wishes that some year the little dwarf could lead. Every spring she asks Grosspapa . . . 'Just this once, Gerhard, just this one year let the little dwarf lead.' But he won't. He always has them go in a straight line with the big dwarf at the head."

14
The Brave Little Tailor

"You always did look like a fairy tale princess," Betsy told Tib, "So I'm not surprised to find that you live in a fairy book."

"I live in a duplex," said Tib.

"In a fairy book," repeated Betsy firmly. "One grandfather has seven dwarfs, and the other one is a tailor. Fairy books are full of tailors. You remember

The Brave Little Tailor? 'Seven at one blow'?"

"That's right," said Tib, and laughed.

They were walking to Grosspapa Hornik's ahead of the rest of the family so that Tib could help Aunt Dolly and Grossmama with dinner. It was midway of Christmas morning. At breakfast Betsy had given the Mullers the presents she had brought for them . . . except Tib. Tib had had hers earlier.

Returning from Grosspapa Muller's, the night before, Betsy had insisted upon hanging her stockings.

"But we don't hang stockings," Tib had protested.

"You're you, and I'm me," Betsy had returned. "I'm hanging my stockings. And if you have a spark of feeling, Fräulein Muller, you'll fill them with those packages I brought from Deep Valley. By the way," she added, "if you should happen to hang your own you might find something at the bottom of it in the morning."

So Tib had hung her stocking, too, over the foot of the bed, and there had been a mysterious scurrying about after the gas was turned out. In the morning they had taken the stockings into their bed and unpacked them jubilantly.

Betsy's gifts had included photographs from Tony and Irma at which Tib had gazed long and earnestly. The Deep Valley Crowd seemed as story bookish to Tib as the Milwaukee grandfathers seemed to Betsy.

"The Brave Little Tailor," Betsy repeated musingly now, pleased with her fancy.

To reach the tailor shop they walked toward the central part of the city. Arms hooked, they swung along happily through a white world full of chiming sleighbells.

"Grosspapa Hornik," said Tib, "is a very good tailor. You noticed what handsome clothes he makes for Uncle Rudy. He makes clothes for the very best people."

"The brave little tailor! But why, oh why, is he afraid of Grossmama?"

"Oh," said Tib. "She has the head for money. And besides, they wrangle about Emperor Franz Josef. Grosspapa's father . . . he was Alois Hornik, too . . . was a Forty-Eighter, if you know what that is."

"I should say I do!" cried Betsy, stopping still.

"Grosspapa was only a little boy when he came to Milwaukee, but he hates the emperor and everything about the court."

"He was a Bohemian?" prompted Betsy.

"His father was a Bohemian. His mother was a Viennese, and she's famous in the family because she was so beautiful, with golden hairs. She was a revolutionist, too. Grosspapa looks like her pictures, and so does Aunt Dolly. So do I, a little."

"How romantic!" Betsy exclaimed. "What was her name?"

"Catherine Wilhelmina."

They proceeded in silence, Betsy thinking of the revolutionist, Alois Hornik and his beautiful, golden-haired wife, fleeing from Vienna after 1848. How strange that Tib, her friend, now walking calmly along a Milwaukee street, should look like that distant, lovely Catherine Wilhelmina.

"And Grossmama Hornik?" she asked, after a while.

"Her parents were Bohemian, too," said Tib. "But they lived in Vienna until Grossmama was twenty-five. As a girl she did embroidery for the Court; and she was given the right to use a five-pointed crown on her linens, calling cards and stationery. She is very proud of it. Grosspapa doesn't like it at all, and she doesn't like his ideas either. When he talks against the Emperor, Grossmama says, '*Ach, der pa!*' But they're very fond of each other." She broke off. "Here we are at the tailor shop already."

"Already yet so soon," Betsy teased.

The tailor shop was in a two-story brick building. A sign in gold letters read Alois Hornik, Schneider. It added in English in very small letters, "Tailor." At the right of the door which led into the shop was another door on which two calling cards were tacked. One of them said *Herr* Alois Hornik, and the other said *Frau* Alois Hornik and that bore a tiny five-pointed crown.

"Even a crown you have in your fairy tale, already yet," Betsy said.

Opening the door they walked down a long, dark, carpeted hall. At the end were two doors.

"Dining room and kitchen," Tib said. "The rest of the rooms are upstairs."

She opened the left-hand door and they went into the dining room which was small and dark but papered in a handsome, red, floral design. A table was set for dinner with polished glass and silver on a gleaming damask cloth.

Tib lifted a corner of this cloth and showed Betsy the five-pointed crown again, in embroidery so fine that Betsy wished Carney could see it. No needlewoman herself, she knew she could not appreciate it but she clicked her tongue admiringly.

Turning right through a small hall from which a carpeted stairway ascended they entered the kitchen. It was large and bright and full of savory odors. Shiny copper pans hung on the walls and you could see your face, although a trifle askew, in the polished nickel trim of the cook stove. The stove was covered with sauce pans in which things were bubbling briskly. Three open-faced apple pies sat ready on the table.

"Everybody must be upstairs," Tib was saying, when an exquisite apparition floated in. Yellow curls were piled on top of a small proud head. A pink messaline tea gown clung to a delicately molded figure. Long sleeves, like angels' wings, hung almost to the floor. Betsy saw a pink and white doll's face, blue eyes. It was Aunt Dolly, and she hadn't changed a bit!

"Why, Betsy!" she cried. She tripped across the room and lifted her cheek for Betsy to kiss. She was so tiny and dainty that she made Betsy feel like a giant . . . all the more so, when she said, "How tall you are, child!"

"Wasn't it nice," cried Tib, "that Betsy could come for Christmas?"

"Very nice. It's too bad, though, that you had to find me looking such a fright."

"Why, Aunt Dolly! You look lovely!"

"A perfect fright!" she repeated happily. "Aren't you ashamed, Tib, to bring your guest in before I'm dressed?" Then she began to trip about the kitchen, lifting sauce pan lids and changing dampers . . . capably, too, in spite of the swinging sleeves.

She ought to be wearing an apron, Betsy thought frenziedly, but Aunt Dolly did not soil a single ribbon. She stirred with a practised hand, tasted critically, added salt and pepper, pinches of sugar, dashes of vinegar. Betsy watched fascinated, until she found herself between Tib and Aunt Dolly, going upstairs.

At the top they came out into a room so large and

gracious that you would not have expected to find it above a tailor shop. The carpet was of soft green, strewn with flowers. There were gold chairs, as fragile as Aunt Dolly. There were long lace curtains, and vases of red and white glass . . . Bohemian glass, Tib said. A grand piano stood in one corner, and in another a Christmas tree.

From a door at the back leading toward the bedrooms, Grosspapa and Grossmama Hornik emerged. Tib embraced them both, and introduced Betsy.

Grossmama spoke only German but she did not, Betsy found, present the problem which Grosspapa Hornik did. With Grossmama nothing was expected except curtseys and smiles. But Grosspapa prided himself on his almost unintelligible English.

"How does it happen," Betsy asked Tib later, "that he doesn't speak English better? He was born here."

"Plenty of people in Milwaukee speak only German," Tib replied. "You get on better here with only German than with only English, I can tell you that. Grosspapa likes to speak English but he can't do it with Grossmama, or with most of his customers, so he doesn't get much practise."

Grosspapa Hornik was small but erect, in a glossy cutaway coat. He was as blond as his famed mother had been, but his hair was thin and his graying mustaches turned down. He had a dimple in his chin, a small mouth, and a sweet spontaneous smile which showed even white teeth. There were two deep lines between his brows . . . a result of concentration over the tailor's bench . . . but the look of severity vanished when he smiled.

Grossmama Hornik was large and stately with dark hair parted in the middle and drawn smoothly back. A fresh apron partly covered her black satin dress which buttoned tightly over an imposing bosom. Presently she and Tib started down stairs.

"You wait here," Tib said to Betsy. Aunt Dolly departed to dress, and Betsy was left alone with Grosspapa Hornik.

"Vat tink you of diese Milvaukee?" he asked Betsy. "*Es ist gemütlich, nicht wahr?*"

"I like it very much," said Betsy politely.

"I am here sixty years already," he said. "*Und es ist gut* here. *Ja, sehr gut.* Here is no Kaiser, no *Soldaten* marching, marching all de time. Kaisers are *nicht gut.* Der Kaiser Franz Josef und der Kaiser Wilhelm are de same, *beide nicht gut. Verstehen Sie?*"

"*I verstehe,*" said Betsy.

"*Die Grossmama versteht nicht. Weil* der Kaiser likes her *Stickerei,* her embroidery, de Grossmama *versteht nicht.*" He frowned. "Here in Milvaukee ve have fun, *nicht wahr?* De people has joy mit his wife und *Kinder* und his Christmas tree und his music und his beer."

"Und his kuchen," Betsy added.

"*Ja, ja!*" Grosspapa Hornik's sweet smile broke over his face. He patted her shoulder. "De Grossmama," he said "has made so many kuchens you can't count dat many yet."

"Grosspapa Hornik," Betsy said, "do you have a picture of your mother?"

"*Was? Was sagen Sie?*" Grosspapa Hornik was so startled that he lapsed into German.

"Your mother," Betsy repeated. "I want to see a picture of your mother, the beautiful Catherine Wilhelmina."

Then indeed, Grosspapa Hornik smiled. His face shining, he led Betsy to one of the slender-legged tables and picked up a miniature, framed in chased gold. Betsy took it in both hands and stared. Catherine Wilhelmina did indeed look like Tib. It was the fearless expression in her eyes.

"Oh, thank you, thank you!" Betsy cried, and to be sure he understood she added, "*Danke, danke schön.*"

Grosspapa Hornik struck his chest. "Mit me, *mein Kind*," he said, "you may speak alvays de English. Only mit de Grossmama *müssen Sie Deutsch sprechen.*"

Fred and Hobbie came pounding up the stairs followed by their parents, and Grossmama Hornik and Tib. Uncle Rudy strode in also, and Aunt Dolly's fiancé arrived, a dapper pleasant-faced young man, called Ferdy.

Wearing a trailing blue lace dress now, Aunt Dolly tripped across the room to slip her arm possessively into Ferdy's. There were mingled shouts of *"Fröhliche Weihnachten!"* and "Merry Christmas!" Packages were opened with cries of *"Wunderbar!"* and *"Sehr schön!"* and *"Danke, danke sehr!"* Again, as at Grosspapa Muller's, there were presents for Betsy, too.

They all went down stairs to goose with onion dressing, and potatoes, and gravy, and apple sauce, and various vegetables with piquant flavors. The apple pie was heaped with whipped cream. There was beer for everyone, and coffee.

Most of the conversation was in German, but Betsy didn't feel left out. Everyone kept smiling at her, and when they began raising beer mugs and proposing toasts, Uncle Rudy toasted her. Betsy blushed, but she was very pleased.

They toasted Grosspapa and Grossmama Hornik, and Christmas time, and the President of the United States. But they didn't toast a single kaiser . . . not Wilhelm nor Franz Josef.

Grossmama Hornik said something in German and Tib whispered to Betsy, "She says that if Grosspapa were not such a stubborn *Esel* we should drink to the dear Kaiser Franz Josef who appreciates her beautiful embroidery."

"Those who likes kaisers should go back to the *alt* country," Grosspapa Hornik muttered fiercely.

"The brave little tailor," Betsy thought.

She said it to Tib after dinner and Tib answered, "Grosspapa is a very good American, even though he can't speak English. And Grossmama is proud that he was a Forty-eighter, although she would never admit it."

The older people went to take naps, and Uncle Rudy asked Betsy and Tib whether they would like to go skating.

"I'm giving all my girls the go-by on account of you," he said, winking at Betsy.

Fred and Hobbie wanted to go, too, and they all piled into the cutter and drove to the Mullers' house for skates and on to the river. Betsy, a very poor skater, was silently thankful that she hadn't brought skates to Milwaukee. She refused firmly, although politely to borrow any.

"I'll just adore watching," she said. And she did.

For the sun glittered on the ice, a band was playing, and the skaters moved merrily in time to the music. Many glances followed Tib and Fred waltzing together. They made a charming pair for they looked much alike and moved like one person. They stayed until the sun, a round red eye without a single lash, dropped suddenly below the river bank.

Back at Grossmama Hornik's they were all soon eating again. Coffee was made, sandwiches were set out, along with the inevitable kuchen. Uncle Rudy and Aunt Dolly didn't eat with the others. They were going to a Christmas ball.

"Let's watch Aunt Dolly dress," Tib proposed. "She won't mind. I often do." So they went upstairs and knocked on her door, and she called them in.

Her room was all in white and pale yellow. The curtains were white over yellow, the bedspread was white over yellow. There were dozens of small yellow cushions tossed about and a snowy white fur rug.

There were mirrors everywhere. Wherever Aunt Dolly looked she was sure to see her own exquisite reflection. There was a tall, three-sided, pier glass, and an adjustable mirror on her dressing table.

Before this Aunt Dolly now was putting the finishing touches to her toilet: She was wearing a low-cut, green satin ball gown. She had fastened jewels into her ears, and around her neck and wrists. She looked charming, but she gazed into the mirror with a dissatisfied expression.

"This green," she said, petulantly, "makes me look as yellow as cheese." Casually she opened a drawer of the dressing table and took out a round cake of something pink. She took out a soft object, a rabbit's foot, and rubbed it across the pink cake. Then slowly, with complete concentration, she tinted her round cheeks, and the tips of her ears and her chin, which was dimpled like her father's.

For the second time since coming to Milwaukee Betsy was completely astonished. First, the theatre on Sunday, and now this! A hot tide swept up her body coloring her face more vividly than Aunt Dolly was being colored with the rabbit's foot. The blush came partly from embarrassment. It must be, she thought, that Aunt Dolly had forgotten her presence. If she were going to . . . paint her face like an actress . . . she would certainly do it only when she was alone. Betsy didn't know which way to look, and by chance she looked at Tib. Tib was watching Aunt Dolly, and her expression was one of mild interest.

"I'll be glad when I can use that stuff," she said.

"*Ach*, you're too young!" Aunt Dolly put down the rabbit's foot. She picked up a hand mirror for intensive study, took up the rabbit's foot again and gave her dimpled chin another dab.

Betsy's horror was tempered now with a thrill of self-importance. She had seen rouge used, and not by an actress! She could tell her mother and Julia about it.

Aunt Dolly sprayed herself with perfume, and rose. She turned, inch by inch, before the pier glass. She took up a fan, a lace handkerchief, and a small silken bag . . . it was called a vanity bag . . . which she slipped by its cord over her wrist. She handed Tib her white opera cloak and floated out of the room.

Ferdy and Uncle Rudy were waiting in the drawing room. Ferdy's face flushed when he saw Aunt Dolly. Both he and Uncle Rudy had changed into evening clothes, and Uncle Rudy, Betsy thought, looked dazzlingly handsome.

He sat down at the grand piano, throwing the tails of his black coat clear and ran his fingers along the keys.

"I've a new waltz I want Mamma to hear. She talks so often of the great Strauss. Here is a piece as good as any of his and it is also by a Viennese."

He began to play.

The opening phrases were short and artless. They sounded like a rocking horse. But the swing began to grow longer, the rhythm stronger. The waltz began to ask questions, wistful, poignant. It took on a dreamier sweep.

Then a gayer theme sent Uncle Rudy's fingers rippling over the keys. The melody wove in and out. It circled, swayed, as though it were music and dancer in one. It was irresistible.

Aunt Dolly threw her train over her arm. She smiled that sweet sudden smile like her father's, and asked Ferdy to dance. Tib motioned to Betsy but she shook her head and they both sat silent, watching. Fred, too, was motionless but he smiled as though in his mind he followed every undulating curve.

Grossmama Hornik turned her stately head slowly in time to the music. Grosspapa Hornik and Mr. Muller slowly waved their steins.

"What is the name of it?" Betsy asked Tib breathlessly, after it was over.

Uncle Rudy spoke over his shoulder. "It's 'The Merry Widow Waltz,'" he said.

That night, in bed, before she fell asleep, Betsy chuckled.

"What are you laughing at?" Tib asked.

"I'm thinking of the presents I'm going to take home. I'm certainly going to surprise people."

"What are you going to take?" Tib asked drowsily.

Betsy chuckled again.

"A fairy book to Margaret. And it must have *The Brave Little Tailor* in it, and *Snow White and the Seven Dwarfs*. And 'The Merry Widow' to Julia. And a stein for Papa. And for Mamma . . ." her mirth shook the bed . . . "a rabbit's foot."

"I don't see what's so funny. I think they sound very nice," said Tib as she dropped off to sleep.

15
A Week of Christmases

CHRISTMAS DAY WAS OVER, four days of her visit were gone, and Betsy had not yet begun to change.

"I *must* get started," she thought, lying in bed, waiting for Tib to wake up. "I want to be so completely different by the time I go back to Deep Valley. Of course, I've been busy with Christmas. But that's over now . . ."

Little she knew!

"Everyone's coming here for the Second Christmas Day," Mrs. Muller said at breakfast.

"Where are we going for the Third Christmas Day?"

"What is planned for the Fourth Christmas Day?"

Betsy listened in bewilderment. "How many Christmas Days do you have, for goodness' sake?" she demanded, and everyone laughed.

"New Year's puts a stop to them," Mr. Muller said.

The reason for this week of Christmases was clear. It would have been impossible in any lesser period to exhaust the holiday spirit which foamed in the city by the lake. Everyone must see everyone else's tree, and these visits of tree-inspection were virtual parties, with coffee and a great display of kuchen. Betsy learned to recognize a few different kinds . . . *Pfeffernüsse, Sterne, Kipfel* . . . but some of the most delicious had names she never mastered. She and Tib were not able to attend all these gatherings . . . too much must be crammed into two short weeks . . . but Fred and Hobbie reported on the kuchen every night.

Betsy reflected sometimes on how different Tib's life was from her own. Here the telephone did not ring all day. There wasn't perpetually a crowd of boys and girls around. But that did not mean Tib's life was empty. It was crowded with uncles, aunts, cousins and grandparents . . . and with other interests which the rapidly passing days revealed.

One afternoon they took the trolley to Tib's school. Tib was pleased to be showing her Sem to Betsy. When they crossed the Milwaukee River she said eagerly, "We have a regatta every June. I wish you could see it." When the turreted buildings loomed in sight among bare elms, she remarked with a sidelong glance, "It's prettier, of course, when the trees have leaves."

"I like it now," said Betsy, gazing about. The red-brick walls were clothed warmly with ivy. There were towers and friendly bow windows, and roguish gargoyles peering down.

Tib pointed out the athletic fields, the tennis courts, and when she had received permission from the resident teacher to show Betsy around, she took her first to the gymnasium.

"At basketball games," she said, "the girls who aren't playing sit in that balcony, and when a basket is made they yell out the spelling of the name of the one who made it."

"Like T-I-B?" said Betsy.

"That's right," Tib answered, smiling.

"They'd never call B-E-T-S-Y," Betsy said.

They looked in at the chapel, the library, the dining room. They peeked into the Dorm.

"I'm getting boarding school fever," Betsy said. Of course she knew in her heart that no school could ever be more than second best to the Deep Valley High School.

Tib chattered happily of beach parties on nearby Lake Michigan, of plays for which the girls themselves made scenery and costumes. She showed Betsy the large hall with a stage at one end where plays were produced.

"We have our dances here, too," she said.

"Do the girls ever go out with boys?" Betsy asked when they were walking toward the lake.

"Oh, yes, but you take a chaperone and you have to be in by 'second winks.' And Browner girls are allowed to go to only certain places. I remember when . . . one of the girls . . . was 'campused' for sneaking out to a restaurant not on the approved list." Betsy wondered over Tib's momentary hesitation. Could the girl have been Phil Brandish's sister?

"If I were a boarding pupil," Tib continued matter-of-factly, "I wouldn't do a thing like that. Browner is a school with high standards. And schools are like people. They have to have standards and live up to them, or they don't amount to much."

The lake was in sight now. Betsy and Tib clasped hands and ran. It was Betsy's first glimpse of the big inland sea, so different from the gentle, willow-fringed lakes of home. She felt very small standing on the sand, with the gulls swooping overhead and that vast expanse of water before them. The water was gray today, with whitecaps in a neverending race.

Betsy liked Lake Michigan, but best of all she liked downtown Milwaukee . . . the shops and the trolleys and especially the crowds which, like the whitecaps, were never ending. She liked the shipping in the bay, and the Milwaukee River nosing its way so determinedly through the city streets. Tib took her to see the statue of that Solomon Juneau who had started the whole thing.

They went downtown several times, once to a matinee at the Davidson Theatre called *Father and the Boys*. As they waited for the curtain to go up, eating caramels busily, Tib said she saw almost everything good that came to Milwaukee.

"If Uncle Rudy doesn't buy me tickets I buy them out of my allowance. I go alone. I like to, and Papa doesn't mind. I've seen Otis Skinner, and Sothern and Marlowe, and Minnie Maddern Fiske. Betsy, I even saw Sarah Bernhardt!"

"You did?" cried Betsy, and began to laugh. She told Tib about Julia's quarrel with Hugh as to who was greater, Sarah Bernhardt or Rose Stahl.

"Why, I saw Rose Stahl, too!" Tib exclaimed.

"Didn't you love *The Chorus Lady*?"

"Adored it! Betsy, do you remember when I played Meenie in *Rip Van Winkle*?"

"I'll never forget it. You were perfect! Tib, do you think you might like to be an actress when you grow up?"

Tib did not answer immediately. She swallowed a caramel, licked her fingers and looked thoughtful. The orchestra was tuning up now. Fiddles were twanging on the G string, flutes were making rippling excursions into the stuffy, scented air.

"Maybe," she said. "I like to dance, too. But it all goes together."

"I only thought . . . if you're going to be an actress, when I'm a famous writer, I'll write a play for you."

"I'd love that!" cried Tib, and then the theatre darkened, and the curtain went up.

On another afternoon they went shopping for Betsy's presents, the fairy book for Margaret, the stein for Mr. Ray, the score of *The Merry Widow* for Julia. They bought Anna a sewing basket, lined with purple silk, and Tacy fancy hat pins.

Betsy did not have courage enough to buy the rabbit's foot. But Tib, as usual, had courage for two. With Betsy trying to act as though they were perfect strangers, Tib danced up to the drug counter and made the shocking purchase.

"I'd better get Mamma something else," said Betsy,

"and pretend that this is just a joke, in case she doesn't like it." So they bought her a vanity bag like Aunt Dolly's.

Betsy bought dozens of postal cards for the Crowd . . . views of Lake Michigan, of Juneau Park, of Browner and the famous Schlitz Palm Garten. On some of them she wrote, "I want you to meet my friend, Miss Muller, otherwise known as Tib." And Tib scribbled in, "Pleased to meet you," and sometimes, *"Prosit!"*

All these expeditions unfailingly led to a coffee shop called Webers. Every afternoon at four, as Betsy soon learned, that part of Milwaukee which was not at home to put the coffee pot on, gathered at places like this one. There was a bake shop in front at which, on your way back to the tables, you selected a cake from tantalizing displays. Almost everything was covered with drifts of whipped cream.

"Whenever I see whipped cream, all my life, I'll think of Milwaukee," Betsy said.

Choosing a cake required the weightiest concentration. But when they had finally made their selections they proceeded to the tables where one could have either coffee or chocolate from silver pots, with, of course, a bowl of whipped cream handy.

"What a nice custom this is!" Betsy sighed blissfully. "Coffee in the afternoon!"

"But the women in Milwaukee are mostly very fat."

"This is worth getting fat for!" cried willow-thin Betsy. "Let's go back and choose another cake!"

Many of Tib's relatives strove to make Betsy's visit pleasant. One of the stout aunts took the girls to the Turnverein to hear Handel's *Messiah*. A stout uncle sent them to *The Rat Catcher of Hamlin*. Grosspapa Muller took the family and Betsy to dinner at the fashionable Deutscher Club . . . Johann in livery on the box of the carriage. Grosspapa Hornik, not to be outdone, took them to the Schlitz Palm Garten.

On New Year's Eve Tib invited all the cousins to a party for Betsy. While dressing Betsy had an inspired idea.

"Tib, do you know what I think we ought to do?"

"What?" asked Tib.

"Stay up all night tonight, and talk."

"You mean, all night, until morning?"

"Yes. I never did it; did you? And New Year's Eve is a perfect time for it, such a mystic kind of evening. Besides I'm going home day after tomorrow, and goodness knows when we'll see each other again!"

A curious expression crossed Tib's face. Then she replied, "All right. I'll make coffee to help keep us awake. After Papa and Mamma are asleep of course. We'd better not mention it to them."

"Oh, of course not! *Natürlich*."

The evening was passed pleasantly with cousins large and small. Even the twins and Hobbie stayed up for the New Year. They sang and played games, and there were ice cream and two kinds of cake for refreshments.

When the cuckoo clock started to sing for twelve o'clock, everyone made a fearful racket. They yelled at the tops of their voices, "Happy New Year!" and *"Prosit Neujahr!"* They shook hands, and laughed, and Heinrich threw up the window in order that the gaiety of the surrounding houses might come in.

Betsy put out her head. Whistles were blowing, bells were ringing.

"Ring out the old, ring in the new . . ."

But the new Betsy had not yet been rung in. She didn't even seem to be on the way.

"She is, though," Betsy resolved, staring firmly at a star. "I'll start with the new year."

"If you want to get married, Betsy," Heinrich called, "this is the year for you. Nineteen hundred and eight is Leap Year, you know."

"There'll be another in four years."

"But you may not have me around then."

"I'll have to make a special trip to Milwaukee."

This banter made her feel almost as though she were back in Deep Valley.

With the New Year, the party broke up. Singing out good wishes, the cousins departed. Fred took a sleepy Hobbie off to bed. Mr. and Mrs. Muller, too, retired. Tib and Betsy undressed, put on bathrobes and sat down to wait. When the house was quiet, Tib whispered, "Now I'll make the coffee." And they tiptoed toward the kitchen.

While the coffee boiled, they loaded a tray with cream and sugar, kuchen, and what Tib called *Butterbrot*, slices of buttered bread; also some cold beef, two or three kinds of cheese, what was left of the cakes, and dill pickles. The coffee reached a fragrant boil . . . all too fragrant.

"Heavens! Mamma will be sure to smell it!" Tib opened a window and Betsy waved her hands frantically, trying to push the smell out into the night.

Tib took the tray, and Betsy took the coffee pot, and they tiptoed back to their room. The cuckoo clock sang one.

They closed the door and pushed a rug against it and arranged their dishes on a little table. Tib had even brought a lace-edged cloth and two napkins. Neither one was very fond of coffee but they diluted it liberally with cream and spooned in sugar. They made themselves sandwiches from the *Butterbrot*, beef and cheese. Betsy realized suddenly how much fun it was.

"Tib," she said, putting down her cup. "I've had the most glorious time visiting you."

"I've loved it, too," Tib answered soberly. "I wanted you to come. I like the girls at the Sem very much, and I like my cousins, but there's never been anyone like you and Tacy."

"We've never gotten over missing you."

"I was so afraid you wouldn't come," said Tib. "I know how much you think of Christmas in your family. And besides, you have so much fun in Deep Valley during vacation."

"Oh, I was wild to come," Betsy answered. "I was wild to see you. And there was another reason. Tib," she said earnestly, "I want to change myself. I want to get a different personality. And I thought that going away, especially to a romantic place like Milwaukee, would give me a good chance to do it."

Tib stared. "But you're only here for two weeks."

"I know. But two weeks seems like a long time when you're away from home. Do you think I've changed any?"

"Not a bit."

"I was afraid not," said Betsy. "I think I've changed inside though. You couldn't see and do all the things I have, and not be a little different. And when I go back to Deep Valley, I'm going to be changed on the outside, too, so that people will notice it."

"How? What are you going to be like?"

Betsy put her hands behind her head.

"I can't decide," she said dreamily, "whether to be Dramatic and Mysterious, or Ethereal and Intellectual . . . sort of unhealthy in an attractive way, like Elizabeth Barrett Browning. Being tall like I am is good for the first thing, and being so thin is marvelous for the other. Which one do you like best?"

"The first one," said Tib. "Dramatic and Mysterious." She looked at Betsy keenly. "I know a wonderful way to do your hair."

"How?"

"Come here and I'll show you."

They went to the dressing table, and Tib asked for Betsy's biggest rat. She pinned it on firmly, and erected a magnificent pompadour, topped off with a high, pointed knot.

"Marvelous!" cried Betsy. "I ought to stick a jeweled dagger through it. Oh dear, I wish I had one!"

"I haven't got a dagger," said Tib, "but I'll give you this." Rummaging through her jewel box, she brought out a rhinestone pin which they poked into the knot.

"Stunning!" cried Betsy. She stalked about the room acting Dramatic and Mysterious. "A darned shame," she remarked, stopping before a mirror, "that I'm too young to wear ear rings. But I'm going to drench myself with perfume. And I'm always going to use the same kind, so that whenever anybody smells that odor they will know it's me . . . like Mama with violet perfume, only I want something more exotic."

"I have some Jockey Club," said Tib. "Would that be exotic enough? Somebody gave it to Aunt Dolly, but she said it didn't smell a bit like her, so she gave it to me. It doesn't smell like me either, and I'll give it to you if you want it."

"Jockey Club is perfect!" Betsy doused her flannel night gown rapturously. "And Tib, I've read that women of the kind I'm going to be always match their eyes in clothes and jewels. So I'm going to start wearing green."

"Your eyes are hazel," Tib objected. "And blue is your best color, Betsy. Always has been."

"Blue!" scoffed Betsy. "It's namby pamby. And there's lots of green in my eyes. Green for jealousy," she cried in a thrilling voice, resuming her stroll around the room.

"Whom are you jealous of?"

"Oh, nobody! I just like the sound of it. Pour me another cup of coffee; will you?"

Tib poured. "But, Betsy," she said, "you can't throw all your clothes away and get new ones. Can you?"

Betsy shrugged. "I suppose not. Fortunately, though,

my new sailor suit is green. And I can start wearing green hair ribbons and neck bows. I'm going to, too. Gee, I wish I'd bought some green ribbon to wear home!"

"Mamma has a whole bolt of green ribbon. She'll give us some."

"My jewels, from now on, are going to be emeralds."

"Well, that's one thing I don't have," said Tib. And the cuckoo clock sang two.

Betsy sipped her coffee meditatively.

"I'm going to try not to laugh so much," she said. "I'm laughing all the time. And when I'm not laughing, I'm smiling, which is worse. Oh, *why* did my teeth have to be parted in the middle!"

Tib looked at her critically. "You might paste white court plaster over them," she said.

Betsy, forgetting her recent resolve, burst out laughing. She laughed so hard that Tib said, "Hush! Be quiet, *Dummkopf*! you'll wake Mamma."

But Betsy rocked with mirth. "Let's try it. Do you have some court plaster?"

Tib obligingly found some. She measured Betsy's two front teeth, cut the court plaster meticulously, and pasted it on. But by that time she was laughing, too, and they heard a door open down the hall. They grabbed for handkerchiefs, stuffed them into their mouths, and waited tensely. The door closed again, and they removed the stuffing, but alas, the court plaster was gone!

"It's getting cold in here," said Tib. "I wish I dared heat up the coffee. But we'll have to wait until Mamma goes back to sleep."

"Let's move our chairs over to the radiator. There's a little heat left, and we can wrap up in blankets. Let's raise the shade, too. I'd like to see the dawn."

They tucked themselves in cozily on either side of the radiator.

"Betsy," said Tib, "I believe I'll change myself, too. What shall I be like?"

Betsy gazed at her through half closed lids.

"You," she declared, "are the silly type."

"What do you mean?" cried Tib. "I'm not a bit silly."

"That's just the trouble. You ought to be. You disappoint boys, probably, all the time. You look so little and cute and foolish, and they don't like to find out how sensible and practical you are."

"Don't they?" asked Tib.

"No, they don't. You ought to laugh lots . . . just the opposite of me . . . a silly little tinkling laugh. You ought to act too helpless to pick up your own handkerchief. And don't let on that you were ever inside of a kitchen."

"Oh, dear!" said Tib. "I thought boys would like it

that I'm such a good cook."

"Tib," said Betsy. "For a boy who was in love with you to see you making *Hasenpfeffer* with potato dumplings would be an absolutely disillusioning experience."

They started to laugh again and grabbed their handkerchiefs. The cuckoo clock sang three.

"I'm simply frozen," said Betsy then. "We have to warm up the coffee; that's all there is to it." So they took the rug away from the door and tiptoed down the hall again. To their great relief they could hear Mr. Muller snoring.

The rooms of the house were silent, cold and empty, and beyond the windows they could see the ghostly snow. The flame on the gas stove was comforting somehow, and so was the warm pot. They carried it back to their bedroom.

And now waiting for morning began to be hard. They were both very sleepy. They turned down the gas and stared out the window, but they saw only snow and a cold starry sky. There wasn't a trace of dawn. The cuckoo sang four times.

They turned the gas up again and talked some more about their new personalities, but even this fascinating subject could not keep them awake.

"Let's say the alphabet," Betsy proposed. And they did.

"Let's say the multiplication tables," Tib suggested.

"Heavens!" said Betsy. "I don't remember them." But she tried, and it took time. The cuckoo clock sang five.

"Perhaps we might get into bed," Betsy conceded. "It's so darned cold. We'll leave the gas high though, so we won't fall asleep." They jumped into bed gratefully. Then Betsy bounced up. "If we don't turn out the gas," she said, "we can't see the dawn, and I particularly want to see the dawn."

"I'll turn it out," said Tib hopping out of bed. Tib was always quick to do disagreeable things.

They lay in bed staring at the gray square of window. And suddenly Tib spoke. Her voice didn't sound sleepy any more. It was serious, grave.

"Betsy," she whispered. "Can you keep a secret?"

"Yes. Very well."

"I'll tell you one then. Mamma told me. Papa doesn't even know I know it. He came back to Milwaukee because Grosspapa Muller likes his sons around him. But Papa and Mamma like better to be independent, and to raise their children in a more American way. That's why we haven't bought a home, or horses here in Milwaukee. We still own our house . . . the one you always loved so much . . . back in Deep Valley. Maybe, just maybe, we're going back!"

"Tib!" cried Betsy. She sat up in bed again in spite

of the cold. "Why, that would be glorious! Divine! Wait 'til I tell Tacy! Oh, dear, I can't tell her."

"Yes, you may," said Tib. "You and I and Tacy have kept secrets before. But not anyone else."

"Oh, Tib, Tib! Won't we have fun? The Crowd will be crazy about you. Who do you think you'd like to go around with, especially? Dennie is cute. And Tony, of course."

Tib grasped Betsy's arm. "Look out the window! It's beginning to get light."

It was. The stars had faded. The sky was the color of smoke, just a little darker than the gray city snow. And behind the rooftops to the east a fire seemed to be burning.

"We've done it!" Betsy cried softly. "We've stayed awake all night. Happy New Year!"

"*Prosit Neujahr!*" answered Tib sleepily. "And now, for goodness' sake, let's get some sleep!"

Betsy snuggled down. "When I get my new personality," she said, "I'm going to throw in foreign phrases all the time. Things like '*nicht wahr*' and '*wie geht's*' and '*Prosit Neujahr!*'"

"*Prosit Neujahr!*" murmured Tib, plainly too far gone in sleep to understand.

After a few minutes Betsy said, "And I'm going to add an 'e' to my name. B-e-t-s-y-e. Would you like that?"

"Um! What did you say? I was asleep. Good night, dear." Tib turned over.

Betsy laughed. "When you come to Deep Valley," she said, "we'll make a wonderful team. Me, so tall, dark and mysterious, and you so blond and silly." But this time Tib did not answer at all. So Betsy, too, closed her eyes.

The cuckoo clock sang six.

16

Betsy into Betsye

ON NEW YEAR'S AFTERNOON they called on Grosspapa and Grossmama Muller and the dwarfs, and on
Grosspapa and Grossmama Hornik above the tailor
shop. Uncle Rudy said that it was Leap Year now, and
wasn't Betsy going to ask him for a kiss? Aunt Dolly
invited her back to Milwaukee for her wedding.

"I hope I'm coming back sometime," Betsy said,

and meant it heartily. The following morning she started home.

She and Tib went to the depot alone on the trolley. In spite of the consoling secret they shared, they felt sober about parting. Tib wheedled the conductor into letting her go through the gate and aboard the parlor car.

"See what I can do when I act silly like you told me?" she asked with an airy trill of laughter.

"That reminds me! Dramatic and Mysterious," said Betsy, drawing herself up.

They laughed as they embraced, but both of them had wet eyes.

"See you in Deep Valley," said Tib and went quickly down the aisle. Outside the window she smiled and blew kisses, a gay little figure in her purple coat.

The trip to Deep Valley was different from the trip to Milwaukee. The flavor was different. Anticipation was there, of course, but now it was for home. For the first time Betsy dared think wholeheartedly of home.

Her company in the parlor car was different too. There was no sociable Mrs. Gulbertson today. There were five bridal couples, and bridal couples, Betsy discovered are not sociable at all. She looked out the window. It had rained the night before and then turned colder. Every twig on every bush and tree was sheathed in ice. They looked like clouds of silver in the sunshine as Wisconsin hurried past.

Betsy took out a tablet and pencil, but instead of writing a story or a poem as she usually did to amuse herself, she made a list.

"*List,*" she wrote, "*of Things I Must Do to be Different.*"

She smiled as she began for the list reminded her of the glorious time she and Tib had had staying awake all night. But she grew serious before she had finished.

1. *Start signing your name Betsye.*
2. *Don't laugh so much.*
3. *Seldom smile.*
4. *Keep your voice low.*
5. *Wear green.*
6. *Wear emeralds . . . when you can get them. (Jade would do.)*
7. *Use only Jockey Club perfume . . . be lavish with it.*
8. *Use foreign phrases . . . be lavish with them, too.*
9. *See that your waists don't pull out at the waist-band.*
10. *Keep your clothes in press, your shoes polished, and your fingernails manicured.*
11. *Take at least one bath a day; two would be better. Lavish with bath salts also.*

She memorized this list grimly; then she tore it up.

She had dinner in the diner, passing through Madison. Supper came at Winona, back in her own state. Expectancy now became joyful suspense. She sat with her hands tightly clasped.

It was dark outside, and the shades had been drawn. She wondered whether the family would meet her. "Just Papa, probably. But the rest will be waiting up, even Margaret." And that proved to be the case. When the porter had finally brushed her as before, and the train, its bell ringing, had slowed down for Deep Valley, she found her father waiting. The sight of him, so tall, ruddy and dependable-looking, with a happy smile on his face, brought a lump to her throat.

"Well, well! Home again!" he said, as Betsy hugged and kissed him.

She tried to talk about her trip, but he kept stopping her. "No! I promised the family I wouldn't let you tell a thing. They're half crazy, waiting."

Betsy felt half crazy herself as they neared High Street. Welcome lights streamed out across the snow. Margaret's small erect figure with the hair bow and the English bob was outlined in the big front window. The door opened and everyone rushed out, Abie barking and leaping.

Inside everything looked beautiful.

"Mamma has even scoured the coal scuttle," Mr.

Ray said. He always made that joke when one of them came home after being away. There was a fire in the dining room grate, and a lunch on the table beneath the hanging lamp.

"Did you get anything fit to eat in Milwaukee, lovey?" Anna asked.

"Nothing half so good as this," Betsy replied. But she hardly knew what she was eating. There was so much to tell and to be told.

Margaret brought out the new doll in its red silk dress. Julia told about all the parties.

"That Phyllis Brandish was visiting here."

"Is she nice?"

"She took quite a liking to Harry," Julia said. "But I kept him safely by my side."

"Harry," said Mr. Ray, "spends altogether too much time by your side." He seemed a little disgruntled.

Betsy asked for her grip and, smiling broadly, brought out her presents.

"I want you to know, Margaret," she said presenting the book, "that I've seen those seven dwarfs with my own eyes, and I've met *The Brave Little Tailor*."

Julia seized her *Merry Widow* score and dashed to the piano. Anna exclaimed that the sewing basket was tony. Mrs. Ray loved her vanity bag and Mr. Ray, with a chuckle, put his stein on the plate-rail. Slowly, last of all, Betsy brought out the rabbit's foot.

She held it behind her back while she told of Aunt Dolly getting ready for the Christmas ball.

"And if she can use rouge, you can," she ended, extending the package to her mother.

"Here! Here! Give that to me!" Mr. Ray made a grab. Betsy ran, her father following. Margaret screamed joyfully, Abie barked, and Washington yowled. Eluding her father by a breath, Betsy put the gift into her mother's hands.

"This begins a new life for me," said Mrs. Ray. "From now on I'm going to be different." That brought sharply to Betsy's mind the changes she had intended to make in herself. She had been laughing not less, but more than usual. Her waist had pulled out, and the high peaked knot Tib had made on top of her head had fallen down. But her mother noticed the Jockey Club.

"What is that new perfume, dear? Isn't it a little heavy?"

The new personality had hard going that night, and the next day, too. Tony appeared right after breakfast. Cab and Dennie followed. Tacy came to dinner, was given her hat pins and told the joyful secret of Tib's possible return. The Crowd had gathered by evening for a Welcome Home celebration which did not lend itself at all to Dramatic and Mysterious poses.

Betsy told them all about Milwaukee, especially all about Tib. Tib would never have recognized herself in Betsy's extravagant descriptions.

"Gosh, isn't she coming to visit you sometime?" Tony demanded.

"I must say she's changed since we were in school together," Winona remarked skeptically. "She was just a little white-haired kid."

"I should say she has changed," Betsy replied. And reminded of her own plans, added hastily, *"Aber ja! Unglaublich!"* But nobody seemed impressed.

As the days ran on, she made discouragingly little progress. She had no luck with the hair-do, and her mother objected to too much Jockey Club. Now and then she had a trifling triumph. She heard her father say to her mother, "Don't you think Betsy seems a little serious since she got home?" He complained, too, that he could never get into the bathroom. That, of course, was on account of the two baths a day.

"Do you think I seem any different?" Betsy asked Julia. And Julia's reply was satisfactory but surprising. "Of course. Travel is so broadening. But do *I* seem any different?"

"Why . . . why . . ." said Betsy. She realized that she had been so wrapped up in herself that she hadn't paid much attention to Julia. "I don't know," she added.

"Maybe it doesn't show on the outside," said Julia. "But I've been going through a good deal. Harry is . . . quite serious. I think he's in love with me."

"There's nothing new about that."

"Yes there is. Harry isn't just a kid. He's a grown man; and Bettina . . . I like him, too."

"Julia!" exclaimed Betsy.

Julia looked solemn. "I almost think I'm in love with him. And Bettina . . . what do you suppose?"

"What?"

"Papa doesn't like it," Julia said.

Betsy was inclined to take this lightly, but Julia looked grave and uplifted as she looked when she sang.

"It just breaks my heart to upset Papa," she said. "But I can't help it that I have this wonderful feeling. What do you think I ought to do?"

Betsy warmed as always when Julia turned to her for counsel.

"Have you talked to Mamma about it?"

"Yes. She tells Papa not to take it too seriously. It may be," added Julia darkly, "that it's more serious than she thinks."

"Julia, has he . . . he hasn't . . . proposed?"

"Not yet. I don't think he will until I graduate."

"Then don't worry! Because if you do, you may not even graduate." Both of them began to laugh, and remembered that school started next day with examinations imminent.

Examinations, as usual, quite changed the character of life. After school and in the evening, alone and in crowds, everyone was studying. Julia was memorizing a speech from *Hamlet* for Miss Bangeter's Shakespeare class. It was Polonius' speech to Laertes, his son.

Betsy heard it so often that she inadvertently learned it and would chant along with Julia through the various admonitions to the end.

> *"This above all: to thine own self be true,*
> *And it must follow, as the night the day,*
> *Thou canst not then be false to any man."*

Betsy needed such soothing exercise. She was really worried.

"Usually I can rely on a good grade in English. But with Gaston . . . I don't know what to expect. History and Caesar aren't so bad. I think I can manage if I study *diligentia*."

"*Cum diligentia*," Julia corrected.

"*Cum diligentia*. But oh this geometry!"

Julia explained the proposition in hand. "Do you understand it now?"

"If I don't I can memorize it."

"But Bettina, it would be so much better to *understand* it. Geometry is so *interesting*. It's so much fun."

"About as much fun as the dentist," Betsy growled.

She was in her own room, wearing an ancient bathrobe and decrepit slippers. Examination week was definitely not the time to be Dramatic or Mysterious.

When it was over, with Julia and Betsy passing in all subjects, the Winding Hall of Fate took a momentous twist.

Betsy had an attack of la grippe. And her convalescence was not happy. Usually Betsy, who loved to read and loved even better to write, rather enjoyed being kept in bed. But this time, although she had a new dressing sacque and a pile of notebooks and sharp pencils, she did not have a good time at all. She had been running away from some thoughts from which she could now run no further.

The humiliating truth was that she had not succeeded in changing herself.

She had had fun telling Tacy that she was going to change, and even more fun plotting out with the admiring Tib a thrilling glamorous transformation. But facing the facts in her lonely bed Betsy realized that it was much easier for her to plot out something than it was for her to do it. Just as, when they were younger, she and Tacy had loved to dream up wild deeds but it had usually been Tib who carried them out.

This particular plan was unusually difficult to translate into action. It really amounted to play-acting, and Betsy had never been any good at that. Julia could play-act any time, any place, before any audience. She could be haughty or coquettish or melancholy as the occasion required. But Betsy, in the family circle at least, was always the same. She was always plain Betsy.

Right now, the day before the doctor had said she might get up, she was heartily sick and tired of being Betsy.

"I'm so disgustingly young!" she thought, digging into a pillow. "Not in my age but in the way I *am*."

Harry was practically on the point of proposing to Julia. Carney had gone with Larry for four years and now had Al Larson, the football hero, paying devoted attention. Irma enthralled everyone just by widening her big eyes. Winona was not an absolute siren, but plenty of boys followed gaily along her madcap path. Tacy and Alice, of course, weren't interested in boys.

"But I *am*," thought Betsy, tears squeezing beneath her lashes. She was ashamed and dashed them away. "It isn't that I have a crush on anyone. I haven't. But I'd like to be dazzling, popular, a belle. I always thought I would be."

She sat up in bed violently and blew her nose.

"And I *will* be," she said, aloud this time. She went

on silently. "There's no reason why I can't be. I'm not so pretty as I wish I were, but I'm plenty pretty enough. The trouble is that Tony and Cab and Dennie all know me too well. They see me doing homework and washing dishes and things. I can't put on in front of anyone I know. But I can with people I don't know, sometimes. I could with Phil Brandish."

She remembered her thoughts after talking with Tib the first afternoon in Milwaukee. Tib had said that Betsy could probably get Phil Brandish if she tried. All at once everything seemed to fit into place like the pieces of a puzzle. Betsy felt alert and confident.

"I'm going to get Phil Brandish crazy about me," she said, and began to put her bed in order, flapping the comforter so energetically that notebooks and pencils flew in all directions. Julia just back from a lesson at Mrs. Poppy's, looked around the door.

"What do you think, Bettina? The Metropolitan Opera is coming to St. Paul this spring. Caruso's coming, and Farrar."

"Um . . . is that so?" said Betsy. "Julia, what do you do when you want to get some boy interested in you?"

"I tell him I had a dream about him," said Julia, and laughed, and went on to her own room.

So! That was the way! Betsy plumped her pillow and sat up, very bright eyed. She couldn't very well tell Phil Brandish that she had had a dream about him, for she never saw him. You can't buttonhole a virtual stranger in the middle of the street and tell him that you had a dream about him.

"But you can spread the news," thought Betsy, bouncing with determination. She was, she knew, in an excellent position to spread news. The Ray house was headquarters for the Crowd. At any moment now boys and girls would begin trooping in. In fact, the advance guard had already arrived.

"Yoo hoo! Betsy!" Tacy, Winona, and Carney clattered up to Betsy's room.

"What are you looking so excited about?" Tacy asked at once.

"Girls!" cried Betsy. "I had the craziest dream about Phil Brandish."

"You what?" "Phil Brandish?" "For heaven's sake!"

"Yes, I had a dream about Phil Brandish. But don't ask me to tell you what it is, because I won't." And Betsy began to laugh merrily.

Winona started to tease her into telling, but a voice from down stairs interrupted. "Hello! It's Cab and Irma. May we come up?"

"Irma can, but not Cab until I get beautified," cried Betsy, taking pins out of her hair. Irma ran upstairs, and Cab, joined shortly by Dennie, sat down at the piano to play "Chopsticks."

"Irma," Winona said, "Betsy has had a dream about Phil Brandish."

"What was it?"

"She won't tell!"

"I certainly won't! Will you call Julia, and ask her to come like a lamb and fix my hair?"

"Do *you* know what it is?" Winona demanded of Julia.

"Know what what is?"

"Betsy's dream about Phil Brandish."

"Betsy's . . . dream?" Julia looked at Betsy. "Did you have a dream about Phil Brandish, Bettina?" Julia asked easily taking up the comb.

Cab and Dennie, joined now by Tony, shouted up the stairs. "If we can't come up, some of you women come down."

"Go keep the poor things company," Betsy said. And Carney and Irma rose.

Tacy stayed curled on the foot of the bed, and Winona was too curious to leave. She stared with speculative eyes while Julia deftly twisted and pinned and gave Betsy a hand mirror in which to see the effect.

The boys downstairs were calling for Julia to come play the piano.

"Play 'Dreaming' for me, will you, Julia?" Betsy asked.

"'Dreaming'? That old thing?"

"It's so appropriate," said Betsy, and she and Tacy went off into gales of laughter.

"See here," said Winona. "You *have* to tell me what you're laughing about."

"Nothing," said Tacy.

"Oh, Tacy and I made up words for that song . . . ages ago," Betsy said.

"What are they?"

"Shall we tell her, Tacy?"

Julia had started to play, and Betsy and Tacy began to sing, in parts, with sobs of mock feeling.

> *"Dreaming, dreaming,*
> *Of your red auto I'm dreaming,*
> *Dreaming of days when I got a ride,*
> *Dreaming of hours spent by your side."*

"Betsy!" interrupted Winona. "Do you have a crush on Phil Brandish?"

"I never said I didn't."

"But *have* you?"

"I never said I did."

Winona pounced on her, and the scuffle grew so pronounced that Mrs. Ray came out from her bedroom where she had been sewing.

"Is this the way to behave with la grippe? I'm certainly thankful that you get up tomorrow."

"So am I," said Betsy. "And I can go back to school on Monday. Can't I, Mamma?"

"I expect so."

"I hope so because the class officers are meeting. We're making plans for the sophomore party."

Tony, Cab and Dennie roared up the stairs.

"Is Betsy beautiful yet?" "What's this about your dream?" "Why don't you ever dream about me?"

Betsy shouted appropriate replies, and Winona ran down stairs.

Betsy was up and dressed next day, looking pale and interesting, she hoped. The rest of the week passed quickly, more than a little enlivened by talk of her dream.

"Do you know," asked Winona, again dropping in after school, "it wouldn't surprise me if Tony had told Phil Brandish that you had a dream about him."

"What makes you think so?" Betsy simulated horror.

"I saw them talking in school."

"He wouldn't be so mean!"

"Maybe," suggested Winona looking wicked, "he did it on a dare."

"If he did, I know who dared him. Winona Root, you . . . you . . ." Betsy made a dash.

"Be careful," warned Mrs. Ray, "if you want to go to school on Monday!"

"I have to go to school. I wouldn't miss that offi-cers' meeting for a farm."

"Why? What's so important about it?" Winona asked.

"I told you. We're planning the sophomore party. And I have some ideas," Betsy said. "At least," she added, "I have one wonderful idea."

She went to school on Monday wearing her pretti-est waist . . . its lofty collar was encircled by white ruching . . . green bows in her hair and a green belt around her slender waist. Just before leaving she sprayed herself with Jockey Club and hurried out be-fore her mother could protest.

It was good to be back. She was even glad to see the teachers, she announced as supreme proof of her joy. Joe Willard smiled at her. Notes flew briskly up and down the aisles. A Welcome Back present from Tony, in the shape of a piece of licorice, passed hand over hand to her seat and was much appreciated, in spite of the fact that it left a black rim around her mouth.

A short time later . . . she had removed the rim . . . she passed Phil Brandish in the hall. He looked at her keenly. For some reason Betsy did not think at that moment about her much discussed dream. Meeting his yellow-brown eyes brought back the ter-rible moment when she had discovered him listening to her and Tacy in front of the toyshop. She blushed down to her snowy ruching and Phil Brandish turned away.

The sophomore class officers met after school in the Social Room. The president was named Stan Moore. Cab was vice-president, and a nice freckle-faced girl named Hazel Smith was treasurer. Stan at once introduced the subject of the party.

"This is a pretty important affair," he said. "We need to raise money. Next year we'll be juniors and we'll have to entertain the seniors and do a lot of expensive things. And our treasury is as empty as a drum." He looked around the group. "Any ideas?"

Betsy was almost bursting with her important idea but she thought it better strategy not to speak first. Hazel Smith proposed a bazaar with a candy booth. The response was unenthusiastic. After a suitable interval Betsy looked up brightly.

"I have a brainstorm."

"Good! What is it?"

"Let's hire Schiller Hall and give a dance."

"That wouldn't make money," Stan objected. "It would probably lose it for us."

"Not if we open it to all the classes," Betsy answered. "The juniors and seniors give dances at Schiller Hall all the time."

"But, Betsy," put in Hazel, "we sophomores haven't

started dancing much. I'd adore a dance, and I think most of the girls would, but I don't believe . . . to tell the truth . . . that we'd be invited. A few sophomore girls, like Irma would probably get to go and maybe you would, Betsy," she added politely. "But I don't think most of the sophomore boys would ask girls. Would you now?" she appealed to Cab and Stan.

Before they had a chance to answer Betsy spoke. "Oh, but you haven't heard all my brainstorm. This is Leap Year, and I want to give a Leap Year dance. Let the girls do the asking."

"Hooray!" cried Cab. "And the paying?"

"Certainly the paying. Of course, if you are gentlemen you'll return the party soon."

"That would make two parties! Fine for the treasury," grinned Stan.

It was unanimously decided to announce a Leap Year dance for the coming Friday, the last one in February.

Betsy went straight home and up to her room. Since the trip to Milwaukee she had kept a pad of Jockey Club sachet in her stationery which was, of course, pale green. On one of these heavily scented sheets, she wrote a note . . . but not until she had written several trial versions on tablet paper.

The note, which she immediately sealed, stamped and mailed, was signed . . . Betsye Ray.

17

The Leap Year Dance

NEXT DAY AT SCHOOL news of the Leap Year dance blew like a mischievous wind through the cloak rooms, the Social Room, even the assembly room. Not for four years, not for a high school generation, had girls had a chance to invite boys to a party.

"That was a good idea, Betsy," said Stan, stopping her in the hall. "I didn't realize that girls were so crazy about dances. There's such a rush for tickets that it keeps Hazel busy taking in the money."

Betsy smiled, one of the new smiles she was practising. "I'm awfully glad it's working out," she said. "I hear that Hazel's taking you?"

"That's right. Who are you going to take?"

"I don't know yet," Betsy replied. And that was what she said to everyone. It wasn't, she argued, an untruth, although it certainly gave a false impression.

"Who are you taking, Betsy?" Irma inquired. "I'd like to ask Cab, but not if . . ."

"Ask him. He'll be delirious with joy."

Carney approached her. "I'm taking Al. Who are you taking, Betsy?"

"I don't know. Wish I did."

"While you're thinking," Carney warned, "everyone will be snatched up."

"I'll risk it."

Winona complained good-humoredly that Joe Willard had turned her down.

"You ought to take Pin anyway," said Betsy.

"I will. You're taking Tony, I suppose?"

"I believe Tacy's taking him," Betsy answered evasively, and hurried away.

Tacy knew the secret of the pale green, scented note. She was much more interested in that than in whom she would take. "I wish I didn't have to go, but Alice and I are on the program committee. Alice is taking Dennie."

"Why don't you ask Tony?" Betsy suggested, remembering the talk with Winona.

"I'd like to. I know him so well. But you might want to take him yourself, in case you . . . he . . ."

"No," said Betsy, firmly. "If I get turned down I'll have another attack of la grippe."

Phil Brandish did not seek her out that day. But then she didn't give him a chance. She hurried through the halls like a fugitive, not meeting his eyes, and, of course, during the morning she was not certain that he had received the note.

"He must have received it by now," she thought at the afternoon session. But he didn't speak.

The next day there began to be real curiosity about her plans. Winona cornered her.

"Betsy," she said sternly. "Are you asking Joe Willard?"

"I wouldn't dare to ask him after he turned you down."

"Well then, what do you have up your sleeve?" Winona demanded. But even after all the talk about Betsy's dream, not Winona nor anyone else suggested that Betsy might have asked Phil Brandish.

"Any mail?" Betsy asked, bursting in after school.

"No, dear." Her mother looked up in surprise.

"Were you expecting something? Betsy, I've just been saying to Julia, you ought to make up your mind about that party. Decide on some boy, and invite him."

"Urn . . . er . . . that's so," murmured Betsy, and asked Julia, hastily, "You're taking Harry, I suppose?"

"Unnecessary question!" Julia replied. She looked straight at Betsy and her eyes held a knowing twinkle.

But Betsy was beginning to think that this was not a laughing matter. Today was Thursday. The dance came tomorrow night.

"I may have to have la grippe awfully quick," she thought. At supper that night she refused dessert, paving the way for disaster.

Shortly after supper the telephone rang.

"You might as well answer it, Betsy," Mrs. Ray said, "It's sure to be for you." The members of the Crowd were tireless telephone conversationalists. Betsy answered with a cautious hello, but her heart dropped and rose several times like a runaway elevator when she heard a deep and unfamiliar voice on the other end of the wire.

"Hello . . . er . . . Betsy, do you know who I am?"

"N . . . no," murmured Betsy, "I don't believe I do." Mentally she groped for her new personality, for the list she had written on the train. She laughed the low laugh she had practised in the diner. She tried to make her silence full of mystery.

"I'm Phil Brandish. I . . . I'd like very much to go to

that dance, but . . ." At the "but" her heart sank to the ground floor. "But," he went on, "you haven't sampled my dancing."

"You haven't sampled mine!" In glad relief she gave the laugh again. "I can tell you will be a good dancer . . . from the way you walk, I mean."

"I was just going to say that about you," he answered. This was almost more than she had hoped for. "I'm sorry that my auto is put up, but I'll try to get the local hack."

"Oh, no!" cried Betsy. She could never live down going to a dance in Mr. Thumbler's hack. "Everybody walks to Schiller Hall to parties. It's just at the foot of our hill."

"All right," he said. "I'll be around about . . . eight?"

"Eight," said Betsy.

She walked back to the parlor with a thistledown tread.

"Surprise! Surprise!" she announced to the assembled family. "I'm taking Phil Brandish to the Leap Year dance."

"Betsy!" cried her mother, "Why, you hardly know him . . ."

"I suppose," said Julia slyly, smiling, "he wants to find out about that dream."

"The Brandish boy? How did you happen to ask him?" her father inquired, sounding annoyed.

"Oh, I just wanted to," said Betsy, pacing excitedly

about the room. "You don't mind, do you?"

"I guess not, I don't know anything against the boy."

"I should think you'd take Tony," said Margaret, looking up from *Little Women*. Tony was a great favorite with Margaret.

Betsy patted her head and ran to telephone Tacy. When she returned she and Julia went upstairs.

"It's such fun, Bettina," Julia said, "that you're starting to go to dances. Now we'll be going to them together all the time."

"Isn't it wonderful!" cried Betsy.

"What are you going to do now?"

"Wash my hair!"

"Come into my room to dry it, and we'll talk."

Betsy washed her hair, adding plenty of Jockey Club to the last rinse water. She dried it over the register in Julia's room, rubbed it and brushed it, and put it up on Wavers. Then she and Julia manicured their nails, buffing them to diamondlike brilliance, and Betsy told Julia all about the pale green note and Julia told Betsy about dances at Schiller Hall.

"You go up three flights of stairs," she said, "and there's a ladies dressing room just outside the hall. You leave your cloak there, and beautify yourself at the mirrors. They're always crowded with girls. When you come out into the hall you're given your program, and the boys rush up to ask for dances . . ."

"Rush up?" asked Betsy. "You mean they rush up

to *you*. What do I do if nobody asks me for a single dance and my program is a perfect blank?"

"It won't be," Julia said. "But if, by any chance, there's one dance you're not asked for, you go to the dressing room and spend the time doing your hair. You don't sit out on the side lines and let everybody notice you're not dancing as some dumb girls do."

Betsy made a mental note. "There are going to be fifteen dances," she said. "Tacy and Alice are making the programs. They're terribly cute, with a bar from 'The Merry Widow Waltz' painted on the cover. But fifteen dances, Julia! Cab will ask me for one, of course, and Tony, and Dennie, and Pin, and Al, probably, and Squirrelly, and Harry, but that's only seven. I've fifteen to fill."

"Your escort," said Julia, "always writes his name down for the first dance and the last one, and usually one in the middle. If he really likes you, he asks for four." She laughed. "Harry," she said, "wants me to give him every other dance. But I won't. People would talk and Papa wouldn't like it."

"I can just see my program," said Betsy, "with yawning vacant spots." She did have cold chills of fear that she would not be asked to dance, but right along with them was a warm conviction that she would be. This was her first dance. It just had to be wonderful.

"And, Bettina," said Julia, "I think it's swell that

❧ 569 ❧

you asked Phil Brandish. It's time you stepped out and did something for yourself. But he isn't one of the boys that comes to the house. We don't know much about him, and if he shouldn't be our kind, if he should be . . . spoony going home, let him know right off that we don't do that sort of thing."

Betsy nodded wisely. She remembered something Tib had said.

"Don't worry. I have standards. If people don't have standards and live up to them, they don't amount to much."

She went out with the thistledown tread again.

She was still walking like thistledown when she went to school next morning. The girls in the Crowd came up as soon as she entered the Social Room.

"Betsy," said Winona, "have you asked anyone yet? That party is tonight, you know."

"Why, yes, of course," said Betsy. "Haven't I told you?"

"Of course you haven't told us!"

"Really? I thought I had. Let's see. Who *am* I taking!" Betsy rubbed her forehead.

"You tell us!" Winona shook a warning fist.

"All right! Philip J. Brandish."

For a full moment everyone thought she was joking. Irma said, "Betsy! Tell us, please."

"I did tell you," answered Betsy and laughed but she was really flustered. She began to blush and blushed all the harder when necks craned toward Phil. Betsy did not look his way nor meet his eyes. It would be easier to establish that new personality when they were alone than in front of the Social Room. She was thankful that the last bell rang just then. Everyone had to hurry off.

The boys, at the Ray house after school, were equally bewildered.

"What are you going to take that big stiff for?" Cab demanded. But Betsy only smiled, a cool superior smile she had acquired. Cab didn't find it attractive and he didn't like the green bows either, nor the clouds of perfume nor the *"nicht wahrs"* scattered through her speech. He had told her so several times. "What's got into you, Betsy?" he asked with irritation.

Tony's black eyes were laughing. Perhaps, Betsy thought, he considered himself responsible because of having told Phil about her dream.

"I always thought," he said, "that when you started going to dances, you'd go with me. I'd know enough to take a curling iron along in case it started to rain."

"Dummkopf!" said Betsy.

"Never mind! I can mention to Brandish that he'd better put a curling iron in his pocket."

"Tony! You wouldn't!"

"I won't take you to the party if you do," Tacy threatened. "Come on, Betsy. We have to hurry if we're going downtown."

They were going downtown because Tib, off in Milwaukee, always wore lace stockings to parties. Betsy ran up to her mother's room and searched through the rag bag for a scrap of her pink silk dress. With this in her pocket she and Tacy went down to the Lion Department Store and bought lace stockings of the same shade of pink. Tacy, too, had purchases to make. Reassured because she was going with Tony, with whom she had long since ceased to be shy, Tacy was beginning to feel that she might like a dance.

At supper Betsy refused dessert again.

"It's delicate pudding, lovey."

"Put mine in the icebox for me. Will you, Anna? Maybe I'll eat it after I get home."

Betsy was upstairs ready to start dressing at half past six. By the time she was out of the bathroom, smelling sweetly of talc, her mother, Julia, and Margaret, with the cat in her arms, had gathered in her room. Margaret's eyes were as big and watchful as Washington's while Betsy pinned starched ruffles across her chest, donned her prettiest corset cover, strung with pink ribbons, three starched petticoats, the outer one also strung with pink, the pink lace stockings, her high shoes. Dancing slippers, of course, would be carried in a slipper bag.

Julia, who was never in a hurry to start dressing, and Mrs. Ray who by now knew the entire plot, perched on the bed and made lively suggestions.

"Tell him you dreamed he was patching a tire."

"Tell him you saw him staggering under a big bouquet of roses."

"Tell him you saw P H I L written in letters of fire."

Betsy laughed but for once she did not talk. Her eyes were bright, determined. Slipping on a kimono, she ran down to the kitchen to refresh her curls. As she wound her locks on the iron she thought of Tony and giggled.

"That *Dummkopf*!" she said aloud. It would be fun to be going to the dance with someone she knew well like Tony but not so exciting, not so demanding, not . . . she felt . . . so good for her as this.

She ran back upstairs.

"Want me to do your hair?"

"Will you, like an angel?"

Julia did her incomparable best.

Betsy slipped on the pink silk dress. Julia pinned on the daisy wreath. Betsy sprayed Jockey Club perfume and her mother did not say a protesting word.

Ready, down to a filmy handkerchief. Betsy stared into the mirror. Her pompadour made a dark cloud; her neck was white like Julia's. Her figure in the rosy, flower-sprinkled silk looked slender, insubstantial.

"I love the way I look," she thought. "Thank you! Thank you!" She smiled resolutely into her own eyes.

When the doorbell rang she felt like a racehorse, just ready to start. Anna answered and Betsy went swiftly down the stairs. Her mother did not follow immediately and her father did not look up from the paper he was reading in the parlor. Again Betsy was unutterably thankful. She could not have taken the first difficult steps with her family looking on.

Nobody looked on and the expression in Phil Brandish's yellow-brown eyes made it easy to act her part. She put out her hand; he took it in a large strong grip. Both of them smiled.

Betsy heard herself chatting about the party, the sophomores' need for funds.

"That's so we can entertain you juniors next year. I thought I'd start now and get in practise."

"An excellent idea!"

Smiling down at her, his hat in his hand, a white muffler folded with care inside his overcoat, he was very impressive. He was tall, and a lock of his thick light-brown hair hung over his forehead. His skin was a clear olive tint. His eyes were heavily lashed.

He had very good manners . . . pounded into him, Tom had said, by schools all over the country. But he had none of the easy, foolish give-and-take of the other boys she knew.

"I want you to meet my father," Betsy said, and led him into the parlor. Her mother came downstairs shortly, acting gracious . . . not at all as though she had recently been perched on Betsy's bed and thought up ridiculous dreams.

The great Phil Brandish held Betsy's coat, took her slipper bag. She kissed her father and mother. Then they were out in the icy night, walking along sidewalks walled by snow, his hand protectively beneath her arm, going to the dance.

Talking was easier than Betsy had thought it would be. He told her how sorry he was that his auto was put up. He explained what happened to autos in cold weather. Betsy, looking up, mentioned Uncle Rudy's Steamer.

"Steamer!" He gave a disparaging snort. His car was a Buick, he said, and he wouldn't have anything else. He talked on, comparing Steamers and Buicks in technical detail. No one could have comprehended less of this than Betsy but at least she knew well that when a man talks it is a woman's part to listen. She listened, starry-eyed.

"The Buick must be ever so much better!"

He tightened his grasp on her arm.

"In the spring, maybe we'll go for a whirl."

That brought them to Schiller Hall and the three flights of stairs. At the top Betsy left him and went into the dressing room. It was warm, crowded, smelling of mingled scents. Junior girls like Carney had been to dances before, and so had Winona since Pin was a senior, but most of the sophomore girls shared Betsy's palpitating excitement.

Betsy changed into her dancing slippers; she rubbed a chamois skin over her nose. The mirror was a blur of faces in which she recognized her own shining eyes. Out in the ballroom a violin was being tuned. She went to the door to peek out over the glistening empty floor. There were knots of boys talking here and there.

At all high school dances music was provided by a violin and Mamie Dodd's piano. Mamie was a senior but she never danced at high school parties. She earned money playing the piano for them. No one, not even Julia, could play dance music as Mamie Dodd could. She was up on the platform now, twirling the piano stool to conform to her square shortness, smiling and winking at her friends.

On either side of the ballroom door Tacy and Alice were handing out programs. Tacy hurried over.

"You look lovely."

"So do you."

"Are you scared?"

"Petrified."

"If nobody dances with us, we'll hide in the dressing room together."

"Play 'buzz,'" Betsy said.

Alice called Tacy back to her duties and Betsy took a deep breath. She strolled through the door.

Phil came to her immediately. Taking her program he said, "How many may I have?"

"I believe," said Betsy, "three is the usual thing."

"I want four."

She smiled, and he wrote his name four times.

Other boys pressed in upon them. Pin with senior confidence asked for a schottische . . . they were hard to do. Tony, with typical Tony bravado, asked for nothing but wrote his name down for a two-step and a waltz.

"I brought that curling iron . . ." he whispered.

Cab and Dennie had been watching. They nerved themselves visibly, came up and took her program. The other boys in the Crowd came, and Julia's late lamented Hugh, and Stan. In no time at all her program was full, even the four extras at the end. In fact she had to divide one extra between Al and Julia's Harry who arrived late, of course, because of Julia.

Betsy and Phil went to speak to the chaperones, Miss Clarke and Mr. Gaston. Miss Clarke beamed while Mr. Gaston looked sardonic. Betsy gave him her cool, superior smile.

Then Mamie Dodd brought her hands down on the keys in warning chords. The violinist following, she swung into a waltz. Betsy in Phil's assured arms swung out on the polished floor.

The waltz was one they sang around the piano:

> *"Waltz me around again, Willy,*
> *Around, around, around."*

Phil waltzed her around, and around, and around. He was an easy dancer; not inspired, as Tony was. Dancing was one of Betsy's few accomplishments. She loved it, down to her feather-light toes. She even breathed in time to the music and lifted a radiant face.

All too soon the waltz ended and Cab came up for his two-step. He was annoyed by Betsy's faraway look. But they had fun two-stepping . . . just as they did it in the Ray front parlor.

Pin came up for his schottische.

> *"First the heel and then the toe . . ."*

Away they went, Pin's long legs quick and deft.

Next she danced with Phil again, and the words of the song caused smiling faces to turn in their direction.

> *"Come away with me, Lucille,*
> *In my merry Oldsmobile . . ."*

"Only it isn't an Oldsmobile," he murmured in her ear.

She went from Phil to Dennie, to Tony. Dancing with Tony was cloudless joy as always. She smiled beatifically at Tacy . . . who also seemed to be enjoying herself . . . at Julia, who was dancing with Harry. But Julia looked rapt and uplifted.

"That's the way *I* ought to look," thought Betsy, and remembered her resolution not to smile so much. She quickly assumed a wistful expression. But it didn't last, for next on the program came the circle two-step.

When this dance was under way, the violinist called out to make a circle. The company joined hands and circled gaily around the big room until he called again, "Grand right and left." Then you did the grand right and left until he shouted, "Everybody two-step," and you two-stepped with whomever you found yourself facing, until he cried, "Everybody circle," again.

It was glorious fun. Betsy met Pin; she met Cab; she met Tony.

"Well, look who's here!" "Of all the luck!" "Where did *you* drop from!" Those were the proper things to say.

Blissfully two-stepping, Betsy glanced toward the doorway and saw a familiar blond head. Joe Willard was leaning against the door jamb, hands in pockets. He was smiling, a somewhat superior smile, Betsy thought.

She waved, and he waved back, and she concentrated on her dancing, thinking that if he noticed her admirable performance he would ask for a dance. Of

course, her program was full. But it would be a satisfaction to have him know it. And she might, she just
might, split another extra. But when she looked toward the doorway again, he was gone.

The ninth waltz was her third dance with Phil. He
walked toward her eagerly. He really liked her, Betsy
realized, and not just as Cab and Tony did. He looked
actually . . . infatuated.

"I've been talking with Mamie Dodd," he said.
"I've made some special arrangements . . ."

"What," Betsy wondered, "did he mean by that?"

She soon discovered. Mamie smiled and her fingers, roving up and down the keys, seemed to say,
"You're going to like this one." Then piano and violin together began famous and now familiar strains:

> *"Tho I say not,*
> *What I may not,*
> *Let you hear . . ."*

It was "The Merry Widow Waltz."

Betsy looked up at Phil and smiled. He smiled
back, but neither of them spoke. The waltz rocked
through the artless opening phrases. They whirled in
happy harmony.

Then the swing grew longer, the rhythm stronger.
The words sang dreamily in Betsy's head.

"Every touch of fingers,
Tells me what I know
Says for you,
It's true, it's true,
I love you so . . ."

Betsy was certainly not in love with Phil Brandish. She was well aware of the fact. Yet the words seemed sweetly appropriate. The melody wove in and out in dulcet sadness and their feet followed in glad obedience.

The melody changed. Mamie's fingers rippled as Uncle Rudy's fingers had.

"And to the music's chime,
My heart is beating time . . ."

"Exactly," thought Betsy, swaying.

A deep voice spoke in her ear. "Wasn't it clever of me to ask her to play it?"

"Oh, yes!"

"She might have played it for the thirteenth waltz, the one you'll be dancing with that Markham guy."

He had noticed that Tony took two dances! He was jealous! This was the glittering mountain peak of the evening.

Talking breathlessly during the next intermission

Betsy began to tell about Uncle Rudy. He interrupted.

"The one who owns the Steamer?"

"Yes."

"That's a bum car!" He scowled. He seemed to be jealous of Uncle Rudy, too. Oh, beautiful! Beautiful!

Another two-step, another schottische, Tony's waltz, another two-step, and then Mamie Dodd, still smiling but looking a little weary, began the significant bars of "Home Sweet Home."

Phil found Betsy, as boys everywhere were seeking the girls who had brought them to the party. Everybody sang now as they waltzed. Then the girls broke away from their partners and rushed for the dressing room.

"Wasn't it fun?" "Wasn't it divine?" "We're going to Heinz's; are you?"

Out of the babble of voices, and down three steps of stairs! Phil was holding Betsy's arm. They waited there for Julia and Harry, and when they had joined forces Phil asked casually: "How about the Moorish Café?"

Betsy's glance toward Julia was rapturous. Of course they could not go. But to have been asked!

"It's really more fun," said Julia, "to go with the Crowd."

It was fun at Heinz's. All their friends were there consuming banana splits and Deep Valley Specials and Merry Widow Sundaes. Merry Widow Sundaes were the rage. To be sure Phil did not mix well with the Crowd. He took a table for two and devoted himself entirely to Betsy. But that was all right. It was flattering. She hoped Irma noticed it.

Going home they walked slowly up the Plum Street hill. The night was icily cold under icy stars. And just as Julia had warned her he might, he tried to act spoony. She put her hand into her coat pocket for warmth, and his hand followed.

Betsy wondered what to say. She wondered with an intense concentration that was almost prayer. She didn't want to sound priggish; she didn't want to make him mad. But she had to put a stop to this . . . quickly!

In the bottom of her pocket she felt something soft and silky and pulled it out, upsetting his hand.

"Here's what you're looking for. Something to remember me by."

"I don't need anything to remember you by." He took her hand again. "I'm not going to forget you, and I'm not going to let you forget me."

She answered quickly and, for the first and only time that evening, she sounded like Betsy and not Betsye.

"You might as well know," she said with desperate honesty. "I don't hold hands. I just don't hold hands."

He laughed, and let go.

"What were you going to give me?"

"This."

They stopped beneath a street lamp and he scrutinized the silken scrap.

"Why, it's a piece of your daisy dress!" He put it to his nose. "It smells like you too." He reached inside his overcoat and drew out his purse, opened it, and put the scrap in.

"But it's not," he said, "to remember you by. My only trouble will be to forget you."

They climbed the hill dreamily and behind them Julia and Harry were climbing it dreamily, too.

18

Philip the Great

JULIA ALWAYS SLEPT LATE after dances and Mrs. Ray thoroughly approved. Mr. Ray, having country ways, had objected at first. But Mrs. Ray had counted out for him the hours of sleep a growing girl requires, she had stressed Julia's delicacy and had otherwise talked him down. Now it was taken for granted that although on other mornings the girls must appear for breakfast, fully dressed, on the mornings after late parties they might sleep.

Betsy, therefore, would have been privileged to sleep late the morning after the Leap Year Dance; but she didn't. She was awake very early. While the sky was still leaden she heard through the open slot in her storm window the liquid whistle of a bird; a spring bird, she felt sure. It was amazing how that clear, cool whistle, although it came across a snowy world, brought the whole feeling of spring into her heart.

She could see the snow melting and rushing down the gutters where Margaret and her friends would sail boats. She could see pasque flowers—wind flowers, the children called them—on the soggy green hills, and marigolds goldening the slough. She could see buds swelling, feel the warmth of the sun. It was wonderful to have spring come on and be crazy about someone and have someone crazy about her.

If he really were! Perhaps he wasn't? Perhaps he treated all his girls the way he had treated her? Unable to stay in bed with that awful thought gnawing Betsy jumped up. She dressed swiftly and was out of the house before anyone was stirring, except Anna.

"I'm going up to Tacy's," she told Anna. "I'll have breakfast up there."

Climbing toward Hill Street she walked rapidly, her hands thrust into the pockets of her coat. There was a soft south wind. Early as it was, with a copper fish left over from sunrise still hanging in the east, the snow was beginning to melt. She heard another spring bird call and walked faster. She had to talk with Tacy.

The Kellys, surprised but delighted, made room for her at their big table. Although she had thought she couldn't possibly eat breakfast and had told Anna she was eating at the Kellys' only to avoid dispute she found herself eating with a hearty appetite. She and Tacy talked a great deal, too, happily describing the dance. Mrs. Kelly excused Tacy from the dishes, and Betsy and Tacy went for a walk.

Now Betsy poured out her heart. She told Tacy everything Phil had said and done, even about the scrap of pink silk. She confided more than was her wont, even to Tacy, because she had to have her tormenting fears assuaged.

"It can't be that he's really crazy about me! Not Phil Brandish!"

"I don't see why not. Certainly he is!"

"I think he is . . . and yet . . . How could he be?"

"How could he help but be?"

"I don't see how I can go to school Monday," said Betsy. "I'm so afraid he'll just look at me casually, as though I were any girl. And yet I can't bear not to go. I'd die if I had a sore throat or something and had to stay at home."

"Don't get your feet wet in this slush then," said Tacy, looking down anxiously. But even in the throes of her love affair Betsy had remembered to wear her overshoes, which made them both laugh.

Even harder than waiting for Monday was doing homework. There was actually homework. No teacher was more sympathetic to young love than was Miss Clarke and yet she had inadvertently assigned for this particular weekend an outline of the French Revolution. The only advantage to this blunder was that it gave Betsy an excuse to refuse to see Tony, Dennie, and Cab. She didn't enjoy their company today; they had no conception of her feelings.

"I still can't see why you asked that big stiff Brandish to the party," Cab said frankly.

"Betsy's going to be a heart-smasher like sister!" Tony teased.

Invoking the French Revolution, Betsy sent them off home. But it would take more than this remote upheaval to keep them away on Sunday night.

"After all, Betsy, we don't come here just to see you," said Tony. "We like your father, too, you know."

"His sandwiches, you mean. I certainly *do* know!" Betsy thought.

On Sunday night there was the usual Crowd around. Betsy kept listening for the telephone. When

Phil didn't call, she was almost sure it meant that she wasn't important to him. And yet in her heart she felt sure that she was.

Torn by these confused and contradictory thoughts she was up early on Monday. She dressed with the greatest care, wearing a crisp openwork waist over a pale green under-waist, and her most becoming ten-gored skirt. Her cheeks were so red that her father asked her at breakfast whether she had a fever. He actually looked down her throat. But there were no white spots. She was allowed to go to school.

As soon as she saw Phil she knew that everything was all right. She sensed again that—incomprehensible, astounding as it was—he felt about her as Julia's beaus felt about Julia. She even felt sure that he, too, had been wracked with doubts and fears over Saturday and Sunday. The first glances from both of them were questioning, urgent. They were answered by smiles; and relief poured over Betsy like honey.

During the fifth period he wrote her a note. "You haven't told me what that dream was." This was his first reference to the dream.

Betsy wrote back, "I didn't have a chance over Sunday."

He smiled and scribbled rapidly, "May I see you tonight?"

Fearfully Betsy answered, "It's a school night."

Again he wrote rapidly. "May I walk home from school with you, then?"

Betsy answered yes.

Acting as intermediary between them was that same nice, freckle-faced Hazel Smith who was treasurer of the class. She sat at a strategic point between Betsy's aisle and Phil's. After passing Phil's last note to Betsy, she wrote one herself.

"That Leap Year Dance was a good idea. Yes? No? Yes?"

Betsy smiled broadly and answered, "Very!!!"

Phil walked home from school with her and just to be contrary she didn't ask him in. They stood on the steps talking until it grew so late that the melted snow began to freeze in the late afternoon chill. Inside the house Julia was singing from *La Boheme*, that song in which Mimi, the little seamstress, whose name was Lucia, tells how the flowers she embroidered transported her out into flowery meadows. Betsy felt transported now into a fragrant flowery world.

Tony arrived, said "hello," and went inside. Cab and Dennie arrived and walked past with jeering remarks, trying to act as though they hadn't been headed for the Ray house. When Betsy went in, absent and dreamy, her mother reproved her gently.

"I really would prefer, Betsy, to have you ask your friends inside. Phil must have felt as though he wasn't welcome, and of course, he is very welcome. All your friends are."

"How do you like him, Mamma?" Betsy asked eagerly.

"He has beautiful manners."

"Hasn't he?" Betsy answered rapturously. She hugged her mother and floated upstairs.

After that he walked home from school with her every day and on Friday night he took her to the Majestic. Saturday night Betsy took him to a party at Irma's. Sunday night he came for lunch and after that it was Phil, Phil, Phil all the time around the Ray house, just as it was Harry, Harry, Harry.

Phil separated her from the Crowd. It was hard to say just why. Everyone was polite to him; he was polite to everyone else. Perhaps it was because Betsy acted differently when he was around. Cab said she put on airs, acted la de da. Certainly she didn't sing so wholeheartedly around the piano and when the rugs were rolled up she danced mostly with Phil.

Phil was flatteringly inclined to be jealous. One afternoon she went for a walk with Tacy on the hills. They picked pasque flowers, found skunk cabbage in the woods, saw a chipmunk pale from its winter hibernation. Betsy talked about Phil all the time but, of course, Phil didn't know that. He was annoyed with her for having gone.

And he didn't like her correspondence with Herbert. Ever since the Humphreys moved away, Herbert and Betsy had corresponded ardently. They still called each other C F, meaning Confidential Friend, and Herbert told Betsy all about his affairs of the heart. Of course Phil didn't know that either, and when he and Betsy, coming in from school, found these thick missives waiting, he was plainly put out.

But more, much more than Tacy or the far-removed Herbert, he resented Cab and Tony. Gradually the boys in the Crowd almost stopped dropping in.

Not but what their presence wasn't often felt! Sometimes when Betsy and Phil sat by the fire there were mock romantic serenades under the window. Once they made fudge and put it out to cool. When they went to bring it in, it was gone, and Betsy saw footsteps in the snow.

Those long fireside conversations and all their conversations everywhere dealt with two subjects: Phil and his car.

Betsy dug out of her memory something Julia had said last year. "That reforming line is one of the oldest in the world, and one of the best." Betsy started reforming Phil. He smoked. He smoked a pipe. He was the only boy in Betsy's circle who smoked, except behind the barn. It was a wonderful evening when Phil gave his pipe to Betsy. She hung it on a ribbon over her dressing table.

The second and even more successful topic was the auto. He was counting the moments until he could get it out of storage. Melting snow meant pasque flowers to Betsy. But to Phil it brought nearer the joyful moment when he could bring out his car. He described it to Betsy in the most technical detail, and she paid devout attention.

The warm weather continued and one never to be forgotten day he took the Buick out of storage. He could hardly wait to bring it, polished so you could see your face in its red sides, brass work gleaming, up to the Rays' front door. It was the proudest moment of the spring when Betsy walked down the steps and was helped by Phil into the high front seat.

He went around in front to crank it. All the neighborhood children looked on. After considerable rushing from the crank to the seat to work the throttle he climbed in beside her. They started off, and the wind created by the rapid motion blew her hat so that she had to cling to it with both excited hands.

"I must buy myself an automobile veil," she said. "That is," she added with a sidelong glance, "if I'm going to have very many of these wonderful rides."

"Don't buy it," Phil said, and her heart stood still in dismay. But it soared again when he continued, "I've been wanting to bring you a present. You won't let me bring candy, now it's Lent. What about an automobile veil?"

"Mamma wouldn't let me accept it," Betsy laughed. "She's strict about things like that. It's sweet of you to think of it, though." ("I'll buy myself one tomorrow, a green one," she thought.)

The ride was very bumpy for the roads were still frozen into great deep ruts, and more than once Phil had to get out and do things with wrenches and hammers. But when they were riding they went at a thrilling twenty miles an hour. She half closed her eyes and a blurred enchanted world rushed past. Now and then Phil squeezed a rubber bulb. The deep horn sounded.

"Get out of the way! We're coming! Phil and Betsy!"

They did not ride again for a while. The unseasonably warm spell ended. Flakes as big as pieces of paper whirled in the wind; and snow dressed the world in white once more.

But March could not be obnoxious enough to trouble Betsy this year.

This was entirely different from being in love with Tony. Tony hadn't been in love with her. That affair had consisted mainly of her own wistful yearnings. Phil Brandish—it was still unbelievable—felt now as she had felt then. The ecstatic feeling was mutual, or almost so. Deep inside, Betsy admitted that there was something lacking in her own emotions.

But Phil was big and handsome; he was rich and he was a junior. He was very exciting.

An almost equally great excitement came from her new prestige. The girls in the Crowd were respectful about this affair. And there was no need now for Betsy to worry about who would take her to anything. Phil asked her the moment any sort of party or entertainment was rumored.

The sophomore boys, returning the Leap Year compliment, gave another dance in Schiller Hall. Betsy was almost the first girl invited. And the second dance was almost as wonderful as the first one. Again Phil asked Mamie Dodd to play "The Merry Widow Waltz."

It was understood now that they would be together on Friday nights and Saturday nights, and that he would come to Sunday night lunch, and although they saw each other so often they exchanged notes every day in school via Hazel Smith at the fifth period.

Betsy slaved over these notes which were all signed significantly, "Betsye." She wrote and rewrote them when she should have been doing geometry, and copied them carefully on pale green stationery, heavy with the Jockey Club scent. Phil's notes were mere untidy scribbles; he didn't like to write. But the sight of his handwriting on a paper torn from a notebook made Betsy's heart palpitate. She kept these notes in her handkerchief box.

Betsy slaved over her notes, her hair, her clothes, her fingernails. Although Phil was so enchanted by her, she had a feeling that it couldn't last. She didn't dare just be herself. The common ordinary Betsy that Cab and Dennie and Tony all liked would not, she felt, be sufficient for Phil Brandish. She couldn't imagine him liking her with her hair uncurled or when she was having a riotously good time.

In high school they had formed a Girls Debating Club. Carney was excited about it and anxious for Betsy to join. But Betsy thought debating sounded intellectual, unfeminine. She thought Phil wouldn't like it. She said no.

Miss Clarke asked her and Tacy to sing the Cat Duet at Rhetoricals, as they had sung it every year since they were in sixth grade. Betsy couldn't imagine singing the Cat Duet in front of Phil. She and Tacy always clowned through the Cat Duet. Each one tried to make her yowls worse than the other one's yowls. She simply couldn't do it. Again she said no.

When in mid-March Miss Clarke asked her to be the sophomore representative in the Essay Contest, Betsy had a feeling of being actually torn. The Essay Contest was like debating. It wouldn't seem important to Phil. Her being chosen would not raise her in his estimation. It might even lower her. And it would take time! For if she went into the Essay Contest this year she was resolved to do a good job. It would mean hours spent in the library, away from Phil, and in those hours some other girl might very well take him away from her. Irma, for example. Betsy had a deep-down fear of Irma.

And yet there was something in her stubborn nature which would not let her turn the Essay Contest down.

"What is the subject this year?" she asked.

"James J. Hill and the Great Northern Railroad," Miss Clarke replied.

"James J. Hill and the Great Northern Railroad!" Could anything be more remote from spring and the red auto?

"Do you happen to know . . . who the Philomathians have chosen? I suppose it's Joe."

"Yes. And they seem very confident about the sophomore points. But I am equally confident, if you will represent the Zetamathians, Betsy."

"Of course I will," Betsy replied quickly.

Everyone was surprised to hear that she was going out for the Essay Contest. At home they were surprised.

"I'd rather you didn't do it, Betsy, unless you can do it justice," her father said.

The Crowd was surprised.

"What will Phil do?" "Who's going to console Phil?" "Look out for Irma!"

Phil was surprised.

"What do you want to do that for?" he grumbled. "It's just getting to be good autoing weather."

"I'll take books on James J. Hill along, read them while you patch the tires," she said. But Phil didn't think that was funny.

"I don't have to patch tires as much as you think," he answered sulkily.

Joe Willard was surprised. He actually stopped to speak to her on the way out of class. She was wearing the usual green bow at her collar, a green pin in her pompadour, and was scented with Jockey Club perfume.

He looked mischievous, his blue eyes were shining.

"I hear," he said, "that we're competing again. I didn't know you knew anything about railroads. I thought you specialized on autos."

Betsy blushed.

Troubled, she sought out Julia, but before she managed to make her worries known Julia began confidences of her own. Surprisingly enough they didn't deal with Harry's love, nor her father's objections, nor the rapidly impending proposal. They didn't deal with Harry at all. It came to Betsy suddenly that Julia hadn't been talking about Harry quite so much lately.

She was obsessed with a longing to go to St. Paul for grand opera.

"It's perfectly fantastic, I know," she said, low-voiced. "There isn't a chance in the world."

"Why not?"

"Too expensive! I couldn't go alone. There'd be railroad fare and hotel bills, besides the opera tickets for both Mamma and me." It was indeed a daring wish. Deep Valley's rich and great went to the Twin Cities for shopping, concerts and plays. But the Rays were neither rich nor great. Mr. Ray's shoe store didn't yield an income of a size to support grand opera. Besides, Betsy had recently had her expensive trip.

"Does Papa know you want to go?" asked Betsy.

"No, and even Mamma doesn't realize that I've thought of it seriously. It would never even enter Papa's head to send me. But, oh, how I'm longing to go!"

She took out the folder Mrs. Poppy had given her. Enrico Caruso was there in a clown suit, Geraldine Farrar in a ruffled dress and a poke bonnet as Mimi in *La Boheme*.

"'*Mi chiamano Mimi,*'" hummed Julia gazing at her.

"Don't feel badly," Betsy said, deciding to postpone her confidences. "They aren't coming until the end of April. Lots of things can happen in a month." This proved to be absolutely true.

19
April Weather

LOTS OF THINGS CAN HAPPEN in a month, especially if the month is April. Never, it seemed to Betsy, had April been so full of moods. She was especially conscious of them because of Phil who followed Nature's mutations as a fish hawk follows the ripples in a blue Minnesota lake. This was because of the auto, of course. He wanted the weather to settle and the roads to dry so that the Buick could come out and stay out.

But it rained and it snowed. The sun emerged and the snow melted, but it promptly rained and snowed again, sometimes with hail for good measure. Each time, however, there was a little progress. The bushes greened over; the buds on the maples burst open; and Margaret came down from the hills with small tight bouquets of blood-roots and Dutchman's breeches and pinkish lavender hepaticas.

Slowly the world was getting dressed for spring, and so were the girls in the Crowd. Talk was all of new suits and hats, especially hats. The Merry Widow hat had made its appearance this spring. It was as devastating as the Waltz.

Merry Widow hats were sailors, very wide, the wider the better.

"In New York," Julia said, "ladies get stuck in the trolley car doors."

Miss Mix was at the Ray house making Easter outfits and her visit was as confusing as the weather. The house was filled with the hum of the sewing machine. There were fittings and conferences, pins in the mouth, bright scraps and snarls of thread, touchy tempers and company meals. Everyone was heartily glad to see her go although she left lovely things behind.

For Betsy it was a suit, her first suit, blue serge piped with green. Her Merry Widow hat was blue, extravagantly wide, trimmed with green foliage and ribbon. Betsy doted on that outfit. Of course, she was saving it for Easter and this gave her an interest in the weather almost as acute as Phil's. What if Easter should be rainy? A rainy day, always a minor tragedy because it straightened out her curls, would be a major tragedy this year, when she had her first suit and a Merry Widow hat.

She needed to look pretty for Phil's moods were Aprilish, too; and April at its worst, right now. Betsy was starting work on the Essay Contest, and he didn't like it at all. She had bought a new notebook and written on the first page, "James J. Hill and the Great Northern Railroad." Armed with that, and plenty of sharp pencils, she had set off for the library. She would have been exhilarated if it weren't for Phil.

Books dealing with the assigned subject did not circulate. Miss Sparrow had assembled them on a special shelf in back of the stalls, near a table set apart for the contestants. There were eight of these . . . two freshmen, two sophomores, two juniors, and two seniors. One of each pair was a Philomathian, the other a Zetamathian. The essays were graded on the point system, and the society whose team piled up the most points won.

Sometimes the table was almost empty; sometimes all eight were working busily at once. There was a good feeling of respect at that table, and a pleasant mingling of camaraderie and rivalry. Betsy enjoyed her sojourns there in spite of her nagging worry.

Joe Willard came only in the late afternoon or evening. He was friendlier to Betsy now. He looked up and smiled from under his thick light brows when she came in and when she left. But he didn't, this year, ask to walk home with her.

"And just as well," Betsy thought, although she admitted that she would have been pleased. Phil wouldn't have been pleased. He was more and more inclined to be jealous and Betsy ceased to find it flattering.

The approach of Easter, as usual, brought Tom home. He was Betsy's oldest friend among the boys. Not knowing how Phil had changed the atmosphere of the Ray house, Tom came hurrying up the day of his arrival.

"Grandma's making sour cream cake," he said. "The kind with cinnamon in it, and she said I could bring you back to supper."

"Wonderful!" Betsy cried. "Maybe she'll tell us about the Indian massacre again."

"She's sure to," Tom replied.

She did, and Betsy had a very enjoyable evening. But when she told Phil about it next day he began to act stiff and unnatural. At first Betsy could not make out what was wrong. It was too, too ridiculous to be jealous of Tom. Then she remembered that he and Tom did not like one another because of Cox. Something, she realized, would have to be done about that.

"You and Tom will just have to be friends," she said with what she hoped was appealing frankness. "Our families get together, you know. He brings his violin to play with Julia. Why, during his vacations, he almost lives at our house."

"Just don't expect me to come when he's here," Phil relied.

"But Phil, you wouldn't be coming at all."

"All right, I won't be coming at all."

Betsy was appalled. She couldn't possibly tell Tom to stay away. The whole family would protest. And as for having Phil stay away . . . why, Easter was almost here. What would be the fun of a new suit and a Merry Widow hat if she had a quarrel with Phil?

They were coming, however, perilously near to a quarrel. He left, saying coldly that she might let him know whether or not he would have to run into Slade. Betsy didn't telephone him and he didn't telephone her. The next day, the last before Easter vacation, the fifth period came and went without a note. Hazel Smith turned around in her seat. She raised her eyebrows at Betsy and gesticulated wildly. Betsy tried to smile but the result was feeble. Another evening passed and Phil did not 'phone. She cried herself to sleep.

Betsy was stubborn, but she wasn't so stubborn that she wouldn't have patched up the quarrel if she could have seen a way to do it. She really couldn't see one. It was absurd for Phil to expect her to bar Tom from the house.

"Tom's of no romantic interest to me!" she cried in her thoughts. "Never has been! Never will be!" It was all too utterly silly.

But silly or not she came down stairs Saturday morning with red eyes.

The family had noticed, of course, that Phil hadn't 'phoned or come to the house for several days. Everybody tactfully refrained from mentioning him.

Mrs. Ray and Julia went downtown to shop for accessories for the new Easter suits . . . gloves, jabots, and so on. Anna was baking a cake, and Betsy, remembering all the precepts about doing something kind for someone else when you're feeling down in the mouth, offered to help Margaret dye Easter eggs.

They both put on kitchen aprons, and Betsy twisted her hair in a tight knot out of the way. Unhappy as she was, she could not help enjoying the business of dyeing eggs. She had always loved it. The rich glowing colors brought back a procession of happy childhood Easters. She was telling Margaret gaily about how she and Tacy used to save their Easter dyes and dye sand and have sand stores, when the front door bell rang.

Anna was folding in egg whites. Margaret's hands were dripping purple. Betsy pushed back a wisp of hair and rushed through the music room to answer the door herself. On the porch stood Phil looking his handsomest and most immaculate, and he was not alone. Beside him was a slight graceful girl, beautifully and expensively dressed in a gray suit with a big fluffy fur and a Merry Widow hat so wide that it made the one Betsy cherished in a box upstairs look positively narrow.

She was small where Phil was large, but they had the same heavily fringed, yellow-brown eyes, the same olive skin, the same somewhat sullen faces. Betsy almost collapsed in a heap, for she knew that this was Phil's twin sister, Phyllis.

Betsy had heard that when you are drowning one moment may seem like a lifetime. That was the kind of a moment she experienced now. Beyond Philip the Great, and his even greater sister, she saw the red auto and beyond that the greening hill with the German Catholic College on the top. Behind her she heard Margaret happily calling, "Betsy, come and see! It's the most bee-utiful purple!"

There was another aspect of the moment which suggested drowning, too. Betsy's thoughts went so deeply into the gray waters of the past. She was like a diver going down for a pearl and she found it . . . the almost forgotten incident which could help her.

She remembered a distant afternoon back in the Hill Street house when Mrs. Ray was housecleaning and the minister's wife had come to call. Her mother had ignored the fact that she was in the midst of washing windows. She had not mentioned the towel around her head nor the wildly disordered parlor. She had calmly dried her hands and sat down to chat. When her mother referred to the housecleaning, at last, she had merely said that the hard work made her long for a good cup of coffee. She had made coffee and the two of them had drunk it, with a cookie for Betsy. When Betsy dredged up this memory now, she smiled and put out her hand.

"How nice of you, Phil," she said, "to bring your sister to see me!" And she asked them into the parlor.

Betsy perspired but she tried to hew to her mother's line.

"Margaret and I are dyeing Easter eggs. Did you ever do that? Margaret, dear, bring in the eggs. . . . Aren't they beauties?"

Phyllis Brandish did not help her as the minister's wife had helped her mother. Gracious but chilly, Phyllis managed to give the impression that she thought Easter eggs were silly, that she had certainly never dyed them even as a child (if, indeed, she had ever been a child, which Betsy doubted).

While Margaret displayed the eggs Betsy excused herself, went into the kitchen, washed her hands and took off the stained apron. That was the best she could do. The miserable call ended somehow, just as Old Mag drew up before the house and her mother and Julia came in triumphantly laden with small packages. They helped immeasurably in covering the farewells, but when the callers were gone Betsy both laughed and cried.

"If he's worth a fig, he'll like you just as well this way," Julia comforted her.

"You look cute!" her mother said.

Betsy knew better. She went upstairs finally and blew her nose and combed her hair. She wished Cab and Tony had not stopped dropping in. Their presence would have been cheering now. Tom came, but aware of the great concession Phil had made in ending their quarrel by bringing his sister to call, Betsy didn't have the heart to be very nice to Tom. In fact, she wasn't nice at all, which hurt his feelings and didn't help anyone.

Her mother and Julia went into action. Families can be wonderful sometimes.

"Betsy," said her mother, "we're having an extra good lunch tomorrow night because of its being Easter. Don't you want to ask Phil to bring his sister?"

Betsy nerved herself to telephone him, and somewhat to her surprise he accepted the invitation promptly. He even seemed pleased to receive it.

That brought a little of the glory back to the new suit, the Merry Widow hat, and Easter day. In gratitude, next morning, Betsy went to early church. She hadn't gone for a long time, and it was good to be there.

> "Lift up your hearts."
> "We lift them unto the Lord."

Betsy loved those sentences always, but especially today in a church white and fragrant with lilies.

She went to church again at eleven o'clock, to sing in the choir. Julia sang a solo.

After dinner Phil drove up in the auto and took Betsy for a ride. Neither of them mentioned the quarrel and they were very happy. He said the new suit was spiffy, and the Merry Widow hat a dream. He took pictures of her with his big expensive camera. They drove up to see Tacy, and over to see Irma, and down to see Carney, and around to the rest of the Crowd.

"Time now to go over and pick up Sis," he said, and they turned toward the slough.

The snow was gone except for absurd patches in

shady hollows. The sun was so warm that even the new suit felt heavy. Robins were everywhere, and in the slough, red winged blackbirds swung from the cat tails. Betsy exclaimed over them, and he said absently, "Um . . . pretty; aren't they? Listen to that motor! Did you ever hear anything sweeter?"

The Brandish mansion had a porte-cochere at the side like Grosspapa Muller's house in Milwaukee. Betsy was pleased to be grandly familiar with porte-cocheres.

Phil took her in to meet his grandmother who had bright spots of rouge on her cheeks. Betsy had liked rouge on Aunt Dolly, but she didn't care for it on this small, over-dressed, smilingly tight-lipped old lady. She liked old Mr. Brandish, though. He was a big, warm, alive sort of man with a curly gray beard. He could tell stories, Betsy imagined, to match Grandma Slade's.

"Phil is going to bring you over to dinner soon," his grandmother said, as the young people departed.

Phyllis, Betsy thought, was just like her grand-mother. Betsy seldom had trouble making friends with people, especially with other girls, but she could not feel close to Phil's sister. They spoke of Browner, of Tib, of Milwaukee, but they seemed to speak in a vacuum.

"It's not that way with Phil and me," Betsy

thought, puzzled, for they were, she realized, equally uncongenial. Between them, however, paucity of interests did not matter.

Julia got on with Phyllis better than Betsy did. Phyllis seemed taken with Julia. Yet Julia was not very nice to her. In fact, she came as close to snubbing as you could come and not do it.

Phyllis was interested in Julia's music and while Harry watched Mr. Ray make sandwiches and Phil talked with Mrs. Ray, Phyllis and Julia and Betsy looked over opera scores.

"I suppose you'll be going up to the Twin Cities for opera," Phyllis said.

Betsy knew what a sore spot that put a finger on, but Julia gave no sign.

"I'd be glad if I could," she answered casually. "Farrar will be singing in *Boheme*."

"I'm crazy about Farrar."

"Oh, have you heard her?"

"Yes. Many times." Phyllis circled the group with a daring smile. "They say that she and the German Crown Prince have been having quite an affair."

"I don't believe it, and I don't think it's important," Julia answered. That was one of the times when she came near to snubbing. "Just what roles have you heard?" she asked superciliously.

The sandwiches were never better and the cake was

superb. They had a very pleasant time. To be sure, Phil was not at his best in gatherings like this one. He always seemed a little ill at ease with the family as he did with the Crowd.

But he wasn't ill at ease with Betsy. The quarrel was over and things were as nice or nicer between them than they had been before.

20

Julia Sees the Great World

JULIA WAS SINGING, "*Ni-po-tu-la-he.*" When she had sung it a number of times with a look of critical attention, she opened her copy of *La Boheme* and began Mimi's song about being called Mimi although her name was Lucia.

"'*Mi chiamano Mimi,*'" she sang in her own version of Italian. She greatly preferred the Italian text to the English translation.

"How do you think my voice sounds in that aria?" she asked Betsy, breaking off.

"Fine!" said Betsy.

"I wish I could hear Farrar sing it. Then I'd know what I do wrong."

"You don't do anything wrong," Betsy replied.

Julia sighed and closed the book. She sat still on the piano stool, her hands in her lap.

"They're coming next week, and they're going, and not one soul who will hear them needs to hear them so much as I do."

"You mean the grand opera?"

Julia nodded in profound dejection. Before Betsy could find a word of comfort, Anna poked her head in from the kitchen.

"Your pa hasn't come in yet? I don't like to complain about such a nice gentleman, but Mr. McCloskey always came home on time the night I made cheese soufflé."

"I hear him outside now, Anna," Betsy answered.

"Strike the gong for me; will you, lovey? Then he'll hurry up his washing."

Betsy beat a brisk tattoo, and the family gathered expeditiously. It was light at supper time now, and tonight the windows were open, for the day had been unseasonably warm. The soft yet exhilarating air came into the dining room. Julia began to tease her father.

"I don't know about *your* father, but my father brought me up to be on time for meals."

"Especially," chimed in Betsy, "the nights we have cheese soufflé."

"Anna's soufflé," said Mr. Ray, "actually improves by waiting. And I was busy tonight, Anna. Had to pick something up."

"A birthday present for Betsy?"

"When is Betsy's birthday?"

"You know perfectly well. It's next Thursday."

"By George!" said Mr. Ray. "I'd forgotten. That's bad." He looked worried. "Anna, do you know how to make a cake?"

"Do I know how to . . . what?" Anna stared.

"Make cake?"

"Stars in the sky!" she said. "The man's taken leave of his senses."

"I'm only thinking about a birthday cake for Betsy," said Mr. Ray in an injured tone.

"Bob," said Mrs. Ray. "What are you driving at? Anna makes the best cakes in the world, and for that matter there's nothing wrong with mine."

"But you won't be here."

"I won't be here on Betsy's birthday?" Mrs. Ray sounded amazed.

"It's going to hurry you awfully to get back," Mr. Ray answered. He reached into his inside pocket.

Sudden silence fell on the table. A song sparrow perched on a greening shrub outside gave vent to his joy in three notes and a trill which echoed through the dining room.

In a leisurely gesture Mr. Ray brought out a long envelope. He carefully extracted a pack of papers, sorted them thoughtfully on the tablecloth while Anna and the family gazed entranced. There were railroad tickets. And there were two small packs in rubber bands containing four pink tickets each. And there was that folder Mrs. Poppy had given Julia with pictures of Farrar and Caruso and information about the St. Paul grand opera season.

Julia grabbed Betsy's knee under the table.

Mr. Ray looked the folder over slowly. "Maybe, you can make it home by Thursday night. It will hurry you though."

Julia put her napkin down.

"Papa," she said in a choked voice.

"Bob!" said Mrs. Ray. "What have you done?"

Mr. Ray flipped the tickets thoughtfully.

"I'm just sending you and Julia up to St. Paul to grand opera. That is, if Betsy and Margaret can keep house and Anna knows how to bake a birthday cake."

"Papa!" cried Julia again. This time she jumped up and ran around the table to her father's chair. She pressed her cheek against his shiny dark hair.

Mr. Ray said, "Hey! Do you think I need my face washed?" for a tear was trickling down his forehead to his cheek.

Julia ran to kiss her mother. She kissed Betsy and Margaret and Anna.

"I'm going to grand opera! I'm going to grand opera!" Tears were running down her cheeks, and she didn't even seem to know it.

Mrs. Ray jumped up too to kiss Mr. Ray. And Betsy and Margaret jumped up just to jump up and down. Julia ran into the music room. She sat down at the piano and began to play *La Boheme*. She didn't sing. Suddenly the music stopped.

"Julia, you idiot! Come and finish your supper."

No answer.

"Will you come? Or shall we come and get you?"

"I'll come," said Julia, and she came back, blowing her nose and wiping her eyes. She sat down but she didn't eat any more supper. She just sat at the table, smiling, a faraway look in her eyes.

Anna brought in the dessert, but she didn't go back to the kitchen. As usual on exciting occasions she leaned against the door jamb.

"How long will they be away?" she asked.

"Five days, Anna."

"Where will we stay?" Mrs. Ray wanted to know.

"The Frederick Hotel. Reservations are all made."

"That's where Mrs. Poppy is staying," Julia cried.

"Farrar and Caruso are staying there, too."

"What?" cried Julia jumping up again. "I'm going to be under the same roof with Geraldine Farrar?"

She went into the parlor, out of sight, and sat down.

"Bob," said Mrs. Ray. "Whatever made you think of it?"

"I've got a pretty good think tank."

"You've got a wonderful think tank. But what about Betsy's birthday?"

"You leave that to Anna and Margaret and me. I remember now, I remember perfectly, Anna *can* make cake."

"Stars in the sky!" said Anna, shaking her head, and went back to the kitchen.

Mrs. Ray and Julia left on the four forty-five train. Julia was missing almost a week of school but Miss Bangeter had agreed that the trip was educational. Mr. Ray hitched up Old Mag and took the whole family to the train. Harry came, too, of course.

Mrs. Ray and Julia wore their new Easter suits and Merry Widow hats. Mrs. Ray looked excited, and Julia looked as she had looked when she was baptized, and confirmed, and when she sang. She didn't pay much attention to Harry.

Mrs. Poppy was there, large, elegant and radiant,

and Mr. and Mrs. Home Brandish, and others of Deep Valley's rich and great. They all had seats reserved in the parlor car. So had Mrs. Ray and Julia.

"You shouldn't be doing this, Bob," Mrs. Ray said. "We can't afford to be going up to Grand Opera along with all these millionaires."

"I'd like to know who will appreciate that music any more than you and Julia."

"It isn't a question of our appreciating it. It's a question of your being able to afford it."

"You leave that to me," Mr. Ray said.

Julia came up to her father.

"Papa," she said formally, "I want you to know that I'm going to get everything possible out of this trip. I do appreciate all the advantages you're giving me."

"I know you do, my dear," Mr. Ray replied.

Betsy squeezed Julia's hand. "Julia," she said, "you're going to see the Great World."

"At last!" Julia answered.

Betsy felt important in her new position as lady of the house. She sat in her mother's chair and poured the breakfast coffee. She conferred with Anna about meals and told Margaret what dresses and hair ribbons to wear. She asked Phil to dinner, that he might see her in this new dignity, and he was properly admiring.

As her birthday approached Anna suggested that she ask the Crowd to a party but Betsy thought it better not to. Phil still didn't get on any too well with the Crowd, and he was feeling grumpy anyway because Betsy was working so hard on the Essay Contest.

"I'll just have the girls come in for birthday cake in the evening," she decided. "And Tacy for supper, if that's all right."

"Lovey," said Anna. "On your sixteenth birthday, anything's all right!"

Her sixteenth birthday! It was, Betsy realized, a pretty important occasion! Her father and Margaret awakened her by squeezing a wet sponge in her face which wasn't a very dignified beginning. And Betsy chased them all over the house until she stumbled on her long night gown, which made it worse. And at breakfast she was given sixteen spanks, with one to grow on; and sixteen more, when Tacy came in. All very childish! But the day, as it wore on, grew up, quickly, just as Betsy was doing, to adult stature.

Home presents were to wait until her mother's return but when she came in from school at noon she found two packages.

One was from Tib, a pair of stockings with tiny blue flowers embroidered on them. "Very Frenchy!" Betsy thought. "They look just like Tib."

The second package was from Herbert, a Japanese

print showing a big white bird with a long beak and long legs, among some rushes. Betsy liked it . . . not just because it came from Herbert. It reminded her of the quiet bay, smelling of water lilies, and the faintly rocking boat, in which, last summer, she had started her novel.

She hurried up to her room and hung it over Uncle Keith's trunk. If she left it down stairs she would have to show it to Phil. It was more and more inconvenient, having Phil so touchy.

Before the afternoon was over, however, she forgave him everything.

He walked home from school with her but he did not mention her birthday and neither did she. She could not help wondering, though, whether he remembered it. She did not ask him in, and later Tacy came and they went up to Betsy's room where Betsy changed into a white duck skirt and a white silk waist.

"Just think," Betsy said. "I'm older than Juliet."

"Juliet who?"

"Juliet out of *Romeo and Juliet*. She had a big love affair and died before she was sixteen."

"Well, you've had the love affair," said Tacy who always said the right thing.

And with equal rightness at just that moment the doorbell rang.

The girls hurried down. A florist's boy stood on the porch with a long green cardboard box. Boxes like that had often come for Julia but never for Betsy before. Betsy and Tacy began to squeal in unison, and Betsy seized the box and unwrapped it while Tacy, Anna, and Margaret hovered near.

Inside, in a nest of glazed paper, were sixteen pink roses—sixteen perfect pink roses, surely the most beautiful roses that had bloomed since the world began.

Betsy hugged them, ignoring the thorns. She buried her face in their fragrance. She ran swiftly to telephone Phil while Anna put the roses into a tall vase.

Her father teased her about them all through the supper, and the girls when they arrived, laden with packages, exclaimed and teased too.

Irma ran out to the kitchen and got sixteen cubes of sugar and tied them by ribbons from a chandelier.

"Sweet sixteen!" someone cried.

"Sweet sixteen and never been kissed!"

"She gets pink roses, though."

It was glorious.

There was chocolate ice cream, and Anna outdid herself on the cake.

"What do you think, Mr. Ray?" she asked as she brought it in, candles gleaming, "Can I make cake or can't I? Stars in the sky! You should have heard Charley when I told him what you said."

And before Betsy blew the candles out (at one puff, with a secret wish that Phil might keep on being crazy about her forever), her mother and Julia walked in. They had come from the train in Mr. Thumbler's hack. Mr. Ray had not met them, for the ecstatic jumbled postal cards and letters which had flooded the mails ever since they reached St. Paul had not made clear just when they would return.

Both were radiant and even before Julia took off her Merry Widow hat she gave Betsy her present. The box bore the name of a St. Paul jewelry store. The girls crowded around as Betsy opened it.

"Oh, how beautiful! How lovely!" It was a gold linked bracelet, the first really fine piece Betsy ever had owned. She hung it on her wrist, pushed it up her slender arm.

She wore it over the wristband of her night gown when she sat on Julia's bed later hearing the story of the trip. Her hair was wound on Magic Wavers which always made her face look childishly round. Julia was in bed, her dark hair loose around her shining face.

"It was too unutterably wonderful," Julia said. "I was longing for you, Bettina. I could hardly stand it that you weren't there."

"It would have been over my head," Betsy said.

"Nonsense! You're much more musical than you

let on," said Julia, who had a gracious habit of investing Betsy with all the qualities she most admired.

The first opera had been *Die Walküre*.

"That was over *my* head," Julia said. "I came back to the hotel so blue. I thought, 'Can I possibly be mistaken? Can it be that I don't like opera after all?' But I know now it was because *Walküre* is so hard. It's the ultimate, Mrs. Poppy says."

"The next was *La Boheme*! I saw Geraldine Farrar come in with her candle. I heard her sing '*Mi chiamano Mimi*.' Oh, Bettina how I cried! And I knew then. *Cavalleria* and *Pagliacci* only made me surer, and so did *Aïda*, although that's pretty hard, too. Not like Wagner, of course. He's just the ultimate."

"I thought *Die* whatever-it-is was the ultimate?"

"But that's Wagner. Don't you see, darling? I'm going to send for *all* the scores, and then you'll understand."

"Tell me about seeing Farrar and Caruso around the hotel," Betsy said, reaching for some bedclothes. The room was growing cold.

"Well, I saw them. You did Caruso an injustice in your essay on Puget Sound last year. He isn't really short and fat, and he's *very* magnetic. Farrar is adorable. She was wearing a suit, just as simple as could be. And, Bettina, she does look like me!"

"Does she really?"

"Yes. Or I look like her. It might be more respectful to put it that way."

Julia paused a moment, and when the talk stopped the room was very quiet. For it was late now. Betsy's sixteenth birthday was a thing of the past.

"The trip settled one thing for me," Julia said. "I belong in the Great World. There's no doubt about that. I'm definitely going to be an opera star."

"But, Julia?" asked Betsy. "What about Harry?"

"Harry?" asked Julia vaguely. "Harry?" She sounded almost as though she were asking, "Who is Harry?"

"Oh, Harry!" she said, bringing her thoughts back from far spaces. "Harry will get along all right."

21

Dree-eee-eaming Again

HARRY PROPOSED TO JULIA. He didn't wait for her to graduate. Perhaps he thought the coolness which developed so rapidly after her return from St. Paul would be checked by laying his heart and his hand at her feet. So he only waited for a moonlight night, and laid them there.

Julia refused him. Naturally she was gratified by

having received a proposal . . . her first. Coming into the house, after it happened, she went to Betsy's room and told her all about it, and called her mother who slipped on a kimono and came in to hear, too. Julia described the proposal in detail, but she hardly bothered to mention that she had turned him down. That was taken for granted.

"Poor Harry!" mourned Betsy. "Did he feel badly, Julia? I hope you were nice to him."

"Oh, I was lovely," said Julia, and went out of the room singing *"Mi chiamano, Mimi."*

"We all know your name is Lucia!" Betsy called after her. "What we want to know is how poor Harry felt."

But Julia was already taking the pins out of her hair.

"I must say," said Mrs. Ray, going back to bed, "that Papa does a lot of unnecessary worrying."

Harry stopped coming to the house but Julia didn't seem to mind. She was busy just then with Tacy's lessons. Miss Clarke had asked Tacy again to sing at Rhetoricals and Julia had almost hypnotized her into accepting. Now they were working hard on the song Tacy would sing.

> *"There's a bower of roses,*
> *By Bendemeer's stream . . ."*

Tacy sang it over and over. Sometimes Betsy, in the parlor, heard her break off and say;

"Julia! I just can't do it!"

But Julia would answer, "Nonsense!" and start over again. When Tacy wasn't thinking about Rhetoricals, she sang it very sweetly.

On the great afternoon Betsy was as nervous as Tacy. They walked to school together, and Betsy kept tight hold of Tacy's icy hand. Tacy's eyes were full of misery. Her cheeks which were usually flushed were so pale that Betsy could see the freckles on them. She was dressed up, of course, in her Sunday blue silk, but she wore her red hair just as always in Grecian braids. No one had been able to persuade Tacy into a pompadour.

"Cheer up!" said Betsy. "Maybe the school will burn down. I'd touch a match to it if I weren't so sure that you're going to sing like an angel."

Tacy tried to smile.

Rhetoricals got under way, with a chorus number. Betsy among the second sopranos kept looking anxiously at Tacy among the first sopranos and then accusingly at Julia. It was all Julia's fault, but her expression was guiltlessly bright. Katie looked as grim as Betsy. She and Betsy were feeling just the same.

Alice recited a piece. *"Johnny gets a hair cut."* It

was humorous and people laughed. But Betsy could not laugh, looking at Tacy's stony profile; and neither could Katie. Julia laughed and clapped.

Number by number, inexorably, the program went forward. At last Miss Clarke announced a solo by Tacy Kelly. Betsy twisted her fingers and looked into her lap. She could not watch Tacy going down the aisle, like a sleep walker, white and stiff.

Julia, who was to play her accompaniment, went forward with her usual assurance. She swung the piano stool up to a proper height, sat down and opened her music. The piano was placed so that she could look at Tacy, and she looked up now, full in her face, and smiled.

She played the opening bars and her lips formed the words. She was almost singing. Tacy began to sing.

And Betsy began to breathe again, and Katie gulped and color swept into her face. For Tacy was singing beautifully, as she sang by the Ray piano.

> *"There's a bower of roses,*
> *By Bendemeer's stream . . ."*

Her voice was tender and plaintive like an Irish harp.

She was tremulously happy afterward. Miss Clarke

said, "You're not going to get out of singing solos after this, Tacy. You're going to sing often for Rhetoricals."

Betsy and Katie were radiant, and Julia was proud.

"I always knew she could do it. She has temperament. Lesson tomorrow at three forty-five, Tacy dear."

Julia was engrossed with Tacy's lessons, but being Julia she was soon engrossed also with more romantic affairs. May had warmed up gradually. On the hills around Deep Valley the wild white plum was in bloom, and one fine afternoon the faculty and the seniors had a picnic. It was an annual event, which Betsy considered important because it gave a holiday to the rest of the school. She and Phil had a splendid ride, and he had just left her at home when Julia came in.

She ran up the steps and into the house calling, "Bettina! Mamma! Bettina!"

"Yes, yes!" "What is it?" Mrs. Ray and Betsy came running.

Julia's hair had blown loose and her small hands were grubby. She was holding a gigantic bouquet of purple violets.

"Bettina!" she said, looking mischievous. "You can now have your revenge."

"What do you mean? What revenge? I don't want any revenge."

"Any time you want it."

"But who on?" Betsy demanded.

"Who do you think fell for me at that picnic? And I didn't try, Bettina. I give you my word I didn't."

"Who?"

Julia began to laugh, showing her pretty teeth, set close together like Geraldine Farrar's. She looked more mischievous than ever.

"Gaston!" she cried. "Your precious Gaston!"

Betsy was thunderstruck.

"I don't see how you can even be interested in such a horrid person," Mrs. Ray said.

"But don't you see?" asked Julia. "I can help Betsy get her revenge."

"Maybe you can get me an 'E,'" said Betsy. "I'd like that better. But I simply can't believe it. He isn't human. He cares for nothing but cutting up frogs."

"He cares about violets," said Julia and gave the big bunch to Betsy to smell while she went to get a vase.

It was true. Astounding as it seemed, Mr. Gaston now followed Julia with calf's eyes. Betsy did not think she could count on an "E" but she did notice a marked softening in his attitude. He smiled at her sometimes, a little sheepishly. He reminded her that she was excused from her homework because she was studying for the Essay Contest.

She was certainly working hard on that. Oftener and oftener now she braved Phil's displeasure and went to the library. Almost in spite of herself she had become fascinated by the life of James J. Hill. She came to know the tough-fibered young Canadian who arrived in Minnesota at the age of seventeen and was soon directing the boats on its rivers and the course of silvery rails across its land. She came to see the majestic northwest country, its Indians and trappers, its pine-encircled lakes and the rivers with magic names. Red River of the North! She said that over and over to herself. She read more than she needed to read, everything she could find, and her essay grew and took shape in her mind until she looked with a friendly challenge into Joe Willard's blue eyes.

"I suppose," he said one day, "you're going to put pink apple blossoms into your essay?"

"Don't you think," Betsy returned, "that apple pie would be more in James J's line?"

"An apple in his pocket, I'd say," Joe answered, and they terminated the conversation quickly. Contestants weren't supposed to discuss their subject with one another.

"After we've written our essays," Betsy thought, "I'd like to talk James J. Hill over with Joe."

Phil disliked the subject, and Betsy ruled it out of

their conversation as they bounced, jounced and rattled about the countryside. Apple trees were coming into bloom, and she found herself squinting at them.

"They look pink, but like pink under gray gauze," she remarked to Phil.

"What are you so interested in apple blossoms for?" he asked, and she explained, but he did not vouchsafe an opinion as to their color.

He was interested only in the auto, careening along at twenty miles or so an hour. They went too fast to admire the flowering bushes, the hosts of bright warblers, the brimming streams with violets and strawberry blossoms on their banks. The enchanting scent of May was blotted out by the bitter smell of gasoline.

Yet when they went, it was better than when they stood still. They were constantly getting stuck in the mud, which infuriated Phil. They got stuck going up hills, too; the engine stalled, and they had to pile rocks and pieces of wood behind the wheels. Betsy had always liked hills, but she came to dread the sight of one.

Things happened, too, to a red auto. Tires had to be patched. The insides had to be tinkered with. Farmers had to come and pull it to the nearest blacksmith shop and Phil always thought the blacksmith was an idiot.

A red auto, Betsy decided, was not so nice as a surrey.

The rest of the Crowd was taking picnics out behind Dandy or Alice's Rex. Betsy had loved picnics ever since she and Tacy, at the age of five, started taking their suppers up to the Hill Street bench. But Phil cared no more for picnics than he did for scenery. He talked scornfully of spiders, and sandy sandwiches, and warm lemonade and other inconsequential things. The spring went by, and Betsy hadn't eaten one hard-boiled egg out doors.

The Friday before the Essay Contest, which was always held on Saturday, the Crowd planned a picnic at Page Park. Tacy had had the idea last fall, the day she and Betsy, up on their own Big Hill, had made up the "Dreaming" song. It had never been carried out, but now the Crowd was enthusiastic.

"Don't you think you and Phil could come?" Tacy pleaded. "I know the Essay Contest comes tomorrow, but you must have studied enough."

"I have," Betsy said. "My head wouldn't hold one more fact about James J. Hill. I'd write a better essay if I went out on a picnic today and let the whole thing jell."

"Then you'll come?" Tacy cried joyfully.

"I'll ask Phil."

Phil was reluctant, as Betsy had known he would be. But she was more insistent than usual. Usually, they did without argument whatever Phil wanted to do. But today Betsy so yearned for a picnic, and the Crowd, and Page Park out on the river that she actually teased.

"I can't imagine anything worse," Phil said, but he gave in at last, with bad grace.

Betsy tried to forget about his ill humor. She hurried home after school, took her books to her room, and put out of sight in Uncle Keith's trunk the notebook with her James J. Hill material.

"I'm just going to forget about you," she said closing the lid. She knew she had done a thorough research job, and she would come back from the picnic so full of joy and fresh air that she couldn't help sleeping well, and writing well tomorrow. "I'm going to write the durn best essay in the contest," she remarked to space.

She put on an old blue sailor suit, and dressed her hair in a braid turned up with a big bow. That was the way she had worn it last year; the way Carney still wore hers. She and Anna filled a basket gleefully, and she looked so happy when she greeted Phil at the door that he almost forgave her for making him go on the picnic. They drove around collecting Tacy, Squirrelly, Pin, Winona. The rest were going with Carney and Alice in their surreys.

They drove across the slough and through the high

white gate which admitted one to the glories of Page Park. There was a race track with a grandstand; then a hill with a flagpole, and on the other side a picnic ground with tall swings and a little kitchen. Beyond that the river flowed over its sandy bottom.

The Crowd went to the picnic ground and swung in the big swings. They swung sitting down with someone pushing, and standing, in pairs, pumping up. Tony and Betsy went so high that they could see the river.

They went to the little kitchen, and made coffee in a big pot. They set out on one of the long tables potato salad, potted meat, sandwiches, hard-boiled eggs, a chocolate cake, a cocoanut cake, and a jug of lemonade. It was a marvelous supper, and Betsy ached from laughing at the silly jokes which seasoned it. Everyone was having a very good time. Even Phil was smiling.

When the empty plates had been piled back into the baskets, the Crowd went to the river. The sky was still flushed with sunset. They skipped stones and the boys, to be daring, smoked punk wood. It grew dark and cool and they made a campfire and sat down around it and sang.

They sang the old songs first, "Annie Laurie," "Juanita," "My Wild Irish Rose," and that one about a tavern.

"There is a tavern in the town,
  in the town,
    And there my true love sits him down,
      sits him down."

Tony chimed in expertly in his deep bass. Betsy sat with her arm around Tacy, singing alto and acting as silly as she used to act in the pre-Philip era.

Exhausting the old songs they came up to "Shine Little Glow Worm," "In the Good Old Summer Time," and others of more recent vintage. They sang "Because I'm Married Now," and "I'm Afraid to Go Home in the Dark." When they were almost sung out, Winona sprang up suddenly.

"I know one we ought to sing in honor of Betsy and Phil!"

She started to sing "Dreaming."

Everyone chimed in, and instead of singing the right words they sang the words Betsy had made up. They had learned them the day of her fictitious dream, and had often sung them teasingly since. Winona, Betsy knew, didn't mean any harm. She probably thought that Phil had heard the parody, and that, if he hadn't, it would be a good joke. Tacy turned her head sharply toward Betsy. Her eyes in the darkness seemed to ask whether she should stop it. But it was too late to try to do that now.

The Crowd was singing lustily:

"*Dreaming, Dreaming,*
Of your red auto I'm dreaming,
Dreaming of days when I got a ride,
Dreaming of hours spent by your side.
Dreaming, dreaming,
Of your red auto I'm dreaming,
Love will not change,
While the auto ree-mains,
Dree-ee-eaming."

Betsy sang merrily along with the rest. Phil had never heard the parody, so far as she knew. But of course he wouldn't mind. Yet she had a queer apprehensive feeling. Phil didn't have a very good sense of humor.

He was not sitting near her and she could not see his expression. Walking back to the picnic ground for the baskets he did not seek her out. They went on to the field where Dandy and Rex were finishing their oats and where Phil had left the auto. Still neither chance nor design brought them together.

Calling jokes and farewells, people took the same seats they had occupied driving out. Betsy sat down on the front seat of the auto. Phil cranked and the car began to shake. He climbed up beside her but he did not speak.

They left Winona and Pin at Winona's house, took Squirrelly to his home and Tacy to Hill Street. Tacy had noticed, Betsy knew, that Phil was very silent. Getting out of the auto, she leaned over and gave Betsy a kiss.

"You write a good essay tomorrow. Do you hear? I'll be saying my prayers for you."

"Thanks," Betsy said, and she and Phil drove on.

Betsy felt terrible. Her apprehension had grown into a premonition of disaster. She felt slightly ill as the car bounced along down Hill Street, down Broad Street, and up the Plum Street hill. Phil had still not spoken. Betsy made one or two timid conversational overtures but he did not respond, so she too was silent.

He got out of the auto, and helped her out. They climbed the two flights of stairs to her porch, but he did not hold her arm as usual. She started to open the door.

"Good night," she said. Then he burst out.

"What do you mean by making a fool of me with that ridiculous song?"

"Phil," said Betsy. "You must believe me. I made up that song . . . or Tacy and I did together . . . way last September, before I even knew you."

"It's about me, isn't it?"

"Yes, but . . ."

"I thought I meant more to you than that."

"But don't you see? I made up that song before I even knew you. Tacy and I were out on a picnic. We were just acting silly. You know how silly we act . . ." But he didn't. She had never acted silly in front of Phil . . . until tonight.

"I thought you acted very silly at the park," he said coldly.

"I suppose you didn't like me that way."

"No, I can't say I did."

All at once they were in the midst of a furious quarrel.

Betsy interrupted desperately. "Phil, listen to me. I tell you again that when I made up that song you were a perfect stranger. But I'm sorry. Do you hear? I'm apologizing. I'm very sorry."

Phil jumped off the porch and ran back to his auto.

Betsy went into the house and up to her room.

"Have fun?" came a voice from her mother's room.

"Wonderful," said Betsy. She started undressing. She didn't wash or put up her hair. She didn't even think of doing it. She got into her night gown, and into bed, and started to cry.

She had lost Phil. She knew she had lost him. The proud dazzling structure of the Betsye-Phil affair had crashed about her head. She had lost Phil. Irma, probably, would get him. She cried for a very long time.

When the gong woke her next morning, she felt numb. Her head was aching. In the mirror she saw that she looked as badly as she felt. She couldn't remember a thing about James J. Hill.

At breakfast everyone noticed how badly she looked. The family knew without being told that she had quarreled with Phil. She took coffee, found a pen, and said good-by. Everyone wished her good luck but with almost frightened glances. They knew, Betsy felt, that no one who looked as she looked this morning could possibly win.

She walked to school and found Miss Clarke and Miss O'Rourke waiting in the upper hall. Just as last year, they directed her into the algebra classroom where the other seven contestants were already gathered. Joe Willard grinned when Betsy came in, but when he saw her expression he looked troubled. A bell rang, and they all started to write.

Betsy's essay was not so bad as she had feared it would be. Everything she knew about James J. Hill came back to her and she knew all there was to be found out about him in the Deep Valley Public Library. Yet even as she wrote her well organized and heavily factual paper, she knew it was not good. Not at one point did she kindle to her subject and bring it to life. Not one bit of the emotion she had felt when she read about the Red River of the North came back to her now and transferred itself to paper.

She wrote until twelve o'clock, then turned in her essay and went out into the hall.

Astonishingly, Joe Willard was waiting for her. It had never happened before. He stood brushing his hands over his yellow hair with a worried expression.

"You didn't feel well; did you, Betsy?"

She managed to smile. "Yes, of course. I have a feeling, though, that the Philomathians have won the sophomore points."

22

Betsye into Betsy

She still felt numb, but that wore off at last. She began to be pricklingly conscious of the warm sweet day pushing in at the windows, the smell of lilacs, the song of birds. The telephone too grew harder to bear. It rang and rang, but it was always for Julia, or her father, or her mother; or if it was for her, it was not Phil. Her heart would rush up into her throat when she was called to the 'phone, and her mother and Julia must have sensed this, for they stopped saying just, "Telephone, Betsy." They began to say gently, "It's for you, Betsy, but it isn't Phil."

Late that Sunday afternoon Winona telephoned. She sounded anxious.

"Gee, Betsy, I hope I didn't get you in Dutch starting that song Friday night. I thought Phil had heard it. And anyway, I never thought of it making him mad."

Betsy swallowed. "What makes you think it did?"

"Why . . . er . . . you might as well know. He's called Irma and asked her to go to the track meet. Next Saturday. He wants her to go out in his auto."

So! It had come! But Betsy had known it would come. She had known even before last night when everything toppled. It had always been just a house of cards.

She was silent for so long that Winona spoke again.

"Irma didn't wangle it, Betsy. She doesn't even want to go."

The powerful arm of pride stretched out to steady Betsy.

"Tell Irma for me she's a chump not to go. That auto is fun."

"You ought to know!" Winona gave a relieved giggle.

"Phil and I had a terrible row," Betsy said, "and

we're finished. Tell Irma that if she wants to see the Merry Widow, she can just come up and look at me."

"You don't sound very heartbroken."

"I'll put on my Merry Widow hat for her," Betsy joked. They talked a little longer, and then Betsy rang off.

She went to the closet for a jacket and a tam.

"I'm going for a walk," she called carelessly to the family.

The May evening was poignantly sweet with a moon like a half slice of lemon in the sky. Betsy began to walk, and at the same time she began to cry. She walked and cried for a long time but that was the end of her tears. She found herself at Lincoln Park, that pie-shaped piece of land with a big elm tree and a fountain on it, which stood where Broad Street met Hill. Instinctively, in her trouble, she had headed for Hill Street and Tacy. But she stopped at Lincoln Park. She washed her face and hands in the fountain and dried them on her handkerchief and sat down on a bench and looked up at the sky.

"Well, that's that," she said.

She went back to the thought she had had when Winona told her the news. It couldn't have lasted.

"It couldn't have lasted. It wasn't true from the beginning. It wasn't the real me that Phil liked. No particular compliment in having him crazy about somebody who wasn't even me.

"I'm darned glad I went down to Tom's for that sour cream cake, even though it did make Phil mad, and that was the beginning of everything. I wanted to go.

"And I'm darned glad I did my best on the Essay Contest. The Essay Contest was more important than he was. It belonged to me, not to some person I was pretending to be.

"I'm not even sorry I acted so silly at the picnic. I'm sorry about the song . . . that hurt his feelings. But when I acted silly I was doing what I had a right to do. I was just being myself."

That last phrase brought into her mind something which comforted her. It was the poetry Julia had been reciting around the house last winter.

> *"This above all: to thine own self be true,*
> *And it must follow, as the night the day,*
> *Thou canst not then be false to any man."*

"That's exactly what I'm trying to say!" Betsy cried, and jumped up in her excitement.

"*'To thine own self be true!' 'To thine own self be true!'* That's what I have to do if I'm going to get out and make something of myself. I lost the Essay Contest. But that's all right. I tried. I've done terrible work in school all spring and I have to get busy now if I'm going to pass my exams."

She started walking rapidly toward home. It was hard to go, for she knew her father would be making sandwiches. Julia would have a beau, and there would be singing . . . all the songs she and Phil had danced to. But thinking that, she only walked faster and when she reached home things weren't so hard as she had expected them to be.

For Tacy was there. Tacy had heard from Alice, who had heard it from Carney, who had heard it from Winona, who had heard it from Irma that Phil had asked Irma to go to the track meet. Tacy had had a feeling, probably, that Betsy might like to have her around. Betsy was so glad to see her that she gave her a bear hug. Not that she needed to confide in her now. She had done her confiding to the stars in Lincoln Park. But the loving warmth of Tacy's presence helped.

The family had finished eating but her father made some sandwiches for her, and Betsy and Tacy went out into the kitchen to watch him. They joked about the coming examinations, and stood with their arms about each other acting silly through the singing.

Tacy did not so much as mention Phil. But when Katie and Leo came to call for her, she said good-by to Betsy with a curious and helpful remark.

"Betsy, did it ever occur to you that the better

people know you, the better they like you?"

Betsy thought this over. She thought of Tacy and Tib and Alice and Winona and Carney and Tony and Cab . . . all very old friends now.

"Why, yes," she answered. "I guess they do. What of it?"

"It shows how silly you are ever to act like somebody you aren't," said Tacy, and gave her another hug, and went out.

It all fitted in with what William Shakespeare had said hundreds of years before.

The next day at school Betsy went to Carney. "If you're still looking for members, I'll go into that Girls' Debating Club. I think I'd enjoy it."

A few days later she went to Miss Clarke, "Tacy and I," she said, "have decided that if you still want us to, we'll sing the 'Cat Duet.' We've done it for so many years. It's too bad to break the tradition."

"That's what I thought," Miss Clarke answered eagerly. "I was awfully sorry when you decided against it."

"There's another thing," said Betsy, "I've been wanting to tell you. I really worked on the Essay Contest this year, Miss Clarke. But something happened, and I didn't write a very good essay. I'm sorry."

"Why, that's all right, Betsy."

"I just thought I'd tell you," said Betsy, "so that you wouldn't be building up any false hopes. I'm afraid that next year you'll be choosing someone else to represent our class on the Essay Contest. I wouldn't blame you," she added, "I've let you down for two years running."

Miss Clarke put her arm around Betsy with one of those little girlish gestures she had.

"We'll see about that," she replied.

In the ensuing days Betsy studied. She really studied. She made a game out of seeing how much she could raise her marks, which she knew were bad, by passing good examinations. She wanted to study instead of going to the track meet, but she feared that this was weakness. So she pinned on the school colors and went with the other girls to watch the boys in the hundred yard dash, the two hundred and twenty yard dash, the discus throwing, the high jump, the hurdle races and the pole vault.

She sat beside Carney driving out. Carney had been very nice to her since the quarrel. She hadn't mentioned Phil at all, but she referred to him diffidently now.

"It must be hard," she said, slapping the reins over Dandy's back, "to break off with a boy you've been going around with. It must be something like . . . having him go away."

"I guess it is," said Betsy. After a pause she re-marked, "I'm glad you've started going with Al, Carney. He's an awfully nice kid."

"Yes, he is," said Carney. "But I'm going to tell you something, Betsy. Larry has been gone for a whole year now, and I like him as much as I ever did."

"Do you?" Betsy asked.

"I still like him better than anyone," said Carney. Her dimple didn't show at all, and she looked almost stern.

Betsy thought this over at the track meet, for Irma, looking charming, sat in the red auto with Phil and a big box of candy. Betsy didn't like it . . . but she didn't mind it so much as she had thought she would.

"It can't be," she thought, "that I liked Phil any-where near as much as Carney liked Larry."

She was glad she had seen them together for the first sting was gone. And their appearance at the meet had another good effect. It must have confirmed significant rumors for Tony, Cab and Dennie all appeared as of old the next night for Sunday night lunch.

Everyone was very glad to see them. They went out to watch Mr. Ray buttering bread and slicing onions; they sang around the piano, teased Betsy about her curls. Mr. Gaston came that night for the very first time . . . which made it quite an occasion.

He flushed when he saw the boys, but after a period

of uncertainty he started acting boyish himself. He laughed harder than anyone, made poor jokes. And he must, Betsy thought pityingly, be all of twenty-three! Betsy felt almost sorry for him and hoped that Julia wouldn't really seek revenge.

The next week was filled with examinations, and rehearsals for the commencement exercises. The chorus was singing "Damascus."

> *"Save the holy sepulchre,*
> *A-a-men."*

Betsy and Tacy heard it in their dreams.
Julia was practising her solo.

> *"A rose in the garden,*
> *Over the way . . ."*

"I think it was heartless of you to choose that song," Betsy said.

She and Julia had washed their hair and were drying it out on the lawn at the back of the house. The trees were in full leaf now; the bridal wreath was coming into bloom.

"Why?" Julia asked, shaking her long locks.

"Because of Harry. That's his song. You learned it to please him."

"Oh . . . Harry," said Julia. "I don't feel guilty about turning Harry down. You know, Bettina, I had to be true to myself."

"You what?" Betsy cried. After an incredulous moment she told Julia how those lines from William Shakespeare had fitted into her own life that spring. She said how foolish she thought she had been to try to be different from herself.

Julia listened thoughtfully.

"You're absolutely right," she said when Betsy finished. "Fundamentally, that is. Each one of us has to be true to the deepest thing that is in him. But Bettina . . . a little play-acting has its place . . . with a woman, that is."

"What do you mean?"

"You wanted Phil, and you went out and got him. It took grit. It took determination. It was all right. And you couldn't have done it without a little of what Cab calls 'la de da.'"

"But I didn't keep him."

"Silly! You didn't want to."

Betsy threw down the brush with which she had been conscientiously adding gloss to her hair.

"What do you mean, I didn't want to?"

"You know you didn't. You wanted other things more."

"What?"

"Well, the Essay Contest, for example."

"That's true," Betsy thought, staring at her brush. "And I wanted the picnic more, and not hurting Tom's feelings. I wanted . . . my freedom more."

She did not answer.

"You didn't want to go to the bother of keeping him," Julia continued. "But, Bettina, the whole affair did you a lot of good. You're better groomed, more poised, you have sweeter manners and . . . well . . . more charm than you had before you started it. Don't be scornful of 'la de da,' Bettina. You may want to use it sometime with someone you really like."

"But then," cried Betsy, "surely I wouldn't have to use it! Not with someone who was my own kind!"

"Oh . . . wouldn't you?" asked Julia, and smiled inscrutably, and began to shake her hair again.

This was too confusing! Betsy stretched out on the grass and looked up at the sky, June blue with puffball clouds.

"Life," she said, "is complicated . . . for a woman, at least."

"You have to be wise as a serpent and harmless as a dove," Julia agreed, looking anything but harmless.

23
Julia's Graduation

THE FIRST EVENT OF Commencement Week was the joint evening meeting of Philomathians and Zeta-mathians at which the essay cup would be awarded.

Betsy put on the pink silk dress and the daisy wreath. She wanted to look nice for she would have to sit on the platform with the other contestants, but she well knew, this year, that she would not be asked to stand and bow. Joe Willard who sat opposite her, very blond in a new dark suit, would be the one to rise when the sophomore points were awarded. This year no one would be surprised. Betsy had told not only Miss Clarke but everyone she knew that she could not possibly win.

The assembly room was crowded, even to the bookcases. It was gay with Zetamathian blue and Philomathian orange. Betsy felt festive and untroubled even when, at the end of Miss Bangeter's speech, Joe was announced as the winner.

"That's because I did my best," she thought, applauding.

It was consoling, too, that the Zetamathians won the cup. Competing freshmen, juniors, and seniors had saved the day. The Zetamathians had already won the athletics cup, so now they had two out of three. No loyal Zetamathian could fail to find the evening glorious.

Betsy went up to Joe and offered her congratulations. He smiled.

"This luck can't last forever. It'll be your turn next year."

"Heavens!" cried Betsy. "He's being polite."

"I'm always polite."

"No, it means you're sorry for me. You're hurting my pride."

He grinned. "I do have a few kind emotions. Do you know what I almost did this spring when the apple trees were in bloom up at Butternut Center? I almost 'phoned to tell you not to worry. They were rosy."

"Well, why didn't you?" asked Betsy. She heard her voice growing soft and sweet, the way she had tuned it for Phil. She remembered her conversation with Julia on the lawn, and blushed. Joe Willard laughed.

Betsy looked for him the next night at Class Day exercises. He wasn't there. She looked again at the class play. He wasn't there either. Artfully, late the following afternoon, she went to the library. He was not there.

She asked Miss Sparrow about him. He and Miss Sparrow, she knew, were friends.

"Why, he's left town," Miss Sparrow explained. "He's going to work with a threshing rig this summer. He'll get three dollars a day, he said, and earn all he needs for next year. You know, Betsy, Joe supports himself. Entirely. It's pretty wonderful, I think."

"I think so too," Betsy replied. She heard herself telling Miss Sparrow something of her difficulties with Joe . . . how she had tried to get him into the Crowd, and how he had told her the Crowd bored him.

"I think," Miss Sparrow said, "I can explain that."

They were alone in the library except for some children in the Children's Room. She leaned across the desk, lowered her voice, and made quite a speech about Joe.

"I figure him out this way," she said. "He has no father or mother. He has to work for a living. And being barred from the usual things high school students do, the things requiring money and time, he takes refuge in books. He not only reads them, but he dreams about them. He sees himself as the heroes he admires. He is confident that he could behave as Ivanhoe did, or Marco Polo, or D'Artagnan. Do you know what I mean?"

Betsy said she did.

"He isn't a boy who pities himself. Not at all. He has to work, but he makes that an adventure. He would really like to play football, or baseball after school, but he can't. He has to go to the Creamery. So he just makes plans about playing them in college. It helps that, when he has a spare hour and can play, he is better than average.

"His routine is quite satisfactory to him but only because he puts out of his mind the things he cannot have. And they are the boy and girl pleasures. If he let you draw him into your Crowd, he would be constantly embarrassed. He would be forced to admit that he isn't, perhaps, quite so lucky as he thinks he is. Don't you see, Betsy? Living as he does now, he doesn't mind shabby clothes. But he is a proud boy. He wouldn't like coming to call on you in shabby clothes. When you urge him to come he gets desperate. He just has to be rude. Don't you see?"

"Yes," Betsy answered. "I see."

Walking home she thought over what Miss Sparrow had said. Next year, she resolved, she would find some way to make a friend of Joe . . . and without making things hard for him, either.

Commencement night was drawing very near. The chorus was rehearsing in the Opera House.

> *"Save the holy sepulchre,*
> *A-a-men."*

Presents were flooding in for Julia. She was being fitted to a lace-trimmed, white silk dress with a crushed white satin belt and elbow length sleeves. There was much talk at home about her plans. It had been decided that she was going to go to the state university at Minneapolis. She would take the music course.

"This is the end of something, Bob," Mrs. Ray kept saying. "It's the first break in the family. Next year Julia will be gone."

"Minneapolis isn't very far away," Mr. Ray answered

with his usual optimism. "Besides, she isn't going until fall. We're all going out to the Inn at Murmuring Lake and have one swell-elegant vacation."

"Just the same," Mrs. Ray persisted. "It's the end of something. You know it as well as I do."

He did, and Betsy knew it too. She felt increasingly solemn. Julia was through with high school; next year she would be gone. There wouldn't be any Julia around to play the piano, or to fix her hair, or to tell her to tell boys she had had a dream about them.

Betsy felt tearful at supper, and she could see that her mother did. Mr. Ray acted unusually cheerful, as always when he felt the opposite. Julia put on the white graduating dress.

"You look puny, lovey," Anna said.

"She looks like a bride," Mrs. Ray mourned. "She'll be getting married, the next thing we know."

Mr. Gaston had sent her a gift of pink carnations. Her father had sent her pink roses. Julia mixed them into one superlative bouquet.

They drove down to the Opera House behind Old Mag. Mr. and Mrs. Ray and Margaret and Anna sat together, near the front. Betsy, because of being in the chorus, sat on the stage with the graduates. It was a sweet June night, but inside the Opera House there was only that stuffy opera house smell.

Betsy and Tacy sang with the chorus.

"Save the holy sepulchre,
A-a-men."

Julia sang her solo.

"There's a rose in the garden,
Over the way . . ."

Betsy, sitting behind her, admired the lovely line of Julia's upswept hair.

The diplomas were handed out. The members of the graduating class marched up one by one to fond applause. Julia went up, and Katie, her cheeks as red as the red carnations she carried.

After it was over Betsy and Tacy started home together.

"I don't see why we had to sing that Holy Sepulchre song," Betsy said. "I felt badly enough already."

"So did I," said Tacy. "It seemed like a funeral at our house tonight. Of course Katie isn't going so far away as Julia is. She'll just be going to the college on the hill. But things won't be the same, Mamma says."

"It's the first break in our family," Betsy answered.

"Remember how we used to fight with them when we were kids?" Tacy asked, smiling.

"Do I! Remember the contest for May Queen?"

"And how we peeked and saw them at their club?

And now they are graduating. Life is funny."

"Life is queer."

They reached the foot of Plum Street Hill where they must part, and had just concluded plans for a picnic the next day when Tacy said:

"Betsy! We've come to the end of your Winding Hall of Fate."

"That's right," Betsy cried. "And what a hall it's been! You sang a solo at school. I went to Milwaukee. We found out that Tib is maybe coming back, and I've had . . . you might say . . . my First Big Love Affair. I'll have to go home and write it all up in my journal."

"Make it sound thrilling."

"I will."

"Of course," Betsy said, "that winding hall keeps right on winding. Only now it takes an even bigger turn. We're practically juniors. Can you realize that?"

"To be frank, no," Tacy said. "Good-by, Betsy. See you in the morning."

"See you in the morning," Betsy said.

Maud Hart Lovelace and Her World

(Adapted from *The Betsy-Tacy Companion: A Biography of Maud Hart Lovelace* by Sharla Scannell Whalen)

Maud Palmer Hart circa 1906

Estate of Merian Kirchner

MAUD HART LOVELACE was born on April 25, 1892, in Mankato, Minnesota. Shortly after Maud's high school graduation in 1910, the Hart family left Mankato and settled in Minneapolis, where Maud attended the University of Minnesota. In 1917 she married Delos W. Lovelace, a newspaper reporter who later became a popular writer of short stories. The Lovelaces' daughter, Merian, was born in 1931.

Maud would tell her daughter bedtime stories about her childhood in Minnesota, and it was these stories that gave her the idea of writing the Betsy-Tacy books. She did not intend to write an entire series when *Betsy-Tacy*, the first book, was published in 1940, but readers asked for more stories. So Maud took Betsy through high school and beyond college to the "great world" and marriage.

The final book in the series, *Betsy's Wedding*, was published in 1955.

The Betsy-Tacy books are based very closely upon Maud's own life. "I could make it all up, but in these Betsy-Tacy stories, I love to work from real incidents," Maud wrote. This is especially true of the four high school books. We know a lot about her life during this period because Maud kept diaries (one for each high school year, just like Betsy) as well as a scrapbook during high school. As she wrote to a cousin in 1964: "In writing the high school books my diaries were extremely helpful. The family life, customs, jokes, traditions are all true and the general pattern of the years is also accurate."

Almost every character in the high school books, even the most minor, can be matched to an actual person living in Mankato in the early years of the twentieth century. (See page 331 for a list of characters and their real-life counterparts.) But there are exceptions. As Maud wrote: "A small and amusing complication is that while some of the characters are absolutely based on one person—for example Tacy, Tib, Cab, Carney—others were merely suggested by some person and some characters are combinations of two real persons." For example, the character Winona Root is based on two people. In

Betsy and Tacy Go Downtown and *Winona's Pony Cart,* Maud's childhood friend Beulah Hunt was the model for Winona. The Winona Root we encounter in the high school books, however, was based on Maud's high school friend Mary Eleanor Johnson, known as "El."

Another exception is the character Joe Willard, who is based on Maud's husband, Delos Wheeler Lovelace. In real life, Delos did not attend Mankato High School with Maud. He was two years Maud's junior, and the two didn't meet until after high school. But as Maud said, "Delos came into my life much later than Joe Willard came into Betsy's, and yet he is Joe Willard to the life." This is because Maud asked her husband to give her a description of his boyhood. She then gave his history to Joe.

Maud eventually donated her high school scrapbook and many photographs to the Blue Earth County Historical Society in Mankato, where they still reside today. But she destroyed her diaries sometime after she had finished writing the Betsy-Tacy books, in the late 1950s. We can't be sure why, but we do know that, as Maud confessed once in an interview, they "were full of boys, boys, boys." She may not have felt comfortable about bequeathing them to posterity!

Maud Hart Lovelace died on March 11, 1980. But her legacy lives on in the beloved series she created and in her legions of fans, many of whom are members of the Betsy-Tacy Society and the Maud Hart Lovelace Society. For more information, write to:

The Betsy-Tacy Society
P.O. Box 94
Mankato, MN 56002-0094
www.betsy-tacysociety.org

The Maud Hart Lovelace Society
277 Hamline Avenue South
St. Paul, MN 55105
www.maudhartlovelacesociety.com

About *Heaven* to *Betsy*

Heaven to Betsy is based on Maud's freshman year at Mankato High School from 1906 to 1907. Maud remembered that time well and incorporated many of her adventures into the book.

In 1904 Maud's father, Tom Hart, was elected Blue Earth county treasurer. By 1906 he had sold his shoe store and, as Maud recalled, moved the family "up Fifth Street in order to be nearer the Court House and the high school Kathleen and I attended." Mr. Hart's election to the position of county treasurer and the sale of the store are not mentioned in the book, but Maud found out about the new house in much the same way as Betsy does.

There really was an Anna who worked for the Harts, although she did not stay with the family as long as the fictional Anna stayed with the Rays. And Maud *did* learn about a freckle-removing cream and Magic Wavers from her before she left. In response to a question from a fan, Maud wrote: "Our hired girl Anna told me about them, just as I said in the story. I tried them, too, but I never lost the freckles and there was really nothing magic in those curlers, for a

Maud's house at 428 South Fifth Street, Mankato, was the inspiration for the High Street house in Deep Valley.

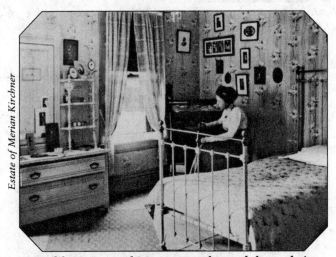

Unlike Betsy and Margaret, who each have their own rooms in the High Street house, Maud and her little sister, Helen, shared this bedroom. Maud is shown here at her desk; the inscription under the photo reads, "Genius is burning."

Maud's parents, Tom and
Stella Hart, appear to
have had as loving a
relationship as Mr. and
Mrs. Ray do.

Maud's older sister, Kathleen.

The Harts did
have a hired girl
named Anna,
but only for a
short time.
Here she is with
Maud's little
sister, Helen.

sprinkle of rain took my curls away." (Of course, Magic Wavers really were popular hair curlers of the era.)

The two school societies described in the book, Philomathian and Zetamathian, had been established at Mankato High School the year before Maud began her freshman year. The yearbook from 1912 describes the function of the Zetamathian Society in this way: "The purpose is to give the students a literary training, and all the students must belong to this society or to the Philomathian. The members of the society must attend the meetings unless excused by the teacher in charge. The meetings are held the fourth Friday in each month, when a literary program is given." Such societies were common in turn-of-the-century high schools.

The institution of Sunday Night Lunch is first mentioned in this book, although it was actually a custom of long standing in the Hart family. As Maud explained, the tradition began soon after the birth of her younger sister, Helen, in order to give her mother a break from cooking. Maud once said: "I loved to put down how many boys came to Sunday Night Lunch each week. You would think from my diary that they came to see me, but that was far from being the case. I wasn't the attraction. To this day when I meet some of those boys, grandfathers now, of course,

Deep Valley High School . . .

. . . looks very much like Mankato High School.

1912 Otaknam

*Maud and Bick probably tried to get
back seats in the Assembly Room,
just like Betsy and Tacy do
on the first day of school.*

*Marney Willard
and Connie Davis
were photographed
together shortly
before Connie's
departure from
Mankato, just like
Carney and Bonnie.*

Estate of Merian Kirchner

they look at me dreamily and say, 'Oh Maud, I can still remember your father's onion sandwiches.'"

Maud once remarked that her high school diaries were filled with "boys, boys, boys." And they were! Mike Parker, the model for Tony Markham, moved to Mankato in 1906, so he certainly qualified as a dark stranger (although he wasn't tall). And Maud did go to the freshman dance with "Herbert Humphreys," whose real name was Helmus Andrews. The typed note of invitation was pasted into Maud's high school scrapbook and is nearly identical to Herbert's note in the book:

> *Dear, dear Maud;*
>
> *It makes no difference to me which way you take the following. Will you accompany me to the High School this evening? My mother said she was going along too and I am glad because then you cant [sic] flirt with me. Of course you will have to pay your own way. If you will answer this and if affirmmative [sic] tell me when to call. I remain*
>
> > *Yours truly,*
> > *Helmus W. Andrews*

Like Betsy, Maud's crowd suffered the loss of three members toward the end of her freshman year: Connie

Jab Lloyd was the model for boy next door Cab Edwards.

The handsome Herbert Humphreys was based on Helmus Andrews.

Betsy's Tall Dark Stranger, Tony Markham, was based on Mike Parker.

Davis (Bonnie) and the Andrews (Humphreys) brothers left Mankato in 1907. In spite of these losses, however, Maud's crowd survived—evolving and expanding—through her high school years and beyond.

Estate of Merian Kirchner

Maud at sixteen

About *Betsy in Spite of Herself*

MAUD'S SOPHOMORE YEAR at Mankato High School (1907–1908) is fictionalized in *Betsy in Spite of Herself*. Not surprisingly, many of Betsy's experiences were also Maud's. Maud *was* elected to a class office during her sophomore year, but she was elected class treasurer, rather than secretary, as Betsy was. And Maud did write a parody to the song "Same Old Story," which she kept in her high school scrapbook. The lyrics are almost exactly the same as those in the book, with the exception of the last two lines of the chorus. Instead of "For she's Deep Valley's High School Girl, / And she's all right," it reads "Hurrah for 'Kato's High School girl, / For she's alright."

Maud's greatest adventure of the year was probably her Christmas trip to Milwaukee. One thing Maud did that Betsy didn't was stop in St. Paul to visit her friend Connie Davis (Bonnie from *Heaven to Betsy* had moved to Paris, not St. Paul, as her real-life counterpart had). Once she arrived in Milwaukee, Maud undoubtedly met a lot of Midge's family, as Betsy does Tib's family. Midge's maternal grandparents, the Iraseks, were both from Austria, where

Maud's crowd loved to visit Heinze's Ice Cream Parlor, which was owned by Ferdinand Heinze.

High school dances were held here, at Schiller Hall.

Grossmama Irasek did embroidery for the imperial house of Franz Joseph, Emperor of Austria. And Midge's paternal grandparents, the Gerlachs, were from Germany. However, Grosspapa Gerlach had died by the time Maud visited Milwaukee, so she wouldn't have met him or attended a Christmas party at his house. But the Christmas party Betsy attends in the book wasn't purely from Maud's imagination. Her sister Kathleen traveled to Europe in 1909 (as Julia does in a later book) and spent Christmas in Germany. Many of the details are taken from a letter Kathleen sent to her family about her experiences there.

Another fascinating detail about Betsy's Christmas visit that is historically accurate is the introduction of "The Merry Widow Waltz." In fact, "The Merry Widow Waltz" *was* brand-new at Christmas in 1907. *The Mankato Free Press* advertised a New Year's Eve performance of the opera *The Merry Widow* in its December 26, 1907, edition—the first appearance of the waltz in Mankato. And when the Merry Widow hat made its appearance the following spring, it soon became all the rage.

Maud and Midge stayed up all night to ring in the New Year, just like Betsy and Tib do. Maud later recalled a Christmas visit to "Tib" in Milwaukee, where she decided to change her personality. "I was going to be tall, dark, and mysterious." In the book, Betsy decides to inaugurate her new personality by going with Phil Brandish. We don't know if there really was someone like Phil in Maud's life; he seems to be one of the "loose characterizations" and may have been based on more than one boy. However, a yearbook note to Maud from Bick refers to a certain auto and reads, "Love will not change while the auto remains," which was a line in Betsy's version of "Dreaming" about Phil. So perhaps there was a red car–driving boy in Maud's sophomore year.

Like Betsy, Maud did add an "e" to her name. In real life, though, she started spelling her name "Maude" when she was a freshman, or even earlier. Although "Maude" lasted beyond the end of sophomore year, she probably discovered that she was happiest when she was true to herself, like Betsy.

Maud pasted her dance card from the Leap Year Dance into her scrapbook.

Waltz. Carl Hoen.
2. Two Step
3. Schottische Ral.
4. Waltz. Herman &
5 Circle Two Step
6. Waltz
7. Two Step Alan F
8. Schottische. Carl Hoen
9. Waltz
10. Two Step
11 Schottische
12 Two Step
13 Waltz
14 Two Step
15. Waltz. Carl Hoen

Will you dance?

1908

Maud's lyrics for her "Same Old Story" parody from her high school scrapbook.

Parody on "Same old Story".

(1) I am going to sing a ditty
Of the little freshman Maid,
Timid, tearful, and retiring,
Flirtacious I'm afraid.
Faithfully she learns her lessons,
And she never, never, cheats
Never sticks a pin into her neighbor,
Or carves initials on the seats.

cho. Same old story, same old High.
Same old bunch of gigglers,
As the years pass by
She's a hummer, shining light,
Hurrah for "Kato's High school girl,
For she's alright

Maud in
her Merry
Widow hat

*Mildred Oleson
(Irma) in her Merry
Widow hat*

*Connie Davis (Bonnie) in
her Merry Widow hat*

Fictional Characters and Their Real-Life Counterparts

Betsy Ray	Maud Palmer Hart
Julia Ray	Kathleen Albertine Hart
Margaret Ray	Helen Hart
Bob Ray	Thomas Walden Hart
Jule Ray	Stella Palmer Hart
Tacy Kelly	Frances "Bick" Vivian Kenney
Tib Muller	Marjorie "Midge" Gerlach
Bonnie Andrews	Constance "Connie" Davis
Irma Biscay	Florence Mildred Oleson
Phil Brandish	Carl George Hoerr
Cab Edwards	Jabez "Jab" Alvin Lloyd
Mamie Dodd	Mamie Skuse
Dennie Farisy	Paul Gerald Ford
Herbert Humphreys	Helmus Weddel Andrews
Larry Humphreys	Robert Burke Andrews
Al Larson	Henry Orlando Lee
Tony Markham	Clarence "Mike" Lindon Parker
Stan Moore	Herman Hayward
Pin	Charles Ernest "Pin" Jones
Winona Root I	Beulah Ariel Hunt
Winona Root II	Mary Eleanor Johnson

Carney Sibley	Marion "Marney" Willard
Tom Slade	Thomas Warren Fox
Hazel Smith	Harriet Ahlers
Joe Willard	Delos Wheeler Lovelace

THE BETSY-TACY SERIES BEGINS

BETSY-TACY
ISBN 978-0-06-440096-1 (paperback)

BETSY-TACY AND TIB
Foreword by Ann M. Martin
ISBN 978-0-06-440097-8 (paperback)

BETSY AND TACY GO OVER THE BIG HILL
Foreword by Judy Blume
ISBN 978-0-06-440099-2 (paperback)

BETSY AND TACY GO DOWNTOWN
Foreword by Johanna Hurwitz
ISBN 978-0-06-440098-5 (paperback)

THE BETSY-TACY HIGH SCHOOL YEARS AND BEYOND

HEAVEN TO BETSY AND BETSY IN SPITE OF HERSELF
Foreword by Laura Lippman
ISBN 978-0-06-179469-8 (paperback)

Heaven to Betsy: In the first of the high school books, Betsy is 14 and a freshman at Deep Valley High.

Betsy in Spite of Herself: It's Betsy's sophomore year and she takes a glamorous trip to Milwaukee to visit Tib.

BETSY WAS A JUNIOR AND BETSY AND JOE

Foreword by Meg Cabot

ISBN 978-0-06-179472-8 (paperback)

Betsy Was a Junior: Betsy (unwisely) introduces the idea of sororities to Deep Valley High.

Betsy and Joe: Betsy's senior year arrives and finally she is going with Joe!

BETSY AND THE GREAT WORLD AND BETSY'S WEDDING

Foreword by Anna Quindlen

ISBN 978-0-06-179513-8 (paperback)

Betsy and the Great World: Betsy sets off for a year-long tour of Europe to start her writing career.

Besty's Wedding: As WWI sweeps across Europe, Betsy hopes she and Joe find happines.

THE DEEP VALLEY BOOKS

EMILY OF DEEP VALLEY

Foreword by Mitali Perkins

ISBN 978-0-06-200330-0 (paperback)

Maud Hart Lovelace's only young adult stand-alone novel, *Emily of Deep Valley,* is considered by fans of her beloved Betsy-Tacy series to be one of the author's finest works.

CARNEY'S HOUSE PARTY AND WINONA'S PONY CART

Foreword by Melissa Wiley

ISBN 978-0-06-200329-4 (paperback)

Carney's House Party fills in the gaps in Lovelace's wildly popular high school Betsy-Tacy books, and *Winona's Pony Cart* revisits Betsy, Tacy and Tib as young girls.